STUNNING PRAISE FOR JULIANA GARNETT'S
PREVIOUS NOVELS . . .

The Baron

"Readers who want their history and romance perfectly blended will find *The Baron* a book they will not want to miss."   —Kathe Robin, *Romantic Times*

"Strong, well-matched, and interestingly conflicted protagonists drive the plot of this intricate tale, which provides not only a compelling, highly sensual romance but also a welcome insight into the characters and political and social realities of the period. . . . This well-written romance is a neat blend of fact and fiction."   —*Library Journal*

"Superb writing with outstanding characters and a fast-moving plot make this one a favorite."   —*Rendezvous*

continued on next page . . .

The Magic

"A brilliant tapestry interweaving shimmering threads of mysticism, intrigue, gallantry, passion, honor and love into a medieval tale that will hold you enthralled till the end." —*Romantic Times*

The Quest

"An opulent and sensuous tale of unbridled passions. I couldn't stop reading." —Bertrice Small

"Filled with the passion and pageantry of medieval times. An exciting read!" —Susan Wiggs

THE
KNIGHT

JULIANA GARNETT

JOVE BOOKS, NEW YORK

THE KNIGHT

A Jove Book / published by arrangement with
the author

PRINTING HISTORY
Jove edition / May 2001

All rights reserved.
Copyright © 2001 by Virginia Brown.
This book, or parts thereof, may not be reproduced in
any form without permission.
For information address: The Berkley Publishing Group,
a division of Penguin Putnam Inc.,
375 Hudson Street, New York, New York 10014.

The Penguin Putnam Inc. World Wide Web site address is
http://www.penguinputnam.com

ISBN: 0-515-13053-2

A JOVE BOOK®
Jove Books are published by The Berkley Publishing Group,
a division of Penguin Putnam Inc.,
375 Hudson Street, New York, New York 10014.
JOVE and the "J" design
are trademarks belonging to Penguin Putnam Inc.

PRINTED IN THE UNITED STATES OF AMERICA

10 9 8 7 6 5 4 3 2 1

To the Merolas—to Salvatore and Francesca, who climbed to the top of Glastonbury Tor with me, and to Jane and Isabel, who waited with Rita for us to come down. Thank you for everything, including our long trek around the summit of Cadbury. At last I have been to Camelot. . . .

With the Quest of Sangrail all you of the Round Table shall depart, and never shall I see you wholly together again.

—Malory
Le Morte d'Arthur

Author's Note

✝

That there was a Briton king named Arthur buried in 542 at what was then known as the Isle of Avalon seems probable, given the records of eyewitness accounts recorded by historian Geoffrey of Monmouth, a contemporary of King Henry II. That it was the King Arthur and Guinevere of legend, is pure conjecture.

If you wish to read the facts I researched for this story, and a brief history of the monks' discovery of the grave at Glastonbury Abbey, please read the Author's Summation at the end of this book.

Part One

✝

ESSEX CASTLE
1189

Chapter 1

✝

LATE MARCH WINDS howled around forbidding towers that bristled in jagged teeth on the horizon: Essex Castle. It crouched atop a spiny ridge of hill as if preparing to pounce upon the fields below. Tendrils of etherous mist curled like dragon's breath around knobby stone feet of the keep.

Stephen Fitzhugh paused in encroaching shadows cast by the massive fortress; thin, filmy wisps of fog slithered in long fingers along the road. Damp air seeped through chinks in his armor, found holes in his wool mantle, chilled exposed skin. His head was bare. His dark hair was a wet, clammy fringe over his forehead and on the back of his neck. A battered helmet hung from a strap on his saddle and banged against the side of his horse, which was dancing from one hoof to another, snorting disapproval.

"I feel much the same, Nero." Stephen bent, soothed his restive mount with an idle pat upon the damp neck, fingers clumsy with the cold. Then he sat back, surveyed the castle with eyes as black as the approaching shadows. It was as he remembered it: brooding, menacing. As menacing as the earl who had summoned him to this bleak pile of cursed stones. Too many memories were lodged in the chinks and cracks of this fortress.

He nudged the weary destrier forward. The dull smack of hooves on wet road was loud in the eerie silence cloaking fields and grassy verges. It would be night soon, and no one would be allowed to enter once the castle gates were closed.

Stephen answered the guard's challenge with his name and was granted immediate entrance.

"You are late, Sir Stephen," was a guard's growling comment as he rode across the wooden drawbridge and into the dense shadows of the gatehouse. "The earl grows impatient."

"It is a long journey from York," Stephen said curtly.

The harsh grating of the portcullis dropped behind him; groaning pulleys and chains that lowered the iron teeth of the gate sounded like the priests' tedious descriptions of the portal opening to hell, albeit a hell composed of icy gusts and howling winds.

It was no warmer inside the castle as eerie drafts moaned plaintive songs down stone corridors and echoes like muted sobs drifted in the dim-lit passageways.

The Earl of Essex did not glance up when Stephen was shown into his solar, but continued to study a huge leather-bound book opened on the table before him. The only sound was the scrape of Stephen's boots and the warm hiss of a fire that burned in a large brass brazier. Heat spread out to lessen the chamber's chill, a welcome respite from the cold.

Stephen stood where the steward had left him just inside the door. Irritation prickled along his spine and tightened his mouth as the earl continued to read and ignore him. Curse the old vulture for his arrogance. It would give

Stephen great satisfaction to leave immediately. It was a bitter gall that he could not.

Finally the earl looked up with penetrating dark eyes that burned like banked coals beneath a shelf of heavy brow.

"You tarried overlong in getting here, Sir Stephen."

The harsh voice was but a disinterested whisper. Stephen did not bother to reply.

Essex continued: "Do you know why I have sent for you?"

"I do not, my lord." Stephen did not glance away from that piercing gaze, but held it until his eyeballs felt scalded, until he felt seared to the bone, a flush of heat scouring him from spurs to brow.

Essex sat back in his chair and folded his hands atop the massive book. The parchment rustled beneath his touch, a dry whispery scratch that sounded oddly ominous.

"I have information that may lead to one of the greatest prizes in all Christendom. Are you interested?"

Regarding him warily, Stephen dipped his head in acknowledgment. "Perhaps, my lord. I would have to know more details."

A short bark of sardonic laughter erupted from the earl, and his eyes narrowed slightly. "You are as cautious as I remember you, Fitzhugh. In some men, a virtue. In others—a vice. Which be you, I wonder. Would you slay a dragon if it be asked of you? Or would you flee with your arse afire, as I have seen so many men do in the face of danger?"

"As you just said, my lord—you remember me as a cautious man. I have not changed overmuch since last we met."

Irritation prickled along his spine at the earl's close regard, as if he still saw a greenling youth or novice knight instead of a man now spurred and proven.

Essex smiled slightly, a tug of one lip upward that could indicate humor or contempt.

"Yea, it seems that you have not changed. I require a man who knows when to be cautious and when to risk all. A man who has little to lose but his life. I have a task. It will earn you a king's ransom if you succeed—the lands and keep of Dunmow."

Stephen's breath filled his lungs to aching. There was a ringing in his ears. *A king's ransom!* Unexpected reward—a fitting compensation after years of struggle, of battle and the stench of death that remained long after the clash of swords and screams of the dying had faded into silence. *But Dunmow!* Could it be true?

His released breath formed a faint misty cloud in front of his face as he asked tersely, "And if I fail?"

"It will cost you all."

Not unexpected. But worth the risk.

Dunmow . . . dare he hope?

"What is the task you would have me undertake to earn Dunmow, my lord earl?"

Essex rose from behind the table. A once powerful man, age had stooped his shoulders. It lent him the awkward grace of a lame horse as he leaned forward, hands splayed atop the crackling vellum beneath his gnarled fingers. He caught Stephen's eyes, held them, his tone hoarse with suppressed excitement.

"Bring me the Holy Grail."

Chapter 2

✝

FOR A MOMENT Stephen stood rigidly still, staring at the earl's face, the craggy features sharpened by the dim flickering light from a branch of candles and the brazier. Then he blew out a harsh breath that sounded even to his own ears like a vicious snarl.

"You mock me with a paltry jest, my lord! A child's trick. A madman's quest!"

"Nay, Sir Stephen." Essex straightened abruptly. On his lips, the title of *Sir* sounded derisive, a reminder of how long it had taken Stephen to earn it, of the years he had spent in brutal conflict where the only rewards were those he had forcibly wrenched from others. Concessions to his prowess were hard-won, yet now grudgingly yielded.

Essex's thick brow lowered over his eyes. "I am not a man to indulge in whimsy or jests, as you surely must recall from our years of acquaintance."

"But to find the Holy Grail . . . it is a farce. A tale concocted for the credulous."

"So. You do not believe there is a chalice?"

"Not as the tales that are told, nay, I do not. A cup with the power to restore life to the dead—to give men immortality? A Holy Grail said to be used by Jesus Christ at the Last Supper? A myth, my lord. A simpleton's fable."

"So you regard me as a simpleton, Fitzhugh?"

More cautiously, curbing his wayward tongue, he said, "Nay, my lord. Never that. But it is possible to be duped."

"Then you consider me easily duped."

Stephen recognized the anger, understood it. "No, my lord earl, I do not. But when a man wishes to believe, he may be convinced to believe in illusions."

"You are a man without illusions, I perceive."

"As you above all would know well. What few illusions I once had have long been proven false, my lord. I believe in only what I see, and not half of that."

Essex smiled. "Whether you believe in it is of no interest to me, Sir Stephen. Indeed, it may well be to my benefit to send a man who cannot be fooled by sentiment or superstition to bring back the most sought-after prize in all of Christendom. I care not if you are a heretic. I leave the state of your soul to the priests."

"Fitting, I suppose, as you damned me long ago. It is easier to leave the salvation of a lost soul to others."

"Now you mock *me*. I will not tolerate insolence from a knight errant whose only purpose in life is to serve his master. Best that you recall your station, Fitzhugh, before I lose my patience."

Stephen did not reply. Angry resentment burned in his throat, tightened his chest. Curse Essex! A man of intrigue and power, as likely to sentence a man to immediate death as to kill him with years of indifference. Did Stephen not know that well by now?

Continuing as if the conversation were amicable, Essex said, "You will bring me back the chalice."

If it were not so insulting to be ordered to achieve the

impossible, the implied assurance that he could do so would have been flattering. Stephen weighed his options and decided that compliance might earn him coin even if not the elusive reward of Dunmow.

"My lord, if I undertake this task, I will require coin for my efforts."

"You are in no position to barter, my cockerel. Dunmow will be your reward for success. You have always thought it your right. Now is your chance to earn it."

Stephen's hand tightened on the hilt of his sword, a gesture that did not go unnoticed, and his tone was gruff. "I decline your generous offer, my lord earl. My empty purse and belly decree that I seek elsewhere for more immediate and certain reward."

"Curse you for a fool! This *is* certain—more certain than any man has ever come to finding it. . . ."

Essex stared at him, eyes burning brands in a sallow face devoid of humanity, empty of compassion for his fellow man, for even those who served him with loyalty, if not love and admiration.

Yet behind those hooded eyes lurked fierce conviction.

Stephen frowned and moved slightly, sword a muted clink against his mailed hip. "Do you claim to know where this chalice lies, my lord?"

"Yea, that I do. But first I would have your reply."

Silence lengthened, stretched into tension unabated by the earl's fierce gaze. Coals hissed in red slumberous eyes beneath lids of gray ash in the brazier, emanating heat that did little to dispel the sudden chill that gripped Stephen. A fool's quest indeed—he would be mad to agree.

His cold hands opened, closed, aching in the damp chill that pervaded the chamber. He exhaled raggedly.

"Yea, my lord earl, I will pursue this illusion."

A satisfied smile etched deep furrows into the thin cheeks. "Ah, I thought you might, with the proper inducement to stir your interest. Do not look so affronted.

All men are the same. Nobility is not inherited, it is a prize of war." He leaned forward, gnarled hands propped into fists on the table's surface, his voice lowered to a hoarse rasp that summoned brief images of hell's gates yawning open.

"Information has come into my possession that the answer to the mystery of the chalice lies with the abbot of Glastonbury Abbey."

Despite his rancor, curiosity stirred. "And the abbot is willing to divulge such a secret, my lord?"

"Ah, the abbot is dead." At Stephen's muttered oath, the earl's smile only widened. "Peter de Marcy, who was for a time appointed by the king to care for the abbey after the good abbot's death, was a man of great . . . curiosity. He came into some information that was most intriguing, but alas, he died before able to impart it to me. A pity. I paid him well yet received little reward for my coin."

"Have you assurance that de Marcy was not just after your money, that he did have this information?"

"I am astounded that you would even ask such a question of me, Sir Stephen."

Essex, whatever else he may be, was not a fool, not credulous enough to swallow a fantastical tale more suited to be told over a cup of wine. Perhaps it was not a fool's quest after all. The earl's tone was too emphatic.

Essex drew in a heavy breath, reached for a silver-wrought goblet of wine and water with a hand that shook in a faint tremor and drank deeply before he looked again at Stephen.

"Take care, Fitzhugh. The last man to pursue the Grail to Glastonbury died in the same fire that destroyed the abbey. I do not wish to waste more time and men in such a manner."

"Nor do I wish to be *wasted* in such a manner, my lord earl."

Stephen's dry tone was lost on Essex, who had turned to gaze again at the book still open upon the table. A draft ruffled the pages in a sound like dry reeds rustling in the wind, and the branch of candles flickered madly, light and shadow an eerie dance across the chamber walls. A soughing wind curled around castle walls, seeped through heavy velvet draperies over the windows, stirred turbid shadows with the pungent stink of moat. It carried with it the taint of perilous promise, and Stephen shifted, his sword clanking dully against the edge of the brass brazier.

Essex looked up with a start. Crimson splotches muddied his face, and his mouth was a bloodless slash as he reached for a sheet of vellum, drew it to him and lifted a quill. Ink stained the point, gleaming as he dipped it into the pot, then scratched a few lines across the clean, spare curl of parchment. When it was sanded, he sealed it with a blob of melted red wax, then pressed his ring into it. Drawing a small purse from the folds of his tunic, he tossed it to Stephen, who caught it in one hand. Coins rattled softly as he looked up at the earl, who watched him with a faint smile acknowledging this compromise.

"Do not fail me, Fitzhugh." Essex held out the sealed message. "This is for you. It holds the key to the mystery. Guard it well. There is another letter here for the prior of the abbey. Give it to him when you arrive."

As Stephen took the proffered letters, he suddenly realized why the earl was so insistent upon the Grail's discovery. Death rode his bony features, a pale spectre, an implacable foe that could only be conquered with the promised salvation of a fabled chalice.

It was Death the earl heard rattling at the windows and recognized in the shadows yawning beyond the waning light. It was Death he hoped to vanquish by the grace of a cup held over a thousand years before in the hands of the man known to the Christian world as the Son of God.

Even as Stephen understood it, he pitied both the earl and the futility of misplaced faith.

Chapter 3

✝

GLASTONBURY ABBEY

A SOFT MAY breeze wafted over tumbled stones and an occasional charred timber that had been pushed to one side. Aislinn of Amberlea stepped cautiously over the debris. Clad in an old blue gown of blanchet, which had seen better days, she moved easily through the busy hum of construction. Warm sunlight seeped through thick beech limbs to heat the back of her bare neck. Her honey-colored hair was parted in the middle to form two plaits, wound atop her head and secured on her crown with pins.

She paused to survey the progress of the rebuilding. It had been five years now since the great fire. Remnants of the disastrous blaze that had ravaged the abbey and chapel were only scattered reminders, which had been carefully saved by the monks. Brightly colored broken tiles were streaked with soot, blackened stripes had been scorched into the altar, massive pillars were seared with indelible images of crosses that had burned to ash.

Miraculously, the sole survivor of the inferno was an intact image of Our Lady of Glastonbury—a sign, the monks said, of God's favor as well as the king's.

Aislinn tilted her head, and admired the graceful framework being erected beyond the new chapel, an immense, soaring skeleton of vaulted ribs and intricate stonework. Scaffolds clung to the walls in intricate webbing. Hammers pounded in a loud, droning rhythm, a constant hum now that the days were longer and the weather permitted.

In the shadow of those stone walls, Ralph Fitzstephen, King Henry's chamberlain in charge of the rebuilding, stood beneath an arched doorway. He frowned down at a sheaf of papers in his hand as the breeze riffled them.

Clutching a wad of blue wool skirt in one hand, Aislinn lifted her hem to avoid tripping as she hopped gingerly over a low trench dug beside unfinished walls of the north transept. Her feet slid on rubble, and when she reached the doorway, she steadied herself with a hand against stone.

Fitzstephen was so engrossed that he took no notice of her, but continued to stare down at the building plans in his hands.

"Master Fitzstephen," she said finally, a gentle nudge to gain his attention, "Prior Thaddeus wishes to speak with you."

"Again?" The papers jerked sharply. Tightly compressed lips indicated his effort at restraining a curse as the steward glanced up at her. Harsh, grizzled features settled into a more amiable expression. His tense face relaxed and took on an ironic cast. "No doubt, the carpenters are not competent or the stone masons build crooked walls, or—" He halted, lifted his shoulders in a shrug. "I'll speak with him shortly. Come, Mistress Aislinn, tell me what you think of the work so far. It progresses swiftly, don't you agree?"

Aislinn nodded her appreciation as she gazed at stone

pillars that rose into the air to form the south aisle of the nave and presbytery, transected by more pillars that separated the areas with a wide crossing. Beautiful stonework was cut into supports, with a magnificent triforium opening for the doors, while the nave held nine bays, pillars on north and south forming clustered stone shafts that curved gracefully upward. Lancet windows boasted arched heads and wide proportions.

Turning to Fitzstephen, she said, "So much has been done in such a short time. Master Fitzstephen, I do believe that this abbey will far outshine even Wells Cathedral."

Pride was evident in his eyes and voice. "Do you think so? It would be most pleasant were Bishop Reginald to be outdone after all that has been said. Perhaps we should mention that to him the next time he visits."

Aislinn laughed. "Oh no, don't include me, sir. I try not to become embroiled in such rivalry. I leave that to the priests and bishops."

"And demanding monks. Brother Prior bedevils me most unmercifully."

"Prior Thaddeus can be difficult, but he's only anxious that all be done perfectly. As prior, he is quite protective of all the abbey affairs."

Fitzstephen's brow lifted, an ironic acknowledgment. He looked so weary, Aislinn thought suddenly, the toll taken of all the details involved in supervision of construction. Lines etched deep into his face, fanning out from his eyes as he squinted against the soft spring sunlight that poured in through roofless bones of stone and wood framing.

"The good prior would no doubt commit near any deed not deemed sacrilege to assure Glastonbury be regarded as the holiest in all of England," he said. "I've warned the king there will be trouble about it one day. Too much competition between monks and madmen."

Aislinn put up a hand to shade her eyes, frowning a

little. "Father Prior means well, Master Fitzstephen. Truly he does. He is very honorable, and would never do anything unethical, I'm certain of that."

"No? You've a gentle regard, Mistress Aislinn. I find him maddening. He weeps over the loss of the original church so greatly that he's unable to see the future in his grief for the past."

"True, but surely you understand. This abbey was ordained by God. While Saint Dunstan's may have been little more than mud and wattle, it was blessed by Joseph of Arimathea and was the holiest of holies. Few pilgrims will come to see a new church. It was the holiness of the old that drew them. Glastonbury needs the funds, especially since the fire. The old church is a great loss."

"A loss, yes, but now we look to the future. Have I not taken the bones of the saints and enshrined them? I even found the bones of Saint Dunstan buried in the ruins of the old church—the greatest find yet, but Father Prior still moans about our losses."

It was a familiar argument, and Aislinn forbore a reply that would only fall on deaf ears. Good men both, Ralph Fitzstephen and Prior Thaddeus were frequently at odds over everything from the design of the buildings to the materials used. It was true that Fitzstephen had enshrined the relics of Saint Patrick, Saint Indract, and Saint Gildas, but now Christ Church Canterbury claimed to possess the true bones of Saint Dunstan. Another feud. There was already an ongoing feud with Wells regarding the churches under Glastonbury's jurisdiction. These conflicts had put a strain between King Henry's steward and the prior, and a strain on the abbey.

"Your uncle would deal with this fairly," Fitzstephen surprised her by saying. "Abbot Robert was a man with great vision."

"Yes, his wisdom is sorely missed, but I miss him even more greatly for his loving kindness."

With brief compassion, the king's steward put a hand upon her shoulder, a gentle squeeze to impart understanding. "He was an excellent abbot. It was most unfortunate that he died so soon."

Aislinn nodded. "As abbot, Uncle Robert was a good man, and most difficult to replace. He was generous to the monks and especially kind to the poor. It was that goodness of spirit that caused this trouble with Wells, I fear."

"More like, it was Reginald of Bath's greed. If not for his persuading your uncle to his folly, there would be no bitter dispute to taint us all now."

"Until King Henry's patronage brought us relief and hope," she said, "I worried the abbey would be abandoned and I'd have no place to go. I've been fortunate to be allowed to remain here in peace since my uncle's death."

Fitzstephen snorted. " 'Tis not good fortune, Mistress, but Father Prior's tight fist that prizes your generosity and hard work. He's a difficult man. Perhaps you would do better to leave here and seek refuge with other kinsmen."

"*Leave* Glastonbury? I could not." She looked down at her hands, turned a small ring on one finger idly, and shook her head. "I have my own portion and no complaints. Prior Thaddeus is kind in his way. I feel useful here, and the tasks I perform are not too burdensome. You know what is said about idle hands, Master Fitzstephen."

For a moment, nothing was said, then Fitzstephen smiled slightly. "You are much more generous of spirit than is the good brother, Mistress. You deserve more regard for your labors than you receive from the prior."

Aislinn felt awkward at his scrutiny. Though they had developed a certain rapport in the years he'd been here, the king's steward was still far above her station in life. He was the natural son of King Stephen, an educated man. But neither was she wholly ignorant. As the abbot's niece, she had enjoyed a higher status than many females, and had been privileged with a level of education many women did not receive. While she had no vast lands or wealth of her own, she'd been born into a family of sufficient means, and had possessed an adequate bride-dower.

Now she was a comfortable widow of no value, but free of maidenly constraints. Yet with her husband's death, she'd been relegated to the rank of expendable female, unimportant to anyone unless she married again.

That option was inconceivable. Her mercifully brief marriage to the son of a wealthy Glastonbury merchant had been a mistake from the beginning. Neither of them had been happy. If not for his untimely death in an accident, they would have spent the rest of their days as strangers in the same household, accommodating but distant.

It was so long ago now. Nearly ten years. The relief she'd felt at his death had been confessed to a priest, but her penance was incomplete. How could she receive absolution when she was unrepentant?

"I am content," she said now, and wondered if she lied.

Master Fitzstephen rattled the papers he held, glanced up at the soaring roofline where laborers toiled on scaffold webbing. "As you say. Tell the prior I'll come to see him shortly, Mistress. I must attend to the stonemasons first."

"I'll tell him. My gratitude, sir."

Fitzstephen grunted, but his glance was kind.

Aislinn returned to the abbot's kitchen with the message and found Prior Thaddeus in another crisis of his own creation, his ire kindled by a basket of leeks.

"Shriveled and rotten!" He raged at a monk, his round face mottled with anger as he demanded, "Do you expect me to accept such fare?"

Brother Timothy quivered under the prior's furious glare, his bony hands held out in a supplicating gesture.

"But Brother Prior, there are only one or two that are not acceptable. The others are quite good."

The offending leeks were spread across a wooden table; white bulbs exuded a pungent scent.

Prior Thaddeus snatched up a leek, shook it violently in the monk's face. Green stalks flopped forward in a light slap against Brother Timothy's cheek, and his eyes bulged with dismay as the prior ranted at him.

"Do you not see this? It is rotten! Dare we serve this to the king's man when Henry is funding the rebuilding? The king will hear that we have misspent his funds!"

The prior was a bulky man, and he loomed over the thin monk with such anger that Aislinn was alarmed. Swiftly, she stepped between the two men to inspect the leeks. "Oh, I see the problem, Prior Thaddeus. These leeks were meant for the almshouse, not here. I must have delivered the wrong basket. I crave your pardon for my error and will exchange these for the proper leeks at once."

The prior's heavy brow lowered over his eyes as he turned his attention to her. An oval of light from the dome opening in the cone-shaped ceiling gleamed on his bald pate.

"Mistress Aislinn, if you cannot do even so simple a task as deliver leeks, perhaps it would best serve us if you were to allow others to have such an important duty."

"Certainly, Father Prior. I'll send Mistress Margaret to you the next time, if you like."

Prior Thaddeus looked aghast, and she hid a smile. It was well-known that Mistress Margaret had a sharp tongue that she wielded without regard to person or station.

"No, no," he said and flapped his hands at her, "take them back, take them back. Do not send that woman here to me. She would try the patience of a saint, and I have no claim to that lofty status. Just be more careful in future to choose edible viands for our tables. We may grow weary of eggs and fish, but neither do we want rancid food."

As Aislinn scooped leeks back into the reed basket, Brother Timothy stood awkwardly, cleared his throat as if to speak, but halted at her swift, upward glance and the slight warning shake of her head. It would do no good for him to invite the prior's wrath on his head, now it would only make matters worse.

Brother Timothy stood silent as she lifted the basket of leeks, but there was an expression of resentment and frustration mixed with relief on his face. He need not be such a mouse, she thought, for it earned him no respect from the prior. He must learn to speak out on his own behalf or grow accustomed to Father Prior's insults.

Aislinn took the leeks to the almshouse built outside the abbey walls. The gate to High Street was open, as was usual during the day, and she could see her own lodgings across the crowded avenue.

Shouldering the reed basket, Aislinn crossed the gutter and entered the storeroom that nestled behind the almshouse. It was dark and musty, littered with the lingering reminder of previous years' stores, the pervasive scent of old vegetables rife in the close air. A stout woman knelt in the far corner, her white coif crumpled and dingy. Imprecations muffled by the swathe of linen and her puffs of labored breathing were mercifully unintelligible. If not for the tone of her voice, those less familiar might think she was praying.

Aislinn stifled a sigh. Mistress Margaret was not known for her patience or her sweet temper. Her husband was more agreeable, no doubt having learned patience from years of enduring the harsh words of his wife. It would have been far easier to exchange these leeks with him.

Now Aislinn put on a pleasant face as she lowered the basket to a long bench cluttered with leeks, turnips, onions and parsnips. Bundles of dried herbs dangled from a low ceiling beam, brushing against her cheek as she straightened up. She peered through a fragrant stalk of leafy fennel.

"Mistress Margaret, a mistake was made with the leeks this morning. These are meant for the almshouse. Father Prior sent me to—"

"A mistake!" Mistress Margaret turned to glare at her balefully, her considerable bulk seeming to fill the gloom as she snatched up a leek and shook it. "It were no mistake! Does the good brother begrudge us decent fare? Aye, and he fills his own fat gut while he be complaining about it!"

Aislinn stepped back to the open doorway as the leek was shoved closer, the sharp scent filling her nose. She strove to keep her tone calm. "The brothers are as generous as possible with provender. The monies granted by the king are to be used for the rebuilding."

"Aye, and what good will gilded columns do us when our bellies gripe? Does the king think of that?"

"God will provide, Mistress."

It sounded trite when she had meant to appease, and Aislinn winced slightly as Mistress Margaret brandished the leek more forcefully. Green stalks whipped back and forth in her hand, and pudgy fingers squeezed the whitish bulb until it was mashed to a pulp.

"God provides for *them* well enough, I trow, but not for those who really need it! Aye, blasphemous it may sound to ye, my fine arbitress, but it only be the truth. Go and tell Prior Thaddeus that even the almonry grows weary of rancid leeks—and ye can take them all back to him, ye can!"

Sensing the next move, Aislinn ducked as Mistress Margaret flung the leek with considerable force. It flew over her head and out the doorway, where it should have landed harmlessly in the gutter.

A choked oath, however, indicated that the mashed leek

had struck a human target, and Aislinn turned. An apology died on her lips, supplanted by a rising bubble of mirth that she could not stem as she saw the irate man wiping bits of spoiled leek from his eyes.

Flecks of white graced thick black eyebrows, and as he blinked leek from his lashes, Aislinn pressed her hands over her mouth to stifle her laughter. An unusual quiet came from Mistress Margaret, who stood as if transfixed in the center of the storeroom.

The knight was garbed in mail beneath a red surcoat with an unfamiliar crest embroidered on frayed wool. A knight errant, no doubt, come to seek refuge and sustenance at the almshouse.

With an effort, Aislinn swallowed her laughter, but there was a betraying quiver in her voice when she said, "We don't always greet visitors so roughly, sir. Shall I fetch a damp cloth for your face?"

There was no reply as he wiped a broad hand over his face and shook aside bits of bulb and stalk. He was a tall man, clean shaven, with a faint scar curving up one cheek. Rough-cut black hair covered his ears and tumbled over the folds of chainmail hood at his nape. His black mantle was fastened at the throat with a gold pin and thrown carelessly back over his shoulders. Flakes of white leek dotted his red surcoat.

Disconcerted by ominous silence, Aislinn met his gaze. Any lingering laughter died swiftly at his taut comment: "It seems that my misfortune has afforded you some amusement, damoiselle."

"Indeed, it has, sir." When his scowl deepened, she added, "But I regret that it's caused you discomfort."

Composed, she did not lower her eyes from his black stare. His voice was low, raspy but not unpleasant. He spoke Norman French in a diction as eloquent as the nobility, but that was not unusual for knights reared and educated in a castle. There was an arrogance about him

that reeked of familiarity with command. He looked—
battle weary.

The mail covering his massive frame had broken links,
his surcoat had rents in the fabric, and his knee-high
leather boots bore deeply scuffed toes. But the gold pin
at his throat was heavy and expensive, and the traces of
gilt that trimmed his mantle were of good quality.

Not always a knight errant, perhaps.

Stirred to sympathy, Aislinn gestured toward the front
gate of the almshouse. "Alms are given out at the gate in
the mornings, sir."

"I did not come here for alms." Insult flashed in his
eyes, and he stiffened. There was silent aggression in
those dark eyes, a hostility that she did not care to test.

"Grant pardon for my error, Sir Knight."

Her simple apology in his familiar Norman French was
meant to defuse his ire; she saw him relax slightly. He
pointed in the direction of the abbey.

"I was told to turn in at the gate to find the prior, but
it's closed."

"The wind must have caught it. It's not locked. I just
left the abbey. Prior Thaddeus was in the kitchens, though
I don't know if he's still there."

"Take me to him." When Aislinn arched a brow at his
brusque command, he had the grace to add, "If you please,
damoiselle."

Damoiselle. It sounded so much more elegant than the
English use of *mistress* that she was used to hearing,
though not quite proper address for a widow. "I am maid
no longer, sir, and past the age of maidenly pretensions."

"Your face belies your years, damoiselle."

It was a courtly reply that meant nothing; the fluid
French language lent itself to flowery phrases.

Mistress Margaret broke her unusual silence, hands on
broad hips as she glared at them. "Take yer wicked speech
out of me hearing, the both of ye! 'Tis the devil's tongue!"

"Careful, Mistress," Aislinn murmured in English, "for he obviously understands our tongue well. It would behoove you to guard your willful chatter before you give offense."

"Offend the likes o' him? I do not think it possible!"

Before Aislinn could offer further argument, the knight said in curt English stripped of civility, "She gives you good advice, Mistress. Heed it."

Mistress Margaret gaped at him, then had the good sense to shut her mouth with an audible snap of her teeth. Aislinn turned to gaze at the knight with new respect.

"I'll escort you to Prior Thaddeus, sir."

Silently he stepped aside, allowing her to precede him from the storeroom. She felt him behind her, a powerful presence that was not diminished by the vast open air of the courtyard. It seemed suddenly close in the passage between lofty abbey walls and the almshouse.

Aislinn quickened her pace, then paused as they reached the abbey gate and turned to gaze at the knight. "It's not my place to grant pilgrims audience with Prior Thaddeus, but I can show you to the refectory where you may await his pleasure."

A dark brow shot up. Black eyes glittered. "I do not wish to dine with the prior, but to speak with him, damoiselle."

"So I understand, but as you can see, construction is afoot. Buildings are being used for other than their common purpose."

"Where are the kitchens?"

Impatient to the point of rudeness, he'd abandoned any attempt at courtesy. Aislinn's lips tightened. She shouldn't have offered to take him to Prior Thaddeus. The prior would be most displeased with her presumption.

"Sir, the refectory is just beyond the new Lady Chapel. I'll escort you there but no farther, though I will take word to Prior Thaddeus of your desire to see him."

For an instant she thought he would argue, then his head tilted with exaggerated courtesy.

"Your generosity is great, damoiselle."

"Yea, near as great as my cowardice," she said with a wry twist of her lips. "I confess to being in the prior's bad graces at present, sir, and dare not risk his ire."

The knight stared at her. Some of the grimness faded from his austere countenance after a moment, a visible easing of tension.

A slight tuck at one corner of his mouth indicated ironic humor, but his tone was grave: "It must be a serious crime, indeed, to have earned you the good prior's wrath."

"Most serious." She lowered her voice so that he had to bend slightly to hear, "It involves rotten leeks."

"Ah." Impossibly long lashes briefly shuttered his eyes, then lifted as he said, "I fear my sympathies lie with the prior."

Aislinn smiled, her first impression of the grim knight softening at his response. "It doesn't surprise me to hear it."

"Yes, I didn't think it would."

A deep clang of bells indicated the ninth hour offices, summoning the monks to tierce and muffling the knight's reply. Aislinn beckoned him to follow her. Even amid all the construction chaos, the offices were still conducted in the lovely Lady Chapel. It was a serene refuge from the constant noise.

At the foot of the chapel steps, the knight caught her sleeve and shook his head. She paused. Inside, soft light gleamed on the new stone and elegant carvings over chancel doors. Richly colored paintings embellished the walls with beauty, depicting holy scenes.

The muted shuffle of feet on the tiled walkway was familiar as the black robes filed past them into the chapel, one after the other. A low, mesmerizing chant began like a soft sigh, growing more audible as the chapel began to fill with monks.

Dominus vobiscum . . .

Et cum spiritu tuo . . .

Aislinn stood silently with the knight at her side as the chant drifted out the open chapel door. Her restless fingers sought and found the small wooden cross she wore around her neck, brought it to her lips as she murmured an inaudible prayer, lips repeating the Latin words by rote: *Et, glorisa beatae Mariae semper Virginis intercessione.* . . .

The undulating flow of black robes was like a stream of ants intent only upon a single purpose, disregarding all else around them as they pursued their own courses, lost in the mesmerizing chant that seemed to fill the world with the lulling melody of praise.

If she didn't have such close acquaintance with them, it would be simple to view them as earthly saints. But human foibles were as common among the monks as among the villagers with their own petty conceits and prejudices. Even men of God could have secular goals, she'd discovered.

Another irreligious thought. Prior Thaddeus was quite right when he had told her that she was in peril of her immortal soul, that for the niece of a former abbot, she took far too lightly the teachings of the church. He had shocked and so shamed her with his rebuke that even the memory of it was scalding.

A gentle nudge roused her, and the knight leaned close to mutter, "Show me to the refectory. I'll wait there for Prior Thaddeus."

She turned to glance up at him, a bit surprised at his grim expression. "You do not wish to hear the Mass?"

"No. I do not."

His tone was emphatic, and left no room for doubt. She hesitated, then gave an uncertain nod of acquiescence. She felt a bit awkward at his close scrutiny as she led the way, so filled the silence between them with commentary.

"It's not far, just beyond the Lady Chapel, and still in sight of the original church that Saint Dunstan gave his blessing in the fourth century. Alas, the mud and wattle chapel burned to the ground five years ago in a great fire that also destroyed our beautiful nave, chapel, and quite a few other structures. Glastonbury Abbey has been the holy place of saints since Saint Patrick visited. Joseph of Arimathea came here not long after the death of Christ, and even the Christ child visited when he was a youth. The bones of Saint Dunstan and Saint Patrick now reside here, along with other saints—"

She paused when they drew near the refectory and added a bit lamely, "But you must already know this, else you would not have come to the abbey."

A surly grunt was his only reply to her litany of the abbey's attractions. For the first time, Aislinn wondered what business he had with the prior.

Most visitors to the abbey arrived as pilgrims or supplicants, but there were also those who came for other reasons, more worldly pursuits. Somehow, she did not think that this knight with his shabby garments and austere manner had come for temporal matters. There was an intensity about him that bespoke spiritual resolution, like so many of the pilgrims who came to Glastonbury. Perhaps he'd come on a quest for atonement, and felt unworthy to join holy services until his penance had been met.

In that case, Prior Thaddeus would be delighted to impose acts of contrition on a penitent, as the prior deemed it his duty to inflict hours of kneeling on cold stone floors in prayer, as well as hefty donations to the abbey funds.

Half finished, the refectory was a long low building diagonal to the chapel. It was only a single structure, but there were plans to enlarge once the main church was complete. It was dim inside, with light filtering in through small, high windows. Long tables squatted in the gloom, with benches tucked beneath. A single oil lamp gave off a fitful glow in a shadowed recess on the far wall. Remnants of past meals spiced the air with a lingering scent.

Aislinn turned to invite the knight to be seated at one of the tables to wait, but he spoke first, "You do not have to remain, damoiselle."

It was a blunt, almost rude dismissal. The gruff words echoed hollowly in the large chamber; he stared down at her with an enigmatic expression.

Aislinn briefly met his dark gaze, looked away and said softly, "Very well. I'll tell Prior Thaddeus you await. He's always pleased to greet new pilgrims to the abbey."

"Pilgrim? No, I am no pilgrim. Not of the kind that you mean."

His cryptic comment brought her eyes back to him, and she frowned slightly. "If you seek sanctuary—"

"There's no place on this earth that offers me the kind of sanctuary I would need. No, I do not seek refuge from the world."

There was something mocking in his tone, as if he thought her amusing, and Aislinn's chin came up at once in a defensive gesture. "You need not mock me, sir."

"I do not."

"Then why are you here, if not as a pilgrim? It's not so common for knights to seek audience with the prior."

"My purpose is not common. Nor is it something I wish to discuss with you."

A flush warmed her face, and she bit her lip to halt a sharp retort. He was correct. It was not for her to question his reasons for coming to Glastonbury.

"Shall I tell him who awaits his pleasure, sir?"

"You may tell him that the earl of Essex sends him an important message."

Aislinn moved to the door and turned. "Ere you greet Father Prior, sir, you may wish to remove the rest of the leek from your face. It has a certain—stench."

His hand went to his face, broad palm raking over his features as he scowled at her, and Aislinn left the refectory. She went at once to the Lady Chapel and slipped inside to stand at the rear.

As the familiar prayers flowed around her, she put the troublesome knight from her mind. Whatever his business in Glastonbury, it had nothing to do with her.

"*Kyrie, eleison,*" rose the chant, and she dutifully responded with the others, "*Kyrie, eleison. . . .*"

Lord have mercy on us.

Chapter 4

✝

LIGHT SLOWLY CRAWLED across the refectory's stone floor. Time limped slow as a one-legged beggar as Stephen waited for the prior to appear. Melodic chants had finally faded, signaling the end of tierce, yet still Prior Thaddeus had not arrived.

Boot steps scraped loudly on the floor as he crossed to the open door to peer out. Black-robed monks filed from the Lady Chapel with unhurried gaits, yet none came toward the refectory. Had the woman even summoned the prior?

Yes, he answered his own impatient question, *she is not the kind of woman to say one thing and do another.* Honesty and frankness had unmistakably shone in her eyes. Through years of bitter experience, he had learned to judge people swiftly; instinct told him that the woman would do what she had promised.

He leaned against the stone door frame and propped a boot atop the threshold. There were no threshes to hold inside the refectory, only clean, gleaming stone floors. No doubt, diligent monks kept it free of food scraps and the usual debris found among the rushes in dining areas. Abbey life was rigid and restrictive, devoted to worship and work with no room left for worldly pursuits.

Scraping a thumb across his jaw, Stephen reflected that he would never have made a good monk. While it was no less strict than the formal training of a knight, it was far too empty of life's gentler pleasures, few as they were.

Weariness seeped into his bones, a vivid reminder of the days of constant riding to reach Glastonbury. To his chagrin, he had lost his way taking a detour to avoid a road collapsed due to rain. The lost time had added to a journey already begun late. The earl had deemed it prudent that he spend a fortnight in making himself *worthy* to retrieve the Grail, and he'd found himself under the pious tutelage of the Bishop of Lincoln. If anything, that town was even colder and wetter than York, nearer to the sea and staggered up steep hills. The warmth of Somerset was a welcome change from the cold, wet spring of East Anglia.

Yet there was something unsettling about this shire, a distinctive difference that summoned illusions of dragons and wizards caught in strange rock formations and the bend of ancient trees. The old tales held more credence here, in stories told by the bards round the fires at night of those days when King Arthur rode the land and dragons slept deep inside caves. Welsh bards had a particular fondness for the old tales. It was a Welsh bard who had intrigued King Henry with the tales of Arthur and the Grail.

In a roundabout manner, it was that Welsh bard who had set him on this quest that led to Glastonbury, where legend whispered the chalice of Christ was hidden. Glastonbury—the legendary resting place of King Arthur after his last great battle. And if he believed the letter Essex had given him, Arthur's grave was also the resting place of the fabled cup of Christ. Another myth.

Stephen picked idly at white flecks of leek still dotting his surcoat, and the pungent scent reminded him of the young woman who had so ungraciously laughed at him. A faint smile curved his mouth. She was too honest to hide her laughter, too poised to seek refuge in denial. Rare traits indeed to find in a female.

It had been a long time since he'd bothered to notice or measure a woman's appeal, yet this woman had intrigued him with her bluntness. Unusual honesty in a world of duplicity, not oft seen in men, was even rarer in the women of his experience.

Frowning, he inspected his sleeve, flicked aside more raw leek, saw himself as the woman had no doubt seen him: a ragged knight, dirt grimed and weary, with no idealistic illusions to soften his nature. It was a true assessment.

Movement on the path caught his attention, and he stood upright, pushing away from the prop of the door frame. This must be Prior Thaddeus. The man was tonsured, with a fringe of brown hair like a ring around his crown, and he walked toward the refectory with a rolling gait that was peculiar to corpulent men—splay legged, his feet planted firmly wide apart with each decisive step. A thin monk scuttled along at his side.

"I'm told that you have come to the abbey to seek an audience with me, sir." Prior Thaddeus had an oddly high-pitched voice for a man so large. Against the dusky hue of his black robe, a heavy gold cross hung around his neck and gleamed like a beacon in the darkness. The faint scent of garlic and leeks mixed with the unmistakable fragrance of incense that clung to his garments.

Stephen stepped from the doorway into light. "This is for your ears alone, Prior Thaddeus. I bring an important missive from the Earl of Essex."

"Your name, sir?"

"Stephen Fitzhugh."

"Ah. Your name is not unfamiliar to me."

"I am flattered, Father Prior."

"Perhaps, though I think not." The prior regarded him with unexpected perception and Stephen returned his gaze with a narrowed stare.

"Do you wish to receive the letter from Essex?"

As he pulled it from his belt, he caught a glimpse of suspicion in the prior's eyes, quickly hidden as he inclined his head in a grave nod and murmured to the monk at his side, "Leave us, Brother Timothy. I will seek you out in the chapel when I am done here."

"Yes, Brother Prior. As you will it."

As the monk left, the prior turned back to Stephen. "It has been some time since I've corresponded with the earl. I trust he is well."

"He is as always." Stephen held out the sealed letter. "You're to read this at once."

Pudgy fingers closed around the vellum, which crackled in his grasp as the prior broke the seal and unfolded the page. The edges of the parchment trembled slightly as he read it, and after a moment he looked up with glistening eyes.

"It is well you came to me, my son. The earl is truly a godly man, and shall be blessed—it is a miracle!"

Stephen's mouth tucked in at the corners as he suppressed a bark of sardonic laughter. He bowed his head so Prior Thaddeus would not see the cynicism that he was certain was obvious in his expression, and when he could trust himself not to betray his true thoughts, he looked back up at the prior.

"I'm not unaware of the contents of your letter, if not the specifics, Father Prior. Essex has sent me to learn what I can of these rumors of the Grail. If it's discovered, it would benefit the abbey greatly, a prospect I'm certain you find desirable after the fire that destroyed Saint Dunstan's original chapel."

Prior Thaddeus nodded soberly, his light brown eyes filled with tears. "It was most holy, a place of worship for pilgrims from as far away as Madrid. This abbey was once quite wealthy. Now—until recently, we despaired of survival here. God heard our prayers, it seems, and good King Henry has taken an interest. With his aid—and our esteemed Earl of Essex—I hope to see it regain its former glory."

Stephen regarded the shorter man for a long moment. At issue was more than just a desire to restore the abbey, he was certain. Did Prior Thaddeus see himself as the next abbot, perhaps? A lifetime position of security and prestige would no doubt be welcome.

"You agree to the terms, Father Prior? No one must know why I am here. *No one.* It could jeopardize our success. I must have the freedom to go as I will, where I will."

"Yea, of course I agree, but with the provision that you'll consult me with your findings as you progress. The rumors have never been proven, though there were those who came before you who searched and failed." He paused, and his eyes gleamed. "This time, the chalice will be found! I have prayed for just such a miracle, and now Lord Essex has sent the means to provide it."

"The Grail has not yet been found, Father Prior. Save your prayers of gratitude until then." Stephen shifted position, and his sword clanked against the stone wall. He saw the prior's glance at his weapon, and the swift shadow that crossed his face.

As he refolded the vellum and tucked it into a fold of his cassock, Prior Thaddeus said, "I trust there will be no undue violence. The abbey is a refuge, a place of peace and sanctuary, a place of worship, not a place for weapons."

"I never seek out violence."

"Perhaps not, but violence oft visits unbidden—be

wary of it, for the devil will seek to destroy those who love God and not him."

"But I have met the devil and fear him not, Father Prior."

The prior made the sign of the cross over his chest. "You must be a godly man, indeed, not to fear the power of the devil, sir!"

Stephen ignored the consternation in the prior's face. "Indeed. Tell me what you know of the information learned by the former prior, if you will."

"You speak of Abbot Robert of Winchester, I presume, not of Peter de Marcy, who was last appointed as prior. *He* learned only what the good abbot had already discovered."

"Yes then, tell me what Abbot Robert discovered."

Prior Thaddeus puffed out his cheeks and blew a long breath. "It seems that the good Abbot Robert was a scholar of sorts and did much investigation into local legends. He listened to the villagers a great deal. When they repeated tales of the old ways, he indulged them. Foolish, I say. He should have rebuked them harshly. He did not, of course. Many in the village still believe in magic and wizards, though we have worked hard to convince them of their error. To no avail, it seems, for though they hide it, they still whisper of the old gods and enchantment."

He paused, wiping his brow. "I find it warm in the sun, sir. Let us go inside where it's cooler."

✝

STEPHEN PERCHED AWKWARDLY on the edge of a long bench pulled from beneath a trestle table as the prior fetched a jug of ale and two mugs, plopping them on the table as he lowered his bulk to the bench opposite. He poured a liberal amount into each mug and slid one across to Stephen with a contented sigh.

"God provides the grain, King Henry the coin to put it before us. Drink, good sir, drink."

Sipping the bitter ale, Stephen observed the prior over the rim of his mug. "What of the Grail? Did the former abbot share what he had discovered with you as well as Peter de Marcy?"

"He did not. Nor do I think he shared it with de Marcy. It would have been foolish for him to do so, as de Marcy was not to be trusted. After Abbot Robert's death, his papers were bundled up and put away. Peter de Marcy studied them, I am certain, and learned enough to convince him that the Grail was hidden in the abbey. Alas, with the fire, it may well have been destroyed along with so many other relics, but I will not yet give up all hope that it was saved."

"Where are the abbot's papers now? Were they saved from the fire?"

"Yea, some of them. I confess that I cannot gain any useful knowledge from the writings, however. It seems that many pages are missing, though I cannot be certain of it."

"If there are pages missing, do you mean they have been destroyed?"

The prior hesitated. "Not all. As you mentioned, Peter de Marcy also sought the Grail. He succeeded Robert as abbot in capacity if not title—it was de Marcy's wickedness that brought about the fiery destruction on Saint Urban's Day." Leaning forward, Prior Thaddeus said, "He was unconsecrated from an act of warfare when he conducted the Mass that Christmas, earning God's wrath and judgement upon us all for his sin. Despite Ralph Fitzstephen's disbelief, it was Peter de Marcy who brought misfortune upon us. Fitzstephen may be the king's steward—and I admit he's been quite generous in his way—but he displays a dismaying tendency to be far too . . . worldly . . . for a man who is in charge of building a holy church to glorify God."

Father Prior blew out a sigh that was rife with ale and shook his head. "It is not my place to judge, but I fear that the very sanctity of our efforts is being diminished by men unworthy to be involved. I have seen the devastation wrought by a man bent upon his own will instead of God's."

Stephen sipped the bitter ale, half hiding his face with the pewter mug; impatience filled him, but he curbed his tongue with an effort when he lowered the mug. "And de Marcy was familiar with the former abbot's papers?"

"He made himself familiar as soon as he arrived."

Another obvious sore point with the prior so Stephen changed his tactics.

"I would see these papers as soon as possible, Father Prior. They are in safekeeping, I presume."

"Safe enough." Owlish eyes blinked at him for a moment, then he leaned forward again as if the walls were listening. "I dared not leave them about with all the confusion. They are valuable, and it seems that too many are aware of their importance. The earl—praise God for his assistance—is one of the few men still alive who know of their existence."

"Then you have hidden them well?"

Prior Thaddeus sat back on the bench, his lips pursed as he studied Stephen. It was warm in the afternoon gloom, window light diffused by lengthening shadows. Beads of perspiration dotted the prior's broad forehead, glistening in bushy eyebrows. Outside could be heard the steady rattle of hammers and shouts of workmen, yet in the refectory it was quiet seclusion.

"Show me the ring, Sir Stephen."

Stephen put a hand to his neck and withdrew a chain from beneath his surcoat. A heavy gold ring slid along the fine links, winking in muted light with shades of crimson. A beveled ruby in the shape of a chalice gleamed in the center of the ring. The prior put out a hand for it, and Stephen relinquished the ring and silver chain.

The chain pooled in the prior's palm, silver on soft white. The ruby glinted as he turned the ring over, then nodded in satisfaction and cleared his throat.

"It is indeed the ring I sent Essex. Very well. No man has been trusted with the papers, but they are safe."

"In Glastonbury?"

"Yea, right under the very noses of those who would seek the chalice for their own rapacious reasons."

This time Stephen could not hide his impatience. "For the love of all that's holy, Prior Thaddeus, where are these important pages kept now?"

"Robert of Winchester's niece has them safely in her possession—Aislinn of Amberlea."

"His niece. You gave them to a *woman*?"

The prior poured more ale. As he lifted his mug, he stared at Stephen over the frothy rim. "Not just any woman. The abbot's niece. She is not like most females, but has common sense and discretion. You have met her. It was she who brought me word of your arrival. A thorn in my side at times, but most trustworthy."

He tilted his mug and drank deeply. Spume spilled over the brim and onto his florid jowls so that he looked like nothing more than a rabid dog.

Stephen stared at him. Aislinn of Amberlea—the woman who had laughed at him. The former abbot's niece. He had not counted upon female interference in his plans. This created an entirely new set of problems.

His hand tightened on the pewter mug, and his voice was flat. "You'll get those pages from her, Father Prior, and I will then—"

"Nay, Sir Stephen." The prior shook his head. "It's not that simple, I fear."

Stephen regarded the monk with a raised brow. "Why is it not that simple?"

"Mistress Aislinn does not know she has the pages. Nor would she know their importance." When Stephen just stared at him Prior Thaddeus said softly, "It's for her protection as well. One man has died here for the mere promise of such a great prize. I could not risk her death on my conscience."

"But you don't mind risking mine, I perceive."

Silence fell. Then the prior said, "You are aware of the risks, Sir Stephen. Mistress Aislinn would not have a chance should there be danger." He paused, and his high voice was nothing but a whisper as he said, "Do not be misled. The danger is there and it is real. I have not forgotten the last man the earl sent, nor have I forgotten how he died. There are men—evil men—who would think nothing of murder to gain such a prize as the holy chalice of our Lord. Those men do not want to find it for the right reasons."

Stephen did not reply; the prior was no judge of men's character if he thought the Earl of Essex meant to allow the church to keep such a prize. But it was not his place to instruct the prior on the frailties of human nature. It was his task to recover the Grail and deliver it to Essex.

No man—or woman—would be allowed to interfere.

Chapter 5

†

IT HAD BEGUN raining in the night, leaving muddy puddles yawning in the street, slick and treacherous as Aislinn picked her way with wool skirts held high. Water sloshed over her feet, ruining her shoes. A light sprinkle dampened the air and her hooded cloak as she crossed High Street to the almonry.

The gates were open. Petitioners huddled under the eaves as they waited for alms to be given out. On Mondays, coins were distributed; Fridays, food was given out to those who came. There was always, she had noted, a longer line on Monday than Friday. For some, coin held higher appeal than bread and cheese.

Aislinn worked past the crowd and, to her surprise, encountered the knight who had arrived a few days before. He stood beneath an overhang of the almonry roof. Leaning back against the wall, his arms were folded over his chest. He seemed so aloof from all that went on around him, ignoring the clamor of the petitioners and even the rain as he waited.

"Bonjour, damoiselle," he greeted her pleasantly, and when she paused uncertainly, the suggestion of a smile bent the corners of his mouth.

Rain misted her cheeks, made her cloak cling heavily as she regarded the knight. The smell of wet wool was strong. "Good morning, sir," she replied in English. "I see you are still here."

"So it seems." He swept a gaze along the wet stones and sodden crowd. His lip curled when a woman's strident voice rang out. "I've found the abbey most peaceful until now."

"Those poor souls are not as fortunate as some to have lodgings and food, sir. Do not judge them too harshly."

"I do not judge them at all. It's not my place to judge them or any other, great though the temptation may be." Eyes as black as sloe berries regarded her without blinking.

Aislinn jerked forward. "Grant pardon, sir, but I have much yet to do this morn."

"You are excused from your regular duties, damoiselle. I have been waiting here for you. Prior Thaddeus suggested you can help me."

"Help you?" Aislinn turned, caught between amazement and irritation. It was not at all like the prior to excuse her from any of her duties. It was more likely, he would simply add tasks, not take them away. She frowned. "I find that most unlikely, sir."

Pushing away from the wall, the knight stepped forward into the rain. She noticed droplets clustered on his lashes until he blinked them away. His head was bare, hair wet and dripping.

"Shall I fetch him to give confirmation to you, damoiselle?"

Aislinn hesitated. There was no reason to disbelieve him, though it was certainly strange that Prior Thaddeus would be so generous with her time.

"That's not necessary, sir. If you are mistaken, the prior will seek you out quickly enough."

Mistress Margaret appeared in the almonry doorway, her face set into lines of disapproval. "Be ye still dallying, Mistress Aislinn? No priest is like to shrive yer soul this week. Best to leave off such wickedness and come tend yer duties."

Aislinn turned. "Your faith in me is most encouraging, Mistress, but I fear that I shall not be able to help you today. The prior has other tasks for me."

Prompted more by irritation with the dour Margaret than a desire to lend aid to the knight, Aislinn briefly relished the expression of dismay on the woman's face. Any twinge of guilt for leaving Margaret alone to dole out alms vanished at her muttered prophecy that females who gave themselves airs were likely to find their penance harsh.

"No more harsh than the penance visited upon those who seek out strife rather than harmony, Mistress Margaret." Aislinn turned back to the knight to say, "I'm ready, sir, to lend what aid I can, since Prior Thaddeus requests it of me."

"An evil-tempered woman," the knight commented as they left the almonry behind. "I find myself most relieved that the prior did not put me in her hands."

Mirth rose in her throat as Aislinn visualized the inevitable result of such a match. "It might have been most entertaining to observe, sir, for Mistress Margaret can be unpleasant company on occasion."

"Truly, I would not have thought it."

His droll reply earned her laughter, and Aislinn felt immensely relieved. Perhaps he was not the stark knight she had first thought him to be, after all. He seemed almost—pleasant.

"What is this onerous task that Prior Thaddeus would have me lend my hand to do, Sir Knight? It must be most dreadful indeed if he sends me in his place."

"Tedious, more like. Or perhaps he dreads my company."

It was a noncommittal reply, and Aislinn wondered if he was being deliberately obscure. "What is your name, sir?"

"Stephen Fitzhugh. And you are Aislinn of Amberlea, formerly of Shepton Mallet."

"Prior Thaddeus has been most informative, I see."

"Very. Your uncle was the former abbot, Robert of Winchester. He died in 1180. You have lived in Glastonbury since you were ten years of age when your parents died in a virulent fever that swept the countryside, leaving you in your uncle's care. You are a widow of some ten years now, having wed at the age of fifteen, and on Saint Nicholas's Day, you will achieve a score and five years of age. Your temper is mild, your nature generous, and you are honest almost to a fault. If you have a major flaw, it is that you are willful at the most inconvenient times, and have a sharp tongue when you are sufficiently provoked—of which I have some experience, I might add."

"Well," Aislinn said when he crooked his brow at her, "I believe you left out a few important details. I have all my teeth, no disfiguring scars save the one on my knee that I received when I fell out of an apple tree when I was ten. A fitting penance, as I was stealing the abbey's apples. Also, I have the annoying habit, I've been told, of saying exactly what is on my mind instead of being prudently silent. Why are you so interested in me?"

"I'm not interested in you save as an assistant. I require someone trustworthy and I'm told that person would be you."

"Of all the lay brothers who come to the abbey, Prior Thaddeus recommended me? I find that most difficult to believe, Sir Stephen."

"Nonetheless, it is true." He halted in the shelter of a

wall, turned to stare down at her. "If you prefer to hear it from the prior, I'll wait for you here."

Silence fell between them. One of the abbey cats chose that moment to approach, and wound around the knight's ankles with a loud purr. He looked down. The cat lifted on hind legs to sniff at his hand, and to Aislinn's surprise, he bent to lift the little animal into his arms. Cradling it in the crook of his elbow, he idly stroked the soft calico fur.

"Well, damoiselle?"

Wry amusement curved her mouth and her hand moved to touch the cross around her neck, a habit when she was uncertain. "Brother Timothy would be most gratified to see you being kind to one of the abbey cats. He cares greatly for them."

"Brother Timothy—do you refer to that thin worm of a monk who grovels every time the prior barks? He could learn much from cats, I think. They hiss and spit, but cower to no one. A powerful lesson for him." He stroked the cat's chin, and lifted his brow. "I'm never kind, but I believe in giving the devil his due. It's a payment with which I'm familiar."

"You're more kind than you pretend, Sir Stephen."

"Only when it suits my purpose. You might remember that for the future."

It was an enigmatic comment that summoned disquiet. Her hand dropped to her side as he released the cat and it minced a nonchalant path away from them. No doubt, gone to find Brother Timothy. Another bone of contention with Father Prior, who argued that he fed them too much for the cats to be interested in ridding the abbey stores of mice and rats. Poor Brother Timothy. His holy visions had earned resentment from the prior, an envy that was unworthy of a man of God.

"Come," she said, "show me what it is that requires my skill. I'm greatly intrigued."

Sir Stephen strode toward the chapter house, and she accompanied him, lifting her skirts so the hem would not be wet by the soaked grass of the cloister. When he unlocked the door and swung it open into the chamber, it was empty of lay brothers or monks, just an organized jumble of furniture and relics crowding the stone floor. Reliquaries containing saints' bones to be put into the new church were carefully stacked. Precious books were chained to tables, awaiting a permanent home in the new scriptorium, and statues and icons lined the walls.

"Do you have permission to be here, Sir Stephen?" she asked as she hesitated in the open doorway. "This area is normally restricted to all but a few."

"Yea, I have the prior's permission to be here. He said you are familiar with some of the records I need to search."

Startled, Aislinn was still loathe to enter. "I have not been allowed in here, Sir Stephen. It's restricted to the consecrated monks alone."

Impatiently, he motioned her inside. "If there was not so much construction, it would no doubt be the same now. None of these new buildings are complete or consecrated yet, so the relics are safe enough from female contamination."

"Best not let Prior Thaddeus hear such sacrilege. He regards females as one step ahead of damnation."

"No doubt with good reason. However, I think he can be persuaded to overlook the dangers this time."

Aislinn stepped tentatively inside, managing a smile that felt stiff. "What records do you seek here?"

"One book. A journal kept by a former abbot. There has been some dissention with the Bishop of Wells regarding certain promises about the churches. Perhaps the abbot's writings will shed light on a solution to the quarrel."

"You are speaking of my uncle. He was involved in

the cause of that dispute, to his sorrow." She frowned, then said, "My uncle has been dead for over eight years. Surely no one seeks to discredit his memory now."

"It's not to discredit anyone, but to settle the dispute as equitably as can be done, damoiselle. Do you object?"

"No, of course not. It has been a matter of contention for far too long. But I cannot see how you hope to resolve the problem by studying my uncle's journals."

"It is hoped that he made some references that will be of use. Where shall we begin our search?"

Aislinn hesitated. It would sound foolish to voice her objections now that he had explained his reasons. Yet she felt strangely uneasy.

"We can start here," she said after a moment and gestured toward a heavy ledger chained to a table. "The lay brothers have listed all the library contents that survived the fire. If there are any journals that may be useful to you, they will no doubt be listed here."

"Excellent. Shall we begin?"

After a brief pause, she shrugged out of her enveloping cloak and draped it over a low bench, then lit oil lamps and fixed them in the iron brackets dangling from the ceiling. Bending, she pulled out a thick volume and hefted it to a table; the thin chain tethering it clinked softly in the gloom.

"We can begin with this ledger, if you like," she said. "It ends the year my uncle died, I believe."

The lamps cast swaying pools of light over illuminated manuscripts salvaged from the fire. There were only a few that had survived the flames, and most bore scorch marks. Vellum crackled dully as Aislinn opened the ledger atop the large table. She smoothed the pages with one hand, brought a lamp closer to shine upon the volume.

Stephen hovered behind her, watching as she perused the ledger carefully; her fingertip skimmed the lines with swift precision, and her lips moved silently.

An educated female, he mused, familiar with reading Latin—an anomaly in his experience. There was much more to this Aislinn of Amberlea than he'd first suspected. It may prove to be more difficult to deceive her than the prior believed.

A low rumble of thunder rolled in the distance, and the rain fell harder, a constant drum outside the open door. A gentle fragrance wafted from her hair. Her head was bent, soft coils of honey-colored hair loose atop her crown as she studied the ledger.

A few strands had escaped from her plaits, straggling down the nape of her neck. Her gown was damp where rain had penetrated her light wool cloak, leaving darker patches of blue across her shoulders. Without a coif, she seemed much younger than her years, the absence of a head cover softening her features. He had observed her from a distance the past two days, but had not expected her to seem so vulnerable when near.

An unexpected, unfamiliar warmth seeped through him, dispelling the damp chill. Impulsively he put out a hand to touch her hair, fingers skimming silky strands in a feathery touch that shocked him.

He jerked back his hand, flushed and unsettled, greatly chagrined at yielding to such a foolish whim. It was futile and dangerous to allow tender emotions to whittle at his hard-won reserve.

Fingers curled into his palm, making a fist as he drew a sharp breath in through his teeth. Treacherous territory lurked beyond his control if he surrendered to even the most basic emotion. It could ruin him. Long ago he had vowed not to allow Essex to defeat him. He had trained himself to feel nothing other than anger, not sorrow nor joy nor need—nothing.

Yet for the first time in years he glimpsed a chink in that armor he kept around him like a suit of new mail, and it was disturbing. To lose sight of his goal for even an instant could spell doom. He would not allow it.

Chapter 6

✝

AISLINN GREW STILL. Had she imagined it, or had the knight touched her hair? It had been so light, a whisper of contact, then gone so quickly that she wasn't certain if he had touched her intentionally, or merely leaned too close. A shiver tickled her spine. Her finger paused atop an entry in the ledger and quivered slightly as she read aloud:

" 'Robert of Winchester entertained Reginald of Bath in September of 1179.' If we can find a journal written by the abbot during that time, it should refer to the details of that meeting."

No tremor betrayed her words as she turned to glance up at the knight, who gazed down at her impassively. There was no suggestion of guilt or any other emotion in his features. A faint flush warmed her cheeks. Truly, she was imagining things to think he had caressed her hair!

"Where would we find such a journal, damoiselle?"

Aislinn glanced around the crowded chamber. "If it did survive the fire, it will be in one of these chests. Only the ledgers and books most often used are kept out, because it's so crowded. When the chapter house is completed, the library will be much more organized, I'm certain. But for now, we must search through all the chaos to find what you need."

"Would the abbot not have left his personal journals in the possession of a family member or trusted friend? It seems more likely that his private thoughts would not be trusted to a journal accessible to any lay brother."

"It's possible, of course. Unlikely, as his only living relative was myself. You will have to ask Prior Thaddeus about a trusted companion. My uncle was very generous and kind and treated all equally. As abbot, he was not allowed the luxury of close friends. It created dissension among the monks if one thought another received higher favors."

"An intrigue to rival that of the royal court, I perceive. There is much more to monastic life than I had ever considered."

Stephen stepped away from the table, his hands clasped behind him. It did not escape her notice that he spoke of intrigue at the royal court as if he had experience of it. She studied him more objectively. The surcoat he wore was in better condition than the last one he had worn. It was of fine red wool, the edges worked in a pretty gilt pattern that was not frayed or worn. A jewelled belt circled his lean waist and looped back over, empty of the sword it was meant to hold.

A warrior. A knight. A man with a purpose. She sensed it like an approaching storm, and wondered what he intended.

"The abbey is more like a village than a sanctuary, Sir Stephen. The greatest difference is the rigid adherence to the spiritual life."

"And the absence of women."

She smiled. "For the most part, yes. There are a few of

us who are allowed in certain areas of the abbey, but only briefly and to tend our duties. No women at all are allowed to remain on the abbey grounds after dark."

"Not even for midnight matins?"

"There are exceptions, of course. Are you considering joining the abbey, perhaps?"

His brief expression of incredulity dissolved into a wry smile as he shook his head. "I doubt that I would be a good candidate to join these godly monks."

"Ah yes, I seem to recall that you say you have no need of sanctuary."

Dark eyes met hers, held her gaze for a long moment. "I never said I have no need of it. I said there's no place fit for my needs."

"And are your needs that different from those of other men?"

"Yea, damoiselle, they are indeed. I require much more than the mere gratification of my belly and a warm fire."

Aislinn stared at him. There was an intensity in his tone and eyes that was unnerving. She turned back to the ledger opened atop the table. In it, carefully penned notations filled the pages, daily details of the abbey a requiem to a life long past. There was a continuity in these ledgers, an implied promise of everlasting life within the simple tasks of lay brothers and monks. It was comforting to think that her uncle would never be forgotten as long as men could read of his kind acts. Robert of Winchester may lie in a tomb on the south side of the chapter house, but his memory would linger as long as there was an abbey.

Was that what this knight meant when he spoke of refuge from the world? Did he seek true spiritual immortality, or only the earthly gratification he scorned?

"I have shocked you," the knight said, and she looked up at him with a faint smile.

"Nay, Sir Stephen, you have not. I was thinking of my uncle."

"Do you compare me to him?"

She laughed. "It would require more imagination than I possess to liken you to Robert of Winchester, I fear. He was truly one of the most spiritual men I have ever known. All who met him admired him."

"Not according to the archdeacon of Wells."

"No, but Reginald of Bath caused that bitterness to flower. It was due to my uncle's unfortunate agreement with the bishop to place the Seven Churches of Glastonbury's jurisdiction under a special officer called the abbot's archdeacon. It benefitted only Reginald to have the abbey under his control. Valuable income was diverted from Glastonbury to Wells, and the monks here appealed to the pope to cancel the agreement. It's an ongoing dispute that's brought you to Glastonbury to investigate. There are none here who wish to be under the bishopric's domination."

"I'll make note of that fact."

Aislinn rose from the stool to face him. "Considerable revenues were earned by the abbey, monies enough to finance the wars of kings. Though funds are much diminished at the present, once the abbey is rebuilt it will support itself again. The fisheries are still here, and there are the baker's ovens, and the mill—if you must judge the future of the abbey, take into consideration all that would be lost if it were dissolved."

"That decision is not mine to make, damoiselle. I'm merely attempting to find the abbot's journals."

"If you're here to resolve the dispute with Wells, it seems logical that you are involved in the final disposition of the abbey affairs."

"Logical, but incorrect." A faint smile tucked the corners of his mouth inward. "Do not invite the wolf when the dog will suffice."

"What is that supposed to mean?" She eyed him with rising irritation. "If you must speak in parables, please be good enough to make them comprehensible."

"It was a mere comparison to illustrate my point, not so ambitious as a parable. I meant only that it is never wise to invite great trouble when a minor inconvenience is the more likely outcome."

"Then you should have said so."

A lifted brow was his only reply. Aislinn turned away, focusing intently on the open ledger, angry that she had let him provoke her into such a reaction. It was never prudent to allow annoyance to supplant discretion.

She read silently, perusing the list of dates and names but fully aware that Sir Stephen was roaming the chamber in restless strides. It was quiet with only the steady hiss of rain outside penetrating the room. Even construction had halted for a time, and it was eerily still in the lamp-lit gloom.

Sir Stephen had paused before an open manuscript, reading silently, turning the pages carefully. After a few minutes, he looked up, and she felt his stare and raised her head to gaze back at him.

"What do you know of these tales of King Arthur being buried in Avalon?" He stabbed his finger at a page. "It alludes here to the fact that Glastonbury and Avalon are one and the same."

"I know the popular tales, those sung by bards and told around a fire at night. Is this important in the dispute with Wells?"

"Perhaps." A faint smile curved his mouth. "If the great King Arthur's grave were discovered here, that would give the abbey an added incentive for pilgrims to come, and make it even wealthier than Wells."

"It still does not relate to the disagreement."

She sat back, brushed ink from her fingers. The pages were damp, and should be more carefully maintained ere they ruined. She would speak to Prior Thaddeus about that.

"It relates to the disagreement should Glastonbury suddenly become the site of such a momentous event." His voice was soft, a purring sound. "Only the discovery of the Holy Grail would be more significant."

Aislinn did not look up from observing slightly smeared ink on her fingers. It would never do to betray by even the faintest flicker of an eyelash a reaction to his comment.

"Neither of which is likely to happen, Sir Stephen."

Does he know of the journal pages among my uncle's possessions? No. He could not. No one knew of them. It was a well-guarded secret, and only she knew of the significance behind other journal entries. Surely, if the prior had guessed their importance, he would never have allowed her to keep them. They were safe now with her, hidden away until she could decipher the mystery of the scrawled entries.

The Holy Grail. It would surely endow Glastonbury Abbey with the favor of the king and pope and restore it to the prominence it deserved. The bones of Saint Patrick were sacred, but not lure enough to bring pilgrims from as far away as the Holy Land. King Arthur would bring them.

But the Holy Grail would bring the world to the abbey gates if it were indeed to be found with King Arthur. . . .

It was enough to make her giddy. The Grail would summon fame as well as guarantees that the abbey wouldn't be disbanded, the monks scattered, the town left to languish. All would be well.

It wasn't selfish to want that, not greedy to want the abbey to survive. If Joseph of Arimathea had truly thought this place holy enough to leave the Grail, then the abbey should endure man's efforts to destroy it. Or to use it for other than the most holy of reasons.

Aislinn lifted her head, saw the knight watching her with a frowning regard. He had come too close to the truth, almost as if he knew what she had found in the pages. But that was impossible. He could not know. No one knew.

Chapter 7

✝

SHE KNEW. IT was a brief impression, a fleeting glimpse of wariness in her eyes that convinced him she knew more than she intended to admit. So much for Prior Thaddeus and his conviction that the woman was too ignorant to recognize the value of the papers she held. Now he must try a different tactic.

"No doubt you're right, damoiselle. It was a passing hope. A fancy, you could say, that the fortunes of the abbey could be restored with such a treasure. Alas, men have been searching for King Arthur and the Holy Grail for over five hundred years without success. It's most unlikely either the chalice or the grave still exists, if ever they did."

"Yes, most unlikely." She met his gaze without a trace of secrecy in eyes of a deep violet-blue.

Uncertainty gnawed at him. Either she was accomplished at deception or she truly had no idea of the value of the pages in her possession.

He moved away from the manuscript to gaze out the

open door. Rain was a gray veil over grounds littered with construction debris and patches of green grass.

Beyond the abbey walls, soaring upward, loomed the Tor. It rose majestically, the summit hidden now by rainy mist, mysterious and brooding, like a watchful hawk that hovered over the abbey and town. Surrounded by marsh-lands and prone to flooding, this region was studded with rounded hills and unexpected crags. The Tor was by far the highest, spearing the sky and clouds, mist shrouded. It must be the warmer clime that made the mist so thick.

Stephen turned away from the door. "The prior says the people here still practice the old ways."

"Some of them. Not many. Have you come to convert them, Sir Stephen?"

"I told you why I've come to Glastonbury. Conversion is the duty of priests."

"And killing is the duty of knights. Yet you are here on a peaceful mission, I'm told."

"How gratifying to know you pay such close attention." He frowned slightly. "My time here will be brief enough, once I learn what I need to know. You needn't fear I have any intention of meddling in abbey affairs for too long."

After a moment, she said, "There are only a few who cling to the old ways. They stay to themselves for fear of being condemned as heretics."

"Which is likely to happen should they speak too often of magic, or gods living in trees," he said wryly.

She smiled faintly. "Yet would it not be better to lead them gently to the right path instead of to the stake?"

"A radical suggestion. It could earn you a place beside them in the fire."

"And you would approve?"

She stared at him intently, as if her life did indeed depend upon his reply. Amused, he shrugged. "My disapproval would make not a shred of difference to those who sought to make an example of heretics."

"That's not what I asked you, Sir Stephen, but I see you prefer a cautious reply. It's growing late, and I have much yet to do today. I've shown you how to find what you need, so I will return to my usual duties."

She lifted her cloak from the bench where she had left it and pulled it around her, tugging the hood over her hair in a graceful, feminine motion that reminded Stephen of the absence of softness in his life. He had been too long in the company of men accustomed to coarseness, it seemed. For the first time in longer than he could easily recall, he felt the need for a woman, even if just for a night.

Cursed inconvenient in this blighted hamlet. . . .

As Aislinn reached the door, he said, "If I don't find what I need, I'll call upon you again."

She paused and turned back to look at him. Lamplight gleamed in her eyes, shadowed the small cleft in her chin. "I have helped you all I can, Sir Stephen."

"No, damoiselle, I do not think you have."

✝

BROTHER TIMOTHY CAUGHT her as she crossed the green, hailing her with a gentle call. "Mistress Aislinn, do you have a moment?"

"Of course, Brother Timothy."

He reached her as they came abreast of the chapel, and they stepped inside out of the rain. Candles burned, chasing shadows with small ellipses of light in holders on the wall. Lovely wall paintings in brilliant colors glowed in the soft gloom, scenes of angels and heavenly choirs.

Aislinn did not take the hood from her hair, but shook it loose of raindrops. "It seems as if it's rained for a week," she said with a little laugh.

The monk flashed a wavering smile, but his face looked strained in the shadows. Fair hair curled around his tonsure, a pale glow in murky light. Thin fingers clasped and unclasped, the wide sleeves of his habit slid over bony wrists.

Aislinn put out a hand to lightly touch his shoulder. "What is it, Brother Timothy? Is all well with you?"

"Yea—well enough." He glanced around nervously. The chapel was empty save for the two of them. The chancel was deep in gloom, but where they stood in the misty light of the open doorway and flickering candles, it was easy to see his distress.

"Tell me what afflicts thee, Brother," she murmured. "I have never seen you so upset."

"It is the prior . . . oh, Mistress, we have known each other since I was a lad and I know no one else I can talk to without fear of reprisal. You must give me some advice."

"Advice? I don't know that I'm qualified to give advice to a holy brother, but I can listen. Will that help?"

He looked wretched. His gaunt face twisted, and he turned away, nodding. "Yea, perhaps just to unburden myself will ease my anger, for I fear I will burst with it if I do not say what I feel!"

A brief silence fell. His narrow chest heaved with his frustration, and Aislinn understood. "Father Prior can be very difficult, I've learned. Is it he who distresses you so?"

"Yes! Oh, I cannot bear it at times, for nothing I do meets with his approval! The basket of leeks—he told me to take with gratitude the largesse that comes to the abbey, and to see that Mistress Margaret does not cheat the almonry. I did so, but she sent me with the leeks that she said the prior had approved. I should not have listened to her. If you had not come when you did—I thought Brother Prior would strike me again."

"Again?" Alarmed, she asked, "Has he struck you before, Brother Timothy?"

"Only once, in extreme anger. One of the cats—Abbey, the calico—had soiled an altar cloth. It wasn't her fault, as she'd been sick. Brother Arnot is teaching me the proper use of herbs, and she's well now, but . . . oh, Mistress, I fear that I will be sent to another abbey if the prior finds me unsuitable. I know nothing else but Glastonbury! It is my home, but as a sworn Benedictine, I must go where I am told. What will I do? Lord have mercy, what will I do?"

"Ease yourself, Brother Timothy. Prior Thaddeus can be difficult, but he's not malicious. He would not send you away out of spite."

"No, no, you're right. It's just that when I have one of my visions—oh, so holy they are, Mistress, and I do not invite them, I swear it! But they come upon me unbidden, the sweetest visions of heaven and love . . . and the holiest of holies at times." A luminous light lit his face, so that he seemed apart from the mortal world as he spoke. "Brother Berian has visions, and he has been set to test the truth of what I see."

"Brother Berian is so old, he has the wisdom of time on him. He will convince Father Prior of your sincerity."

"I hope so, Mistress." He drew in a deep breath. "The prior means no harm, I suppose. It just feels that way at times." He gave her a beseeching look that went straight to her heart. "If it should ever come to pass that I'm to be sent away, will you speak for me?"

"I'm not certain anyone would wish to hear what I have to say, but of course I will. You're a devout man, faithful to the church and your calling, and all know that. Now come. Make peace with yourself."

"Yes, I will do that." He paused. "Take a basket to my grandfather, if you will, and tell him I am well and happy."

"I will, Brother Timothy. You *are* well and happy. You

have your calling here. No one will take you away, I'm certain of it."

"I hope you're right, Mistress." His smile was wan. "I pray that you're right, and that Brother Prior is pleased with me."

She clasped his hands between her own and squeezed gently. He looked so young. She remembered him as a small lad and felt suddenly old. There was a six year difference in their ages, but it felt strangely like a dozen years or more.

Then he drew himself up as if remembering his position, and made the sign of the cross over her. "Go with God, my sister."

From youth to monk in the space of a heartbeat, he had changed before her eyes.

"Grant mercy, Brother," she said softly, and turned to leave the chapel. Rain pelted stone and earth, wet her even through the hood drawn low over her face. A gray curtain hovered over abbey walls and shrouded High Street. It seemed as if the rain would never end.

✝

THE RAIN HAD finally ceased and Aislinn sat by the un-shuttered window in her hall, gazing out into the small courtyard with the carefully tended beds of flowers and herbs. This house had been her refuge in the years since being widowed.

It was a painful memory, those dark days after David's death when she had not known what to do or where to go. If not for her uncle, she might well have been forced to choose a distasteful course. Yet Abbot Robert had rescued her when she was still so young, too young to know that life offered difficult choices to a fifteen-year-old female already wed and widowed. Seven months she had been married when David was killed in a hunting accident. The boar had been vicious, the shaft of his hunting spear weak, and his death violent. A shock to all, his grieving family and his bewildered young wife. Ah, so immature she had been, a child still for all that she was married and expected to be wiser than she was.

Robert of Winchester's perception of her dilemma kept her from an unwise decision. Returning to Glastonbury Abbey with him was meant to be a temporary solution until she had time to choose her future. That was nine years ago, and she still lived in this comfortable, cozy house across from the abbey walls. It was hers for as long as she lived, granted her by the abbey in return for the widow's portion that she had received from David's family in lieu of a claim on his estate. There had been no children, no reason to stay where she was not wanted. And so she had come here. Where had the time gone?

Aislinn slid a fingertip across the wooden windowsill. She spent most nights sitting at this window, gazing into a courtyard mantled with snow or ablaze with summer blooms. It was not a bad life. Master Weaver helped care for her garden and vegetables, for a share of them. He also watched over her. Her free time was spent in quiet reflection and study. Yet tonight she couldn't concentrate. A feeling of restless energy marred her usual serenity.

Rising from her seat by the window, she stepped around an oak dining table flanked by two chairs and set with a bowl of pottage and white bread brought from the abbey. On the wall above it was a small painting depicting the search for the Holy Grail. It was a gift to her from her uncle, given to her when he knew he was dying. It had been crudely painted by a local youth, purchased for a few pence, more as a characteristic act of generosity than a desire to display the painting. The colors were already fading, yet that gave the scene a mystical quality, the light beams streaming from heaven to spill over a mailed knight who knelt with the Grail in his hands, offering it up to a heavenly host.

Carefully, Aislinn lifted the painting from the wall. A loose corner of the thin wood stuck out from the backing, and she pressed it gently so that it was easily removed. Between the painting on wood and the heavier back were pages from her uncle's journal. As always, her fingers trembled when she touched them. She'd recognized their importance at once when she found them and remembered the abbot's barely contained excitement in the months before he died. He had not shared his find with her, save to say he had discovered information that could very well change the Christian world. One day, he'd promised her, he would divulge everything.

Alas, he had died soon after, and his knowledge and the secret he kept had gone with him—until she had stumbled across these pages only a year ago when the painting had fallen and been cracked. The tiny, neat letters so carefully penned on parchment, sanded, and hidden away behind the painting, held more questions than answers. Alone, they were incomplete and puzzling.

Until the abbot's journal, which had been saved from the fire, was given into her keeping, the pages still scorched and stained with soot. Together, the entries in that journal and the missing pages the abbot had hidden were meant to give a complete outline of events that could lead to the discovery of King Arthur's grave—in itself, a marvelous find. If the chalice Christ had used at the Last Supper was found as well, it would be a miraculous discovery.

It was obvious the abbot had feared the discovery would be usurped by others, for much of the information he'd left was written in obscure verse. She had managed to decipher some of it, but there was so much yet she had not been able to comprehend. It was painstaking work.

Aislinn lit a candle and set it on the small table where

a light breeze from the open window made the flame flicker and dance. With her supper of pottage and thick bread, she sat down to study the pages.

Light faded outside, and the candle cast a feeble glow. The abbot's cramped writing was difficult to understand, her grasp of Latin adequate but woefully sparse.

"Between desert obelisks in holy aisles," she read softly, "lie the keys to the Kingdom of God. Tread softly, ere mortal kings rise up with mighty swords to take back that vessel which has been stolen."

An obvious referral to the chalice and the king, but where could he mean? Massaging her temples with ink-smeared fingers, she sighed. Holy aisles—the church, no doubt. But it was gone now, save for memory. She tried to recall the nature of antiquities kept in the old chapel before the fire. Could her uncle have hidden something in that mud-and-wattle hut? Keys to a door, perhaps, or a locked casket?

Desert obelisks—a baffling reference. Nothing had been saved from the fire that fit the description, nor could she recall exotic relics of that nature.

She could recall nothing that might have held the key to finding the chalice. If there had been something there, it was most likely destroyed by the inferno that had consumed the abbey. She shuddered at the memory.

A conflagration that had seemed to ignite the world, and did indeed light the night sky with the brightness of a summer day, had ravaged the abbey and any hopes that Peter de Marcy had held for finding the Grail.

It was de Marcy who had first discovered the abbot's notes on his search for the Grail, and he'd understood at once how important they were. She'd never told him of the pages she found. Peter de Marcy was not a man to be trusted, and she had held her tongue and knowledge to herself, even when the Templar Knights had visited the abbey.

One of them had died most mysteriously in the blaze that demolished the abbey, his body found in the smoking ruins of the chapel. At the time, de Marcy had claimed no knowledge of the knight, though Aislinn knew they had come at his invitation. Messengers and letters were not so easy to hide in a small village and abbey where strangers were more noticeable.

Outside the window, a night bird whistled softly, a low trilling sound like a flute. Aislinn looked up, then gasped as a form suddenly appeared in the window. Brief fear turned to laughter when she heard a soft *meooow* of greeting, and recognized the calico cat.

"Abbey, aren't you?" she murmured, stroking the soft fur as the cat entered the window to sniff at her empty bowl of pottage. "What are you doing away from Brother Timothy? I thought you rarely left his heels, but here you are."

A purr was the only reply, and the cat bent her head for Aislinn's caress, then lifted whiskers and chin to be scratched. Obligingly, she obeyed the feline command until the cat decided it had gone on long enough. With a twitch of tail and last *meow*, the calico leaped from the window back into the garden and disappeared.

Stiff from sitting so long bent over the table, Aislinn stood up and folded the thick pages of her uncle's writings. She stooped to retrieve the wooden painting from the floor where it leaned against the table leg, but a sudden loud knock on her door startled her.

"Mistress Aislinn," a familiar deep voice called, "I would speak with you a moment."

Sir Stephen. . . .

Before she could do more than shove the pages beneath her empty supper bowl and reply that it was late, the door swung inward and he filled the portal. She whirled to face him.

"Sir! You intrude upon a lady's privacy!"

"My pardon, damoiselle, but did you not invite me to come in?"

"Nay, sir, I told you quite plainly that it was late."

The single candle provided scant light; he loomed in the darkness as a black silhouette against the torchlight from the abbey wall across the street.

"Your door is unbarred, or I would not have entered."

With her back to the table, Aislinn rested her palms against the wooden surface to hide the sudden trembling in her arms.

"Your manners are lacking, Sir Stephen."

"Aye, it seems they are. Grant pardon for my boldness at this late hour."

His words were smooth, practiced, a fluid plea for a pardon he did not deserve. Her chin came up, irritation a welcome replacement of the quick spurt of fear he'd ignited with his sudden entrance.

"You are importunate, sir. What brings you to my home at such an hour?"

"A discovery of great importance."

"A discovery that could not wait until the morrow to be told? I'm intrigued, though still annoyed."

The hammering thud of her heart had slowed to a more normal pace, and she relaxed slightly, folding her arms over her chest to gaze at the knight with a faint smile. He still stood in the open doorway, his red tunic a bright splash of color in the gloom. A handsome man, for all his brusque ways and insolence, she thought irrelevantly. There was an air of competence about him that was both comforting and disturbing at the same time. He would make a formidable enemy.

"So divulge this great news, Sir Stephen, ere you burst with it."

Without asking her permission, he stepped inside and closed the door behind him. He seemed to fill the room, his presence suddenly intense and overpowering. It felt as if the air was overheated, though there was naught but a few coals burning in a small brazier to lessen the night chill in the hall.

"Sir!—" she faltered, a hand rising to her throat when he stood staring at her, a shadow against darker shadows, an expression on his face that unsettled her "—the door!"

"It is not news that over-eager ears should hear, you understand."

Alarmed and aghast at his brazen invasion, she eyed him warily. "You overstep courtesy, sir, when you are so bold as to intrude upon a lady's privacy. Tongues will wag far too freely, and I must live here long after you've gone. It's not meet that we should be alone in my lodgings. Pray, be so good as to leave here at once, ere you are discovered."

"Aye, so I will, damoiselle, but first you must promise to name a time and place where we may have private speech."

"I will await you outside the Lady Chapel in the abbey after prime tomorrow morning. Will that suffice?"

"Yea, if it must." He reached behind him and swung open the door, stood framed by oak to stare at her. "If you truly seek to better the abbey's future, you will be there."

For a long moment after the door had closed behind him, she stood staring at the nail-studded oak.

Chapter 8

†

STEPHEN ARRIVED LATE, preferring to stand just inside the chapel doors while the offices were performed. It took a moment for his eyes to adjust enough to find Aislinn in the crowd, but at last he found her standing by an arched column near the front, a graceful coif covering her hair.

During the long night, turning restlessly on the hard cot in the cell he occupied in the monastery, he'd thought of her. He had gone to her lodging with the hope of surprise as an advantage, a way to gain information, but his resolve had quickly frayed. He'd not expected to find her clad in a thin gown, her body outlined by the candle-glow behind her, her hair loose and flowing over her shoulders like wanton silk. It had made him momentarily lose the thread of the reasons he had come, a most unexpected event.

Instead he had been struck dumb for an instant by the glimpse of female curves beneath sheer linen, a powerful reminder of his self-imposed abstinence. Had she noticed?

Bells rang out three times from the altar at the front.

He knelt with the others, though he had no pillow. His knees pressed against cold stone as the prior intoned, *"Sanctus, Sanctus, Sanctus, Dominus Deus, Sabaoth . . ."*

Until forced to attend the bishop in Lincoln, he'd avoided Mass for many years but the responses learned as a child rose unbidden to his lips now, the Latin words familiar on his tongue: *"Benedictus qui venit in nomine Domini . . ."*

Just before the ritual offering of the wine and host, Stephen slipped from the chapel to wait outside. He was unconfessed, unable to partake of communion even if he had chosen to do so.

Misty sunlight scattered the shadows outside the Lady Chapel, lending a glow to the air that was clean and fresh. He sucked in a deep breath that cleared away the sweet, strong smell of incense.

It was Tuesday, market day. Not far from the abbey, in the bend of High Street and Market Street, lay the market with low buildings flanking it on two sides, and the abbey standing opposite. Stephen leaned one shoulder against the chapel cornerstone and listened to the bleat of sheep and raucous honking of geese brought to market. It was sacrilege to liken the noise of the animals to the reflex responses of those inside the church, yet tempting. Once, he had been as they, blindly following the church's traditions.

Until he'd learned the truth.

Voices muffled by closed chapel doors rose in the final response, *"Deo gratias,"* and the doors swung open. Stephen spied Aislinn as soon as she came out into the light and watched her as she searched the crowd for him.

She paused uncertainly on the wide top step and squinted in the morning sun. Her face was framed in pale blue, the coif held back by a fabric circlet of blue and gold gilt twisted in a plait around her head. She lifted a hand to shade her eyes, turned, and saw him. A faint smile touched the corners of her mouth. Relief? Pleasure?

"One would suppose a man of your height and breadth would be difficult to overlook even in a crowd," she said when she reached him, "yet I almost did."

"Walk to the market with me, damoiselle." When her brow rose, he added, "I wish to speak with you. Your good name should be safe enough in such a public place."

"Oft, one's good name depends upon the company they choose to keep." Amusement lit her eyes and pressed at the corners of her mouth when he scowled. "Do not look so insulted, Sir Stephen. I fear no such slander while in your company."

"Perhaps you are overly optimistic."

"Yea," she said with a soft laugh, "it would seem so at times. Once I thought all knights were sworn to courtesy. It seems that I may have been mistaken."

"Do you think me discourteous?"

"Indeed. Or perhaps I'm just not accustomed to being ordered this way and that. I've been told I dislike authority."

There was such frank sincerity in her that it rang in her words, shone from her eyes. He studied her face, the slim, straight nose and full lips that so often smiled. Aislinn of Amberlea represented redemption—and temptation.

Stephen glanced around them but few were paying attention to aught but their own pursuits. The street was crowded with those going to the market, and mud sucked at the wheels of passing carts and ox hooves. The risk of being overheard was great. He looked back down at Aislinn.

"Where may we speak privately, damoiselle?"

"I'm to deliver a basket to the miller's cottage on behalf of Brother Timothy. You may escort me, if you wish."

"A most tempting proposition. I accept your offer."

He accompanied her to the market, where she chose fresh leeks, turnips, a pot of honey, and a loaf of bread

to add to several items in a large willow basket. She doled
out her coins carefully, haggling with merchants who apparently knew her well, a good-natured bartering that
ended with all satisfied and wares tucked neatly into the
basket.

A gentle breeze made leaves on roadside bushes dance
as they walked down High Street, then a steep incline that
took them behind the abbey grounds. Peasant closes were
clustered just beyond the back wall of the abbey. Thorn
hedges ran alongside the road and the edges of the narrow
holdings, and herb and vegetable beds formed long furrows behind each dwelling. Earth banks and ditches separated some of the houses, and the stench from pig
wallows rode the air.

They passed the fishery and orchards, taking the narrow
path that circled the foot of the Tor. It rose steeply against
the bright blue sky. The sloping sides of the Tor were
ridged, but not as if the ground had been plowed. These
were more like terraces, wide and even. At the summit
was a cairn, brooding over the abbey. Cows and sheep
grazed the vertical slopes. The grass was fresh green on
the terraced incline, dotted with yellow buttercups. Fruit
trees twisted by the wind clambered along the lower bank,
blossoms fluttering in a soft breeze.

A feeling of peace enveloped him, surprising and gratifying. He speculated how it would be if he had come for
other reasons.

Would he have met Aislinn of Amberlea? Perhaps, but
it was unlikely he would have done more than form a
distant admiration for her. He was a landless knight and
knew nothing but war. Turning his sword into a plow held
little charm for him. Residing at the abbey held even less.

"What is this matter of importance you wished to share
with me, Sir Stephen?"

Sunlight graced her face, made her blink against the
glare as she looked up at him. A faint shadow was cast

on her brow by the ruched edges of her coif, and her nose boasted a faint spray of freckles on creamy skin. She looked suddenly much younger than her twenty-four years.

He looked away from her. "I found something in the journals that's far more significant than references to the abbey's feud with Wells."

"Did you? Prior Thaddeus will be most pleased."

"Such restraint. Are you not even curious about what I discovered, damoiselle?"

"It's not my place to ask. If you wish to tell me, you will."

"Ah, such indifference is admirable, if not quite believable." When she gave him a sharp glance, he bent his head to meet her gaze. "Perhaps you suspect what I found in your uncle's journal."

"Abbot Robert wrote many things during his years in the abbacy. I can hardly be expected to recall all of them, nor was I privy to many of his writings. Ecclesiastical and secular matters are usually kept separate."

"There are times they merge in purpose, do you not agree?"

"Not often, Sir Stephen." She looked away. "Very well. I'll ask. What do these important writings concern?"

"King Arthur's grave. There was some communication between King Henry and Abbot Robert regarding the possible site of his grave here at the abbey. Apparently, your uncle searched for it, but he couldn't find it and gave up."

A frown briefly knit her brows, then she shook her head and said, "I recall my uncle mentioning a task for the king, but he said nothing of such a search to me."

"Likely not, but he did write about it. I discovered several entries in the journals. Much is missing, I presume because of the fire that destroyed so many books, but there's enough there to piece together a general area

where he searched. What do you know of ancient obelisks?"

Aislinn stumbled in a rut on the road, nearly losing her
balance and upending the basket of goods, and Stephen
barely caught her before she fell. She was a slight weight
on his arm as he held her an instant, featherlight curves
of unexpected fragrance: *roses*. It was a fresh, sweet scent
that summoned images of summer and softness, of soothing climes and contentment. Of happier days, oh so long
ago now.

Stephen's throat ached with a sudden yearning, dredged
up from those long-forgotten memories, and he released
her so quickly that she nearly fell again. He righted her
with a hand on her arm and, with his other hand, caught
a turnip that tumbled from the basket.

"Ware the road, damoiselle. It's uneven."

"So I see, Sir Stephen." The loaf of bread had fallen
from the basket, and she knelt to retrieve it, brushing it
free of leaves and dirt. As she replaced it atop a blush of
turnips, she looked up at him with a frank stare that made
him wonder if she knew how much she disturbed him.
Her coif was slightly askew, and she put a hand up to
straighten it. A graceful motion, pale fingers as slender
and delicate as a noblewoman's tucked blue silk into
place. "I think you'll be most intrigued by the miller's
father you're about to meet. He may be able to enlighten
you if you're truly interested in the tales of King Arthur
and Avalon."

"Indeed? Then I am doubly glad I'm fortunate enough
to be your escort today, damoiselle."

His smile felt false and deceiving. The arch of her brow
convinced him that she saw through his facade to the man
beneath, and it was discomfiting. He bowed slightly from
the waist and held out the turnip he'd caught.

As she took it from him, her fingers brushed against
his hand, and another unexpected memory scoured him—

the bittersweet recollection of a beloved woman's gentle touch.

What was it about this place that summoned such painful memories? Unbidden, they haunted him: a flash of color spun before his eyes, the sound of cherished laughter, then the skewering agony of loss. Ah, he knew better than to allow his thoughts to drift too far. They always brought him desolation.

The road they were on curved around the bottom of the Tor, dipped down a steep hill and rose again, clinging to the very edge of another knoll that fell sharply away. In a bend in the shadow of the Tor, the miller's cottage lay beside an outlet of the River Brue. A huge mill wheel spun with noisy splashing, spilling water into a small pool.

A young boy played outside with a stick and hoop. He looked up at them, then obviously recognizing Aislinn his face brightened. In rough English, he called to his mother that the lady had come again, and he ran to greet them.

From a small pouch, Aislinn produced a sweet, held it out to the boy, who promptly took it with a murmured word of thanks, then scampered off to disappear around the corner of the mill house. She laughed.

"Young Edwin fears he'll be required to share with his older brother, I think."

"Then he is wise to retreat. Older brothers oft take from the younger without permission."

"It sounds as if you have some experience of that, Sir Stephen."

"Yea, to my regret."

"Ah, then you must be the younger." She smiled. "If you were the older brother, you would have no regrets."

"If I were the elder, I would not now be here." He said it simply, a bald truth. When she looked at him quizzically, he shrugged. There was no explanation that would suffice.

At that moment the miller's wife came to the cottage door, and they went to greet her.

Smiling, the miller's wife avoided staring at Stephen, but focused her attention on Aislinn. He knew he must look out of place here, a knight wearing only a leather gambeson under his tunic, his sword belt buckled atop wool instead of mail. But it seemed simpler to discard the garb of warfare while at the abbey, and no overt danger lurked in the quiet town. His concession to the possibility of danger was the sword, donned despite the prior's disapproval. There were some compromises he would not make.

Feeling awkward, Stephen found himself entering the cottage with Aislinn while the miller's wife fussed about them, offering meager refreshment. The smell of freshly ground grain was strong, permeating even the cottage. Jugs of mead were offered, and two cups placed upon a table near the door. The one room was large and continuously filled with the hum and splash of the turning mill wheel. Gears creaked and rumbled loudly.

"Gaven is on his cot in the back," Aislinn said as she beckoned for Stephen to follow them.

A bit reluctantly he ducked his head beneath the low ceiling beams, trailing slightly behind. A separate dwelling had been built in the back, with a steeply pitched roof that attached to the main cottage. It was newly thatched, with bunches of the dried grass still smelling sweet and strong.

The ceiling was low, and Stephen found himself crouching down near the door as Aislinn took the basket to an old man lying on a cot. He looked up, squinting in the close gloom. Age creased his face and gave it the appearance of a wizened apple.

"Aye, so yer back, are ye?" A trembling arm reached up for the basket, but his voice was surprisingly strong. "Did ye bring it? Did ye bring it?"

"I brought leeks, turnips, honey, and bread for you. Brother Timothy does not approve of the old ways, Gaven."

"Pish! He were allus a doltish lad. But did ye bring it?"

She leaned close to him, her whisper loud enough to be heard in the tiny room. "Yea, I brought it, but you must not betray me to Brother Timothy."

A satisfied cackle was obviously meant as a promise, and Aislinn handed over an object that Stephen could not quite see. The old man tucked it beneath a wool blanket spread over him and rucked his body higher on the cot. His head tilted to one side like a bright sparrow.

"Ye're not alone."

"No, Cordelia is with me, and—"

"Aye, I know her, I do. Begone, Cordelia! We have business." With a shrug, his daughter-in-law left the room, obviously accustomed to the old man's whims. Gaven leaned forward when she was gone, his tone insistent. " 'Tis the dark one I cannot see. Be it him?"

When she hesitated, he flapped an impatient hand and demanded, "Be it *him*—the one I saw in the dragon bones?"

Aislinn looked over her shoulder at Stephen. Sparse light from the door washed over her, so that he saw her slight frown. "I do not think so. But perhaps you shall have to decide that, Gaven."

"Bring him to me." The old man beckoned imperiously. "Come, come! Quickly now. I be too old to wait long."

"Sir Stephen, do you mind?" She gestured to a stool by the cot. "It will take but a moment."

A refusal hovered on his tongue, but he swallowed it and moved to squat on the low stool next to the old man's cot. Perched awkwardly, he did not recoil from the eager touch, the clawlike fingers reaching out to catch him by the arm.

Silence enveloped them, save for the sound of Gaven's

labored breathing as he ran his hand over Stephen's arm, up to his shoulder, then touched his brow. His fingers were cold, knotted with age, and slightly shaking, but the touch was light, a mere feather-brush over Stephen's forehead, then his hand fell away. He drew in a sharp, hissing breath.

"The pouch! Give me the pouch! Quickly now, ere I be too late. . . ." He waggled an impatient hand at Aislinn. She put a small leather pouch in his hand, and his fingers closed over it. He held it next to his chest for a brief moment, eyes closed, then he pulled open the strings to pour a small powder into his palm. It glistened with an oddly brittle light.

"Put out your hand," he demanded, and Stephen glanced at Aislinn with a lifted brow as he did so. Gaven lifted a pinch of the powder between his thumb and forefinger, then sprinkled it on the back of Stephen's hand. Unexpectedly, it began to glow, brighter and brighter, tingling on his skin. A brilliant light suddenly shot up from the back of his hand like a beacon, illuminating the entire room.

Aislinn gasped, and Stephen jerked. The powder fell free and the light vanished. It was silent. No one spoke for a moment.

Then, from the shadows, the old man's voice said in a reverent tone, "It be him. He be the one."

"The one for what?" Stephen said irritably. When the old man did not reply, he turned to look at Aislinn. Her face was a pale orb in the gloom, eyes wide and glistening in the scant light. She leaned forward, the words hushed.

"The one he prophesied would find the Holy Grail. . . ."

Chapter 9

✝

WAS IT POSSIBLE? Aislinn stared at Stephen Fitzhugh in the dim light. He sat stiffly, an expression on his face that could only be called wary. It was unlikely that this man was the one Gaven had long dreamed of coming. Gaven was an old man, known for his whims, and she'd been in the habit of indulging him. Yet this was uncanny, that he would decide that this particular knight was the one he'd predicted would find the Grail. Had he somehow heard of Sir Stephen's persistent inquiries?

That must be it. Certainly, Stephen Fitzhugh, with his hard cynical eyes and irreverent philosophy, was not the virtuous man she had dreamed would arrive to resurrect such a miracle.

"I felt the light," Gaven said in a reverent whisper. " 'Tis the true light . . . he *is* the one!"

Sir Stephen sat like a stone, his face impassive. His hands were curled into loose fists, resting atop his bent knees. It was a small room, and his large frame dwarfed the furnishings, the narrow cot and low stool, the table in one corner with a cracked pitcher atop it. Behind him, the glow from the open door surrounded him with an ethereal light. A brief memory of the crude painting in her hall flashed in her mind: just so did light surround the painted knight who held the Grail. It was an unnerving thought.

Uncertainty seeped through her. Perhaps . . . hadn't she thought him a pilgrim at first meeting? He hadn't seemed so irreverent to her then, but a man come to seek spiritual absolution. Could she be wrong to have changed her view of him?

"I'm flattered by your faith in me," Stephen said to Gaven, "but I do not think I'm the one you seek."

Sagging back in his cot, Gaven smiled blindly. "Ye be the one."

A muscle flexed in the knight's jaw. "You're said to be familiar with tales of King Arthur and the Holy Grail. Don't confuse me with those fables."

"I may be old, but I am not yet foolish," Gaven said sharply. "And not all be fables. Ye be a knight, be ye not?"

"I am."

"And have ye not heard of Arthur and his knights?"

"Yea, I have heard the tales that are told. Geoffrey of Monmouth is said to have set down a history of King Arthur and of Guinevere, his queen."

"Aye, lad, so he did. But he told only part of the tale, ye ken."

"Monmouth drew upon old histories to recount his story, but it's said by some that he created his own version of the truth."

"So it has been said." Gaven hitched up higher on his cot, smacked his lips, and gestured for the jug on the table to be brought to him. "I have a tale of my own to tell ye, lad. Listen well, for ye'll have need of what I know."

Aislinn watched Sir Stephen's face as Gaven related the old tales, of how Arthur was born at Tintagel in Cornwall to Briton king Uther Pendragon and the Duke of Cornwall's wife, Ygerna; of how the wizard Merlin took him to Brittany to be reared for his future role as king, and how he grew up to become the greatest king Britain had ever seen, vanquishing the Picts, holding the Saxons at bay, and defeating enemies in Gaul and Denmark.

These tales were familiar to the knight, she knew from Stephen's expression. Gaven paused to drink deeply from the jug, his voice hoarse as he continued. He told of how treachery was afoot in Arthur's absence. His nephew Mordred had taken the queen, Guinevere, as his wife and claimed his kingdom. Then Arthur returned to Britain and his fate at the Battle of Camlann.

"Mordred were dealt a mortal blow, and Arthur given a grievous wound. A sad day it were, for those who loved the king." Gaven's words were a raspy whisper now. He leaned toward the knight. "They took him to the Isle of Avalon, for 'twas there the cup of life was kept—the chalice that grants the power of life to those who drink from it. 'Tis said both cup and king never left. I know it to be true."

Scrubbing his open palms against his knees, Stephen stared at Gaven skeptically. It was obvious from the curl of his mouth that he had reservations.

"If 'tis true, then where now is the king and Grail, old man? Why has no one seen them?"

"They wait. For the right time. For a worthy knight to free them from the shadows. It be ye, lad. Ye have come here for the Grail, have ye not?"

Silence greeted his query, yet Gaven lay back on his cot with a satisfied smile. Aislinn looked at the knight. He sat stiffly, staring at the old man. His posture was rigid, intent. No denial sprang forth from his lips.

So—it's true! she thought, *his real reason for coming to the abbey is the Grail. . . .*

Hope soared. *The Holy Grail*—never before had she put

much weight to Gaven's ramblings, but now she dared to hope for a miracle. If this knight was worthy, together they could find the Grail.

Gaven's whisper caught her attention: "It be where it be left, lad. Find the true king, and ye find the Holy Grail. They lie in sacred ground still, that much I can tell ye." He collapsed back onto the cot, his eyes closed and his breathing unsteady.

Aislinn rose and went to him. He slept peacefully, the slumber of a weary old man. She turned back to the knight.

"We should leave now."

Sir Stephen rose from the stool and followed her from the cottage out into the light.

Clouds scudded overhead, shadows racing across grass and road as they skirted the Tor. Neither spoke until they reached the thorn hedge that separated the peasant closes from the abbey. Then Stephen paused, put out a hand to touch her arm. She turned to look up at him. His expression was grave.

"There are missing pages of your uncle's journal. They are vital, if the grave and Grail are to be found."

She searched his face for a sign that she could trust him. It was perilous placing trust in a man she knew not at all, a knight who had given false reasons for his presence at the abbey. But she could understand why he would not want it known that he sought the Grail. Nor did she want others to know how many nights she sat hunched over the pages of her uncle's journal in an effort to solve the mystery.

But in the year past she had not come close to finding the Grail. Could she do it by herself? Would it not be welcome to have help in unraveling the few clues she had managed to gather?

"Why do you want to find the Grail?" she asked bluntly and saw his brow lift.

"For much the same reason as do you, damoiselle. It's the greatest prize in all Christendom. Why would I not want to find it?"

"Yes, it is a great prize, but there are men who want it for reasons other than good. It would bring immeasurable wealth to the man who held it, and immortality. No man who drinks from it would ever die."

"If it's true it lies with King Arthur in his grave, it wasn't able to save him from death."

She blanched. "Blasphemy, sir!"

"No, not blasphemy. Logic. The cup is sacred for many reasons, but I believe that men have given to it a power it does not possess. It should be treasured for the more humble reason that it once belonged to the Son of God, not because it offers wealth and immortality."

Aislinn drew in a deep breath. He sounded so sincere, his reason for finding the Grail noble. Did she dare trust him?

Surprising her, he lightly touched her cheek, fingers a soft stroke along the curve of her jaw, his voice a low murmur. "You are wise not to trust too easily."

"Can I trust you, Sir Stephen?"

"Nay, I am no more to be trusted than any man who comes here seeking an illusion."

"Then you do not believe the Grail exists."

His hand fell away from her face. "I believe it should. It has yet to be seen if the legends are true."

Aislinn put out her hand, placed her palm against his chest. His eyes narrowed slightly, and his jaw grew taut. The thud of his heart was steady and strong beneath the cup of her hand.

"Your heart is strong, Sir Stephen, and your faith is stronger than you dare to think. Perhaps together we can restore the chalice to a place of honor in the church's grace."

He took her hand in his, held it to his mouth, and she

shivered at the intensity of his gaze. For several beats of her heart she held his eyes and saw something in the dark depths that touched her soul.

"Together, damoiselle," he murmured against her trembling fingers, "we can achieve any dream we dare to have."

It was the answer to more than one prayer, and Aislinn felt suddenly as if she had stepped from darkness into the light.

✝

STEPHEN LEFT HER at the door to her lodgings, crossed High Street to enter the abbey gates and return to the small cubicle he occupied. Clouds bunched darkly now, threatening rain. The wind was brisk and smelled damp. It fit his mood.

He was a fraud. A cheat. The taint of his deception was a bitter taste in his mouth. How easily the lies had tripped from his tongue, the promises meant to cozen and seduce. It was a travesty to think himself worthy to pursue the Grail. Yet the old man had been so certain . . . a foolish certainty, for his search was not for the noble reasons they believed.

How could he betray the vows he had sworn as a knight? Vows of honor, truth, reverence? Yet how could he lose Dunmow . . . it was his by right of birth, the only legacy he had ever sought, the desire to possess it a constant, burning ache inside for longer than he could remember. It seemed that he had been born wanting it. The only happiness he had ever known lay within those stone walls, a life once of promise.

Ah, Christ's blood! But how fiercely he wanted that rough stone keep!

Rain began to fall, a light shower that promised to be heavy. He quickened his pace, moving past the rising stone walls of the new church. Construction did not pause. Perched atop a maze of scaffolding, laborers paid little heed to the drizzle, but continued to use hammer and awl.

Prior Thaddeus sought him out just as he reached the cell he had been given to sleep in. "Sir Stephen, a word, if you please." Hope gleamed from the prior's eyes. "Have you learned aught of the Grail?"

"Not yet enough. Abbot Robert did much laborious work, and he left information that is most promising."

"Excellent!" Clasping his hands together, Prior Thaddeus drew in an excited breath. "You will keep me informed, will you not, Sir Stephen?"

"It would be most difficult to keep good news quiet. Do you pledge the discretion of Aislinn of Amberlea?"

A slight frown darkened the prior's face. "I've always thought her to be most discreet, but—she is a woman, with a woman's frailties. It may well be a burden she cannot bear should she be trusted with too much knowledge. You will have to be the judge of how much to divulge, Sir Stephen. Do you have reservations about her prudence?"

"I have reservations about the discretion of anyone, man, woman or child, when it involves such an extraordinary find. It may best serve our purpose to avoid any undue discussion about my explorations, even between ourselves."

"Oh. Of course. I had not thought of that." The prior glanced around as the rain misted on his bald pate, his tonsure a pale gleam even in the gloom of the cloister walls. His voice dropped. "It has certainly proven to be dangerous in the past. Men have died in the quest to find the Grail."

"Yea, and I do not intend to be one of them." Stephen met the prior's startled gaze with a steady stare meant to impress upon him the vital need for secrecy. It would negate the need to perpetuate lies if Thaddeus could be convinced to wait patiently for information—information that he had no intention of sharing should the Grail's location be found.

"Nor should you be one of the fallen, Sir Stephen." Father Prior smiled, his hands forming a steeple, and his fingertips supporting his chin as he studied Stephen. "It's my fervent hope that you survive and succeed in this quest. As you may know, there was talk of closing the abbey, but I now envision such great things for Glastonbury in the coming years. Possession of the Grail would be the ultimate honor in her crown of glory, and assure our future. This abbey has been here in some capacity since the days of the Celts, when the first priests struggled to bridge the gap between pagan and Christian. To disband now . . . it's unthinkable. I would do whatever I must to prevent that. Finding the Grail—it will save us all, and inspire those who still doubt its power, nay, its very existence."

A light of conviction burned in the prior's eyes. It bordered on fanatical, though Stephen supposed that his perception of the prior could be due to his own cynicism.

"If the Grail is found, Father Prior, it will indeed prove that it exists."

He seemed taken aback. A frown drew thick brows over his eyes. "That is an ambiguous reply, Sir Stephen. Do you not believe in the sacred powers of the Grail? That it will be the source of all things pure and holy?"

"I believe it has already been the source of impure and profane deeds, Father Prior. Men who profess holy intent act in unholy ways to gain custody of saints' bones, and the search for the Grail summons even worse depredations."

"An interesting view, considering that you are sent to find the Grail, sir. Is your heart in this search?"

"Yea, my heart and all my energies are devoted to this

search, Father Prior, never doubt it. I intend to find the Holy Grail if it still exists."

Silence fell between them. The wind was a mournful wail over stone walls, and the rain had at last sent the laborers inside. Seeing indecision was written on the prior's face, Stephen recognized his inner struggle and waited.

In the distance, thunder rumbled, and several monks fled for shelter, dark robes briefly illuminated by a flash of lightning. One of them he recognized as Brother Timothy, scurrying along with several cats at his heels.

Finally the prior murmured, "May your quest be truly blessed. Go with God, sir."

Stephen watched the prior cross the cloister, hood pulled up to protect his head from the rain. Father Prior expected too much if he expected the Grail to be delivered to him. Essex was not a man to willingly relinquish that which he wanted. It mattered not if it was holy or unholy, if the earl lent his attention to the task, it would end as he wished it to end. It never seemed to matter what God or man wanted.

Alone at last in the stark comfort of the cubicle, he sat on the edge of his cot. A cross hung on one wall, a simple wooden symbol of sacrifice. Shame burned at the back of his throat. It had been too long since he had allowed any soft emotion past his guard, since anger had consumed the man he might have been.

If he yielded even the smallest fragment of resolve, he would lose all. He could not. Not now. Not now when he had gone so far and come so close to achieving a dream. *Dunmow.*

Damnation yawned before him, but it could be no worse than the damnation he had endured in his score and ten years of life. There was no redemption for him.

Not even in the arms of Aislinn of Amberlea.

He sucked in a sharp breath, laughing bitterly at the

direction of his thoughts. He wanted her. Yea, he wanted
her as he had not wanted a woman in years, perhaps ever.
She represented all that he had never had, the honesty and
love between a man and a woman that was so precious
and rare.

But he was a fool if he thought such would ever be for
him. It was not his lot to be granted such a boon. And
that knowledge burned worse than the depredations of the
past years.

It was not just Aislinn's fair face that drew him to her
like a moth to the flame, but what lay in those eyes the
color of soft spring violets. Truth and honor shone like a
beacon in the night, a light to guide the lost and weary
home. For so long now he had wandered alone, a wayward knight in search of deliverance.

Now he had found the promise of release from exile,
but it was out of his reach.

Fate's cruel jest made him want her when he knew she
could never belong to him . . . yet nothing diluted the tormented need that left him burning. If salvation lay in denial of that need, he was damned indeed.

Chapter 10

✝

PARCHMENT CRACKLED BENEATH their hands as they studied inked letters that formed comprehensible words and incomprehensible sentences. Aislinn stared morosely at the journal pages.

"I cannot make sense of this. The meaning eludes me."

Stephen did not lift his eyes from the pages. "There must be a key to the message he sought to convey. It's here in his written words. We just have to detect it."

Lamplight sprayed over the table they used in Aislinn's hall, their seclusion being a bold risk to protect the privacy of their task. The good beeswax candles gave off a pleasant scent that was preferable to the usual tallow candles she used. Stephen had brought them with him, a practical gift she suspected he'd taken from the abbey stores.

"It is obvious," she said slowly, "that my uncle feared what may happen should the wrong men discover his journal."

The knight looked up. His eyes probed hers, opaque and intense. "If he took such care to disguise his meaning, then it's probable that he had an idea of the actual location of the Grail."

"Old tales decree that Joseph of Arimathea buried it at the foot of the Tor. Others say it was taken elsewhere and thrown into a bottomless well. Gaven insists it lies with King Arthur."

"Gaven dreams of a resurrected king. He is Welsh. All know the Welsh are mad, and despise the English. They would like nothing so much as to see King Arthur return and save them from English rule."

"Some, perhaps, but not all. Gaven is often right."

"Abbot Robert dug and didn't find the grave. I have no intention of heeding the impossible dreams of an old man." He sat back on the stool, relieving his cramped limbs with a leisurely stretch like a large cat. Aislinn did not let him see that the derision behind his words stung.

"While the old man may dream of impossibilities, he has knowledge of the ancient legends. Gaven was once a bard, until age made him infirm and robbed him of his sight."

"He sees more than he tells, I think." Stephen smiled crookedly. "His eyes followed me."

"Perhaps. Or perhaps he sees with more than his eyes." She rose from the small stool beside him, moved to the open window. It had been a warm day and the heat still lingered beyond purple shadows that cozied up to the garden walls. Faded light lent a softer hue to the herbs and flowers of Master Weaver's garden. She leaned on the stone sill, drew in a deep breath of fresh air, then turned back to Stephen. "To credit the old legends often contradicts what the church teaches. Yet there are truths that cannot be ignored. You spoke of Geoffrey of Monmouth. Perhaps he has added to the truth. Or perhaps he recorded the truth as he perceived it."

"You confuse truth with pleasant diversion, damoiselle. One cancels the other."

"Do you see the entire world so starkly, Sir Stephen? Is there no room in your life for dreams?"

He rose to his feet in a lithe motion, an uncoiling of his lean body that was slightly intimidating. She did not retreat, but stood still as he approached.

"Dreams?" He put out a hand to touch her cheek, a light caress. "Once I dared to dream. A foolish extravagance that cost me dear. I do not recommend it."

"Without dreams, life is too dreary to endure. Better to be a beast of burden, an ox under the yoke, than to live with the capacity for dreams and use it not. It is what distinguishes us from sheep and—"

"Savages?" His hand fell away from her face, but came to rest upon her shoulder, a warm weight that was firm but not threatening. She did not pull away.

"I would think even savages must have dreams, or they would not seek to better their lots, Sir Stephen."

"You mistake dreams for greed. It's not a trait unique only to savages. *Civilized* men have been known to do far worse."

For a moment she did not reply, but stared up into his eyes. Beneath the mocking words she detected bitterness and wondered at it. Impulsively, she lay her hand against his chest, an instinctive gesture of comfort.

His hand went at once to lay atop hers, pressing it against his velvet tunic. There was an intensity to his grip that was vaguely alarming, and when she tried to gently tug her hand free, he did not release her.

"Sir Stephen—"

"Nay, sweet lady, do not withdraw."

It was not a command, but almost an entreaty. She grew still, wide-eyed as he held her close. There was an awkward grace in his touch, a restraint as if he was unused to being gentle. With his free hand, he traced the slope of her cheek and the outline of her mouth. A shiver trickled down her spine, as her breath was trapped in the back of her throat, so that her lungs ached for air. She closed her eyes.

It was an unseen motion, felt in the soft feathering of his lips over hers, the barest contact, but one that sent hot spears of fire bolting through her entire body. Shuddering, she knotted her hand into a fist, clutching velvet between her fingers as she clung to him in breathless anticipation.

Abruptly, he released her and her eyes snapped open. She swayed slightly, reached out blindly with one hand to steady herself against the table.

In a hoarse voice, he said, "Someone comes."

Her spacious hall seemed suddenly far too small, and she took a step back away from Stephen. His intense gaze was heated, scalding her, and she heard as if from a distance the tapping upon her door.

Master Weaver called out to her: "Mistress Aislinn, I have a message for ye from the prior."

"Just . . . just a moment, Master Weaver." She shot Stephen a glance, and he leaned forward to blow out all the candles save one so that the room was darkened.

When she opened the door, a brisk wind swept into the room, a cooling balm against skin that was flushed with heat and contrition. Master Weaver paid no notice, when she was certain her guilt must be evident upon her face. He held out a small rolled parchment.

"Prior Thaddeus allowed as ye would need this tonight, Mistress, or I would no have disturbed yer rest."

Numbly, unable to meet his eyes, she murmured an appreciation that was barely audible. Agitation made her awkward as she closed the door and moved to the table to fumble with the parchment.

Sir Stephen came up behind her, stepping from shadows into the small wavering pool of candlelight. He gave no indication of what had passed between them, and his tone was neutral.

"Perhaps it's the information I requested earlier from the prior."

She broke the seal and unrolled the parchment. "Yea, it is indeed a list of the relics destroyed in the fire. And a letter—look at this!"

Stephen sat back down at the table, relit several wax candles; they burned with a steadier flame than tallow, illuminating the pages he held to the light.

"This is a letter to the abbot from King Henry, dated 1179. The king reports that Arthur's grave lies between two stone pyramids on the abbey grounds—Abbot Robert's desert obelisks, no doubt. Apparently, the abbot couldn't find a grave, though there's only one attempt recorded. Are there two pyramids in Arthur's honor erected in the old cemetery? If there is such a grave, it lies at the south door of the new chapel."

He looked up at her, his face revealing nothing when she said, "Of course! Where Saint Joseph's old church stood is the old cemetery. I know those pyramids, but the writing on them is nearly illegible. They've been there since the days of Merlin, or so I've been told."

He lay the letter down on the table. "If that's true, they were put there to honor a dead king, not the immortal one of which the tales boast." He looked amused. "That would mean the bards were wrong about Arthur's immortality, of course, reducing the tales to unlikely dreams."

"Men must have their dreams, sir. There's no harm in them, save possible disappointment."

"The futility of dreams is harmful enough, I'd think." He studied her in the gloom, his face unreadable. "But I would know nothing of that."

Confused, she shook her head. "It's no dream to want to find King Arthur's grave. It's a necessity if the abbey is to flourish. What can we do?"

Stephen frowned, drummed his fingers against the letter as he mused, "Prior Thaddeus insists he doesn't wish to draw too much attention to our efforts. Yet digging for Arthur's grave without doing so is nigh unto impossible."

"Yea, it would seem so." She sighed. Perching upon the edge of the stool next to him, she leaned forward to study the pages. All her senses thrummed as an unexpected response to their proximity lingered—the residue of that brief flare of heat he had ignited with his kiss.

Had it not affected him? There was no sign of it in his manner or face, and she felt suddenly foolish. A meaningless gesture to him, perhaps, if not to her. She should not endow the moment with more importance than it deserved.

"Now that we've both stated the obvious," she said in a tone that was remarkably calm, "perhaps we can come to some agreement on what to do next—unless you deem it too risky."

Stephen raked a hand through his hair, and the resulting tumble made him look surprisingly youthful in the flickering light. Dark eyes reflected pinpoint flames as he studied her in silence.

Long-forgotten dreams of maidenly fancies returned for an instant, a reminder of those innocent days when life had promised so much more than it gave. . . . There were no regrets, only a faint sense of loss, an emptiness where once those dreams had brightened lonely hours.

Yet for one moment, Sir Stephen had filled that void.

It was exhilarating, uncertain, terrifying.

Then he put out a hand, dragged his knuckles from her ear to one corner of her mouth, tested the cushion of her bottom lip with the pad of his thumb.

"You are watchful as a cat, damoiselle, and as curious. I only meant that there are too many prying eyes about to take unnecessary risks. Cats are an allegory, not a parable, should you wonder. Have I distressed you?"

Nay, but your touch unnerves me. . . .

"No, Sir Stephen," she said aloud, "I only consider our choices and find them lacking."

His hand fell away. "Perhaps the king's information is wrong. He details what the Welsh bard related, but there are other facts that must be known if we're to succeed."

"Do you intend to dig between the pyramids?"

Stephen blew out a harsh breath. "Yea, though 'tis like to be a waste of time and effort. To search for the grave of a dead king and a legendary chalice is the height of folly."

His mockery was irritating, and Aislinn's tone grew sharp. "You came to Glastonbury to find the Grail, Sir Stephen. Do not exploit the legend if you don't believe in it."

In a sudden move, he surged to his feet, glared down at her with his eyes narrowed. "Exploit the legend? It's hardly exploitation to sit here night after night poring over near incomprehensible notes made by a doddering old man, or to listen to the ramblings of another in his dotage, knowing all the while that the probability of truth is nil. It's a fool's quest, and I am set upon it to my misfortune."

White lines bracketed his mouth showing his anger, but beyond the anger was frustration, fueled by a sense of futility. She understood it, even as she resisted it.

"I will not surrender hope, Sir Stephen. Neither should you. All the legends cannot be wrong, nor can so many who believed in it be wrong. The Grail's discovery will save us all. It would be greater even than finding King Arthur's grave."

With a soft sound similar to groaning laughter, Stephen turned away from her, moved to lean against the wall, his arms stretched over his head and his palms braced against the plaster. He bent his head to stare down at the floor.

"Sweet damoiselle, you defeat me with your logic. Or lack of it." His words were muffled. For a long moment he stood that way, in a posture of discouragement, then finally he levered his body from the wall and turned to face her again. A faint smile with no hint of mockery curved his lips. "I yield to your superior wisdom—and apparently endless faith."

She regarded him with an emotion akin to cautious affection. The past three days they had spent together with her uncle's journals had been enlightening, for beneath his gruff attitude was a man tormented by his own demons, yet compassionate enough to listen patiently to an old man's boring recitations of years long past. He wavered between irritation and consideration with unnerving regularity, so that she too often had trouble discerning his mood.

Yet she had seen him cradle a cat with the same hands that wielded a sword. Which man was he?

Sir Stephen Fitzhugh was full of contradictions. Yet she must believe that he was the man she needed him to be. It would be so much easier.

Chapter 11

✟

STEPHEN SUPERVISED THE digging done by laymen, while Prior Thaddeus hovered about as anxiously as a hawk over her brood of chicks.

"Do compose yourself, Father Prior, lest you give away our true purpose," he finally muttered, and the prior gave him a sharp glance.

" 'Tis most difficult to be composed when the key to the greatest find in Christendom lies near at hand!"

"Perhaps it does. They have dug down farther than most graves, yet have found nothing." Stephen stared darkly into the hole, ostensibly dug for a new grave. Though none had questioned the grave without a corpse, there were those who would wonder at it.

He looked up, stared at the ancient pyramids with the etched writing so badly deteriorated it could not be read. If the tale was true, the pyramids reported the king's burial here, an unwelcome truth to men who preferred to believe the great king would return England to the Britons. An unlikely fable, fabricated by desperate men, or the dreamers of which Aislinn spoke so fondly.

At last the hole was much deeper than a man's height, and Stephen said wearily, "No point in continuing, Father Prior. It's obvious that the king of legend is not here. And of course, neither will be the Grail."

Near tears, Prior Thaddeus nodded, his fleshy jowls quivering with misery. "After finding the letter, I had hoped that we had found the prize," he said in a whisper. "But you will not give up yet, will you, Sir Stephen? The earl is most convinced that—"

Stephen made an impatient motion with one hand to indicate a need for silence. Brother Timothy approached, his thin face reflecting bewilderment.

"Father Prior, I have not heard of the death of one of our own, yet I see a grave being prepared—"

Prior Thaddeus whirled around, his tone biting. "It is hardly your place to question me, Brother Timothy. Go you now, as the bells summon the faithful to vespers. I'll join you shortly."

As the monk nodded obedience, a flash of rebellion gleamed in his eyes. With hands tucked into the wide flowing sleeves of his cassock, he turned toward the chapel. Narrow shoulders were hunched, as if against a bitter wind. Behind him, three cats followed like shadows, graceful and wary.

"He oversteps his bounds too often," the prior muttered irritably. "Brother Timothy has been a thorn in my side since he came here, but the bishop saw fit to appoint him as my steward."

"Another thorn? You are truly beset, Father Prior."

He glanced up at Stephen, composed his face in what was obviously meant to be a more pious expression. "All men must bear their crosses gracefully if they are worthy to serve God and the church."

Stephen ignored that and stepped to the edge of the yawning hole. The evening shadows were growing deeper, the smell of raw earth rich and pungent in the damp air.

"That's enough," he said to the men down in the grave, "come out and refill the hole."

Disbelief stared back up at him, and one of the men muttered a complaint that was swiftly shushed by his comrade as they set to work.

"Useless to try and silence them. Owein cannot be the only one here questioning this madness today," the prior said with a sigh. "It seems that we have been misinformed, Sir Stephen."

"So it seems."

"Yet we cannot fail!" Prior Thaddeus gripped his arm, a tight hold. "*All* depends upon finding the Grail."

Stephen stared at him irritably. "Compose yourself, Father Prior. You draw attention to us."

The prior released his arm. "I'm certain you'll pursue this matter to success, as the earl was most emphatic in his letter to me that the chalice is here. He would be most displeased were I to report your failure."

"Is that a threat, Father Prior?" Stephen's brow rose in a lazy arch, but his smile was feral as he gazed at the portly monk.

Prior Thaddeus seemed taken aback. "Indeed not, sir. I do not resort to threats. I merely sought to remind you of your duty."

"I am well aware of my duty, and need no reminder from you, good brother."

The prior hesitated, then inclined his head with stiff dignity. "I'm certain of your eventual success, Sir Stephen. See to it that these men have their pay before they leave."

Stephen stared after him as the prior stalked toward the chapel. It had taken the better part of a day to arrange the digging, and only a short time to end the hope for success. Another disappointment. The abbot's letters were not proving to be as beneficial as he'd hoped, written so obscurely that it was difficult to decipher most of it. Only the reference to the pyramids had been plain enough, and that was obviously wrong.

There must be another solution.

✝

IT WAS WARM for the end of May. Stephen perched on the edge of the stool beside Gaven's crude rope cot, impatient and fidgeting. Aislinn was to meet him here, and she was late. The residue of past meals permeated the close air; the strong fragrance of beer emanated from a pewter jug atop the table. It was stifling in the room, far too confining for his comfort.

"D'ye see the jug, lad?" Gaven asked.

Stephen nodded, then recalled that Gaven could not see him well, and said, "Aye, 'tis on the table."

"Pour us a mite. There maun be two cups next to it."

Grateful for an excuse to move about, Stephen rose and moved to the table, where he poured an ample amount into one of the cups for Gaven, but none for himself.

He held it out, then reached for the old man's hand to bring it to the cup. Gaven's twisted fingers curled around the wood bowl with surprising agility.

"Thankee, lad. It be dry and warm today."

"Tell me again about ancient obelisks," Stephen said when the cup was half emptied. "Is there another meaning?"

Smacking his lips, Gaven settled back with the cup held tightly in one hand. Pale eyes reflected dull light, blindly staring at the opposite wall. "Long ago, when time was still young, this land was surrounded by water. It was called by the Welsh name of Ynys Gutrin, or the Isle of Glass. 'Twas when the Saxons came after Arthur's time

with their own language, that it became Glastinge-
bury. . . ."

Stephen let his mind wander, accustomed by now to
the ramblings. He'd heard it the last time he was here, the
tales of Arthur's prowess in battle and his dealings with
his knights and queen. Now Gaven related how men had
come to Somerset to build a mighty fortress near the River
Camel, and the ruins were said to hold the sleeping king
and his knights until England should need another savior. . . .

Leaning forward, Stephen put out a hand to stop the
old man, then said, "This fortress—it is Arthur's?"

"There are those who say it be. Climb to the top of the
Tor, and ye can see to the ruins if the day be clear."

Could it be Arthur's fort? And if a sleeping king did
lie among the ruins . . . so could the Grail.

Stephen sat back. The Grail wasn't at the abbey. If it
was buried with a dead king, it may be at this fortress
Gaven mentioned. Most likely, it would be another futile
search. Another empty gesture in the earl's service. Hot
frustration rose in the back of his throat. He could not go
back without the Grail. It mattered not if it was the right
grail, as long as it sufficed. As long as Essex accepted it
and then granted him Dunmow. That was what mattered.

Should he tell Aislinn of the fortress? It would be so
easy not to confide in her, to search on his own. If he was
alone when he found the Grail, there would be no dispute
over where it should go. Aislinn expected it to remain at
the abbey in a place of honor. To her, the Grail was a
miracle, a spiritual mystery and a marvel.

But there were more practical concerns. While he had
no illusions about supposed miracles, he did have very
real experience with the harsher aspect of life. The closest
he had come to a miracle was this opportunity to seize
Dunmow for his own.

He could not relinquish it all for the sake of a pair of

lovely violet eyes and a sweet, honest smile.

Stephen suppressed the urge to laugh aloud at the direction of his thoughts. *Fool!* He would be a fool indeed were he to yield to any mad impulse that prompted him to be soft. It would gain him nothing.

Instead he said, "So the dead king lies among the ruins of his castle, not on abbey grounds as the king was told."

A soft cackle accompanied Gaven's shrewd smile. "Not all the old ways be lost, lad. Not all honor be lost. Nay, nor all kings be dead—'tis Arthur's castle that lies neath the rowan trees and sheep hooves—but where lies he?"

"You speak in riddles, old man."

"A wise man hath no fear of riddles."

The cryptic comment was accompanied by a waggle of his empty cup, and Stephen rose to refill it. Gaven was a garrulous old fool, and it was obvious he enjoyed being vague. More than likely, many of the old tales were created as the jug was drained.

As he gave him back the full cup, he saw Gaven's eyes flicker. Yea, he saw much more than he would admit. A crafty trick to beguile the unwary, this deception that lent Gaven an advantage with those who thought him blind, slight though it may be.

Stephen straddled the rickety stool again. "Where lies this fortress?"

"Some say 'tis in Cornwall."

"And what do you say?"

" 'Tis hard to miss the highest hill beyond the River Camel. Folk there say that on Midsummer Eve, gates open and the king can be seen, that he and his knights ride from the hilltop through the ancient gateway, and their horses drink from the spring beside Sutton Montis church . . . and on winter nights, South Cadbury rings with the ghostly sound of hounds and hoofbeats . . . Ah, but what do I know? I am but a fool, an old man to spin foolish tales, be it not so?"

It was disconcerting that Gaven knew the direction of his thoughts, but Stephen said only, "Telling tales passes the time well."

"Yea, lad, that it does. Listening to the tales may earn a man his heart's desire if he be bold enough to seize the prize." His rusty voice dropped lower, and he sat up on the cot to the creaking protest of the bed ropes. "Be not faint of heart, and ye shall win all that has waited for ye these many long years. Gold is not the true reward, but ye know that more than do most."

Stephen had an eerie feeling that Gaven knew more about him than he told, that somehow the old man knew the reasons behind his search for the Grail. It was unsettling.

"It's said that the chalice gives everlasting life and vigor, not gold. The value is in the legend, not the vessel. Is that not true?"

Stephen waited silently for Gaven to reply, and it was long in coming. Flies buzzed and tiny gnats drawn by the rich smell of beer hazed the air. A recent rain had bequeathed damp heat that lingered in the stuffy room.

"There be gold, and there be gold, lad. Ye maun decide the worth. Ye have stood at the mouth of hell—go now 'twixt the stones at heaven's gate to seize the prize."

Another enigmatic reply that told him nothing. He gazed at the old man in rising frustration.

It was a relief when Aislinn finally arrived, heralded by the joyous shouts of two small boys. He could hear them greet her, no doubt running to collect whatever sweet she had brought them. Greedy lads. Children left him impatient and uncomfortable.

By the time she entered the musty room, Stephen was at the door. He leaned against the wall, a silent nod his only greeting. Aislinn moved past him to the cot.

"Ye brought it, lass?" Gaven asked eagerly and held out one hand, his palm cupped expectantly. As soon as she placed a small leather pouch in his hand, gnarled fingers closed around it. He made a small sound of satisfaction.

"Be sparing," she said, "for 'tis difficult to get."

When she straightened, she looked over her shoulder to Stephen. "Good day, Sir Stephen. I trust that you and Gaven have been able to help one another."

Beneath a blue head rail framing her face, her eyes gleamed a welcome and her full lips curved in a smile that was genuine and intimate. His reaction was instant.

Heat flooded him. His belly knotted, and blood surged to his groin. It was unexpected and dangerous. He wavered, torn between an honest response and caution.

Awkwardly, he muttered, "I helped him empty the beer jug."

"Did you?" She laughed. "It is the first time I have ever known him to need aid in reaching the bottom of a jug, but I'm pleased that he has had good company."

"It be uncertain if yon knight has been good company, lass," Gaven said, "but he be a good drinking companion, I warrant. 'Tis well enow that he leave more in the jug than do most men."

Stephen waited, wondered if the old man would tell her about the fortress at Cadbury, but though Aislinn lingered to read from her uncle's journal, Gaven said nothing else about King Arthur or the Grail. The old man was tiring, his eyes closing as he slipped lower in the cot, obviously ready for a nap.

"We will come again, Gaven," Aislinn said softly, and the old man just bobbed his head in mute response.

"He tires so easily these days," she said when they were once more out in the mill yard. The noise of the wheel splashing was loud, the gears and pulleys a steady, grinding hum.

"He's old." Stephen shrugged when she glanced up at him. "It's the way of it."

He still felt damnably awkward, though the taut ache in his groin had eased. What was it about this woman that so stirred him? Or was it only the fact that it had been so long since he had last lain with a woman that made him edgy?

"Gaven may be old," she was saying, "but his mind is yet keen. He knows more than he tells about the Grail."

He sought a neutral topic, something to divert her attention from the Grail.

"What did you give him? The last time we were here, you gave him something in a small pouch . . . what's so important to him?"

Aislinn paused beneath the spreading branches of a chestnut tree, where spikes of white flowers bedecked thick limbs, vivid against green leaves. A wind shook loose snowy petals to frost her blue head rail; the color was vivid against her pale skin. She made him suddenly think of a pagan queen, graced by nature and wreathed in mystery. She reached up, tugged at a white-flowered chestnut candle as the leaves fluttered.

"Gaven seeks comfort in the old ways. There's a crone who lives in a hazel coppice that makes a potion for him to ease the ache of his many years. He barters flour for what he needs. A fair enough trade."

"Yes, unless the prior hears of it. Isn't this mill a possession of the church?"

"It is. A certain amount of the grain belongs to the miller and his family, in payment for their labor."

"Yet the grain comes from abbey fields."

"Do you intend to tell Prior Thaddeus?"

Blunt, direct without being accusatory, she waited for his reply with an arched brow and steady gaze. He shook his head.

"No, I have no reason to bear such news. It would only do an ill."

It was the proper reply. Aislinn smiled. " 'Tis fitting that you extend such courtesy."

"More fitting that the abbey share with those who labor long and hard to provide food, damoiselle."

"Perhaps. Yet the brothers eat meagerly for the most part. Fish and eggs are the staple on communal tables."

"Father Prior does not seem to suffer from any deprivation that I have noticed."

His dry comment earned her soft laughter. Releasing the chestnut spike, she brushed away the mantle of white petals from her sleeves. "No, he does not. It is a source of great satisfaction to him that the king's generous allotment also includes funds for the nourishment of the brothers."

"Yet I was told that funds are low."

"The Welsh wars pinched royal coffers, but Master Fitzstephen is a fair steward. He's accomplished much in the rebuilding of the abbey, despite occasional reverses. It's long been my heart's desire to see it restored to the glory it enjoyed when my dear uncle was abbot. Perhaps soon it will be. King Henry has been quite beneficent."

As they walked along the road that curved around the foot of the Tor, Stephen hardened his resolve. It was plain that Aislinn of Amberlea would never yield the Grail to Essex willingly. Prior Thaddeus could be cozened, but she wouldn't relinquish any claim to it for an instant. No, it would be foolish to allow her more knowledge of his plans than necessary. And it was increasingly important that his search take him away from Glastonbury.

Before I lose all my sense and even Dunmow. . . .

✝

AISLINN STOOD IN gloom brightened by a single candle and stared at the painting. They were gone. The pages she had kept so carefully hidden were not behind the wood.

A chill shivered down her spine. Only one other person knew where they were kept. It was inconceivable that he would have taken them. But who else would realize the importance of such papers? Who else would come into the privacy of her own hall and remove them?

Trembling with anger and disappointment, Aislinn took a deep breath. She would ask Sir Stephen before she accused him of so disloyal an act. There may be a logical reason for it, if he did, indeed, take the journal pages.

Borrow the journal pages, she corrected herself. Surely he would allay ugly suspicion with a simple explanation. Or an honest denial.

But it must wait until morning, as the abbey gates were closed and no women were allowed past the chapel after dusk. It was a rule the prior enforced quite strictly.

She readied herself for bed, carefully removing her outer garment. It was her best gown, Flemish cloth of soft blue, embroidered on the cuffs of the long sleeves and at the neck with amethyst thread. Beneath it, her undergown was of fine linen. An impulsive choice that morning, prompted by some imp of mischief to appear at her best when she met Stephen Fitzhugh.

He had not even noticed.

Clad in only her thin shift, she washed herself with tepid water from the pitcher and a pot of scented soap. The smell of her favorite rose fragrance was soothing. Finally, her ablutions ended, she packed away her gown and laid out garments for the morrow. Pride had earned her a deflating lesson. No more would she seek to impress any man. There were more worthy goals to covet.

Kneeling on the hard floor, Aislinn clasped her hands in prayer. Her unbound hair was a warm weight in the chilly gloom of her darkened bedchamber. Outside, it was quiet and still. She prayed earnestly that she would overcome the sins of false pride and vanity, that she'd find the way to bring glory upon herself and the church, and that all those she had lost would intercede with the saints on her behalf. Then she prayed that no harm would befall the brothers of the abbey and that Glastonbury would rise to honor again.

By the time her evening prayers were finished, her legs were numb from kneeling so long. She rose stiffly and blew out the guttering candle. Even with the shutters closed over the window, the air was so cool she moved hastily to her bed and snuggled beneath the warmth of heavy wool. The mattress was thick and comfortable, stuffed with fragrant herbs and straw, cushioning her weary body.

In the darkness broken by only a sliver of thin light that pierced the shutters, she thought again of Sir Stephen. She had not prayed for his soul, when perhaps she should. It may be that Fitzhugh had greater need of prayers for his deliverance from temptation.

As do I, Lord, as do I. . . .

Scalding shame seared her at the direction of her thoughts. It was unexpected and alarming to find herself reflecting upon the knight as she did, to remember with such vivid clarity the warmth of his mouth and the dark heat in his eyes. . . . It was surely a sin to feel the way she did, this strange restless yearning that burned brightly whenever she was near him, or even thought of him.

No, she must remain steadfast in her pursuit of the one goal that was most important. Squeezing her eyes tightly closed, she envisioned the painting and the golden light that streamed from heaven to surround the Holy Grail. That was what she sought, the assurance of faith, of sacred love.

Wasn't it the reason her uncle had left her such an important trust? By leaving those pages in her care, he had known she would do her best to achieve his goal, would find the sacred cup. It would ensure Glastonbury's future, and also her own.

Aislinn slept fitfully at last, yet when she dreamed, it was not of a dark knight holding a golden chalice, but of Stephen Fitzhugh holding her in his arms.

Chapter 12

✝

SOFT LIGHT WAITED beyond the narrow, dark tunnel of road he traveled, a beckoning promise beyond the trees. It was early yet, dawn still a misty shimmer. Stephen's horse picked a careful path on the rutted track beneath elm boughs that formed a leafy cloister overhead. The creak of saddle leather and soft metallic chink of harness was swallowed by dense shadows on each side of the narrow byway.

Glastonbury lay just behind, the Tor rising in a steep mound from marshy levels that surrounded the town and abbey. It would be his guide on this trek toward South Cadbury.

If Gaven had told the truth—a supposition that was not certain—the castle ruins should lie within sight of Cadbury village and be easily visible. A fortress would of necessity be built atop a high hill.

It was midday when he reached the small village of West Camel beyond the river. Morning mist had long been burned away by a sun that was hot on his bare head and shoulders. He wore his familiar mail but no surcoat. A gust of wind blew the hair back from his face.

An undulating curve of hills beyond meadows, woods, and fields rose in slumped shoulders above the village, cupping a few shops and farmhouses in a wooded palm. There was no indication which hill might have once held a castle. He studied the terrain with growing irritation. Gaven could have made it easier, but the old man seemed to delight in his riddles.

West Camel was little more than a narrow street with a small cluster of single-story stone buildings. Dismounting in front of one of the houses, he asked for a cup of water from a youth. The boy gave it to him silently, eyes big as he regarded the mailed knight before him.

When his gaze moved to the broadsword, Stephen said over the rim of his cup, "I was told that once there was a castle near here. Would you know where it lies?"

A shrug and shake of head was his only reply. The boy's eyes were riveted on the sword, fascination evident in his face. Stephen shifted slightly so that the sword swung temptingly against his thigh.

"Would you like to hold it?"

Startled eyes flew up to Stephen's face, gleaming. A jerk of his chin indicated agreement. He reached out eager hands as the sword was unsheathed with a metallic rasp of tempered steel against iron casing. The sheath was plain, with engraving forming the only decoration. No jeweled hilt or precious gold disguised the purpose; it was a weapon of death unadorned with beauty but beautiful in its simplicity.

Stephen held it out, hilt presented forward. When the youth grasped it, the blade immediately sunk to the ground in a heavy arc. The unexpected weight of the weapon startled a cry from the boy.

"Saint Jerome! 'Tis heavy!"

"Yea, it takes practice and strength to wield such a

weapon. My first sword was much lighter. Hold it like this, and balance the weight in both hands."

He pressed the boy's fingers around the hilt, one fist above the other, and the sword drew level, the wicked blade gleaming brightly in the sunlight. Awe filled his eyes as the lad held the weapon, the strain obvious as he tried to keep it level.

"It be heavier than I thought 'twould be," he said at last, and Stephen reached out to take the sword from his trembling hands.

Hefting it easily, he slid it back into the sheath at his left side, smiling slightly. "It takes years of practice to learn how to hold a sword and tilt at the quintain. A lad such as you would find it hard work at first, but you seem sturdy enough to succeed."

An impossibility that both of them knew, as the most this youth could hope for was to become a soldier, or perhaps an archer if he was good with a bow. More probable, he would spend all his days in this village tending cows or sheep, working in the fields.

"I met another knight once," the boy offered. "He came to find the castle, too."

Stephen smiled. "Did he find it?"

A shrug was the indifferent response. "Not so many come here now, though I've heard me mum tell as how once the castle was home to knights, aye, and a king, too."

"Have you heard all the tales then, lad?"

"Some, when a jongleur passes through. I swapped a small cheese for the last bit of tale." Brown eyes were suddenly shrewd as he looked up at Stephen. "It maun be worth a coin to find the castle, d'ye no think?"

"Greedy beggar," Stephen said without rancor, and tossed the boy a copper. "Tell me which hill hides this fort that was once home to a king."

Biting the coin to test its value, the youth smiled in satisfaction. "South Cadbury be the place to find it. Just beyond the south side of the church, ye'll find the old road that leads up to the top. It passes through a cow byre."

He turned, pointed east in the direction that Stephen was to go. "If ye search for the king and his knights, seek them beneath the hill."

"Beneath? Yet the castle ruins lie atop the hill, I'm told."

"Aye, but the king sleeps in a hidden cave beneath. No one has ever found them. 'Tis said no one will."

"Then there are those who search still."

"Oh aye, there are always those who search." The youth lifted his shoulders in another shrug, glanced around him as if suddenly wishing to flee, then looked back at Stephen.

"Not all," he muttered softly, "be so noble a knight as ye. Others have come in search of Camelot. . . ."

Before Stephen could ask him if other knights had come recently, the boy was summoned by a woman.

"Wat! Keep to yerself!" Indignation and fear laced her voice, and she stormed toward them, a stout cudgel gripped in one hand. "Get to the lambing, lad, and leave the knight be. . . ."

"Be at peace, beldame, for he has suffered no harm at my hands," Stephen said sharply when she jabbed the stick in his direction. "I but sojourn here."

Wary, the woman glared at him as he gathered up the reins to his grazing steed and mounted. He felt her staring after him as he rode down the rutted street, the rhythmic clop of hooves against hard dirt mingled with the bleat of sheep.

Sunlight was harsh on his bare head, warm enough to make him uncomfortable. It would have been more practical to leave his mail at the abbey. He could have garbed himself in a cassock of the brothers, or even worn a simple tunic and braies and not drawn any notice. Perhaps he was too used to defending himself, preferring the security of armor to the risk of discovery.

If others had come here recently, then the trail of the chalice was more common than he had been led to believe. It would be a trick worthy of Essex to set him unaware against a host of foes, for he had done it to him time and again.

South Cadbury was composed of a church and three stone houses, one of them substantial, but the others mere huts. Sheep and cattle grazed broad green fields. Just beyond the church, a steep escarpment rose sharply. Opposite was a sprawling house, boxed in with stone fences and white-faced sheep. Smaller hills ringed the farm.

Stephen pulled his mount to a halt at the mouth of a thin cattle track across from the house. It then climbed the hill between overhanging trees. Ducking limbs, he nudged Nero up the hill. The destrier's great hooves churned up clods of dirt and pebbles, muscles bunching with effort. Tree roots snaked across the track while hartstongue and lady fern straggled in dusty green clumps up the banks. Primroses and bluebells bloomed. Nesting crows circled overhead, shrieking a raucous protest at his trespass.

Evidence of a fort was visible through dense trees. He could see four lines of bank-and-ditch defenses that left the unmistakable outline of a moat, quarried stone walls, remnants of cobbled roads. But was it Camelot?

Near the top, he dismounted to lead Nero the rest of the way up. It was hard work for man and beast, the incline arduous. At the crest, he paused in the shadow of the trees, panting from the climb. The weight of his mail was pressing.

Just beyond the wooded track, a broad expanse of green grass studded with tiny daisies lay in bright sunlight. It was an immense enclosure, cradled within earthen banks. A stone wall curved at one side, red rock tumbled haphazardly.

With the prick of light in his eyes, he started forward,

then abruptly halted. A blur of motion caught his eye. His hand flew to the hilt of his sword, half drew it, then he heard a familiar voice:

"You took overlong to arrive, Sir Knight."

Aislinn of Amberlea. . . .

Chapter 13

✝

"WHAT ARE YOU doing here, damoiselle?"

Cool and composed, she arched her brow and gazed at the sweaty, dust-grimed knight. A massive destrier stood docile at his shoulder, and patches of sunlight gleamed on Stephen's bare head.

"I thought to ask you the same thing, Sir Stephen. What are *you* doing here?"

Anger simmered just below the surface of her calm. She held it in with an effort. It had been a grievous blow to discover the knight gone this morning. More grievous still to realize that he must have learned important facts from the journal pages and chosen not to share the knowledge, but meant to conduct a search on his own.

"You've been talking to Gaven," he said curtly.

"Nay, not since last we visited him." Releasing the reins of her small palfrey to allow it to graze on tufts of buttercup-strewn grass, she moved closer to the knight. "I'm surprised to find you here."

"Yet you arrived here before me, it seems."

"Yea, so I did. The palfrey is swift and I'm familiar with the road to Cadbury."

"You rode near twelve miles alone? What a brave little mouse you are, but very unwise."

"Perhaps. But you were not far from my sight for much of the way. Do you doubt me?" She smiled. "I saw you talking to the shepherd lad in West Camel."

His face darkened, and he demanded, "Why did you not mention this fortress to me?"

"It didn't seem important until now." Anger made her voice vibrate slightly. She steadied it with a deep breath. "Perhaps you would like to share with me what you learned from my uncle's journal pages. It must be important indeed to lure you here so swiftly you could not pause to impart your plans to me."

Silence greeted her thinly veiled accusation. He looked hot in his mail. Perspiration dampened a lock of hair on his forehead and formed tiny rivulets that trickled from temple to jaw. His mouth was a harsh slash, dark eyes narrowed.

When the silence stretched too long, she snapped, "Return my uncle's journal pages to me."

"I have nothing that belongs to you." He moved at last, looping his reins over a tree branch to tether the destrier, then warned, "Best keep your mount at a distance. Nero is trained to savage anything he perceives as a threat."

"There are strong similarities between master and horse, I see. Why did you take those pages? They were left for me by my uncle. They are *mine*."

"As I said, I have nothing of yours."

"Do you consider them yours, Sir Stephen? Do you think that because I was foolish enough to share with you that you have a claim upon them? Shame on you, sir, for your fraud!"

He took a step closer to her, his voice taut. "If there has been deception, it lies with you. I haven't taken your uncle's pages, but you have kept them secret from the prior. Isn't that true?"

Heat flooded her face and bound her tongue. It was true that she hadn't told Prior Thaddeus of the pages. His zeal was so often misplaced, overbearing in its intensity, and she'd feared he would share the knowledge with those who did not have the best interests of the Grail at heart. But how did she explain her reasons to a man who had come to the abbey at the prior's behest? It would serve no good purpose to further alienate him, nor help her retrieve the journal pages.

"You don't answer, damoiselle. Why is that?"

"I do not answer because you're right, Sir Stephen. It shames me to admit it, but you're right when you accuse me of secrecy. My reasons may seem sound to me, but would not be so to others, I suppose."

Moving from the shade of the trees into dappled light, she turned back to face him, said frankly, "I'm guilty of the sin of omission, but not of commission. That sin must lie with the person who took my uncle's pages."

"I have said I didn't take them."

"And you have also said you came to Glastonbury to seek information about the dispute with Wells. Why should I now believe you when you swore falsely to me before?"

"Your point is well-taken." He sketched a mocking bow. "It seems that we have much in common after all. I didn't tell you the entire truth, nor did you tell Prior Thaddeus the entire truth."

"I have admitted that," she said irritably. "But that doesn't excuse either of us."

"Ever the surprise, m'lady. Your unexpected honesty is refreshing, if a bit questionable."

"Do you doubt me?"

"Why shouldn't I?" he demanded rather peevishly. His mouth was set in a sulky line, his eyes moody. "It's too much of a coincidence that you just happened to know my direction today. I wouldn't be a bit surprised to learn you and Gaven thought it would be rather amusing to send me off on a wild-goose chase."

"Credit me with some sense, Sir Stephen. If I wanted to amuse myself at your expense, I'd hardly take the trouble to follow you. It would be much more amusing to be lounging about on cushions and eating dainties when you returned to the abbey weary and empty-handed."

"I suppose there's some sense in that."

It was said grudgingly, and she shook her head. "Once I found my pages gone, I waited until daylight to talk to you. But when I arrived at the abbey, you were gone. Then I saw you leading your horse from the stables."

"And so you followed me." His gaze flicked to her palfrey grazing on tufts of bright green grass beneath an oak. The trappings were simple but sturdy, and a small scrip hung from the saddle, filled with dried apples and bread crusts hastily gathered. Stephen's brow lifted.

"How intriguing that you would have such easy access to a swift mount of your own."

"The palfrey isn't mine. It belongs to the abbey. Brother Timothy was kind enough to ask no questions."

He gave a faint snort and glanced back at her. "What a facile tongue you have. It was still dark, and I told no one my plans. What if I'd been on my way to London? Would you have followed me there?"

"The London road lies northwest. You took the southwest road around the Tor. I knew when I saw you ride toward the River Camel where you were going. And it became just as obvious that you must have deciphered my uncle's pages. Why else would you be here?"

"Your uncle's pages are worthless. I learned of Camelot from the old man—though his veracity is suspect." He took a step closer to her. For the first time, she saw how angry he was—fine lines bracketed his mouth, and his eyes were cold and hard.

Instinctively, she took a backward step and he followed her, intimidating in his stance. His voice was low, harsh.

"The time for lies is over, damoiselle."

"I agree," she said, a little surprised at how steady her voice remained, "the truth would be welcome. *Where* are my uncle's journal pages?"

"Why would I want worthless pages? Your uncle's conclusions are too vague and present too many unanswered riddles, just as does the old man. By all that's holy, I begin to think all of you have concocted a tale to lure the credulous to the abbey. There's no magical Grail, no grave, and more than like, no King Arthur as the tales report. There's only an abbey full of monks desperate to draw pilgrims and their money so they can continue to rebuild."

"If you believe that, why do you continue to search?"

"Because there are others who believe in it. Because there's an off chance it could be real. Because I'm a fool. I must be, or I wouldn't be here now."

He was a bare hand's breadth away now, towering over her angrily, frustration evident in his seething dark eyes. His intensity was intimidating but not frightening; she did not back away, but held her ground, stared up at him with sudden compassion.

"Perhaps it cannot be found because the Grail means more to the monks you name as so desperate than it does to you."

"Nay, sweet lady, the Grail means everything to me."

He said it with such conviction that she hesitated. "I wish that I could believe you."

"Believe me," he said quietly, convincingly, "believe it when I tell you that finding the Grail would be my reward and my salvation."

"What of your reasons, Sir Stephen? For whose glory do you seek the Grail?"

Sunlight filtered through laced branches overhead; it was windy at the summit, steady gusts that whipped at her skirts and ruffled the knight's drying hair. Light reflected in his dark eyes with an odd gleam.

"As I've said before, it's the greatest prize in all Christendom. Why would I not want to find it?"

"You seek it for your own glory, then."

"Perhaps. Would it not be a triumph to be the man who found the celebrated Cup of Christ?"

"Your answers are ambiguous, sir. Do you consider the Grail to be miraculous? Do you seek miracles for yourself?"

"Finding the Grail would be miracle enough. I have no need of other miracles," he said shortly.

"Do you not?" Aislinn inhaled warm air spiced with the scent of sweet privet. Sunlight was warm on her back, bright in her eyes. "It's my thought that all mortals are in need of a miracle in their lives."

"And are *you,* damoiselle—are you in urgent need of a miracle in your life?"

"You mock me, but aye, the miracle of the Grail would be most welcome, Sir Stephen." She faced him squarely. "Yet if it's to be, it will be. I must trust in a higher will than mine to direct me. I've done that all my life."

"Apparently it's been a futile trust, if you still await a miracle. If your faith were enough, you wouldn't be here now searching desperately for a miracle, would you."

It was a statement of fact, not a question. She could not disagree, hateful as that was to admit. Why must he persist in tormenting her? In forcing her to see truths that she found so unpalatable? Sir Stephen Fitzhugh was a cynic, a man who had lost his faith and perhaps even his soul—yet she could not surrender her hope.

Twisting her fingers together, she looked down at her

hands, then up at him, a swift glance that caught a strange expression on his face. What was it? Frustration? Anger?

"Tell me," she said, "is it so wrong to want to find a miracle? You, beau knight, also seek a miracle—the Grail."

"Yea, that I do, though not for the same reasons as do you, it seems. I want no guidance in my life."

"All lives are guided by something, whether it be by higher principles or by greed. Which is yours?"

"Greed isn't one of my vices. I want nothing that's not due me."

"And what are you due, Sir Stephen? You speak as if you have not been rewarded in life with your just due."

"No, I have not, though there are those who consider my just due to be hellfire and brimstone. I do not agree, of course." Reaching out, he lifted one tail of her twin plaits in his fist, his thumb testing the confines of the cloth that bound it.

His expression changed, became intense, his tone husky as he murmured, "Some prizes are just out of my reach, it seems."

Dark eyes bored into her face, potent and riveting, and she couldn't look away. There was an odd wistfulness in his voice that she had not heard before, a yearning that bespoke matters beyond her ken. Behind the stark features she caught a glimpse of the man, his uncertainty masked by harsh words and mockery. It was fleeting, an impression swiftly replaced by a stronger reaction. Light-headed, her chest began to ache and she realized she was holding her breath. She swayed, and he caught her arm, holding it fast, his other hand drawing her close by the tether of her bound plait.

Anticipation swelled, and her limbs began to quake as he cupped her chin in his palm.

"Sweet lady . . ." His voice was a husky whisper, so soft she could barely decipher his words, but there was gentle intent in his touch, in the caress of his hand on her face and her throat. She trembled beneath his warm fingers.

It seemed as if she balanced on the edge of a dangerous precipice, and if she moved too fast or not at all, she would tumble into the waiting unknown. She should move away from him, step back and out of his reach.

But she could not.

He drew her into him, easily, so that it felt natural for him to put his arms around her. A tremor went through her body. Ah, she was not as impervious as she had thought herself to be, not to this man's touch.

His kiss was light at first, a mere brushing of his lips over her mouth, a teasing caress. Aislinn leaned into him, aching with unnamed and unfamiliar response, a desire to have more, yet fearful of it, too. What was this strong emotion that gripped her when he touched her? It was like no other feeling she had yet known . . . but a man's intimate touch was not unknown to her. It was a duty, merely a wife's submission to her husband with the begetting of a child the only purpose. But she was not wed to Stephen Fitzhugh, nor did she want a child of him.

Why then do I crave his touch?

Confusion muddled her mind, the heat inside did not abate, but grew hotter and higher as his kiss deepened. The gentle kiss changed subtly at first, became insistent, a demand for her response. And she gave it, tentatively, not certain how or what to respond, opening her lips for him at his prodding.

Stephen's hands gripped her tightly now, held her hard against him, his hands splayed across her back to hold her close. The length of his body pressed into hers; he probed her mouth with his tongue, heated strokes that were shocking and tantalizing. It was not what she expected, nor did she anticipate her own reaction.

A moan trembled in her throat, and her arms rose to

curve around his neck, to hold him even closer. On her toes now, she pressed harder against him, her body singing with a pulsing need that obliterated caution.

She heard him groan, felt his arms tighten around her and his hands move to cradle her head, fingers stroking back her hair as he kissed her with a growing ferocity that was forceful and frightening.

From deep inside, she summoned the strength to remove herself from his embrace, to take a step away. He released her grudgingly, his breath harsh gusts between his teeth, but he did not try to hold her against her will. His arms dropped to his sides, hands curled into fists, and his face was a careful mask when she dared look at him.

She found her voice, a little strained but perfectly coherent, remarkably so considering her inner turmoil.

"If we're both here to find the Grail, Sir Stephen, we would do well to begin our search."

"Ah yes. The Grail. A miracle awaits us, damoiselle. We should not tarry longer in—less fulfilling pursuits."

He swept her a low bow as if she were a court lady, a practiced gesture that spoke of familiarity with such courtesies. Her cheeks flamed. He mocked her.

Flustered, she moved past him into the bright sunlight that flooded a huge plateau of green grass ringed by stone and dirt ramparts. Evidence of the once-huge fort was still visible in the concentric earthen banks, the tumbled piles of red stone erratically scattered, and two careful cairns of white stone that squatted amidst daisies and bluebells. Buttercups like chips of sunlight nodded brightly in tiny crevices between the rocks. She inhaled deeply, striving for calm.

Somerset stretched below the summit in green fields and thickly wooded copses, with neighboring hills billowing like sea waves beyond an emerald valley dissected by hedge fences and sheep.

"Perfect site for a fortress," Stephen commented as he passed her, "but not to bury a dead king."

Aislinn was silent. The wind was brisk, tugging at her skirts, loosening the plaits she had bound so quickly in her haste that morning. Crows swooped and soared below the hill, riding air currents with outspread wings, loud in flight. In the tops of tall trees, nests bristled with fledglings.

Stephen walked the boundaries of the fortress, pausing at times to examine tumbled rock, then approached one of the stone pyramids in the greensward and knelt beside it. Bright sunlight lent his hair the blue-black sheen of a raven's wing as he bent his head close to the cairn. Tussocks of grass cradled the stones as if intentionally placed there. He looked up at her, a hand indicating another cairn across the grassy bowl.

"Two of them. More pyramids. The Welsh bard failed to mention they are mere wells."

"The bard also claimed Arthur lies at the abbey." She approached the cairn. "My uncle's journal could mean either the abbey or Camelot, I suppose. Do you think it's here?"

"I do not." He stood up, kicked idly at a rock so that it came loose and rolled away, revealing red earth beneath. "Mary, I must be insane to have come here! We follow wisps of smoke. There's nothing here to yield evidence that King Arthur or his grave ever existed. Or that the Grail is anything more than a fanciful dream. The only certainty is the waste of time and effort in pursuit of such a foolish myth. I should have known better."

"What did you expect to find here?"

"Expect?" He shook his head, indicated the hill with a wave of his arm. "Something other than crows and dirt. I don't know—a sign of some sort, a pyramid or a cross— it's obvious to me we've both been deceived."

She stared at him uncertainly. "Do you not want to even dig?"

He shot her a vicious glance. "Dig where? Between the cairns? Do you truly think a king is buried atop a fortress wall? It seems cursed unlikely."

"Does it? Not to me. It seems as if we stand near the very gates of heaven up here. Even the crows fly below us, their nests in tall trees that we look down upon instead of looking up. Why not bury a king so near heaven?"

Stephen stared at her. A muscle throbbed in his jaw. "Near heaven's gate . . . it sounds almost plausible when said like that. I must be delirious."

"Well, you did ride all this way for a reason. There's no point in giving up before you even start. Did you bring a tool to dig for the Grail, or shall we use your sword?"

"A spade serves better than a sword when it comes to digging, unless there are vicious voles to slay. Just where do you suggest we begin this noble effort?"

Aislinn chose to ignore his obvious sarcasm. "If Abbot Robert was correct, the grave is betwixt two pyramids." She looked across at the other cairn. "Perhaps we should begin in the very middle. A trench of sorts could be dug, going from one pyramid to the other."

Stephen looked at the distant cairn, then back to the stones where they stood. It was a distance of nearly twenty feet.

"Of course, I presume you intend to help dig." His brow was cocked up, but he didn't linger to hear her reply. He returned to his tethered destrier, and when he came back to the cairn where she waited, he carried a small spade. With a single thrust he shoved the sharp edge into the ground.

A protest that digging should begin in the middle died on her lips at the expression on his face. He shot her a look of frustrated anger as he began to disrobe, unbuckling his sword belt and removing his mail coif, then struggling with his tunic. She lent her aid by unfastening tunic straps and buckles he found difficult to reach, ignoring his growl of protest.

Heavy mail was soon doffed and laid upon the ground, and he stood in white linen undertunic and braies. The laced neck of his tunic was loose around his throat, pale against his dark skin. He stretched, extending his arms backward, and an instant's glimpse of sculpted muscle beneath the linen was unexpectedly unsettling.

Aislinn stepped away from him. The unfamiliar heat surged through her again, flushing her face.

Stephen slanted her a look from beneath black lashes, his gaze smoldered as if he sensed her reaction. A taut, queer smile tucked in the corners of his mouth.

"It's plain that you have no desire to help dig. I'm not surprised. Anyone with sense would hang back."

She stood awkwardly as he lifted up the spade and walked to the center of the ground between the pyramids. Unexpected chagrin, unfounded confusion—why did she feel so flustered? He was only a man. Yet he was a man she had dreamed unholy dreams about, dreams so vivid and real she'd awakened with a restless yearning seething inside her that nothing had quenched. Not even the discovery that Stephen left the abbey without telling her had abated that turmoil.

It was disconcerting.

The spade dug into the red earth with a hefty *shunk*. Occasionally there was a sharp clunk when the metal hit a rock. Shortly, the linen tunic he wore was damp enough to cling to his upper body, the mound of dirt was high, and Sir Stephen knee-deep in a trench.

Aislinn brought him a skin of water, held it out with a smile to soothe any lingering ill will. He straightened, looked up at her as he accepted the water skin. Damp hair straggled onto his forehead and clung in wet strands.

After he drank deeply, he poured water over his head

in a cooling splash. He sucked in a sharp breath, blinked away water from his lashes, and drew his forearm across his face.

"The water is most welcome, damoiselle."

"Yes," she said faintly, and took the water skin he held out to her. "I thought it would be. It's unexpectedly warm after so many days of rain."

"It's hotter than the priests' description of hell," he muttered. Before she realized what he intended, he stripped off his tunic and tossed it up to her. Shocked, she caught the wet garment, staring at him.

He was bare from the waist up, the cords of his braies tied low around his midsection. Sunlight gleamed on his damp skin. Powerful male, muscled and hard, dark skin a burnished, elegant gold. Ropes of muscle on his belly flexed as he bent for the shovel again. Her mouth was suddenly as dry as the red earth he scooped from the trench, and she stood clutching his discarded tunic for what seemed an eternity.

Stephen seemed not to notice her sudden immobility.. He continued digging, the spade biting deeply into earth dense with rock. Uprooted buttercups and daisies lay scattered on the ground around him. He worked steadily, taut muscled body gleaming in the sunlight while she stood silently watching, trying to gather her composure.

Slowly, the knot that was her stomach loosened, and she moved away, feeling as if her legs did not work properly as she put distance between them. Draping his tunic atop the crumbled remnant of a stone wall, she smoothed it out to dry in the sun. The light was bright atop the mound, hotter and more intense.

Spread out below, the green valley was thick with trees and sheep. Crows wheeled gracefully with wings outspread under oaks that towered over white-laced May trees. A sweet fragrance filled the air with promise. With her face upturned, she let the wind blow through her hair, cool the turmoil inside. It was restorative, to stand on what felt like the top of the world and admire its beauty. She stood there for some time, while the sound of digging continued behind her, interspersed with a few muttered curses and the occasional clang of iron spade against rock.

At last she returned to the edge of the trench where Sir Stephen was chest deep in the excavation. Black hair was plastered to his head from his exertions, and his taut muscles flexed, gleamed in the sunlight. He stabbed the sharp end of the spade into the ground with another heavy scrape of iron against rock. He swore softly when the spade glanced off a large rock, and looked up at her with weary frustration.

"No tomb lies here." He wiped sweat from his eyes with an open hand. "All I've found are ancient coins and a few pottery shards. Nothing else. Now I've hit a flat rock. I do *not* intend to dig all the way to the bottom of this hill."

"The legend says Arthur and his knights sleep in a cave beneath this hill. When England needs them they will rise to fight again."

"England has needed them more than once in the past six hundred years. For what in Mary's name do they wait?"

He climbed out of the hole in an easy, graceful motion. Smears of red sandstone stained his braies and stuck to his boots. His bare chest was distracting. It was even more distracting than his mockery. She looked away and indicated with a careless wave of her hand the cairn still yards away.

"That may mark the spot. It does seem that a tomb said to hide the great king would be well hidden, or his enemies would take care to find him and dishonor his memory."

He snorted disbelief as he brushed away dirt. "If the king lies in a tomb, then all the legends are wrong anyway. A dead king won't rise to fight again."

"The church has credited many such miracles, and—"

"You cannot be that big a fool!"

His bare chest heaved with exertion and irritation. A glob of dirt smeared his jawline, mingled with the dark stubble of his beard-shadow. She stared at him.

"It's not foolish to have faith in miracles. You're in danger of sounding very much like a heretic. Men have been burned at the stake for less."

"Yea, and died innocent."

"Do you not fear for your mortal soul?"

"My soul has been damned for too long to fear reprisal from a dead king. It's the living that gives me pause."

"I thought we were talking about the church, not men without honor."

"They are too often one and the same, damoiselle."

Nonplussed, Aislinn fumbled for a reply. Never had she been confronted with such blatant blasphemy. All men in her experience were well aware of the perils that befell those who dared question the holy order of the world.

Hesitant, she ventured a question: "Do you not believe in the goodness of God, sir?"

"Yea, that I do most fully believe. It's the wickedness of men that makes me tremble. How many of the holy brethren of Glastonbury abbey do you think are truly pure? Even the good brother prior has his vices, from petty envy to flagrant greed. He would lie and steal to gain the glory of the Grail for himself, do not doubt it."

"Nay, for the abbey, for the Holy Mother Church!"

A dark brow cocked in sardonic amusement. "Only for the church? You're a naive child, Aislinn of Amberlea. I thought you more clever than that. But perhaps you just do not wish to see the truth about the prior because it's too close to how you feel."

Stung, she retorted, "And *you*, Sir Stephen? Do you want the Grail for holy reasons, or for your own?"

"For my own, of course. I've made no bones about it. We both have our own reasons for finding this Grail, do we not? Do you deny that your reason is to bring pilgrims with heavy purses to the abbey?"

"I don't deny that it's one of the reasons, though not the most important. But is it so bad to want the Grail to bring pilgrims to the abbey? The reason we offer the bones of saints for worship as relics is so that those who come may be blessed."

"You mean, so that those who come may pay well to be blessed."

She sucked in a sharp breath. "It sounds so selfish when you say it like that, but there are noble reasons behind the desire to draw pilgrims." She paused, searching for words that would justify the logic she had long accepted without question. "Many people depend upon the abbey for food as well as their souls' nourishment. The abbey must support itself. King Henry may withdraw his patronage one day, or die before the abbey is rebuilt. What then would we do?"

His lip curled. "You'll do like other abbeys all over England, I imagine. Extol the astonishing deeds of the bones of your saints to those who believe and will pay well for an elusive miracle."

"You are profane," she snapped. "I had not thought it of you. Gaven was wrong, I fear. You're not worthy to find the Grail, and you are not the righteous knight of his vision!"

"No, I'm not. I never pretended to be." He gave her a scalding look from eyes dark as pitch. "You lent me virtues I told you I don't possess. I warned you."

"But I didn't think . . . I never thought you meant it. I assumed you were merely being modest."

He gave a hoot of sardonic laughter that brought heat and wrathful tears to her eyes, and she couldn't help a slight quiver in her voice, though she steadied it quickly.

"I believed in you because I thought you worthy to find the Grail."

For a long moment, Stephen was quiet. He looked away from her, kicked at a clod of dirt with the toe of his boot. "By the Holy Rood—you really are a trusting romantic." He shoved a hand through his hair, blew out a heavy breath and shook his head. "It grows late. I am hot, weary, and hungry, and I've nothing to show for my efforts but an empty hole to be refilled."

"And is that my fault?"

He glanced up, a searing look. "No. It's my own cursed fault that brought me to this idiocy. I'm to blame for that. It doesn't mean I have to listen to your lunatic notions." When she just stared at him without speaking, he muttered, "I spoke out of turn. Words said in anger were not meant to offend you."

"They have, Sir Stephen. Your weariness and hunger are not acceptable excuses for your impiety."

"It's not impious to question your reasons for finding the Grail, is it? Or even to question my own?" He moved to the stone wall where his tunic was spread to dry, shrugged into it, then turned back to her. "I'm but a man beset with uncertainty of my own humanity. I question it, as I question the faith of others."

Aislinn wanted to believe him. But the words tripped off his tongue so effortlessly, as if by rote. As if he had said it too many times before and did not believe it either.

Before she could form a reply, he said, "It's too late to go back to Glastonbury tonight. I intend to stay here, but you should seek lodging below. Inquire at the church."

"I have no intention of leaving you up here alone," she said calmly. "If you stay here tonight, I shall stay also."

A faint smile curled his mouth. "Are you not afraid to stay alone with me, damoiselle?"

"I am in little danger from you, Sir Stephen."

It was not a complete lie. Body and soul, she was more in danger from herself than from him. . . .

Chapter 14

✝

A SHOWER OF sparks rose and faded as a log popped, then collapsed into the glowing embers of the fire. Stephen knelt, poked at the flames with a long stick.

"After the heat of the day, the night is near cold," Aislinn said behind him, and he pivoted on the balls of his feet to look at her. Firelight reflected gold in her eyes, cast a rosy glow on her creamy cheeks. The plaits of her hair had come loose and she worked to free them, combing her fingers through the pale silken strands that waved over her shoulders and down her back. It was a feminine gesture that hit him with the force of a hammer, and he sucked in a sharp breath at the poignancy of it.

Memories rushed back in a flood, of evening hours spent watching another woman brush her hair. Just so had she sat with her feet tucked beneath her, slender arms drawing a brush through her hair, the long tresses flowing in a river of fragrant silk around her face and over her shoulders. It made his heart ache to recall it.

He looked away. "You would have done better to lodge below with the village priest."

"I'm comfortable enough. I thought to bring my wool cloak with me."

Stephen tossed a stick into the fire, watched it burn. As he burned. The chill of the evening did not touch him. He burned with a need she had awakened in him, and resented it.

"Your comfort is not the reason you should not be up here tonight," he said abruptly.

Silence answered him. She knew. Curse her, she had to know what he wanted from her. It was a relentless need in him now, this inconvenient lust.

To allay it, he sought refuge in argument.

"On the morrow, we return to Glastonbury. I will leave you there and return to York and my own business."

He heard her swiftly indrawn breath, then the anger in her voice: "You deny your moral duty just to deny me!"

"*Duty?* I have no moral duty here, save that of my own choosing. And I deny you nothing. You may continue to search for the Holy Grail as you like."

"You yield hope after so short a time? I thought you a man of purpose and conviction, Sir Stephen. I'm grieved to learn how wrong I've been."

"Yea, you have erred most grievously, Aislinn of Amberlea, for I'm not the man you want me to be. I am not the knight who has come to rally a fabled king to life and produce a mythical cup. It's all fables, tales to entertain bored nobility and kings. I question King Henry's mind that he should so earnestly seek such a grave, though I do know his reasons for it."

"Do you? Pray, enlighten me, Sir Stephen, since you are so familiar with the king's mind!" Angry eyes flashed, and her hands were small knots in her lap as she glared at him.

"Happily. It takes no special gifts to know the king's intent. If you'd but give it a moment's thought, you could reason it yourself. Even after a hundred and twenty years of Norman rule, there are men who hope for escape from under the Norman boot. Arthur saved Britons from the Saxons five hundred years ago, and some say he will rise to fight his enemies again. In this case, the Normans." He arched a brow at her and ignored her muffled comment to continue: "Should Arthur's grave be discovered, it's proof to the Welsh that he's truly dead and that Angevin rule is secure. A simple truth, to benefit good King Henry. It's the obvious reason for him to want King Arthur's grave to be found. Forget a more noble reason."

"And the Grail?"

"That is a different pursuit." He paused, said in a carefully neutral tone, "I search for the Grail because it's a challenge. I was told it lies with Arthur in Avalon. That is the reason I came. It wasn't to find ancient bones."

Silence fell, flames crackled, and night birds hooted softly in the trees. A chill wind swept over the hill. He felt the weight of his deception heavy on his shoulders, and was suddenly tempted to tell her all. Why not? It would mean an end to the necessity for lies.

Eyes the peculiar hue of spring violets studied him gravely, reflecting the leaping flames. In the shadows, her face was the pale ivory of an early snow, pristine and pure. A sense of peace enveloped him, lured by silent beauty. She was so fair, with the swirl of honey hair over her shoulders and framing her face; a complex blend of innocent faith and worldly wisdom. Perhaps she had faith enough for both of them. He should tell her the truth. He *would* tell her the truth. It would be a relief to share the burden, a relief to believe in something and someone other than men's perfidy and his own. Dare he share that part of himself with her? It wouldn't shock her. She stared at him with all the wisdom of the ages in her unblinking gaze, as if . . . as if . . .

Christ above, but she looks at me as if she reads my very soul. . . .

"It must be sad to believe in nothing, Sir Stephen."

Her soft, blunt words shocked him. They shouldn't have. He'd always known that he was alone. It had been foolish to hope, for even an instant, that someone would see and share his pain.

A smile curled his lips, and he was fully aware that it was a parody of amusement, full of irony.

"Oh, I believe in many things, but not illusions." He stood up. "I believe that there are those who will stop at nothing to gain their own desires regardless of who they must destroy in the process. And I believe that there will always be fools who allow the destruction. I don't intend to be in either camp, and I will never again allow myself to be deluded by useless dreams."

"Or guided by faith, it seems." She leaned forward, held out her hands to the fire, waggled her fingers. "Do you intend to spend eternity without hope?"

"I'm spending this life without hope. That's enough."

"Then you do not believe in eternity?" She turned to look at him, eyes wide in the flickering light.

"It doesn't matter what I believe—"

"It does to me."

Her simplicity jolted him into honest response. "No, I do not believe in eternity as you do. Death is the end of it all. No chalice can resurrect dust and bones, or give a dead man life where there is none. It's an entertaining fable, but a fable nonetheless."

"Then you do not believe in heaven or hell."

"Oh, I believe in hell because I have seen it, lived in it, fought in it. I know the sounds, the sights, the smells of hell. I am as familiar with them as I am with my own hands."

He held up his hands, stared down at them as if he saw demons there in the hills and lines of his palms. Flashes of memory skidded through his mind, flickering images of battle and the aftermath, scenes that had lost their power to shock him, but not to torment.

For a long moment she said nothing, then: "By that logic, you don't believe in heaven, as you haven't seen it."

His hands dropped to his sides, and he shrugged. "On the contrary. I have seen it. I know what it's supposed to be. But I also know it doesn't last."

"The church teaches eternal life, not just the life in this world. There's the hereafter—"

"There is no hereafter. Once we die, we are dead. I've seen more dead men in my lifetime than you will ever see, damoiselle. Not one of them rose again or showed signs of life."

"Not perhaps as you mean, but the soul is eternal—"

He waved an impatient hand, crouched by the fire to poke at it with a stick, watched sparks fly. "You are a victim of the distortions of priests. You would do better to place more faith in the tangibles."

He knew how he sounded: Sacrilegious. Blasphemous. A heretic. It was dangerous treading so close to the edge of the abyss, but pain and frustration drove him. He must keep Aislinn at arm's length. He had to put barriers between them ere he yielded to the strong desire to hold her again.

But Aislinn moved closer, rising to stand beside him with a serious expression. "You are wrong, Sir Stephen. We all have souls."

He swiveled on the balls of his feet, stared up at her with an emotion akin to pity.

"Once dead, we're dust. Old bones. There is nothing of life left. I have yet to see a man rise after death."

Her face was pale, her mouth taut with determination as she shook her head. "No, no. Oh, you are so wrong. How can I explain it so you'll understand?"

Her hands twisted in a knot as she struggled for words,

and he watched her with a detached sense of sympathy. Once, he had felt as passionate as she did about something, but it had been so long ago that he'd almost forgotten how it felt. Save for Dunmow, nothing had mattered in twenty years. A lifetime.

Aislinn held out a hand as if about to touch him, and he almost flinched. She halted at his withdrawal and said earnestly, "Death is not final. There are other forms— compare the oak tree. Even when it's been cut down, it lives on. It may be in the form of a chair, or a table, or a cup, or even this cross, but it still exists, albeit in a much different form."

She held up a wooden cross, tethered round her neck on a slender ribbon. "This was once part of an oak, but now it lives on in a different form from the tree, much as we will live on after death in different forms from those we know now. Do you not see?"

He stood up and held out his hand, and she placed the cross in his palm, looking slightly surprised. He held it briefly, then pulled it free of the ribbon and threw it in the fire, where the flames licked it greedily.

"Now it no longer exists, mouse." He meant it kindly. A lesson on the reality of life, perhaps. Or because he hurt and he felt like hurting her. . . .

She said nothing, but stared silently into the leaping fire, watched the cross turn to red and gray ash. It was a searing moment. Now she would understand, would no longer be so vulnerable. Would no longer try to convert him with her pervasive faith. Would realize he was lost to her and even to himself.

"Ashes to ashes, dust to dust. Sweet mouse, your faith is strong, and I admire that. But don't seek to change me."

Turning, she met his gaze steadily. Her light wool cloak draped loosely from her shoulders, framed her slender body.

"Change you? You give me too much credit, sir. I seek

only to give you another choice. You've chosen death, but I wish to show you how to live. True faith cannot burn to ash."

Amazed, he could only stare at her. She humbled him. She made him feel suddenly small and insignificant. There was an unexpected generosity in her words, a sincerity that left him floundering for a reply.

He laughed, a hollow sound.

"Sweet Christ, what manner of woman are you, Aislinn of Amberlea? You're like no other I've ever met. . . ."

She smiled. "Yea, I believe that, Sir Stephen. As you pointed out when we first met, I've been rightly accused of being stubborn. So now I'm being stubborn. You don't really believe all that you claim, for all that you would like me to think that you do. I perceive intrinsic goodness in you, a purity of heart that you deny."

"One must be virtuous to have purity of heart," he said tersely, "and I've never been accused of that. Virtue is not my habit."

"You deceive yourself. But you don't deceive me, though I admit you do irritate me. All these protests mask your true heart. I know what you really want."

"Do you?" He took a step closer to her, near desperate with need and frustration. "No, I don't think you know what I really want, Aislinn, or you wouldn't be here with me now. By the Holy Rood, I've done my best to convince you of my iniquity, but you're fool enough to tempt me yet. For your own sake, keep your distance from me. I'm at the end of my tether."

Her eyes widened, absorbed light like a mirror, gleamed in the deep shadows and flickering flame. Her tongue came out, wet her lips in a nervous gesture as she stared at him silently, a slender enchantress with loose hair tumbled around her lovely face, smelling faintly of apples and roses.

He ached for her. His blood sang through his veins and

pounded to his groin. His hands curled into fists at his sides. No greater test of his restraint had he suffered.

"Yea," she said softly, "I know what it is you want of me, Sir Stephen. It's in your eyes when you look at me, in your voice, in your touch—and in my dreams. Oh, yes, I know what you want . . . it is not unknown to me."

"But is it unwelcome?"

He saw that the question startled her as his declaration had not. Color stained her face, and her voice quivered slightly.

"Unwelcome? I—I—" Her voice trailed into a breathless silence fraught with confusion. Trembling hands rose to her throat where the empty ribbon still lay, fingers touching it as if searching for the cross. Protection against a profane intent, perhaps. . . .

Forestalling her retreat, he put out his hands to grasp hers, held them tightly in his fists. "Ah no, Aislinn of Amberlea, do not decry your words now."

"Sir, you take too much meaning from my words. . . ."

"Nay, I know what I heard. You speak plain enough when you like. Speak plainly now—do you tremble with need when I touch you?"

A whisper: "No. . . ."

"Then why are you shaking now?" Fisting both her hands in one of his, he marveled at how small they were, fingers as slender as the delicate bones of a sparrow. With his free hand, he touched her face; her brow, her cheek. The heart-shaped whorls of her ear were rose-petal soft as he pushed honey-colored hair back from her shoulder.

A shiver rippled through her at his light touch, challenging her denial: "I do not shake. . . ."

"Your honesty has fled, and you deceive only yourself." He lifted her face to stare into her eyes. Uncertainty stared back at him.

His hand closed in her hair, let it slide through his fingers, silky and soft, tempting him to bury his face in it and forget everything but the scent of roses and Aislinn.

"Sir Stephen—"

He put a finger over her lips, pressed lightly. "No, do not say it. You'll break the spell of enchantment you have put on me."

"Enchantment?" She made a soft trilling sound. "If 'tis magic that summons such feelings, then I fear we are both bewitched."

Stephen went still, for he had just been handed the keys to the kingdom. Her confession amounted to permission to pursue this driving desire that obliterated any other goal.

He wasn't gentle as he pulled her harshly against him and slid his hands under her arms. His fingers spread over fabric, testing the cushion of her firm flesh beneath. When she didn't resist, he kissed her. As his hands explored her slender curves, his tongue explored her mouth. Blood surged through his body, and he pushed her down onto his pile of furs close by the fire.

His open mouth absorbed her gasp, met her tongue with a wicked thrust of his own. His grip tightened on her waist, pulled at the wool of her gown.

Aislinn twisted in his embrace, but did not attempt to break free. He deepened the kiss and slid his hand upward to cup her breast in his palm. He felt her stiffen at his intimate touch. She gasped when his thumb and finger closed over her nipple and blue wool, and a shudder went through her body.

When she arched upward, her hips pressing hard against him, his restraint wavered. He fumbled with the hem of her gown, tugged it above her knees. Then he was caressing soft bare skin of her thigh while she quivered.

"Sir Stephen," she gasped into his ear, "this is . . . I'm not ready."

His hand moved to cradle her chin, tilted her face up for another kiss. She was so fragile, his open hand a dark sacrilege against her pale skin. He kissed each corner of her mouth, then the small cleft in her rounded chin. Her body trembled in an arousing blend of seduction and denial.

"Do you really want me to stop?" he murmured against her ear.

"No . . . yes . . . this is too soon, too soon. . . ." Her lashes fluttered against her cheeks like small brown wings, darker against the creamy hue of her skin.

Reason was fraying, slipping away from him, for all he could think was how much he wanted her. All of her, not just her body, but the very essence of what made her so different from all the other women he had known. He wanted to possess her physically and emotionally, wanted her to want him as fiercely as he wanted her . . . wanted her to see him for who he was, not who he pretended to be.

But perhaps if she saw the true Stephen Fitzhugh, she would flee into the night. . . .

He released her with a suddenness that startled both of them. Surprise leaped in her eyes, and her lips parted. She did not move but gazed up at him in confusion, the firelight illuminating her face.

Hoarsely, he muttered, "You are set free. I would not hold you against your will, even when bewitched—but you will have to set me free."

Eloquent silence answered him. Beyond the fire, shadows mantled the earth; a bird sang sweetly in treetops below the knoll, and the dusky sky held countless stars that shimmered in pricks of light against dark blue. It was as if they were perched at the very edge of the world. It waited, breathless anticipation quivering in the hush as he hesitated.

Aislinn was temptation, both a curse and a benediction. If he had any sense at all, he would walk away, roll up in his own cloak and go to sleep. He should have demanded she stay the night at the church. He was a fool to relax his vigilance for even a moment.

Rigid discipline held him back when need prodded him to take her, to strip away garments and restrictions, to put himself inside her and take them both to an elusive pleasure that hovered just out of reach.

"I hold you not, Stephen Fitzhugh. You are not a man that can be held for long," she said into the heavy hush, which stretched painfully. "It would only end badly were we to yield now to baser desires."

A reply stuck in his throat, so that he watched in silence as she rose with innate grace and dignity and moved to her bed by the fire. Silhouetted against the flames, she sat with her back to him, nestled in the pile of furs. He knelt, still, words and action locked inside him. He had lost the opportunity to gain a far sweeter prize than any he had ever had before. There was much more to life than the pursuit of the tangibles. . . .

In the distance, he heard the lonely hoot of an owl, a haunting, eerie sound that echoed his mood. He had rarely felt so alone in his life than he did at this moment.

Chapter 15

✝

AISLINN AWOKE BEFORE the sun was fully risen, and she lay still and quiet for a long moment. Fingers of hazy light limned the humped hills beyond, so that an eerie glow lay upon the land, a rising pearlescent sheen so fragile and lovely it made her eyes sting. Birds went merrily about their morning business as peace hovered in a mantle of shadows and fresh promise.

Across from her, Stephen lay still sleeping. She turned her head on the lumpy pillow of fur and wool to gaze at him. One arm was flung out to the side, his fingers curled inward in a loose fist, combative even in slumber. Dark hair lay in a mussed fringe on his forehead, and his face held none of the mockery and wariness it did when he was awake. Asleep, he looked very young and very vulnerable.

But last night . . . ah, last night he'd been intimidating, not vulnerable. Yet it was not intimidation that coaxed her to yield to the temptation to lie in his arms. Nay, there had been a singing need that bade her surrender all to him. If he had not withdrawn when he had, no doubt she would have found herself in his blankets.

It was a mystery, this emotion that drew her to this knight, for never had she felt so about her lawfully wedded husband. David had never hurt her and had been patient with the maiden she was when they wed, but neither had he stirred the sense of breathless urgency that teemed within her now.

A mystery indeed, that bid her to respond in such a way when she knew so little about Stephen Fitzhugh.

What she did know . . . was confusing.

A knight, yet neither wealthy nor penniless, nor yet a pilgrim, though he sought the Grail. While he had come to Glastonbury under false pretenses, he didn't bother to hide his pursuit of the Grail from her. It gave her hope to think that he intended it for the glory of the church, but if so—which church? There was often strife enough between churches in pursuit of holy relics to draw pilgrims. The ongoing conflict over the bones of Saint Dunstan was evidence enough of the possible furor, but a prize like the Holy Grail would be revered over the entire Christian world, pursued to the point of danger. It had already drawn dangerous men to the abbey. Was Stephen Fitzhugh one of them?

He was no Templar Knight as were the last men who had come to the abbey in search of the Grail, yet was no less persistent. Death had ended the last search, while this search promised to end more safely, if no less vainly.

But at what risk? At the least, she risked her peace of mind, but at the most, she risked her soul.

Closing her eyes against the sleeping knight, she prayed for the strength to resist her own wayward heart. Yet a niggling protest whispered insurrection, and she could not help but wonder what might have happened if Sir Stephen had not retreated when he had. Would she have yielded all?

"Do you sleep the day away, mouse?"

Stephen's voice jerked open her eyes, and she stared at him with burning cheeks, wondering if he'd seen her watching him sleep. He sat up, his cloak draped over his shoulders, sleepy eyes half lidded against growing light.

"I'm awake," she replied stiffly. "My belly gripes."

"Complaints? Perhaps you should have taken my advice and stayed below with the village priest." He rose, lithe as a cat, stretching as leisurely. "We have bread and cheese to break our night's fast, and a few of the apples are left."

A brisk wind rife with the sweet scent of May trees cooled Aislinn's hot cheeks. She took the hunk of bread and cheese he produced from his pack and held out to her, tore off a piece and stuffed it into her mouth to keep from saying anything unwise. There were three apples left, and he gave her two of them.

She ate slowly, watching him as he kicked dirt on the dead embers of the fire, burying the ashes of her cross. Only the empty ribbon was left, a reminder of his derision.

He glanced up at her, a smoldering gaze that brought back the vivid memory of her near capitulation, but she did not look away, lest he guess the direction of her thoughts.

"I feel like a cursed fool," he growled, "bothering to search this desolate ruin with no more hope of success than the rambling words of an old man drunk on mead."

"Beer," she corrected, wiped her hands on her skirts, and rose to gather up her cloak and the ruins of her bed. "Gaven prefers beer to mead. He says mead is too sweet for his tastes."

"I don't doubt it." Stephen buckled on his sword belt over his tunic. "Beer is more potent than mead, more adaptable to concocting improbable tales for his own amusement. He must truly be enjoying the thought that I

took him so seriously, made a gazing-stock of myself by
haring off up here to this empty hill."

She studied him. He was too angry with Gaven and his
own chagrin for it to be a ruse, so perhaps he hadn't taken
the pages of her journal after all. But if not Stephen, who
then would have taken them?

"You truly didn't take the journal pages, did you," she
said, more to herself than him, but he snorted.

"I swore I did not."

"You have sworn a lot that wasn't true."

"No, I've said a lot that could be misconstrued, but I
swore no lie to you, mouse."

"As near as!"

"Yes, as near as—but not quite. Think on it. You assumed I came to Glastonbury to settle the Wells dispute,
and I allowed you to do so. Recall, if you will, that when
you said I was here to settle the dispute, I told you that
you were incorrect."

Irritated, she vaguely recalled the conversation between
them in the chapter house that rainy day, and suspected
he was right. It would make little difference to lie about
it now.

"So you intend to leave here without searching more
for the Grail," she said, tucking the last apple into her
mouth as she turned away. "How convenient. It's not easy
to find, so you just give up the effort."

"Easy?" He raked a hand through his hair, said curtly,
"I don't think it's so easy to dig halfway to the bottom
of a hill. My aching back is testament to that fact. A
plague upon Gaven for his lies. This is more like the gate
to hell instead of heaven."

"What exactly did Gaven say that led you here?"

"It was what he didn't say—you know how he runs on,
and uses riddles when he should speak out plainly. He
said that the dead king was said to lie beneath this hill,
and on Midsummer Eve, comes out to—"

"Ride to the hounds with his knights. Yes, any child over the age of two years has heard that tale. But what of the Grail?"

He shot her a sullen glance. "He said it lies with the dead king. Therefore, if the dead king lies here—it stood to reason, the Grail would be here. That was my greatest error. I tried to make reason out of Gaven's foolery."

Aislinn removed one of her shoes and shook loose a pebble from it, frowning. "My uncle brought me here a long time ago. We searched for the cave wherein Arthur and his loyal knights are said to lie, but we didn't find it."

"And did he dig between the cairns?"

She shook her head. "No, he knew nothing then of the grave being between two pyramids in the cemetery. But as we know now it's not there, either, I thought you had certain knowledge of it being here."

"We've been foxed, damoiselle." He sounded disgusted. "The Grail and the grave are nothing but hoaxes. Idle tales to while away long winter nights. Or send people haring off like imbeciles in search of illusions. Christ!" He swung his cloak over his shoulders and pinned it, viciously jabbing the cloak pin through wool. "I'm the biggest fool of the lot, it seems, for I had begun to believe that perhaps the story of the Grail was true."

"It is." She shrugged when he made a rude sound. "It *is* true, Stephen Fitzhugh. Don't ask me why I believe it, but I do. You may name me a fool if you like."

"I thought we'd already established that fact." He gave her an insolent grin, ignoring her exclamation. "But you're not the only fool standing atop this bloody hill. It seems a bit too odd that so many from different places repeat the same tale, and even those with nothing to gain save idle amusement claim that King Arthur lies on abbey grounds."

"Then that takes us right back to where we began," she

said, vexed that he took it so lightly. "We haven't found the grave."

"Haven't you noticed that no tales mention the Grail lying in that grave with the dead king? I've not heard them if they do. Only a very few even connect it to Arthur, save to say it lies on Avalon with him—Gaven perhaps, but I've come to the regrettable conclusion that he's a madman who enjoys sending us off on harebrained chases."

"You think the Grail lies elsewhere?"

He knelt to scatter the dead ashes of the fire. "In truth, I no longer know what to think. King Henry believes the grave of King Arthur lies at the abbey. Prior Thaddeus believes it, and so did your uncle, a respected abbot. Who am I to disbelieve such noble intellects?"

He stood up and dusted black ash from his hands. "I'm but a landless knight with nothing to call my own save my horse and armor. My duty is to retrieve the Grail and not ask inconvenient questions. Of course, no one has yet been able to tell me how to do this if it doesn't exist, but I suppose I'll just have to work on that obstacle myself."

Her irritation faded. Despite his mockery there was an undercurrent of tension that betrayed his frustration. He stood gazing over the tops of the trees below the summit, his eyes distant, mouth a downward curve of discontent. The faint scar on the angle of his cheek stood out starkly on dark skin, a pale crescent. A muscle throbbed in his jaw.

She suppressed the urge to reach out and touch him, to trace the scar with her fingers, to offer comfort.

He turned to look at her, dispelling her brief surge of sympathy with a terse command: "Make ready, mouse, or I'll leave you here with the ghost of a dead king."

Silent, she gathered the furs she had slept upon and yielded them to his care, then made her way to a private thicket for her morning ablutions.

When she rejoined him, he was with their tethered horses, her palfrey well out of reach of his destrier. He'd already saddled both horses; several feet apart, the animals munched contentedly on tufts of grass and buttercups.

Stephen paced in a lunging circle through a small patch of buttercups, hands clasped behind his back. There was an arresting tension in his posture, in the impatient strides. Yellow dust powdered his boots, left there by the tiny yellow flowers. Faery dust—the childhood explanation of pollen distributed by buttercups suddenly summoned another memory.

She looked up when Stephen came to her and held out her palfrey's reins.

"We must be on our way, damoiselle. Mount swiftly."

Dawn radiance caught his face in shades of gray and gold light; black lashes cast shadows on strong cheeks as he narrowed his eyes at her. Her heart gave a peculiar thump that she ignored. She took the end of the reins he held out.

"Gaven once told me a tale of the king of the Faeries," she blurted. Stephen's brow rose, and to forestall sarcasm, she added swiftly, "It has bearing, so do listen. The king is said to live beneath the Tor. Gaven also mentioned a sacred vessel guarded by the faeries. It could be that king he speaks of in his tales."

"He said King Arthur, fey little mouse. This is the first I've heard of faeries. Have you taken a fever?"

Stubbornly, she ignored his mockery. "Plainly, or in one of his riddles?" When he just looked at her, she said again, impatiently, "Did Gaven *say* it was King Arthur, or did he tell you about the grave in one of his riddles?"

He shrugged impatiently. "Gaven said where the king lies, we would find the Grail."

"It would be like Gaven to be illusive. He believes in the old ways, the Celtic ways of the ancient ones that lived here once. He's told me of the Druid priests who gave

Joseph of Arimathea land to build the first above-ground Christian church in Britain. It was those priests who told of a sacred vessel buried beneath the Tor. The king of the Faeries is said to lie beneath the Tor. I believe there's a connection between the two."

"It would be like the old goat to speak of one king and mean another," he muttered. "But why? What does he hope to gain, other than amusement?"

"Gaven presents us with a test. If we—you—pass it, then you're worthy to find the Grail."

"I thought Gaven has already pronounced me as the Chosen One," Stephen said mockingly.

"That does not necessarily mean you're immune to his trials. Even King Arthur, who was chosen by Merlin, failed all tests in the end," she replied gravely.

"If that's meant to encourage me, it doesn't." He spoke gruffly, but not unkindly. His hostility seemed diminished, his tone wry.

She smiled. "I would settle for not *discouraging* you at this point."

"Despite my obvious unsuitability, you intend for me to still search for the Grail, I see." He shook his head, a bit ruefully, his smile slow. "I fear your faith is misplaced."

"Perhaps I am just desperate, Sir Stephen."

Ignoring his amused smile, she moved to mount the palfrey and was taken by surprise when he lifted her up in a swift, smooth motion. With his hands on her waist, he set her atop her mount.

Instead of moving away, he remained beside the palfrey without removing his hands. His fingers spread on her waist, and she felt their heat even through the kirtle and undertunic she wore.

"If there is a grail to be found," he said softly, "I will find it. Do not expect more of me."

Aislinn stared after him as he turned away and went to

his destrier, mounted with graceful ease, turned the horse around, and led the way down the track. She followed behind him, her palfrey stepping daintily over the ruts.

The sky was cloudy, shadows drifting, and the light erratic. At the foot of the hill, instead of taking the road back to Glastonbury, Stephen rode round the base slowly, as if searching.

"If you look for a cave," she ventured finally, "none has ever been found."

A tangle of briars snarled the path, and he reined in his mount. Just beyond, a tiny village lay nestled in the shadow of the hill, green fields spreading around it.

"The spring of Sutton Montis—where does it lie?"

"Near the church. My uncle and I once searched that area, thinking perhaps that if Arthur and his knights are said to ride down the hill to the spring to water their horses, a cave opening must be directly above. We found no sign of it."

"Nor will we now, I imagine." He sounded disgruntled, but not surprised. "Since we must water our own mounts, it seems a likely spot."

She eyed him skeptically, knowing there were too many places along the road to water their mounts to go out of the way now, but she said nothing as she followed him. It was quiet, save for the plodding steps of their horses.

In the cloudy hush, with the air aquiver with waiting, as for a storm, the likelihood of King Arthur and his loyal knights rising from five hundred years sleep to water their mounts seemed almost possible.

They found the stream, a mere trickle seeping between rocks not far from an ancient stone church. A spire pointed a wooden cross skyward. Crows perched atop, cawing angrily at the trespassers, wings beating against the wind as if the birds would take flight at any moment.

Stephen let the horses drink, then refilled their water

skins, eying the birds with a frown. "Bloody scavengers," he muttered. "Carrion crows."

"There must be a dead animal nearby." Aislinn took the water skin he gave her, tied it to her saddle, and settled herself firmly. The wind had grown cooler, and without the sun to warm the air a chill seeped through her woolen cloak. She pulled it around her body and gathered up her reins. "Do we ride on for Glastonbury now?"

"Yea, we ride." Stephen mounted, and she followed him on the narrow road that wound through a canopy of trees that grew thickly on each side. It was close, isolated, a tunnel of green that was hushed and protected from even the wind. The beat of hooves on hardpacked road was muffled by old deadfall and the occasional snap of a small branch or twig.

The road curved beyond Cadbury, stretched through trees to meet with the road to Glastonbury just beyond the village of West Camel. The forest was deep here with marshlands brooding on each side of the road beyond the hedgerows, a strangely silent landscape of twisted trees and stagnant pools. Trees bent and swayed with the rising wind as clouds swept blackly overhead, scoured the sky clean of any blue. The air smelled of rain and brackish water.

"Why do we take this road?" she was moved to ask, but Stephen did not reply. After a moment, she ventured, "It's much longer this way, when it would be easier to—"

"This road is safer."

His flat reply surprised her.

"Safer? Where lies the danger? The most vicious thing I have yet seen today were the crows."

"Yea, and did it occur to you to wonder why there were so many in that one place?" He half turned in his saddle to glance back at her. "*Carrion* crows, Aislinn."

"A dead animal, most like, though—" She halted,

struck by his implication. "What did you see, Sir Stephen?"

"I saw nothing. It was what I did *not* see that gave me pause."

"Speak plainly, sir!"

"A ring of stones as for a fire, yet no fire was lit. A patch of grass beside the stream flattened as for a bed, yet no one lay asleep. Crows waited impatiently for us to leave, greedy for a feast. Yet no carrion."

"Is this another of your obscure parables? You accuse Gaven of obscurity, yet you are more so!" Fear battled with frustration. Her hands tightened on the palfrey's reins, and she felt as if the very air shimmered with danger.

"Someone slept below the hill last night, but did not light a fire for fear of being seen. That reeks of stealth. I would like to know the reason for it."

"There could be any number of reasons a man would make a bed for the night beside a stream."

"Yea, but none that would draw so many hungry crows."

She sucked in a sharp breath. "Was there—but if there was someone lying there dead—"

"There was not."

"Then why—"

"Damoiselle, it is far too often the danger that is not seen that is the most lethal. Risk for myself is one thing, but to risk you is another matter."

"Is that why we take the less-traveled road back to the abbey?"

He reined in his mount to allow her to come nearer, but kept a firm hand on his destrier's bridle. "I am by nature a cautious man. I prefer avoidance to the necessity of dealing with the unexpected."

"You did not strike me as a man who would avoid

danger, Sir Stephen. Rather, I thought you a man to encourage it."

"Then you were mistaken. I am not fond of risking my
life or the lives of others."

After a moment she said, "For that, I am grateful. I fear
I'm not very brave."

"It does not take bravery to avoid confrontation, but
good sense." He twisted to look at her, a faint smile curving his mouth. "If there was danger, I believe you have
sense enough to do what must be done."

She felt a wave of almost giddy pleasure. Foolish of
her, to be so pleased at a casual comment, but it was an
acknowledgment of her worth that was both unexpected
and welcome.

"A most surprising compliment, Sir Stephen. I must
confess to amazement at your generosity."

"I amaze myself." He paused. "Nothing is as it seems
at times. Even this quiet road can be deceptively dangerous."

A tension vibrated in his odd comment that caught her
attention, and she frowned slightly. Trees stretched on
each side of the road, dense shadows in brooding silence.
It was suddenly still, a hush without even the sound of
birds. Only the thud of hooves muffled by thick deadfall
could be heard. A shiver crawled down her spine at the
eerie silence.

"Are you trying to frighten me, Sir Stephen? There is
nothing here to—"

"Be quiet." His harsh command was low pitched, and
he brought his mount to an abrupt halt a few feet ahead
of her.

Vexed at his curt rudeness, she had to rein in her mount
to keep distance between them.

A sudden loud crashing startled her, and her hands
jerked reflexively, prompting her palfrey to surge forward
into Stephen's destrier. The warhorse screamed, a fierce

sound, and whirled to attack the smaller beast. Stephen sawed at his reins, brought the horse under control with some effort, but not before a massive hoof clipped Aislinn's leg. Then, incredibly, he leaned forward and slapped her horse's rump.

It happened so quickly she had no time to cry out and barely managed to keep her seat as the palfrey bolted. The horse darted forward, hooves a rapid thunder on the path that snaked through crowded trees. Aislinn held on tightly, breathless with pain from the blow. With her free hand, she finally managed to slow the panicked animal to a calmer pace.

Her cloak hung awry, tangling over her arms. She gave it a few jerks to straighten it, then turned the palfrey back around. How dare he make her horse bolt! Furious, she intended to demand an explanation.

But what she saw made her blood go cold.

Astride his destrier, Stephen Fitzhugh was surrounded by three men wielding swords and hacking at him viciously. The lethal clang of steel against steel rang loudly on the leafy road, and the plunging destrier screamed a savage challenge. Frozen with terror and apprehension, Aislinn could only watch in horror.

Then, above the tumult, she heard Stephen: "Aislinn, take flight! *Now!*"

Fear urged her to obey, but concern for Stephen made her hesitate, loathe to leave him to the uncertain mercy of these outlaws. The brittle clang of steel assaulted her ears and, ebbing courage, she yanked at the palfrey's reins, turned in circles as she struggled between concern and the urge for escape.

Stephen glanced up and toward her, and his inattention earned him a glancing blow from an attacker. He reeled, but did not fall. A scream hung in her throat, held back by the sheer force of will. She must make no sound, as her presence was a distraction that could see him slain.

Anguished, she made the most difficult choice she had ever been forced to make. Wheeling the palfrey, she drummed her heels against the animal's sides and sent it careening down the coiling road.

As the palfrey fled, the wind of flight whisked away the hot tears streaming down her face. Grief clogged her throat and blurred her vision, mixed with frustration at her helplessness.

Oh God, I am such a coward! Never had she dreamed she would be so spineless as to leave a man to his certain fate. Yet she left Stephen Fitzhugh behind as he had bade her do, and prayed she would see him alive again. . . .

Chapter 16

✝

I T WAS A fierce struggle. Nero swung to meet each threat
with lethal hooves and gnashing teeth, earning yelps of
pain and curses. Stephen's sword flashed, disappeared in
a tangle of rough brown robe, reappeared smeared with a
thin crimson stain. A blade glittered in deadly promise,
swung toward him, and he met it with his own, leaning
weight into the blow. Hands attempted to capture Nero's
bridle and drag him down, but the destrier was too well
versed in battle to allow enemies that close.

Christ above, these were no ill-trained outlaws with
clumsy weapons, but men well accustomed to the weight
and balance of their swords. He cursed his decision not
to wear full armor, for now no helmet protected his head
from murderous jabs of their blades. One of the men went
to his knees, and Stephen pressed home his advantage,
brought his sword around in an arc so the flat of the blade
caught another in his ribs. It sliced easily through brown
wool, earned a shriek of pain.

Their monks' habits did not protect them from good

Spanish steel, it seemed. Stephen rose in his stirrups, saw
a patch of freedom open before him, but held back. Aislinn was still in sight, her horse hieing away on the ser-
pentine road. He spared a moment's grim satisfaction that
Aislinn possessed the good sense to heed his urging to
flee, then turned his attention back to the work at hand.
Even afoot against a mounted knight, these men were determined to bring him down. He was dimly aware of slicing blows against his leg and torso, only superficial cuts
that did not deter him.

If desperate, they would use their swords on Nero. A
trained destrier would bring them a small fortune, but if
their goal was a hostage knight, they may forfeit the beast
to unhorse the man. It was not a risk Stephen wished to
take.

Viciously he brought his sword down, heard a man cry
out hoarsely, then felt a harsh blow against his head from
another quarter. He reeled, recovered his balance and dug
his spurs into Nero's ribs. The horse bounded forward
immediately, trampling one of the men with wicked cuts
of his massive hooves. Another man lashed out with his
sword in an attempt to bring down the horse, but Nero
leaped forward, then screamed as the edge of the blade
sliced across his hocks. Stephen swung backhanded,
caught the man with the edge of his sword and sent him
screaming as the destrier thundered away.

Ahead, the narrow winding road was empty. The trees
had swallowed Aislinn. Sweat trickled into his eyes, and
he wiped it away, shook his head to clear his vision. Behind him he heard angry shouts and knew the outlaws had
not yet given up. A backward glance showed him a single
horse in pursuit, a cowled outlaw atop.

Few outlaws used horses, nor yet boasted the skill these
had shown with swords. They were no rude peasantry
turned to outlawry. These men were either former soldiers

or had some formal training in warfare. They fought too well.

Nero stumbled, lather flecked his sides and neck, but he recovered and went gamely forward. The horse was wounded. If not tended, it wouldn't be long before he could go no farther.

Stephen slowed the animal. Just ahead was a small copse where trees were thin enough to afford him fighting space. He turned, hefted his sword in one hand, ignored the stabbing pain that shot up his arm as he waited for the lone outlaw to reach him.

This was familiar to him, the wielding of swords and hate in combat, the smell of blood and danger overriding any thoughts of fear or death. He had been too long in Essex's service, fought even in the Welsh campaigns for King Henry, and knew his business well. Aislinn of Amberlea was right when she said that killing was his duty. It had been this way since he was but a lad of twelve, large for his age and nimble with a weapon, filled with enough hate to slay any who opposed him.

Time may have tempered that hate, but it had not dulled his instincts.

With a roar of challenge, the cowled outlaw burst upon him, sword uplifted to meet Stephen's blade. Horses, wild-eyed and snorting, muscles bunched and haunches quivering, performed the combat dance upon a forest floor cushioned in aeons of debris. Leaves muffled the hard beat of hooves, but could not absorb the ringing sound of impacting steel.

With no shield, Stephen had to parry the murderous bite of the sword with his own. He caught the blade and took it down with a mighty swing of his arm, continued the motion and brought his weapon back in a half circle to catch the outlaw on his ribs. There was mailed resistance beneath the robes.

With no time to reflect upon an outlaw wearing armor

under the robes of a monk, he deflected the next blow, thankful it was slower than the last, the wound he had inflicted a telling toll on the outlaw's agility. Breathing in harsh gusts of air between his teeth, Stephen blinked sweat from his eyes, and he knew his strength was also failing. He must end this swiftly or lose all.

Summoning a burst of power, he urged Nero forward with the pressure of his knees to knock the other mount off balance, stood up in his stirrups to bring down the sword and bite deeply with the edge of his blade. The force of the blow toppled the outlaw to the ground, where he struggled to gain his feet.

With a piercing scream, Nero lashed out in a lethal kick that caught the outlaw on one side of his head. He spun about, then sprawled motionless on the ground. The destrier would have trampled him to gore had not Stephen reined him sharply in.

Freed from restraint, the outlaw's horse careened away before Stephen could catch the dangling reins. He dismounted slowly, his sword at the ready as he approached the still man on the ground. Blood gushed from a gash on his temple. His mouth was open, eyes already glazing over. He would not rise again. Stephen looked up. It was still. A hush lay in the small clearing now, an absence of sound that was complete and waiting. A sense of urgency bade him make haste, and he knelt beside the fallen man, cut free a purse on his belt, searched him quickly but found nothing else to indicate his position or purpose.

Sweat clouded his vision again, and he wiped a hand over his face, then stared at his palm. It was smeared red with the outlaw's blood, bright against rising blisters. With no gauntlets to protect his hands, his skin was rubbed raw from the sword hilt. He wiped his hand quickly on his tunic, but there was still a crimson haze in his eyes.

It was not the blood of the outlaw, but his own.

He stood there a brief moment. There was no pain, only a distant ringing sound in his ears. The blood still beat briskly through his veins, his heart thudded, and his breathing was swift and shallow. The other outlaws would be in pursuit of their comrade. He must go quickly, for he could not survive another encounter.

Nero nudged him, and Stephen turned to the horse. A wicked gash oozed blood on the sleek hocks and would need tending, but was not deep enough to lame him. Heaving himself into the saddle with an effort, he urged the horse off the road and into the verge. Bracken and marsh obliterated any path, and the branches snagged horse and rider with clinging tendrils. Hooves sunk deep into the muck of soggy mud where marsh orchids bloomed in the shelter of fallen tree trunks, and lousewort sported pinkish blossoms atop straggly stalks.

Nero's hooves crushed the delicate blooms underfoot. The destrier was winded and weary. Stephen urged him onward, deeper into the marshlands and desolation. When the fallen man's comrades reached him, they would then search the road. If fortune was with him, by the time they realized he hadn't taken the road, any sign of his passage through the marshes would be obliterated by the elements.

A canopy of thickly intertwined tree branches overhead could not keep out the rain that began to fall. It trickled through, wetting Nero's neck, bouncing off leaves and glistening on tree trunks and limbs. Wind moaned through the marsh. Stagnant pools wet the feet of massive trees, crept over lush green bog moss. Dragonflies hummed among voracious sundews and flitted through rush beds.

Stephen shivered with chill and dizziness. He fought encroaching waves of nausea, ignored the throbbing pain that radiated from his shoulder to his head. His left arm hung numbly, and he pulled it in front of him, rested it on the pommel of his saddle. Nero stumbled, and Stephen clutched at the thick mane to keep his seat, urging the horse upright and on through the shallows of the bog.

Water splashed heavily, and once out of the shelter of the trees, rain came down in sheets. In the distance thunder growled ominously. Stephen slumped over the horse's neck, shoulders hunched against the rain. Oddly, despite the cool and dampness, heat slowly seeped through his body, dispelled the chill so that he felt flushed and warm.

He was losing strength, losing awareness, and clung with desperate tenacity to his saddle as Nero trudged on in the driving rain. There was no sense of direction, nothing but the need to continue, to make his way back to the abbey and be assured that Aislinn was safe. He had bought her time with his stand against the outlaws, and he prayed she had used it wisely.

Feverish now, he peered through the thick gray mist, breathed in a mouthful of rain. Spectral shapes loomed in the murky light. Rain was a thick veil that obscured all but indistinct outlines of trees and bushes. It clogged his nose and throat, seeped through his cloak and tunic and even his armor.

He cursed the rain, the outlaws, and Essex, impartially and inflexibly. A fool's quest indeed, this search for the Grail. He should have refused Essex. This was a futile task.

A lake spread like shattered glass before him, and Nero came to a halt at the water's edge, head hanging low. Over the drumming beat of rain that pocked the water's surface, a dim sound drifted on the wind. A song, perhaps, for it was lovely and lyrical.

Old tales told of men taken by water faeries, never to be seen again, spirited away for all time. The Lady of the Lake had given King Arthur a sword, and Stephen peered at the lake numbly, vision blurred, half expecting an arm to rise from the water and present him with such an object.

Reeling, he held tightly to the saddle with his good hand and fought the overpowering shadows of oblivion that waited. Then, out of the shadows, appearing as suddenly as the Lady of the Lake was said to have done, a woman glided toward him. A long cloak billowed behind her, and pale hands were held out to him as if beckoning. He squinted, blinked at the rain in his eyes, and tried to form words that would not come. His lips would not obey, nor would his body.

Motionless, he waited for her to reach him, but the dark shadows came to claim him first. He could no longer resist them and slipped into the darkness with a groan, falling, falling, while the lovely singing faded into silence.

╪

IT WAS THE song that woke him. Lovely, low and sweet, it filled his ears with haunting melody. He tried to open his eyes but his lids felt weighted, far too heavy to lift. So he lay there and took stock of his surroundings.

It was dry where he lay though he could hear the hiss of falling rain. The tang of smoke filled the air, and he was warm beneath a pile of furs. There was a faint fragrance of herbs to tease his senses, and his belly knotted with hunger.

The song ended, and it fell silent save for the drum of rain on a shutter. He was inside then, though he could not imagine how he had gotten there—or who was singing.

The rustle of a garment drew near, and he felt the weight of a body kneel beside him. A hand came out to stroke back the hair from his forehead, fingers pressed lightly on his brow.

"Sweet knight," a voice he recognized murmured, "thou art so noble. Do not die, for I fear I could not bear it."

He wanted to assure Aislinn that he had no intention of dying, but could not summon the strength. It was as if he lay imprisoned in his own body, able to hear and comprehend his surroundings, but unable to stir.

So many questions needed answers, and he wanted to warn her of their danger should the outlaws find them. But try as he might, no sound emerged from his mouth, though to his great chagrin, he made guttural noises.

Aislinn pressed a cooling hand to his cheek, drew her fingers along his jaw in a soothing motion. "Do you wake, Sir Stephen? You are safe here, as am I. None will find us, and you may mend as you will. . . ."

If she spoke more, he did not hear, for the shadows swooped to claim him again, ushering him into oblivion.

Slumber seduced the wounded knight, and Aislinn put her hand lightly over his nose and mouth to reassure herself he still breathed. Two days had he lain sleeping in a slumber far too akin to death. She feared for him, but took heart that he had roused enough to attempt speech. It was an improvement over the empty silence. His breath warmed her palm and she sat back with a sigh of relief.

More rain fell, hampering her efforts to patch holes in the leaky roof of their shelter. It was near a ruin, a rough cottage that had once housed a woodsman or hermit, no doubt, and in poor condition. But it had been godsend enough to her to find it, for she'd despaired of saving Sir Stephen. The guilt of leaving him behind still gnawed at her conscience.

After overcoming the immediate problem of dragging the fallen knight from the danger of drowning in the rising lake, she had managed to get him to higher ground. To her surprise, the destrier had followed behind as obediently as a tame dog. *Nero.* A savage name for a savage beast, but he had stood as docilely as a lamb when she finally dredged up the courage to attempt to remove saddle and supplies from his back. With her own palfrey safe inside a rickety hedge enclosure that must have once held sheep, she had tended the wounded destrier gingerly and found no resistance. Now he grazed beneath a protective canopy of trees, content to be left alone.

Nothing in her life had prepared her for the harsh circumstances in which she found herself, but she was thankful she had learned the usual medicinal remedies and been fortunate enough to find interest in Brother Timothy's studies of herbal potions and tonics, under Brother Arnot's tutelage. But she was not proficient. Her potions were clumsy, and no doubt not the right strength or mixture. Oh God, she felt so helpless. If she dared leave him, she could make her way to the nearest church or village and seek aid for his wounds.

But in his present state, he was too vulnerable to risk leaving alone. Why did he not wake? His wounds were many but not severe, save for a wicked gash on his head. It wasn't deep, but it was nearly the length of her ring finger, and had oozed blood for the first day.

She had stripped him with some difficulty, tended the wounds with strips of clean cloth torn from her undertunic and soaked in a solution of woundwort she had found growing in the marsh. Nero had been treated first with the potion, a test to be certain she hadn't mixed a harmful dose. A bound bundle of the pinkish purple flowers lay near the fire to dry, and a small metal pot she'd found in Stephen's pack was set upon the coals of a low fire in the disintegrating hut.

A rude hut, with chinks in the woven walls, much of the roof thatching rotted or gone, yet it was a welcome refuge. A pit in the center held the fire. She had found dry wood in a part of a crumbled structure that may have once housed animals or stores—it was difficult to tell. She had hung her cloak over the empty doorway, and managed to close a wooden shutter over the single window to keep out some of the rain-laden drafts.

Weariness made her sag. Aislinn dragged a hand through her hair and blew out a sigh. It seemed she had worried without end since the outlaw attack. Her gaze

drifted back to the knight sprawled on a bed of furs. He
was so still. What would she do if he—

No. I cannot even think it!

Tension made her ache. She sat with her knees together
and her elbows propped on her thighs, fingers pressed to
her temples to stem the throb. Hunger gnawed. A thin
pottage simmered in the iron pot, made with dried meat
and some wild herbs she'd gathered; mint and watercress
lent it a pleasant aroma. She hoped to get more of it down
Stephen. As yet, she had been able to trickle only a small
amount down his throat before he clamped his jaws shut.
That he resisted was a good sign, she thought, for it meant
he was vaguely aware of her.

She ate some of the pottage, reserving most for Stephen
if—when—he awoke, then curled up before the fire in
one of the furs and tried to get comfortable. It was growing late, and soon night would fall again. The horses were
safely up, and there was enough wood to last until morning if she was careful.

Slowly she relaxed, and some of the ache in her body
eased. It was warm by the fire. Stephen slept peacefully,
his breathing regular and no longer labored. The fitful
blaze sent up tiny sparks and curls of smoke that burned
her eyes, and she closed them against the sting.

When she opened her eyes again, the fire had died to
a dull glow, and she roused herself to slide the last piece
of wood into the coals. It caught slowly, but flared bright
as she looked across the fire toward Stephen.

He stared back at her, his dark eyes reflecting the
flames. No longer lying supine, he was propped up on
folded furs, his chest bare above the furs spread over him.
Golden light and hazy shadows played over his face, and
when he spoke his voice was rusty from disuse.

"It is good to see you safe, mouse."

Unexpected tears stung her eyes, but she smiled as she

leaned her chin into her palm. "It is good to see you awake, Sir Stephen."

"How long have I slept?"

"Two days now."

"Two days! I rival King Arthur for the sleep of the dead, it seems."

"You are shy a few hundred years, I believe, but it must seem that long to you. It certainly has to me."

"Where are we?"

"In the marsh. I'm not certain where, but once you have recovered, we can follow the river to a village. Do you feel pain?"

"It feels as if Nero has been standing on my head." He paused, looked at her, and she assured him that the horse was well. He nodded. "How did I get here with you?"

"I had to drag you. It wasn't easy, but you had fallen from your horse and were in danger of drowning. You were half in the lake by the time I reached you."

"So it was you. In the rain, I thought it was the Lady of the Lake who had come for me."

"And I thought you had come to rescue *me*." She laughed softly, her earlier fear diminished since he was awake and lucid. Relief flooded her. He would know what to do now, and the situation was suddenly much less threatening.

"You did not follow me here?" He looked surprised.

"No. If my horse hadn't stepped in a rut and gone lame, I might well have ridden all the way to West Camel, but the storm and my lame horse forced me into the marsh." She paused, aware how fainthearted she sounded for fleeing, but it was the truth. How craven she was! He might as well know all: "I was terrified. I worried for your safety, but I feared the outlaws would set upon me as well. So I fled."

"Which they most certainly would have done had you not obeyed my command to flee. Good sense overcame courage, I'm pleased to see. If not, we might both be dead by now."

Heat scoured her face and her hands knotted in her lap. "How kind of you to commend my cowardice."

"Did you expect me to condemn you for it? You obviously consider me an idiot who prefers some demented sense of valor to be wiser than flight. Not I. There is no shame in fleeing when odds are against you."

"Yet you did not flee."

"I had a sword and a battle-trained destrier. You must admit my odds of victory were a bit higher than yours."

"Did . . . did you slay them all?"

He grimaced. "I regret that I did not. It's a miracle we weren't both slain. They caught me by surprise, when my mind was on other things. I fought near as skillfully as a ten-year-old serving wench."

"But you kept them at bay, and we escaped—"

"Not because of my skill," he muttered, "but because of their impatience." He blew out a heavy breath, frowning as he mused, "They were too eager, too confident of success to prevail. Yet if they hadn't been, we might both be lying in the road now."

She shuddered. "Instead, we are here together, alive and hale. Or nearly so. Your wounds must still pain you."

"A bit. Most are shallow cuts, I think. Only my head is near ruined."

"Yes, most of the cuts are shallow save for a deep gash on your upper thigh." She met his startled gaze calmly. "You must know that I tended your hurts. Did you think you arrived here clad in only your braies?"

"I didn't know the tending of wounds to be among your many talents. I'm impressed, Aislinn of Amberlea."

"You should be, for tending wounds is *not* among my talents. It's fortunate that I could tend your horse's wounds with my potions first, and so test their strength. Brother Arnot would be most proud of my competence."

"Christ's wounds—I didn't think! What will they think at the abbey? You've been gone for three days now."

"You needn't curse," she said primly.

"If I truly cursed, your ears would blister. Are you avoiding answering my question?"

"No. I told Brother Timothy I'd been called to the side of a needy parishioner. It's happened before. He has no need to question my absence, though I admit this is the first time I have been gone so long without first telling Prior Thaddeus."

"There will be talk, damoiselle."

He gave her a keen look that bespoke volumes, and she felt herself flush.

"Yea, no doubt there will be those like Mistress Margaret who will relish the opportunity I have given them."

"I've noticed that Mistress Margaret doesn't always wait for opportunity to arise before she spews venom." He moved slightly, and grimaced. "I feel a pressing need for privacy outside."

Aislinn understood at once and rose from her furs to go to him. "Lean on me if you need to, Sir Stephen. I'll help you outside."

"Cursed awkward to depend upon another even to rise from a bed," he muttered, but accepted her offer as he got clumsily to his feet.

His weight was warm and heavy as he put an arm around her shoulders for balance, and when she had walked him out to a screen of bushes, she discreetly left him there and returned to the hut.

She stirred the fire, set the pot back on the flames to heat the pottage, and waited. Smoke curled toward holes in the roof, spreading out over the frame that had once held thick rushes. She'd patched one of the holes with a fur from Stephen's pack, but the other holes were much smaller. The wood was near gone. On the morrow, perhaps she could cut some peat and dry it in the far corner. If she was able.

Turning her hands over, she stared ruefully at her palms. Blisters rose below her fingers, and cuts left thin red lines. She was unaccustomed to the harsh abrasion of reins on ungloved hands, as well as the misuse they had suffered in patching the roof and breaking wood. Never again would she offer complaint for the insignificant tasks of preparing vegetables and pulling weeds.

A noise at the door startled her, and she turned to see him in the opening, her cloak half hiding him as he clung to the door frame. The bruises on his torso were deep purple with tinges of yellow, hideous and painful to look at. His skin was damp, his hair wet and dripping. He shuddered, an involuntary contraction of his muscles in a shiver.

Alarm brought Aislinn to her feet.

"What have you done?" she demanded more sharply than she intended. "Fallen in the marsh?"

His laugh was rusty and ended in a grimace of pain. "I must be delirious. Or mad. I felt the need to wash myself. There's a bucket on a stump that served the purpose well."

"Doltish man, you were to call me to lend my aid," she scolded as she went to him, "It will take you time to regain your strength after so many days abed."

"Yea, I begin to feel the wisdom in that."

He dragged in a ragged breath. His skin was pale, and beads of sweat dotted his upper lip. The healing cuts on his chest, shoulders, and ribs were a vivid red against the dark bruises. She helped him back to the bed of furs, heard his stifled groan as he lay down. She handed him a torn strip of her undertunic.

"Dry yourself," she said, "and I'll bring you a cup of pottage."

"Pottage? Another talent you have kept hidden from me." He dragged the linen strip over his face, then his chest and belly. "Where did you find food? There was not much left in my pack, I fear."

"There was enough dried meat to use as stock, and I was able to find wild mint and watercress to make it palatable, if not tempting." She poured a small amount into a wooden cup and took it to him. "You have not been very cooperative with my efforts to feed you. I'm relieved you're awake at last and can feed yourself."

He peered into the cup. Steam rose in a wreath around his battered face to lend him a hellish appearance. "It looks delicious."

"You're a bad liar, Sir Stephen. But it will fill your belly. Tomorrow, perhaps you can stomach bread and cheese."

"Too bad there are no dried apples left." He sipped from the cup, lifted a brow, and looked at her over the rim. "It's much better than you credit, mouse. I'm amazed that you have been able to be so efficient."

A rush of pleasure warmed her. "I amazed myself. Never did I think I could survive such an ordeal. Or that I could drag a man weighing at least fifteen stone up a hill."

"Then all these bruises did not come from outlaws, I perceive." He shrugged when she stared at him in dismay, and muttered, "It was a poor jest. It's doubtful you could have done any more damage than was already done."

"Then it's good you weren't awake enough to remember the logs you were dragged over," she said lightly to dispel the memory of how she had been forced to ignore his pitiable groans as she worked his heavy body up the hill to the hut. "It took far too long, and I despaired several times."

"But you persevered. You succeeded, when many others would not have." His lashes lifted, and dark eyes met hers. "I owe you my life."

Flustered, she looked away. "You would have done the

same for me, sir. Nay, you did do the same for me. You risked your life with the outlaws to give me time to flee. Don't think I'm unaware of your reason for staying to fight. You were mounted and they were not. You could have easily escaped them."

"Not so very easily, as it turned out," he said dryly and then frowned. "They did have mounts. Or at least one horse, for the outlaw that I killed gave chase. Any fool knows that a mounted man has a better chance against another man afoot. Experienced outlaws would hesitate in attacking an armed, mounted knight, with only their short swords to recommend them. Yet these did not."

"Perhaps these outlaws are inexperienced."

"Perhaps. Or perhaps they are not outlaws."

"But who would want to attack us? We had done nothing save sleep atop a ruined fort—do you suppose they knew why we were there?"

"It's possible, but not probable. If we had found the Grail, there would have been reason to attack us. But we found nothing save crows and buttercups." A faint smile tucked the corners of his mouth inward. "And faery dust."

"You mock me, but you remember faery dust too, I see." An answering smile curved her lips. "Childhoods seem to be remarkably similar all over England."

"I hope not. Mine was not very pleasant."

It was not what he said, but the flat tone of his voice that betrayed past hurts, and Aislinn gazed at Stephen as he finished the cup of pottage. His lashes lowered, hiding his eyes and thoughts from her. What had he suffered to leave him so bitter?

She pleated the folds of her kirtle between her fingers and wondered. She should ask. It was her nature to be forthright, yet with this man she was strangely reluctant.

When he finished the broth and Aislinn took his cup from him, he reached out to grasp her by the wrist and hold her in a light clasp. She grew still and looked up to meet his eyes. There was an intensity in his gaze that was riveting. He turned her hand over, lifted it to his lips, then paused. A muscle worked in his jaw.

"You wear the badges of your courage here," he murmured as he lightly touched a blister on her palm, "and shame me for not protecting you better."

"You protected me well," she whispered, "for I am here with you now."

He pressed a kiss into the cup of her palm. His breath was warm, yet she shivered. He looked up, light from the low fire illuminating his face.

"Aislinn, you need have no fear of me. I would never harm you."

"I do not fear you. I fear only these strange yearnings you provoke in me. You need not feign surprise, for you are well aware of it, Stephen Fitzhugh, as I am aware of your desire."

"Plainly spoken, Aislinn of Amberlea. You yet surprise me. Where is your maidenly restraint?"

Though his tone was light, an obvious attempt to ease his discomfort, she answered honestly.

"I am maiden no longer, but widowed these ten years past, as you well know. You call me damoiselle when you know I am no maid, but calling a ewe a lamb will not make it so. I'm a widow, sir, and not inexperienced in the marriage bed. Don't insult me with honeyed words and vows of restraint, for we both know the truth of what we desire."

"*We* desire?"

A taut silence followed his query. Aislinn stared at him without replying. The truth lay between them now, open and admitted.

Still holding her hand, Stephen drew her toward him, but she resisted.

"No, while your mind may be willing, your body has

its limits, sir. Do not test either of us. It's not the right time for it."

His gaze smoldered. "I am the best judge of the right time for me, Aislinn."

"But you are not the best judge of the right time for me. Rest now. Do not waste strength you can ill afford to exhaust. While we are safe enough here now, who knows what the morrow may bring."

Releasing her hand, he lay back upon the furs. "Yea, the morrow may bring more surprises."

She smiled at his disgruntled tone. "It very well may, Stephen Fitzhugh. It very well may."

Chapter 17

✝

SHE WAS SINGING again. Her voice was lovely, pure and sweet, the lyrics to a French verse drifted through the marsh. Stephen sat upon a stump, watching dragonflies dance. The rain had ended, and sunlight filtered through the leaves to flicker on bright green bog moss and pools of dark water.

It was disconcerting to discover that Aislinn had been right: his strength was badly ebbed. He slept far too much, and even when awake, the short stroll down the hill taxed him. The cuts he had sustained were minimal, but the blow to his head still affected him. He had bouts of dizziness that left him staggering.

It was a testament to his usual run of fortune that he found himself near helpless and being tended by a woman—a woman he wanted in his bed, not as a nurse. By the rood, it was humiliating enough to be rescued by her. Must he be forced to endure her daily touch and not respond? It left him raw, with a barely contained savagery churning inside.

Tossing a stick into the lake, he watched it float. On the chewed lip of a grassy bank, an upright white sundew blossom trembled as an insect landed on the plant's leaf and remained there, trapped by tiny sticky hairs while the reddish leaf began to curl inward to digest the helpless winged victim.

Stephen empathized. He felt just as helpless, devoured by his own indiscretion. Devoured by burning need.

Christ above! but he was snared by his own cravings. It did not help that Aislinn admitted to similar desires, but had only created this ferocious need to appease the hunger. He ached with it. He could not bear to be close to her and not act upon that need. So he avoided her company.

And she knew why he did so.

He saw that knowledge in her eyes, in the solemn regard with which she viewed him, and cursed himself for a fool. It might be amusing if it weren't so frustrating. He had for too long prided himself on being aloof from sentiment, but now an entire range of emotions were raw as a new-laid goose egg, and just as hot.

He threw another stick into the lake, watched it float lazily toward a patch of reeds. A soft, distant thudding caught his attention and he looked up. A hobby swooped from the sky toward a swarm of dragonflies. There was a flash of dark blue- and gray-winged falcon, a desperate buzz, then a dragonfly lost the race. The hobby climbed upward, wings swept back, the dragonfly clutched in its curved beak.

"It's nesting season." Aislinn came up behind him. "The hobbies feed their young." She perched on the curve of a fallen log that lay near the stump where he sat, looking all grace and concern. A lovely woman, wearing serenity and faith as a protective crown.

He felt like hitting something.

"Are you feeling well, Stephen?"

"Well enough." The dragonflies had returned to feeding, the loss of their comrade ignored. He threw another stick into the water, took angry pleasure in depriving a dragonfly of its intended victim. "I've been sitting here observing the carnage that goes on right under our noses. Dragonflies eat and are eaten. Even the flowers in this bog devour their prey live."

"Is this another of your parables?"

"No. It's an unwelcome truth—politely ignored by most of the civilized world—that we do more butchery in a single day than most dragonflies do in their lifetimes. And for what cause? Power. Wealth. Lust. It's a wonder we still exist. If there was a just God, all mankind would have ceased to exist long ago."

His glance at her was as savage as he felt. She stared back at him uncertainly. Brows like the delicate markings of a forest creature drew together over the bridge of her nose.

"I think your fever has returned," she said.

"Do I detect mockery, little mouse?"

"Dismay, perhaps." Silky lashes lowered over a gleam of distress in her eyes. "You sound angry."

"Why would I be angry?"

"I wondered that myself."

He flicked his fingers, waving away the suggestion. "I'm not angry. Not at you."

"You're angry at the dragonflies."

"Among others."

"Ah yes, there are the predatory flowers, and no doubt the voracious falcons that also deserve your wrath."

An unwilling smile flattened his mouth. Some of his anger eased, and he sucked in a deep breath. An amusing absurdity. As was he. A complex woman, Aislinn of Amberlea, who could go from pious to playful in the space of a single breath.

Her smile was intimate, a shared confidence. It ignited

the hot, fierce need in him. Despite his best intention, he recalled the smooth feel of her skin beneath his hand, the soft yielding of her in his arms, and the tempting swell of her breast in his palm.

It was torment sleeping so near to her yet not touching her, for he had no intention of making a fool of himself again. Danger was inherent in allowing anyone to guess how he truly felt, how the hunger inside was so darkly intense. He was perilously close to breaching his own defenses, to removing the barriers that had long kept him protected.

Such turmoil left him raw inside.

He looked away from her, pulled himself to his feet, and stood unsteadily for an instant. When she put out a hand to steady him, he pushed it away.

"I'm not yet an invalid. I think I can manage to totter up the hill on my own."

"Very well, Sir Stephen."

Her meek reply didn't fool him. She waited, watchful as a hawk, ignoring his peevishness. It became a matter of pride that he make it up the hill without pause or revealing his discomfort. Treacherous tree roots snagged his boots as he trod the path up the steep slope, but he didn't falter.

The summit was reached, the tumbledown hut but a few steps away, the pain in his side was now a throbbing ache. He halted beside a tree and waited for the pain to ease and his breath to return. Weakness seeped through his body, made his knees quake as he leaned against the tree in imitation of a casual pose to wait for her to catch up.

"Have you made your point?" she asked when she reached him, and he glared at her.

"I have. It seems I didn't require your assistance to reach the top of the hill."

"No, but you look as if you're about to collapse. If you

do, I don't think I can drag you into the hut without causing both of us a great deal of pain. I would deem it a personal favor if you would be so kind as to at least lean upon my shoulder for the last few steps."

"As a personal favor? Very well. Since you plead so prettily for my favor. . . ." He smiled. "I will allow you to be my crutch for the last few steps."

"I'm overwhelmed by your generosity, Sir Stephen. Put your arm around my shoulders, just so." She arranged his arm to drape over her shoulder, then tucked her other arm behind him, gripping his belt. "Are you ready?"

"It would do me no good to balk, I see."

"No." She laughed softly. "I admit it wouldn't do you much good to refuse. Keep your steps small, if you will, so I can stay abreast of you."

They moved slowly. She was warm under his arm. He was tempted to lean heavily on her. It would serve the little baggage right to stoop beneath his weight. His hand dangled over the curve of her breast, fingers brushing against blue wool. Another temptation. Since coming to Somerset, his world had been full of them.

Cotton grass swished against his legs, hiding tangled tree roots. Aislinn's grip on his belt was firm, and it gave him stability.

The hut smelled of stale smoke. He detached himself from her once they entered, and limped to his pallet near the fire. Lowering himself to the pile of furs, he stretched out and folded his arms behind his head.

It had exhausted him more than he intended to admit. He should have recovered by now. It worried him, this unusual weakness.

Aislinn brought him a cup of pottage, thinner now than it had been, stretched with more wild vegetables and herbs but near empty of meat. He took it from her, sipped at it as he watched her.

Despite their travails, she was composed, her gown rent

in places but fairly clean for all that they habited in a bog
marsh. Pale hair was loose, pulled back from her face in
two coils that tied on her nape as if ribbons. The blue
wool of her gown fit her slender curves loosely, the long
sleeves tied above her elbow, her undertunic gone for
bandages and clean cloths. Only her shoes showed extreme wear, scuffed and worn in places.

He realized he liked watching her. He found it peaceful.
She worked silently, using her small eating dagger to chop
up more herbs she'd gathered, tossing them into the small
iron pot he'd brought in his pack. Her movements were
graceful, and she seemed absorbed in her task. She
hummed a melody he didn't recognize as she worked.

There were new hollows in her cheeks, and faint bluish
circles beneath her eyes. He felt a twinge of guilt. He'd
been so involved with his own aches and pains that he'd
failed to notice Aislinn's weariness.

"Can you set a trap if I fashion one?" he asked her
when she looked up and caught him staring at her. "We
could do with a goose or a duck for dinner."

"Is that a complaint against my pottage?" She smiled
slightly. "I grow weary of it as well. We have a small bit
of havercake and cheese left, if you want it. I was saving
it for desperation."

He frowned. "You've grown thin as a reed. We need
to return to the abbey before you waste away."

"If we leave too soon, I'll be dragging you over logs
and rocks again. No, another day or two, until you're no
longer dizzy. I don't fancy watching you fall from your
horse. Nor do I fancy trying to saddle that evil-tempered
beast. He bit me this morn when I tried to move him from
the path."

"Did he do damage? Let me see—"

"Just a nip to warn me away." She slung the pot over
the coals, positioned it carefully so it wouldn't tip, then
wiped her hands on a strip of linen. A lock of her hair

had come loose from the twisted coils, and dangled in her eyes. She pushed it away, looked back at him and smiled. "We have an uneasy truce, Nero and I. It does not include familiarity of any kind."

"He has made a bad bargain, then. Familiarity can ease us all."

"At times, beau knight, but not always. Here. Chew this if you like." She handed him a mint leaf, and he took it. It was not the sweet mint of gardens, but a wild, strong scent and flavor that was hot on his tongue.

Easing back on the cushion of furs, he chewed the mint slowly, watched her as she set about female pursuits, busily tidying the small hut. Strange, that in times of crisis, the women of his experience seemed more concerned with neatness than anything else. A feminine trait, perplexing but fairly harmless. Aislinn was no exception it seemed. She went about setting all aright with unwarranted energy.

It was exhausting to watch.

Warm now, he shrugged free of his tunic, lay back down clad in only his braies. Cushioned by furs, his belly full, an unfamiliar peace stole over him. It was a comfort being with her, an unexpected sense of serenity that he'd not experienced since he was a lad in leading strings. Aislinn reassured him that life could be ordinary.

Then she began to sing.

It was a French lay, a tale of two lovers ill-fated and destined for misery. The melody was haunting, the story of Heloise and Abelard sorrowful. He closed his eyes, let her lovely voice wrap around him like a soft cloth. His mind drifted, the ache in his head and thigh eased, and muscles relaxed.

For the first time since he was a child, he felt safe. An illusion that would vanish quickly enough, but for the moment, one he intended to indulge. Why not? There was cursed little enough in life to offer security.

Life would intrude with unpleasant truths whether he willed it or not. Soon this respite would be only a pleasant memory. He intended to take full advantage now of this opportunity. It was unlikely it would ever come again.

Chapter 18

✝

SMOKE CURLED UPWARD, drifted in a hazy layer near the ceiling. Stephen slept, his breathing deep and regular. Aislinn put another piece of peat on the low fire. With approaching nightfall, it grew cool. Days were longer now with the coming of summer, for it was June, near Midsummer Eve, a time of festivals and celebration, though the church did not approve of such pagan revelry. The church would honor Saint John with a feast day and ignore the old ways, the old gods that still held allure for some.

What would the prior say when she returned? It could not have escaped his notice that she and Stephen were both gone—would he hold his tongue? She didn't worry that Brother Timothy would betray her, for she knew he would not. But there would be talk—Stephen was right enough about that.

A brisk wind filtered through the cloak over the door, and she huddled deeper into the warmth of a fur, pulled it close around her shoulders. Beyond the fire, Stephen stirred in his sleep, and his foot thumped at the fur covering him, sent it sliding free. She watched as he slumbered on, heedless of chill wind on the bare skin of his chest.

It wasn't natural for him to sleep so heavily, as if he had drank poppy juice. She worried about his head wound, the deep cut that had oozed blood for near two days. The blow to his head could have been fatal. It was a miracle that he yet lived.

Drawing her knees up to her chest, she rested her chin on them, studied his supine form. A tremor contracted his bruised chest muscles in a shiver, yet he did not wake nor draw the fur back over his body. He slept too deeply.

Aislinn rose and, hugging the furs around her, moved to where he lay. She knelt, pulled the furs over his chest to his throat, and tucked them around him. Stroking her hand in a leisurely glide along the soft fur, she fought a wave of almost overpowering emotion.

How was it possible to feel so about this knight she had known a scant few weeks? There were men she had known all her adult life that did not generate such powerful emotions, such powerful yearnings that led her to feel the need to be near him, to touch him . . . to want to be with him in the most basic capacity.

It was such a strong desire that she ached with it.

Stephen lay on his side, one arm tucked beneath his head and the other flung carelessly to the side, fingers resting only inches from the hilt of his sword. Firelight danced across his bare forearm and glinted on his half-opened hand. She could see the blisters he'd gotten when wielding his sword against the outlaws, proving the wisdom of wearing gauntlets. The pale swellings were now almost healed.

Her heart lurched at thinking how close he had come to being killed on that road! It was frightening to contemplate, to remember the stark terror of those moments when she had watched helplessly as he fought for his very life.

Nothing in her life had prepared her for the savagery of the attack. She'd been sheltered from acts of violence, though not the inevitable aftermath. There were always accidents, drownings, the occasional murder, none of which she had witnessed before.

Stephen's brutal fight, the very ferocity of it, had shocked and horrified her. The deadly strike of steel against steel, the grunts of pain and harsh curses, had all combined in a mélange of images that would haunt her nights for a long time.

She thought of all the years he'd spent in waging such mortal battle. How did he live with it? With knowing that he must kill or be slain himself? She had been near paralyzed with fright. Action had been unimaginable.

He shifted, and the fur slipped from his bare shoulder again, revealing dark burnished skin and muscle that gleamed in firelight that slanted over him. The contour of his body beneath the fur was powerful even in repose. She considered replacing the fur, but didn't. Instead she watched him. The smooth curve of muscle in his arm belied his strength, for it took a strong man to so expertly wield that heavy sword.

It lay beside him within easy reach, a lethal length of steel that he had spent the better part of a day cleaning. He'd used a strip of her undertunic to carefully wipe the blade clean, taking care to polish the surface as if it were a fine mirror. It had caught rays of thin light piercing the roof, glinted in wicked promise. She had seen the promise at work.

She had seen Stephen at work.

He was a knight. Killing was his duty, his purpose for existence. Knights were invaluable. King Henry had hundreds of them at his disposal, and hundreds more roamed the country as hedge knights, often turning to outlawry just to live.

Which was he? Honorable knight? Hedge knight?

She studied him, his thick dark hair and strong jawline, his broad shoulders and blistered hands.

Tentatively, she brushed his hand with her fingertips, a light touch. A large hand, capable, strong, competent. Broad palm, brown skin, corded tendons on his wrist— hard fingers that swallowed her own pale hand in a tight grip.

She looked up. Dark eyes glittered beneath tangled black lashes. Her throat clenched, and the breath left her lungs in an explosive sigh.

She did not try to remove her hand from his grasp. He rubbed his thumb across her knuckles and smiled, a sleepy curve of his lips.

"What is it, mouse?" His voice was husky. "Are you well?"

"Yes," she answered in a whisper, because she could not find the voice to speak more loudly, "I'm well."

His hand opened, and his fingers laced between hers. Dark lashes lowered as he looked down at their joined hands. Flexing his arm, he drew their hands to his mouth, pressed a kiss on her knuckles, then her fingertips, leisurely kisses.

"Wild mint," he murmured, "and peat. A heady blend."

Laughter caught in her throat. "Heady, indeed."

His eyebrow arched in a subtle curve. "I prefer it when you smell of roses." He turned her hand over, dragged his thumb over the hill of her palm to her wrist, tested her pulse with a light pressure of his lips, and said against her forearm, "Your skin is as soft as the furring of a rose petal. No, don't pull away. You don't really want to, do you?"

She couldn't breathe. Her body throbbed. The air was suddenly heated, strained.

"No," she said, a mere whisper of sound.

His lashes lifted. "I'm through with waiting. The time is right."

She closed her eyes. Blindly she felt him shift, felt the heat of him draw near, his hand moving to touch her on the cheek.

"Aislinn. . . ."

Her name was soft on his lips, trailed into silence. She opened her eyes. Dark eyes burned into her face. Light danced over him in gold and orange shadow. The burning peat provided a pungent hum. The air seemed to shimmer with anticipation. Indecision sank beneath the weight of his expectation.

Would it be so wicked to yield her body when she had already yielded her heart? Losing her heart permanently was the only risk.

But it was not that loss that held her back. He was a knight, a man who would not stay. If she yielded, she knew full well there would be no future for them.

Oh God, never had she felt this way, this excitement that pulsed through her body when he was near. There was so much to lose—and nothing to gain but memories.

Stephen waited in potent silence. Sweet Mary, but his gaze was spellbinding, a heady promise and a challenge.

Dare she accept?

She turned his hand over in her own, lightly traced the fading blisters on his palm. *Badges of courage.* She looked up at him and took a deep breath.

"Yes," she whispered, "yes, it's time."

Chapter 19

✝

HE PULLED HER hand down from his mouth, pressed it against his chest and held it there beneath his palm. A fierce need pushed heat through his veins. His chest felt tight.

She was so soft and so lovely, a sweet female with eyes a man could drown in . . . he wanted to take her fiercely, but held back, a hard-won restraint.

"Lie with me." His voice was hoarse. "Lie next to me, sweet mouse. I won't rush you. I won't do what you do not want me to do." He inhaled the sharp tang of peat smoke and desire, blew out a shaky breath as she slipped the wool cloak from her shoulders.

She had loosened the side laces of her gown, and with her undertunic gone for bandages, she wore nothing beneath but light hose. Bare skin gleamed a soft ivory along the curve of her ribs to her hips; a promise of paradise waited.

He moved over to afford her room on his pallet, stroked her hair back from her face as she lay on her side facing him. Behind her the fire cast her in shadow and silhouette.

"Lovely lady," he murmured, letting silky strands of her hair slip through his fingers, "you are more fair than any I have yet seen."

She came up on one elbow, her fingers pressed against his lips as if to silence him. "Fair? I have never been named a beauty. It's most pleasing to hear. Say it again."

Laughter rose in his throat, seeped into his voice. "You are more fair than any woman I have yet seen—nay, more fair than any woman alive. You are Venus, Helen of Troy, a goddess—"

"Pray, do *not* go on," she said wryly, "for you have little practice at love-talk, it is plain."

"And you do, my dove?" He leaned forward, blew softly on her earlobe and smiled when she shuddered. "Now I am most intrigued by the thought of your vast . . . experience. Perhaps I shall just lie here and allow you to share your extensive knowledge of the carnal arts with me."

"Knave. Blackguard." Her fingers flicked lightly against his lips. "I was once wed, but my knowledge of the marriage bed ended before I was sixteen. It is my thought that you are far more educated in these matters. But if you like, I can lie here stiffly with my eyes tightly closed and allow you to do as you will. While you are at work, I can plan the morrow's meals and recount to myself the other tasks that need doing, or perhaps think of the love sonnets sung by the jongleurs and wonder how they can be so wrong. When you fall asleep atop me, I'll push you to one side and then go wash myself. See? I am indeed well versed in passion."

"Yea," he murmured, "so I see. I fear I'm not like the other man of your experience, for I require a bit more of your encouragement and participation."

"That," she said softly, "you will have to earn."

"Ah, a challenge. I have always"— he kissed the lobe

of her ear, then the side of her neck—"been a man to welcome challenges."

"I'm not surprised, beau knight." Her head tilted back and she sighed, a luxurious sound as he pulled away the neck of her kirtle to kiss the smooth white curve of one shoulder and the soft upper swell of her breast. "You may refine your love-talk with me, if you like. Practice, and I shall tell you when you sound more believable than the jongleurs."

"Your generosity is commendable." Caught between laughter and fierce need, he pushed a skein of light brown hair behind her shoulder, let it slide through his open fingers, fine filaments like raw silk crackling slightly in the cool air. "Very well. First, I'll begin by telling you that your hair is like golden moonlight, pale and mysterious and rare . . . soft as silk in my hands." He brought a curl to his mouth, kissed her through the strand so that it clung in a veil to their lips, and drew it slowly to the side as he deepened the kiss. Finally he lifted his head, stared at her with an arch of his eyebrow.

With a little catch in her voice, she murmured, "A bit too fantastic, I think. Something believable, please. Speak of my eyes, perhaps liken them to deep pools."

He smiled. "Better to name them as the stars in the sky for they are as bright . . . or as spring violets, for they are the same fragile color."

"Ah, much better. I like being . . . compared to violets." She arched her throat when he kissed the line of her jaw, then he moved lower to dip his tongue into the hollow of her throat. "Yes," she said, a bit breathlessly, "I think you're managing quite well now."

"Oh lady," he said softly, "I've only just begun."

"Really." She smiled, eyes half closed. "I'm delighted to hear it. Pray, go on."

"If I were a minstrel, I would sing the praises of your soft white skin, compare it to"—his lashes flicked up, and he smiled wickedly—"manchet bread."

"Manchet bread?" She hooted softly. "Best try again, my poor excuse of a minstrel, for that's a pathetic comparison, indeed."

"You are a hard taskmistress, lady fair. Let's see . . ." Trailing his fingers over the bare skin of her shoulder, he murmured, "Soft as a summer breeze, as pale as the wings of a snow-white dove . . . rich as silk to touch, to caress, to—kiss." His mouth moved lightly over her shoulder, the barest of kisses from the curve of her neck to her throat, then lower. She shivered—he felt it beneath the hand he pressed against her side. Loosened laces dangled under her arms, and he tugged at one of them until it came free, until blue wool parted. Only the sleeves held her gown to her body.

Curling his fingers into the edge of her gown, he pulled it down and away. His throat tightened.

Perfection. . . .

He swallowed hard, found his voice, kept it light with an effort. "Ah, a masterpiece of perfection . . . silky skin like alabaster—delicate and fine, so lovely, so lovely . . . God, so lovely." He paused, unable to go on for a moment, his hand on the swell of her breast, and throat tight with rapt admiration. "Beautiful breasts, so round . . . nipples like tight rosebuds, blushing pink. . . ."

"I think," she said on a whisper, "that your poetry is much improving, beau knight."

"Yea, lady, though I fear I need more practice in the art of love-play."

"And I think," she murmured, "that you are very adept at this after all. . . ."

"Flattery"—he kissed her, tasted mint on her mouth and tongue, reveled in it as he murmured—"is best served warm and fresh, m'lady." Lacing his fingers through hers, he pulled her hand to his chest, pressed her palm against his bare skin, watched her intently as he slowly dragged her hand downward.

Her eyes widened. Her lips parted. Fingers trapped beneath his palm trembled, but did not pull away as he brought her hand to the corded waist of his braies. He sucked in a deep breath when she unfastened the cords. Her lashes quivered, lowered as she watched what her hands were doing.

He closed his eyes, shuddered when she found him, light exploratory caresses that excited and teased, even through linen. He pressed his mouth against her hair, breathed in, let sensation take precedence over everything else as she explored his body with delicious curiosity.

"Stalwart knight," she murmured, a little breathlessly, "I find your—flattery—most impressive."

"Do you . . ." he said, striving to steady his breathing, ". . . have to . . . do that. . . ."

"Do—this?" Clever fingers slid up and then down, cool and arousing against his bare flesh as he stifled a groan.

"Wicked woman," he muttered fiercely, and caught her by the wrist, "continue this torment, and you will hurry what should not be rushed."

"Is it sweet torment then, beau knight?"

"Yea, lady fair, most sweet—but now 'tis my turn to torment you." Before she could protest, he rolled to his side, pushing her beneath him, his weight holding her down. "We shall see how well you enjoy sweet torment."

"I give myself up to your uncertain mercy, sir. . . ."

"A most"—he kissed her mouth, leisurely, until the rhythm of her breathing was ragged—"lovely"—his tongue traced the outline of her lips—"prisoner. . . ."

Her arms lifted to curve around his neck, holding him, and he kissed her until he felt as if he would explode.

Enough of that, or he would indeed rush the moment. It would hardly be to his credit to finish ignominiously when he had waited for this moment for near a month. Nay—for his entire life.

But she needn't know that.

Slowly he dragged his fingers over her collarbone, shaped the fragile bones, bent to kiss the madly beating pulse in the hollow of her throat. Warm, female scent . . . arousing and luxurious. His lips moved downward, tasting, teasing, tracing a path to the shadow between her breasts.

He watched her as his tongue swept lower. Round, firm breasts fit his palms generously. His mouth went dry. Blood surged, throbbed in his loins until he ached with it.

Cradling her breasts, he touched his tongue to a taut nipple, circled it in leisurely strokes before he turned his attention to the other. She sighed, a soft sound, said in a faint voice, "Oh, my. . . ."

Yes . . . oh, my indeed . . . such sweet pleasure lies in this one slender frame, such a promise of peace. . . .

Her hands tangled in his hair, fingers moving in light restless touches. Her lips parted, gleaming where her tongue wet them. Neck arched, her head tilted back as she rested on her elbows. Blue wool was scrunched around her waist. Each breath she took lifted her breasts. There was an erotic abandon in her posture that was arousing. Enticing.

Captivating.

"Poetry, sweet lady mine," he breathed against her breast, "you are pure poetry."

Slowly, he pulled her dress away, then her hose, until she lay bare and shivering on the furs of his pallet. Atop her small belly, he spread his fingers, so dark against such white purity that it felt like sacrilege. God, she was a miracle. She had to be. There was no other good reason that she would be here with him this way if she was not. . . .

"Aislinn . . . God, you're so beautiful . . . so . . . very . . . lovely."

Words failed him, trailing into silent fervor as he caressed the sweet curve of her thighs. Small, firm breasts . . . a slender waist tapering to luscious female hips . . . ivory thighs that curved to dimpled knees and well-formed calves . . . and her ankles . . . delicate and fine-boned.

Gently he parted her thighs, heard her catch her breath as he did, and looked up at her. Her eyes were wide, absorbing light from the fire to gleam in the shadows. He held her gaze, moved his hands to touch the rich crop of light curls between her legs.

"Threads of silk," he murmured, his voice a hoarse imitation of his normal tone. He wanted to say more, but the words would not come easily now. His mouth was too dry, his thoughts too muddled with desire.

His thumb skimmed the melting center of her, so hot and damp . . . she arched upward, a moan trembled from her throat. Her hands twisted in the fur, grasping folds of it in tight fists, holding as her body strained into his touch. Soft, dewy folds under the press of his clever fingers, a slick temptation. The breath came harsh between his teeth, heated and shallow, nearly suffocating him when she cried out at last and collapsed into blissful oblivion.

He rose suddenly and knelt between her thighs to slip his hands along her legs to her hips, slid between fur and flesh to cradle her in his palms. His head bent, and he stroked the inside of her knee with his tongue, a flickering touch.

Her eyes opened, blue daze in the soft gloom, her face still flushed with passion. "You are . . . most skilled, after all . . . beau knight," she said with a little catch in her voice, and he met her gaze with desire fierce on him.

"It is not skill that drives me now, sweet lady, but a need I can no longer delay."

"Then ease us both, Stephen Fitzhugh—give me all."

Aislinn lay in candid invitation, arms and legs open to receive him, and he slid over her. She sucked in a sharp breath at the weight of him, the pressure of him against her open body hot and hard—ready for her.

Heat suffused her entire body as she looked up at him. He watched her, lashes shadowed against his dark skin, his eyes hot with passion. Slowly, he arched his head back and pushed into her, a searing slide that took away her breath and sent sweet spears of flame coursing through her.

Heavy invasion, hot and powerful, potent thrusts that filled her with pleasure and awe. Braced with his hands splayed on each side of her, his shoulders and arms shook with strain. His mouth was a taut slash, and muscles corded in his throat. His chest rose and fell in a labored struggle for air, the sculpted curve of his body a burnished gold in the firelight.

This was nothing like she had expected. Her brief marriage hadn't prepared her for the overwhelming excitement that filled her now, the growing frenzy that built to fever pitch until she was moving with him, hips thrusting to take him, hands gripping his shoulders as she panted urgency and need. Release washed over her and she cried out. It was an uncontrollable, startling ecstasy that caught her by surprise and left her shuddering. Nothing had prepared her for this, this sweet, blind abandon.

Stephen caught her hard to him, drove into her in a last powerful thrust that dragged a groan from deep in his throat, a harsh, guttural sound in her ear as he abruptly pulled free and lay panting atop her. His weight was heavy, his breath warm against the side of her neck.

She struggled to catch her breath, felt curiously weak and lethargic, unprotesting as he rolled to one side, his arm still across her body. Clumsily, he pulled the edge of the furs over them both, then collapsed back beside her.

His free hand tangled in her hair, tugged gently to turn her face toward him.

"Never," he murmured, kissing the corner of her mouth, "let it be said that I don't—rise—to a challenge. . . ."

Aislinn laughed softly. "Never," she agreed in a whisper. "Never."

Chapter 20

✝

EARLY MORNING SUNLIGHT filtered through the holes in the walls and roof, lending a hazy glow to the hut. Aislinn stirred, tucked into the angled embrace of Stephen's arm and side. He was warm against her, his breathing slow and easy.

She felt so strange, as if the entire world was new. It all seemed as a dream, save for the chill that permeated the hut with the heavy, damp scent of the bog.

There was no shame in her for what they had shared, though by the church's standards, they had both committed a sin. Should she be brave enough to confess it to a priest, she would earn a heavy penance. She had no desire to tarnish what had been so special with the risk of condemnation.

Snug beneath the fur, she rose to one elbow, gazed down at Stephen. Thin morning light played over his face, glinted on the dark stubble of beard-shadow. She bent, blew softly on his ear.

Still asleep, he brought up a hand, flicked at his ear, then relaxed again.

She laughed softly. Using the tip end of her hair, she brushed it lightly across his cheek and mouth, the barest of touches. His lips twitched. She waited. Still, he slept on. Again she drew a lock of her hair over his jaw, down his throat to his chest, swirling it in idle patterns. His skin was so dark beneath the yellow and purple bruises, the pelt of chest hair black and curly, narrowing at his belly.

Below his waist . . . oh, below the waist, he wore nothing but the fur flung over him. During the night, he'd discarded his braies, and they lay to one side atop her kirtle. She thought of pushing away the fur that covered him. A splendid man, beautiful in his masculinity, intimidating even in his sleep. He awed her at times—

"Shameless wench."

Startled, her gaze flew to his face, found him watching her with an amused gleam in his eyes. She flicked fingers against his chest, tugged lightly at a curl of hair.

"If I were truly shameless," she retorted, "you would be stoking the fire and fetching food to break our fast."

"Then I should have said selfish wench." He caught her hand, bent his arm to draw her across his chest. "You awake early, when I thought you may sleep this morning."

"Those who sleep late, go hungry."

"You are ruled by your belly, I see."

He pushed hair from her face, held it loosely in his fist as he smiled up at her. She was struck by the absence of his usual mockery. He teased, but it was with genuine amusement, not his more familiar sarcasm.

How appealing he can be when he wishes. . . .

She turned her face, pressed a light kiss upon the hand he held at her cheek, said easily, "I'm ruled by good sense, beau knight, and it bids me wash myself, then prepare us a nourishing meal of bread and cheese—of which you have only a small amount now left in your pack."

"Ah, a bath and food—shall we do as the nobles do, and combine the two?"

Intrigued, she stared at him. "Whatever do you mean?"

"Just that, lady fair. A feast in a bathing chamber."

"You are inventing this tale!"

"Nay," he said solemnly, and took her hand to lightly kiss her fingertips, "I swear it is true. In fair weather, bathing vessels are set up under arbors—in intemperate weather, of course, such revelries must be held indoors. A long banquet board is stretched across the vessels, and bathers sit across from one another while food is served. There is also much wine—preferably strong—and delicacies to whet carnal appetites as well as physical." His eyebrow waggled impudently. "A most delightful pastime."

Uncertain as to his truthfulness on this subject, she just stared at him for a long moment. "I have never heard of such a thing," she said at last. "It sounds preposterous."

"I can well imagine you have not heard of such deeds, fair lady. Not hidden away in a hamlet such as Glastonbury, at any rate."

"It seems much too wicked to be true. Men and women do this—unclothed?" She felt suddenly naive, and a bit foolish when he grinned at her.

" 'Tis the usual method of bathing, is it not? Or is it done so differently in Glastonbury?"

"Do not jape at me, odious man." She cuffed him gently on the arm with a loose fist. "I am not worldly as you are. I have not lived in court circles, nay, nor even met the king. I have made the acquaintance of two bishops and a Welsh baron in my time. I imagine you have dined with earls and even kings."

His smile grew strained, his eyes wary. "On occasion."

"Was it so very different? Wondrous?"

"I would say it was—tedious." He pushed to a sitting position. "Hardly worth wasting time discussing."

Curiosity was piqued by his reticence, but she did not

pursue it, instead said lightly, "I assume you did not bathe with the king, then."

He grinned. "It was not suggested that I recall, but then, it was a long time ago."

"I should think you would remember being invited to share a tub with King Henry."

"I would be more likely to remember being invited to share a tub with Princess Joanna." He pulled her to him, said against her mouth, "I would never forget sharing a tub with you, however."

"And I am certain you say that to all the ladies you—" His lips smothered the last of her sentence, and in a moment it no longer mattered.

Exerting pressure, he pushed her to her back, wedged his knee between her thighs while his kiss deepened. He tasted faintly of mint, heated and fragrant.

When she was breathless from his kisses, he entered her with a swift thrust of his body, no preliminaries needed or wanted. His heavy fullness was delicious friction inside her body, the thrust and drag of his hard body eliciting a shuddering response. She clung to him fiercely, curved her legs around him to meet his thrusts with answering passion.

Already she had learned his rhythm, matched it with her own. It was a savage storm that made the peace that came after so much sweeter.

And she realized, when they lay at last in each other's arms once the storm passed, that these hours were the most precious she had ever known.

✝

STEPHEN CROUCHED IN front of the fire, turning the spit that held a roasting heron. It had taken patience more than the crude trap he'd fashioned, but now they at last had meat instead of thinning pottage.

Soon his strength would return, and so they must return to Glastonbury. He found to his surprise that he would prefer to remain in this bog marsh as long as Aislinn was with him.

Perhaps his fever had returned, for the thought made him smile. There was no future for them together. He was a knight sworn to the service of his overlord, and she— she was an abbot's niece, gently reared in the church that he had grown to despise. It would never work. She'd tested his limits with her pious prattle, but he recognized the faith and sincerity in her.

It was the insincerity and hypocritical posturing of those professing to act in the name of God that angered him most, that had driven him from the church with no regrets.

That had killed his mother.

But what had he expected? He'd known what kind of world it was at an early age. A harsh realization for child or man to discover there were those who would destroy a person for no better reason than a malicious whim.

Outside the hut, Aislinn was singing, this time a song learned from the holy brethren, no doubt. How different they were. An abbot's niece and a heretic. . . .

He turned the bird again, scooped grease from it with a thin wooden spoon roughly carved from a willow branch. It was green willow that supported the plucked, browning bird over the fire, charred now from the flame.

With a twinge of guilt, he thought of Aislinn's oaken cross, and how quickly it had burned. He would purchase her another to replace it. If he could not restore his lost faith, he could at the least replace the symbol of her trust in things he found impossible to believe.

He gave the spit another turn; grease hissed as flames heated it, and the tempting aroma made his belly knot with greedy anticipation. No peat fire this, but good dry wood to lend a pleasing scent and flavor to their meal. It was near impossible to recall any meal more eagerly awaited.

Aislinn came up behind him, carrying a cloth of cleaned and chopped wild herbs and vegetables. She echoed his silent sentiment: "I don't think I have ever awaited a meal more eagerly than I do this one. I'll be much more appreciative of my usual fare in the future."

Humor tucked at the corners of his mouth as he regarded her with a lifted brow. "You'll soon forget. I always do."

"So you've been this hungry before, then." She wrapped wild onions with wild parsley and thyme and slipped them into the small iron pot on the edge of the fire. "I never thought I would miss haslet or garbage pye quite so much."

He laughed softly. "You have a fondness for entrails, I see."

"Only when properly cooked. Brother Daniel sneaks me some of the prior's fare on occasion."

"Ah yes, the privileges of the church. I thought the Benedictine order was under strict mandate to eat sparingly, eggs and fish only at communal meals."

"The abbot is not required to abide so strictly to that rule, and Prior Thaddeus fulfills the role of abbot." She scooped some grease into a small wooden cup, added it to the iron pot and herbs. "While Father Prior is not quite generous with provender, Brother Daniel is more so. He sends me surplus delicacies as well as the usual fare I am owed."

"You are fed by the church, then."

She looked up. "Yes. It was a stipulation in the terms of the grant my uncle provided for me."

"How is it that your dead husband did not provide for his widow?"

"We were wed so briefly, and there were no children for which to provide. He was the eldest son, and his younger brother would inherit the manor. I cared not to be viewed as a millstone around the family's neck. We were not close." She paused, frowned a little as she stirred the pot. "They were good enough people, I suppose, but— distant. I think they regarded me as beneath them, though my parents were of good family and left me with an ample dowry. As the abbot's niece, I was a valuable asset while their son lived. As a childless widow, I had no value at all. So they settled a sum upon me that my uncle agreed to, and in turn, I signed a grant deeding my worldly possessions to the church in exchange for house and keep for the duration of my life. Or until I wed again."

"And have you been tempted to wed again, mouse?"

She looked up. "No. I've been content with my lot."

"Content to be alone?"

"Content to be *left* alone." She smiled. "There is a vast difference, beau knight."

"You are truly an unusual woman, Aislinn. Most women in your place would be eager to marry again."

"Yes, I suppose they would. I have no explanation that suffices. Save that few men would be patient with a female who is—as Father Prior insists—unbiddable."

"Father Prior is unbearable."

"He means well most of the time, though I do wish he wouldn't be so harsh to Brother Timothy. Poor lad. He has always wanted to be a monk, I think, though Gaven set up a howl that was no doubt heard all the way to Canterbury."

"Gaven? What has he to do with Brother Timothy?"

"Did you not know? Gaven is his grandfather."

Stephen laughed. "That must curdle the old man's hide, to have a grandson at the abbey, when he believes in the old ways."

"He's grown resigned by now, though he did create quite a fuss at first." She peered into the iron pot, sighed.

"If I had some ginger or cinnamon, this might be tasty indeed."

"How do you reconcile the two, mouse? You show no disapproval of Gaven, though you follow the strictures of the church."

"Hypocritical of me, isn't it? It's one of the reasons Prior Thaddeus lectures me so strongly." She sat down near the fire, her bent legs tucked to one side, a graceful pose. "I have found that for the most part, both religions are much the same. They require self-discipline and reverence, as well as regard for others. If I do not agree with the old ways, that does not mean I am intolerant of them. Gaven does not seek to convert me, nor I him. We respect one another's right to disagree."

"A most enlightened view."

"And you, Sir Stephen? In what do you believe, if you do not believe in God?"

"I've never said I don't believe in God. I said I don't believe in an infallible church. There's a difference."

"How so? The church belongs to God."

"But it is built by men, and men are not always worthy of respect or regard."

"Yet men are appointed as representatives of God." She studied him across the fire, a puzzled expression on her face. "The Holy Mother Church was formed to comfort and to instruct, to offer solace in times of strife, to remind men of an all-encompassing love."

"The Holy Mother Church has been corrupted by men who offer torment in place of solace, contempt in place of love. Do not be misled by a few."

He knew he sounded harsh, but the words were jerked from him, burned in him, a constant affliction.

"Stephen," she whispered, "who has so betrayed you that you would believe such a thing?"

Fiercely, he said, "I was betrayed by man and church.

It was a lesson I learned young and well. The details are not important."

"They are to me." She leaned forward. "Your pain festers. It touches all your life. Ease it as you can."

"A confession of sorts?" He snorted. "It will not be my own misdeeds I confess, but those of others. Is that what you want to hear, Aislinn? How men of God can behave with such ungodly intent?"

"I want to understand. . . ." She held out a hand, palm up as if awaiting alms. "I want to share the burden you carry."

"No," he said savagely, "I do not think you know what you ask. You have your dreams, your illusions. You don't need me to shatter them for you."

"Did you ask to have your own illusions shattered?"

He stared at her. "No."

"Then grant me sense enough to know what it is I ask of you. I do not ask idly. It is not idle curiosity that bids me want to know more of you, Stephen Fitzhugh." Her eyes met and held his, a deep blue in the sunlight that filtered through roof and rotting thatch. "You have won my heart and my high regard. I ask nothing of you in return but your trust."

"My trust . . . God. Oh, God. . . ." At a loss, he stared at her with rising alarm. "It is not my trust that needs be earned, Aislinn, but your high regard."

"I have said you have that already."

"Yes, but how long will I keep it once you know the truth of my life? Your faith is important to you—I will never share it."

"And I would like to know why."

"Christ Almighty, *must* you? Must you persist? Is it not enough that you've already made me into a besotted fool?" He stood up, angry, more at himself than her, angry that he had betrayed how he felt, betrayed the past hurts that still gnawed at him with depressing regularity.

"If you are besotted, you are no more so than am I," she said quietly. She stared up at him through fragrant smoke, not releasing him from her gaze. "I have told you all about myself that you have asked. Return the courtesy if we are to be honest with one another."

"Honesty! Be ware of what you ask, mistress, for you may well get more than you bargained for in return." He raked a hand through his hair, paced the uneven floor of the hut, long strides that ate up the space in three steps. She remained motionless, watching him, silent when he turned at last to face her, his voice grim. "My father was Hugh of Lincoln—a bishop of the Holy Church."

"A bishop—but . . . but . . ."

"Yea, his vows of celibacy were ignored at least once, it seems." His mouth twisted with bitter humor. "By all accounts, he was a gentle soul, though weak willed. I knew him not, and never felt the lack. My mother was enough for me as a child. She was strong, beautiful, the daughter of a knight. Her name was Eleanor, the same as our queen's—I'll never know why she loved my father, but she did. She loved him beyond reason. She must have, to risk damnation and scorn as she did."

He fell silent. His mother's memory was precious, and as painful now to indulge as it had been when he was a child.

"You hate the church because of one man's weakness?" Aislinn's question startled him.

"Yes. Unfair, perhaps, but true. It could be that I just despise the hierarchy. I view it without the reverence and awe that is required."

"You contradict yourself—or have I heard wrong?"

"You misunderstand. I can respect the foundations of the church, the purpose behind it, and still detest those who corrupt it."

"Now I begin to understand. It is not God you despise, but profane men."

Shaking his head, he muttered, "You've oversimplified it, but I should have expected that. Sweet Aislinn, you are indeed pure of heart. You cannot conceive of duplicity and dishonesty."

Indignantly, she said, "I am not a fool! I'm well aware—and acquainted with—men who profess faith for the sake of expediency. One more reason I find you more noble than you will judge yourself is your honesty."

He flinched. If she knew how very dishonest he was, she would not view him with such regard. She had asked for the truth. Now was the time to give it to her.

With brutal efficiency, he said, "I came to Glastonbury under false pretenses, Aislinn. I was sent here to find the Holy Grail and take it with me. My reward for that is not a place in heaven, but my mother's ancestral home—Dunmow. It was seized years ago, taken from her and from me for her sin—a sin she did not commit alone, but which she paid for alone."

When she did not comment, but only stared at him over the fire, he added harshly, "I never had any intention of giving the Grail to the church."

Heavy silence fell between them. The roasting heron began to char, and he knelt by the fire to turn the spit. It was blackened on one side, but not too badly to eat. Nothing was said. He concentrated on turning the spit.

"I wondered," she said at last, softly. "I hoped, of course, that your intentions were honorable."

"Now you know the truth."

"It is not such a harsh truth, Stephen." When he looked up, she added, "I understand why you want the Grail, and it's not for purely selfish reasons."

"Good God, must you give me noble motives that I do not possess?" He jerked at the spit and the bird lurched, nearly tumbling into the flames. He grabbed it, burned his fingers, swore harshly, but managed to save it. He looked up at Aislinn. "Dunmow is a small keep surrounded by a

hundred hectares of land. It is worth little to anyone but
me. The income is small, its position of no strategic use.
I want it for purely selfish reasons. It was taken from my
mother by the church. She was turned out to starve, while
I was taken from her and sent away. Yea, I want it for
selfish reasons. It was hers. It is all I have to remind me
of her."

"Surely your mother could have gone to the church
to—"

His laugh was harsh and bitter. "A woman scorned?
Whose bastard clung screaming to her skirts before being
ripped away? She was a pariah not even the church would
shelter. A knight's daughter, by God, reared gently, but
with the foolish misfortune to fall in love with a weak
man. He abandoned her, abandoned us both, with the
sanctimonious blessing of the Holy Mother Church."

He knelt by the fire, gave a vicious stab at the fowl
with the wooden spoon. "Forgive me if I find it a bit much
to come over all devout and pious about giving the church
anything, much less the Holy Grail. If it does exist, I fully
intend to use it to barter for my meager inheritance. I'm
cursed weary of eating other men's bread."

She stared at him, pale of face and obviously shaken.

Ferocious motions dismantled the spit, slid the bird off
to the waiting cloth; his burned fingers arranged it so the
long neck did not fall off the cloth.

"I've ruined our meal," he said flatly. "Bile is a foul
dish to serve hot or cold."

"Yes. It is." She leaned forward, rearranged the bird on
the cloth, her movements deft. "This fowl will taste much
better than hatred."

Silent, he watched while she carved the heron with her
jeweled eating dagger, swift sure strokes that dissected it
cleanly and efficiently. She served steaming slices atop
bread crusts, spooned boiled onion and herbs over it, and
said, "Eat before it grows cool."

A bit disgruntled by her composure, he looked down at his food; his belly growled, reminding him that despite it all, he was hungry. A mundane need. How ignoble.

Aislinn had begun to calmly eat with dainty motions, spearing chunks of bread and meat with the tip of her dagger.

It was deflating. At a loss, his anger and frustration dissolved, and he began to eat. When he was done, he looked up at her, said tonelessly, "We will go back to Glastonbury tomorrow."

"Yes," she said, "it's time to return."

Part Two

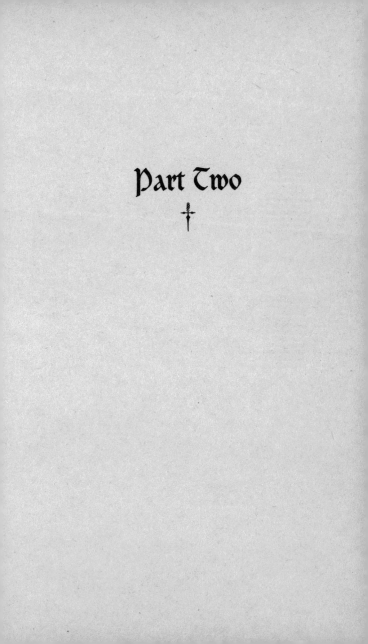

Chapter 21

✝

BROTHER TIMOTHY BURST unceremoniously into Aislinn's hall, trailed by two of the abbey cats. Distress ravaged his face, and he wrung his hands in so agitated a manner that she surged to her feet without regard for the needlework in her lap. It tumbled to the floor unheeded.

"What is it? Brother Timothy—is it Gaven?"

"No, no, my grandfather is as well and peevish as he always is—Mistress, we are ruined! The king is dead!"

"The king . . . King Henry has died?"

"Yea, word has just come . . . Richard has been named as his successor. There will be no more funds for rebuilding, and Brother Prior is beyond bearing." He turned his face, pointed to a red mark on his cheek. "When I dared suggest that Richard might yet continue his father's work, Brother Prior struck me."

"My heavens." Aislinn sank back to the chair. She thought of Stephen, wondered if he was affected by the king's death. It had been near five weeks now since he'd left Glastonbury behind.

An awkward farewell, strained and distant, as if they were strangers again, when both of them yearned for a return to the sweet familiarity they had enjoyed in the bog marsh. He'd worn a haunted look in his eyes when he departed, the residue of regret. For both of them.

There had been no angry words, no misunderstanding between them. Indeed, it was the complete understanding of each other's minds that put them apart.

Stephen had gone to Cornwall—Tintagel, he said, to search for King Arthur's grave and the Grail. He would not give up the search, would not give up his determination to barter the Grail for his mother's lands.

And she understood.

Yet she could not agree, could not condone the use of the Grail for any but spiritual purpose.

It wasn't just the Grail, for that was still only a dream that may never come to pass. It was the fundamental differences between them that now separated them.

Oh, she had no regrets for their time in the marsh, for it had given her sweet memories. Her regret was for what would never be.

Brother Timothy began to pace the floor, wringing his hands, highly agitated. She bent, retrieved her needlework from the floor and curious cats, then put it on the table before she went to him.

"Calm yourself, Brother. Perhaps all will be well. King Richard may yet prove to be diligent in carrying out his father's wishes."

Brother Timothy gave a disbelieving laugh. "Richard of the Lionheart? Nay, he thinks only of Crusades and killing, of using the sword to convert heathens."

"A drastic method that deprives them of life rather than conversion, I think," Aislinn said wryly. "Yet, it is a noble endeavor in conception if not deed."

He paused, looked at her strangely. "Those who refuse

to hear the true word deserve death, Mistress. It is written so."

"But it is not our place to judge or send them to their fates. That judgement belongs only to God, Brother Timothy."

His thin face sharpened, grew taut. "God directs us to act for Him, Mistress. It is our sacred responsibility."

Aislinn nodded. "No doubt you are right, Brother. Come. Let me pour you some wine. You are distraught with worry. All will be well."

"I dare not linger. Brother Prior would be most upset were he to learn I have been here."

"He is still angry with me, then."

"Yes, Mistress. And with me, for not telling him that you left soon after Sir Stephen. He suspects you were not visiting the sick, but with the knight, and considers it a sin, an immoral act of lewdness. If he knew for a certainty you were alone with Sir Stephen for near a week, he would no doubt cast you out of your home."

She did not confirm nor deny the prior's suspicions, for it would only put Brother Timothy in an awkward position. Instead she said calmly, "He cannot cast me out. I have a charter from the abbey giving me the right to remain in this house for the duration of my life. I would have to be condemned as a heretic to rescind that charter."

"Mention it not to Brother Prior," he said softly, "for he seeks any excuse to vent his frustration and fears. Witness my cheek, Mistress. He is beside himself with grief."

"What of Ralph Fitzstephen? Does the king's chamberlain remain here?"

"Praise God, yes. Though he has been called to speak with the legatine council regarding Glastonbury's future."

Aislinn sighed. "What we feared has come to pass. We must pray for the abbey and for England."

For a moment he stood silent, then inhaled as if for

courage and said, "Mistress, I know you search for the Holy Grail."

She said nothing, but arched her brow at him, and he continued in a tumble of words, as if they had been pent up too long.

"I am not as ignorant as some seem to think, nor am I so young that I do not recognize the importance of such a holy discovery. It is my fervent desire that the abbey be allowed to continue in peace, that I be allowed to remain here near all I know and love. You know me, Mistress Aislinn, and have known me since I was but a young lad. I grew to manhood listening to the tales of King Arthur. My grandfather saw to that. Yet I tell you, as important as the king's grave may be, it does not hold the Grail."

"How do you know this, Brother? Have you knowledge to share?"

"Perhaps." He looked away, tucked his hands in the flowing black sleeves of his habit, and blew out a heavy breath. "Perhaps. Or perchance it is just my dreams that bid me believe in the survival of a sacred chalice. It has been nearly twelve hundred years since our Lord and Savior died. If the Grail still exists in this world, should it not have been found by now?"

He looked up at the painting on the wall, the depiction of the knight offering up the chalice to angels, and an expression of utmost reverence and ecstasy altered his face as he said, "But perhaps the Grail awaits an uncorrupted man. A man worthy of the honor."

Aislinn thought of Gaven's test, his proclamation that Stephen was worthy of the discovery. He had been wrong. So wrong. Stephen Fitzhugh was not the man to find the Grail. Nor was she worthy. An unrepentant sinner, fallen from grace and unconfessed—she would surely pay for her sin, but she could not find it in her heart to regret it.

"Yes," she said when Timothy turned to look at her, "a worthy man should be the one to find the Grail. Have you thought that it's not meant to be found? Perhaps it's meant to remain a goal for the faithful, instead of an ending to a search."

"If that were so, it would not be here."

There was an intensity to him that penetrated at last, and she looked at him sharply. "What have you found, Brother Timothy?"

He stepped closer to her. His tongue flicked out to wet his lower lip, and he glanced around as if afraid to be overheard. "I have found nothing yet, but I—I know where to look."

"To look for—the Grail?"

"Yea, Mistress. The sacred vessel of Christ. . . ." He clasped his hands together, bony fingers laced into a tight ball that he held against his chest. "But I will need your help to retrieve it."

"*My* help . . . you honor me with your trust, Brother Timothy. Tell me what you'd have me do."

"Meet me after matins tonight at the foot of the Tor. I will wait for you at the cattle gate on the western slope. Should you arrive before me, hide yourself. I want nothing to happen to you."

Her brow rose. "What would happen to me? Do you fear danger?"

For a moment he didn't answer, then he said, "There were men who arrived with the messenger today. They stay now at the abbey. Prior Thaddeus offered them lodgings and respite from their journey. One of them—" He paused, then blurted, "One of them I have seen before. He was here when the abbey burned four years ago."

"Did you tell Father Prior?"

Timothy shook his head. "No. He is too busy to grant me audience—another sign of his disfavor. But Mistress, I know this man is the same, though he comes here now as a Knight Templar."

"A Templar—" Her mind went immediately back to

the year of the great fire, when the Templar Knights had come to Glastonbury in search of the Grail. It had been a time of disquiet, ending with the destruction of the abbey. And the death of a Templar.

"Why would Father Prior not recognize him?" she asked. "If he was here four years ago—"

"He was a common foot soldier then. He now wears the garb of a Templar."

"A soldier?" She shook her head. "You know that Knights Templar must be noble born, and born in wedlock to be able to become one of that sacred order. He cannot be a common soldier, Brother."

Sighing, Brother Timothy nodded. "It . . . it seems so true. I feel I cannot be mistaken."

"Time plays strange tricks with memory, Brother."

"Yes, Mistress. I know." A faint smile touched his mouth, and for a moment he was the young lad she had known before he took the cowl. "Do you think my visions true? Are they sent by God? I feel sometimes as if they have been sent by the devil, to trick me."

She paused, then nodded. "I think your visions are true and real, Brother. I cannot explain or understand, but I think you honest."

"Brother Prior has doubts."

"Prior Thaddeus resents visions that set you apart from the others—and him. He cannot help his feelings of envy, I fear."

"Yes, I feel you must be right. Bless you, Mistress. I so often doubt my own visions." He paused, gave her a keen glance that seemed to read her soul. "You have your own holy pursuits, whether you will admit it to me or not. I think we are of the same mind."

When Brother Timothy was gone, Aislinn moved about her hall restlessly. How could he know? How could Timothy have discovered the Grail—or known she sought it as well?

She thought of Stephen then and his angry search for the Grail. And she thought of all that he'd told her about himself, about his reasons for wanting it. While it hadn't been as much of a shock to her as he obviously had thought it would be, it was an illumination into all the reasons why they would never suit. She didn't blame him. It was easy to understand why he felt as he did about the church.

But she could not alter a lifetime of faith, and would not if she could. Despite everything—perhaps *because* of it all—she would not now abandon the principles that formed the very fabric of her nature. It would be more of a tragedy than she could bear, to lose both God and Stephen.

And lose them both she would, for she could never forgive a man who expected it of her.

To his credit, Stephen had not asked nor expected it of her.

And that made his loss even harder to bear. . . .

Hot tears stung her eyes, but she blinked them back. It would do no good to weep. What was done was done. One more dream shattered. Now she understood why Stephen refused to dream—the destruction was overwhelming.

Unable to bear remaining alone with her thoughts, she scooped up a basket and left her house for the almonry. Even Mistress Margaret's caustic nature was preferable to her own misery.

It was hot and damp in the almonry storeroom, where the rich scent of fresh herb bundles dangling from the ceiling was a pungent welcome. Aislinn stood for a moment in the open door while her eyes adjusted to the fragrant gloom. July sunlight was bright outside, the storeroom shadowed and familiar.

Across the tables stacked with drying herbs and baskets of cabbages, Mistress Margaret worked with the sleeves of her bliaut rolled up to pudgy elbows. Sweat trickled down cheeks flushed with heat, and limp strands of hair straggled from beneath her plain linen cap. She looked up, and her mouth crimped into a smirk.

"What do ye here? Come to taint us all with yer wicked ways?"

"I have come for cabbages and apples," Aislinn replied, ignoring her derision. "Master Weaver said there was a small amount put aside for me."

"Aye, there be a few bits o' cabbage and some small apples ye can take with ye, but no' much. There be guests to feed. Prior says as ye're to have yer allotment, but no more than that."

"That is all I require, Mistress," Aislinn said coolly. "Where have you put them?"

Mistress Margaret jerked her head to indicate a basket shoved beneath a table in the far corner. "Put them there, I did, out o' the way o' decent folks provender."

"Your kindness is overwhelming."

"More than ye deserve, it is, when ye've turned out as I always said ye would—a trollop, right enough, loose in yer ways and yer manners."

"Your opinion is of little regard to me, for I learned long ago that your bile is careless as it is bountiful. You take no care where you spread your malice."

"Leastwise, it not be my thighs I spread so freely, as ye do, Mistress Leman!"

Aislinn whirled around to face Mistress Margaret and took brief satisfaction in her tiny squeak of alarm. "One day your vile tongue will see you undone, mark me on that," she warned softly. "You strew lies as freely as you do venom. Be wary, for it will turn back on you."

"Retribution has already come upon yer head, 'tis plain to see," Mistress Margaret said bluntly, though some of her bluster faded. "Where be yer lover now?"

"If you refer to Sir Stephens—which I presume you

do—I am not privy to his comings or goings. Best ask
Father Prior about that. Or do you accuse the prior of
being his lover as well? They spent much time together,
I understand."

"Blasphemer!" the woman hissed between her teeth.

Snatching up her basket, Aislinn marched to the table
and dragged out the basket that held cabbages and apples
set aside for her. Withered apples lay among hard green
ones, and the cabbages were limp and brown. Poor fare,
indeed.

She rose and moved deliberately to the tables bearing
more acceptable vegetables. She chose two round, firm
heads of cabbage, and a half dozen small ripe apples from
the lot, then looked up at Mistress Margaret.

"I would prefer these," she said.

Standing with arms crossed over her ample bosom,
Margaret glared at Aislinn. "Take them then, and be gone
wi' ye! I'll petition the prior to keep ye from here, for
'tis no' right that decent folk should be made to consort
with sinners!"

"Mistress, I heartily agree," Aislinn said softly, and left
the almonry with her basket before she betrayed her anguish. The woman would tell all of Glastonbury—if she
had not done so already—that Aislinn was a fallen
woman. A fornicator. A lewd harlot . . . Mistress Margaret
would spare no words in her self-righteous condemnation.
Any uneasy truce they had previously enjoyed was gone.
Malice burned in the woman's soul, crowding out her occasional act of generosity and kindness.

High Street was crowded, and Aislinn paused at the
edge before crossing. Carts lumbered past on the way to
market, oxen straining at yokes and cartmen bellowing
encouragement. The roads were dry, but still bore deep
ruts from the last rain. Summer heat warmed the air. July
would soon be gone, and August was near at hand. Soon
it would be Michaelmas and the time of harvest before

winter set in with days of brief light followed by endless
hours of night.

Perhaps she should visit Gaven soon. The old man
waited for her visits and greeted her with relief each time
she came, but had not asked about Stephen since their
return from Cadbury. It was as if he knew.

She stepped into the street as a cart piled high with
peddler's wares was pushed past by the owner, a man
roughly clad. He eyed her as he passed, nodded courte-
ously.

Aislinn acknowledged the courteous gesture with a nod
of her own and a murmured greeting. Pilgrims and peddlers frequented Glastonbury, drawn by the abbey relics
and new construction. Now that construction may cease,
the laborers would move on to other work. Stonemasons,
carpenters, and common laborers contributed greatly to
the economic welfare of the town and abbey. How would
it survive if construction ended and there was no great
church to offer sustenance?

And how would she survive if the abbey dissolved, for
she would have only her hall and meager funds left to
keep her fed and warm?

Lost in dismal thought, Aislinn didn't hear the clatter
of hooves until the horse and rider were upon her, and
her head jerked up with a startled cry as the beast veered
just shy of striking her.

An angry rebuke rose to her lips, but as she looked up,
she recognized first the horse, then the rider. *Nero.* And
staring down at her, Stephen Fitzhugh.

Chapter 22

✝

"Could you not find a more public manner of renewing our acquaintance?" Aislinn asked, a little tartly, staring at Stephen as he dismounted in the street.

"Acquaintance? Hardly that trivial, I thought. At least to me, it was not so insignificant." He took her arm, led her to the side of the road, and paused.

He was weary, bones aching and sore, but at this moment as he studied her flushed face and eyes suspiciously bright, he felt as if he could linger forever. How did he tell her that? No words were appropriate. Nor would mere words erase the invisible barriers between them. Those *he* had put there, carefully, stone by stone had he erected an insurmountable wall between them.

And he regretted it.

Christ above, but how he regretted it! There had been few enough regrets in his life, but this was one that he had no idea how to surmount.

"I did not expect you to return," she said. There was a faint challenge in her gaze. "You must have been successful in your search."

He smiled, but it felt stiff. "No, I was not. I'm sure
you're relieved to hear that I failed."

"Not relieved—surprised, perhaps." She paused,
seemed about to turn away, then said, "I never wanted
you to fail."

"Did you not? No matter. It's only a temporary failure.
I fully expect to succeed very soon. Aislinn—" He put
out a hand when she took a step back, let it fall to his
side when she made no move to take it. "Aislinn, I cannot
surrender now. I'm too close . . . tell me you understand."

"I told you before, Sir Stephen. I understand your reasons very well. I harbor no anger or resentment toward
you, you must know that. I simply cannot agree with
you."

Beside him, Nero stamped a hoof, snorted wearily. Stephen had ridden most of the night. Now he wondered if
it had been to reach the abbey, or to reach Aislinn. Scant
welcome at either, it seemed.

"The abbey stables are full," he said. "Messengers from
the new king, I presume."

"You know, then."

"Yes." He nodded. "I heard it just before I reached
Devon. Such news travels swiftly. So Richard is now
king. God help us all."

Her head tilted to one side. "You do not think he will
make a good king?"

"I think he could. It remains to be seen if he devotes
his time to England or to his lands in France. He cares
more for the holy city in Jerusalem than he does London."

"Treason, sir," she said softly, smiling, and some of his
tension eased.

"Truth, damoiselle."

"So *you* say." Her smile was warmer, almost wistful, a
sweet curve of her lips into gentle humor.

He recalled the touch of her mouth against him, the
heady taste of her, and felt slightly unsteady. It was a

potent memory. A brand that burned within him constantly.

"I've missed you, mouse," he said softly, and saw her smile waver. He grimaced. "I see that doesn't set well with you. No matter."

As he gathered up Nero's reins and turned away, Aislinn put a hand on his arm, then took it quickly away. "Stephen—I've missed you. I'll never forget you or our time together. I wish—I wish what we both wanted from life wasn't so very different."

"What we want from life isn't that different, just our notions of how to achieve it." He stood for a moment, stared at her with regret gnawing a hole in his heart. He wanted to tell her that he didn't give a damn about the Grail, that he didn't care if it adorned a church or an earl's hall, but the words wouldn't come. And if they had, she wouldn't have believed them. Rightfully so. Oh, it was true enough that he didn't care where the Grail went once he found it, but he did care that it mattered so much to her. He cared that it had come between them. He cared that Dunmow was an obsession now—and that he'd been such a damned fool about it all.

"God," he muttered, at a loss. He shifted his feet; mud caked his boots, and dried chunks broke free. A reminder of his hard ride to reach Glastonbury. He should tell her what he'd learned. Should tell her that once Dunmow was his, he intended to come back for her, to marry her.

Tell her that I love her too much to ever give her up. . . .

But he couldn't tell her that. Not now. It wasn't the right time. She would only try to dissuade him from using the Grail in exchange for Dunmow.

He moved to mount, and when seated in his saddle, he looked down at her. "I'll see you at the abbey."

She didn't reply at once, but looked up at him with a faint flush that pinkened her cheeks and made her eyes seem even brighter. "Perhaps," she said at last, "we shall meet again soon."

"Christ above, Aislinn, don't be so stubborn," he said before he could stop himself. "If we don't agree about some things, there are other things we have in common. Can you not give me that? Do you have to keep me entirely from your life?"

"No. No, it's not that. It's . . . I don't visit the abbey as often as I did."

"No?" He snorted. "Not from some high-minded notion about sin, I hope. Go to confession. A priest will give you a heavy penance and absolution, and all will be well."

"It's gratifying to see that you haven't changed in the weeks you've been gone," she said, but a faint smile eased the sharpness of her tone. "Will you be staying here long?"

"No. Not long at all."

"Then I may not see you again before you leave. Go with God, Sir Stephen."

She turned away, swinging her basket in front of her as she moved toward her house. The half-timbered structure was neat and trim, a compact, comfortable home. But it belonged to the abbey, not to her. He wanted to give her more than that, more than a life on the fringes. He wanted her to be a knight's lady, mistress of her own hall. He wanted to give her a babe in her belly, and that thought shocked him most. Never had he wanted children. But he wanted this woman's children. He wanted daughters with fine hair the color of new honey, and honest blue eyes that kept no secrets.

He felt dangerously near yielding to the temptation to lift her atop Nero and just ride away. Instead, he nudged the horse forward to intercept her.

"Aislinn, grant me time to make all right."

She paused at the door to her hall, turned to gaze up at him with a smile that looked sorrowful. "That is beyond your ability, I fear. But you have given me sweet dreams, and those I will always have."

"Sweet Christ, will you—"

She put up a hand as he started to dismount. "No, do not! Please. If you care at all for me, do not come to see me again. I cannot bear it."

The oak door swung open, then slammed shut behind her. It sounded as final as nails in a coffin.

His mouth hardened. She would listen to him. She must. He had no intention of freeing her. She was his now, and his alone.

Turning Nero, he set off at a brisk trot up the incline of High Street.

The sharp clop of Nero's iron-shod hooves could be heard inside the hall, where Aislinn stood with her back against the oak door as if to keep him out. Slowly she slid down the door until she sat upon the floor. Her basket, forgotten, tipped over and spilled out cabbages and apples. They rolled across the floor.

With her head leaned back against wood, she sat in the silence of her hall. Echoes of hopes and dreams sounded in her ears, and she thought of the days before Stephen had come to Glastonbury. Life had been smooth, uneventful, save for the occasional overflow of war's detritus. King Henry's constant struggle with the Welsh had its inevitable effects. But that had all seemed so distant, so removed from her safe world.

In less than three months, the fabric of her life had come unraveled so that she no longer recognized it or even herself.

The search for King Arthur's grave and the Holy Grail seemed senseless now, futile. She didn't believe Stephen had found information that would help, nor did she think Brother Timothy would succeed. It was obvious now that the Grail was meant to be a goal, an elusive dream, an aspiration for perfection. It was not meant to be found by man.

Drawing up her legs, she bent her arms over her knees and rested her forehead against her crossed wrists. It was foolish to grieve for what would never be. What had begun as a search for King Arthur's grave had evolved into a nightmare.

Abbot Robert could not have known. He had thought only of the grave, not of the more precious prize of the Grail. It was her foolishness, and that of others, who had read more into his journal than was there.

Tonight, when she met Brother Timothy, it would only be another disappointment, another proof that the Grail would not be found. She would offer him comfort as best she could, and praise the monk's faith, and never let him know that she had lost something much more precious to her than the discovery of the Holy Grail.

Blasphemy, indeed.

Mistress Margaret was right, after all.

✝

IT HAD GROWN chill, the wind brisk over the foot of the Tor. Aislinn shivered, glad of her warm wool cloak, and pulled the hood more tightly around her face. No moon lit the sky this night, for the clouds were too thick. In the inky darkness that swallowed familiar landmarks, she had to feel her way along, running a hand over dry stone walls beside the road.

She'd come the back way, passing the peasant closes, and the stench of the pig-wallows lingered in the air. The back of the abbey was on her right, the Tor just ahead on her left. She slowed her pace, feeling for the cattle gate that should be close by.

A pale sheen was her only light, the reflected glow of torches staggered along abbey walls behind her when she reached the outcropping that was the gate. No sound broke the thick silence, save the low murmur of cattle grazing on the steep slope of the Tor.

Never had she worried for her safety in Glastonbury, for it had not seemed a dangerous place, even when the Welsh wars had drawn close and the wounded were brought to the abbey infirmary for treatment.

Yet tonight there seemed to be something sinister in the air. Perhaps it was the black night, or her own worries that left her feeling uneasy. She felt now as she had in the forests surrounding Cadbury, that same sense of sudden dread that had burst upon her without warning, the air trembling with the smell of peril.

But tonight there was no stalwart knight to send her to safety, but only her own prudence to keep her protected. She should have refused Brother Timothy's request to meet him so late. Compline would have been a better hour, for the night fell earlier now with the end of summer drawing near. It would have been dark enough to hide, but light enough to feel safe.

Still, she was here now, and would meet him and have it done and over.

"Brother," she called softly as she swung open the gate and stepped through. "Are you here?"

There was no answer. The wind rattled tree limbs, a dry sound like the clacking of old bones. . . . *How fanciful I have become!* she thought with self-mocking derision, and moved to the shelter of the wall to wait.

Trees were a faint black silhouette against the murky shadow of the Tor. It rose, silent and mysterious, forbidding in this late hour, a witness to aeons of time. She crouched, her back pressed against stone wall, head tilted to gaze up at the sky. Once, years before when she had been young, she had gone with Aline to the top of the Tor one summer night. It was an act of daring, of defiance against authority, of independence.

They had lain on the furrowed sides of the Tor in awe at the mystery of the night, of the thousands upon thousands of stars that spread across the velvet sky, twinkling lights that blurred together so brightly they seemed as a seamless band of brilliance. Aline, her companion and confidante, had spoken of her dreams, her wishes for the future, and her fear and anticipation of her coming wedding to the son of a comfortable landowner near Bath. They had whispered long into the night, until Aline's father had finally found them and taken them home, scolding all the way.

Unrepentant, they had held dear the memory of that night and promised one another they would do it again soon. But Aline had wed and moved away, and word had come a year later of her death in the childbed.

Aislinn stood up, flexing her cramped muscles. Surely, Brother Timothy would arrive soon. Matins had long been over and even allowing for errands, he should have stolen away by now.

Perhaps he had thought better of it, and not been able to send word to her. She may have come here for no reason. A fitting penance for being foolish. She almost laughed aloud. How silly she was!

Moving from the shelter of the wall, she made her way toward the gate, careful to avoid cow piles that would be scattered in the grass. Creatures of habit, cows gathered at the gate at the same time each day, waiting for the cowherd to come and take them to be milked.

As she trod gingerly over grass wet with dew, peering down at her feet and straining to see in the dense shadows, she heard a faint growling sound. Hair on the back of her neck prickled, and her heart hammered in alarm. She paused. It must be the wind in the trees, or perhaps even the thud of apples or pears shaken loose from the branches. She heard nothing, though she waited for what seemed an eternity.

But when she moved forward again, the growling was loud and distinct. Frozen with fear and apprehension, she weighed her choices. Flight could be fatal. Animals gave chase when prey fled. Yet to stay could mean certain harm.

Warily, she took another step, and a bone-chilling screech erupted from beneath her feet. A scream locked in her throat, and her hand flew to the eating dagger at her waist. She drew it. Small though it was, it may afford some protection against attack.

Her right foot nudged against something on the ground, and she drew back slightly, then stumbled, nearly falling to her knees. Off-balance, she threw out a hand to catch herself and encountered something warm and inert. The growling was followed by a hiss, then another screech, as of a cat.

A cat . . . Aislinn drew in a sharp breath. What lay beneath her hand was wool, as found in a monk's habit. She quickly explored, and realized as her fingers shaped an arm, then a shoulder, that she had found Brother Timothy. Guarded by his cats, he was sprawled upon the ground near the cattle gate, still as death.

"Brother Timothy . . . oh, Christ have mercy . . . what has happened to you?"

When she tried to turn him over, to search for signs of life, she encountered a warm, sticky pool. It smeared her palm, and when she jerked her hand away, she recognized the smell of blood.

Her dagger dropped from her hand, and she stumbled to her feet, nauseated by her grim discovery. She must find help for him, for if he still lived, he might yet be saved.

Whirling, she skidded slightly in something slick and wet, realized she'd stepped in cow dung, but did not stop. Panic drove her, fear for herself and frantic worry for Timothy. She tore the flesh on her hands in her haste with the gate, shoved it open violently, near breathless and half sobbing with distress. Slatted wood flung outward. Iron hinges shrieked a protest at the mistreatment, and the gate shuddered as it struck something solid.

"Christ above!" came the harsh oath, and Aislinn went cold with new fear.

A hand clamped down on her arm, fingers a steel vise that would not free her despite her frantic struggle. She lashed out, regretted the loss of her dagger, and aimed a vicious kick at her assailant.

Her boot caught him in a soft portion of his body, sunk into flesh and muscle, and she heard a retching groan as he released her with startling swiftness. Poised to flee, she took only a few steps before she recognized the owner of the voice, heard his muttered curse and her own name.

"Sweet Jesus, Aislinn, do you hate me that much?"

Pausing, she whirled back around, not quite daring to believe. "Stephen? Is it . . . is it you?"

"What's left of me . . . you've near crushed my stones."

A bubble of hysteria rose in the back of her throat, and she went swiftly to him, knelt in the dark to peer at him, saw the blur of his face in dense shadows.

"I didn't know it was you . . . you must help!"

"Christ, you need no help . . . I need the help . . . what ails you, to try to unman me?"

Pain seeped into his panted words, but she gave him a brief shake, her hand on his shoulder. "Never mind that, you must help Brother Timothy."

"*Never mind*—you've run mad on me. A foot in my crutch is not so easy to ignore. . . ."

"Count yourself fortunate that I dropped my eating dagger. Stephen, listen to me—Brother Timothy has been badly injured and is like to die if we do not get him help!"

Slowly he heaved himself to his knees. "I seem to be asking this of you far too often, but help me to my feet and I'll do what I can."

"Lean on my shoulder," she said impatiently, "and be quick about it."

His hand came out, warm and familiar, to rest upon her shoulder. "You smell like cow dung," he muttered as he used her as leverage. "I much prefer roses."

"So you have said before. Come swiftly now. If he is not already dead, he is like to die before we can get him to the infirmary."

"What are you doing out here in the dark, or need I ask that?" He moved at her side, stepped through the gate and knelt beside the prone body on the ground. He put a hand out to touch the side of his neck, and after a moment said, "He still lives. I'll carry him. You had best be concocting a plausible reason for being out here in the middle of the night with a monk."

"Do not think you are above suspicion yourself," she said shortly, "for I have no doubt you will be asked the same question."

It was a truth he did not have to deny.

Chapter 23

✝

BROTHER TIMOTHY LAY upon a narrow cot in the infirmary, pale as death, his bloodless face so still he looked like a waxen image. Brother Arnot had been summoned and tended him with herbs and skill, intent upon his work.

"How did you find him, Sir Stephen?" Prior Thaddeus drew him into the hallway outside the Infirmary. Small tufts of brown hair stood straight up on his scalp, and he looked haggard. "Did you hear him cry out?"

"No. I found him by accident."

"By accident? On the slopes of the Tor?" The prior's brow rose in disbelief. "It is well after matins, sir. I would be intrigued to know what business you had in a cow pasture this late at night."

Stephen regarded him coolly. "Of all men, I would think you would be reluctant to ask such a question of me, Father Prior."

Thaddeus colored slightly and glanced into the chamber crowded with curious monks in various stages of shock and distress. In a low voice he said, "I must ask, Sir Stephen. You realize that."

"I realize that one of your brothers has been struck with a knife and nearly killed, and may yet die. The sheriff will be here soon enough, asking his questions. I do not care to repeat myself endless times."

The prior looked uncertain, then determined. "For my own knowledge, I wish to know what business you had with Brother Timothy that required you to meet him alone on the Tor after midnight."

"I cannot answer that. He lay this way when I arrived."

"Then you *were* to meet him there."

Stephen arched a brow, his silence an eloquent lie. Let the prior think what he would. It diverted suspicion from Aislinn. She must be kept safe—though he fully intended to ask her these very questions at the first opportunity.

It had taken brutal persuasion to convince her to leave Timothy in his hands, to allow him to report the injury and see him safely to the abbey. Her distress was genuine, and he didn't really think she had anything to do with the attack, but he was extremely interested in her reasons for being on the Tor so late at night. And with no adequate protection, save a youthful monk and her eating dagger, for the love of all that's holy. . . .

A cold chill went down his spine. He had not retrieved her dagger, nor had she, to his knowledge. If it was found there in the daylight, it may yet be recognized as hers. It was a fairly distinctive dagger, with a jeweled hilt and an etched cross in the blade. He remembered it well, slicing into the charred skin of a roasted heron.

"It might be best, Sir Stephen," the prior said, "if you do not leave Glastonbury until we have made inquiries into this matter."

"I have no intention of leaving Glastonbury until I've completed my business, Father Prior, never fear."

"And that is another matter we must discuss as soon as

possible." Brown eyes studied him dispassionately. "I fear I may have made an error in judgement."

"Pray for guidance, Father Prior, pray for guidance," he said with a curl of his lip.

"I've had a letter from Essex. He grows impatient with the delay, and is concerned about your failure to achieve success."

"My lord Essex has taken great pains to ensure the success of our joint venture, Prior. If I am to continue, I must have your cooperation. And I must have the freedom to go about undisturbed. Should I be watched, as you insinuate, then there is the great chance that others will usurp the discovery from under our very noses. Do you wish to take that risk?"

Indecision was plainly writ on the prior's face. He struggled with it, chewed his bottom lip, and frowned blackly before he gave a curt jerk of his head in assent.

"Very well. You have leave to move about freely, but not so freely as to venture from Glastonbury farther than a mile. Should you take advantage, I will hand you over to the sheriff without a qualm."

"I've told you what I learned in Cornwall. If you wish to continue the search yourself. . . ." He let the sentence trail into silence, and was rewarded with a shake of the prior's head.

"You know that is not possible, especially not now, with the arrival of the king's envoy. Knights Templar have little patience or tolerance for transparent excuses. I would never be able to deceive four of them."

Stephen scraped the pad of his thumb across his jaw with deceptive indifference. "You did not tell me the envoy included Templars."

"It should not matter."

"No. It should not."

"Go, go," Father Prior said impatiently, waving his hands at him, "before I change my mind and see you delivered up to the sheriff after all. This has desecrated the peace of the abbey, and I begin to think it all useless. Brother Timothy lies near death with a stab wound, and I've wasted time searching journals and old letters for the past weeks without success, and even imperiled the soul of a widow left in my charge. It is a heavy burden laid upon me, and I'm not certain I wish to continue. God may not want the—may not want us to succeed."

"That has crossed my mind as well," Stephen said with deliberate calm, "but I hardly think you have imperiled the soul of a widow in your efforts, Brother Prior."

"No, *I* have not. I cannot say the same for you, it seems, Sir Stephen. Do not deny it. It is hardly coincidence that both you and Mistress Aislinn left the abbey the same day, nor that you were both gone a sennight. She has sinned, and goes unshriven of it, in peril of her immortal soul. You must account for your own soul, but she is my duty. I do not take my duties lightly."

"I do not deny that we were both absent during the same time, but so, too, was the soap peddler. Do you consider him in danger of his immortal soul?"

"You mock me, Sir Stephen!"

"No, Father Prior, I merely wish to enlighten you. It is a sin to judge others. Leave that responsibility to God."

Silence fell between them. Beyond the hallway where they stood, frenzied activity centered around the fallen young monk on the table. The pungent scent of betony and woundwort hung in the air. Prior Thaddeus heaved a great sigh.

"It is nearly time for lauds. Mark my admonishment well and see that you are cautious, Sir Stephen."

"I am always cautious, Father Prior."

A lie, of course, for of late he had been anything but cautious. If he hadn't been so careless, perhaps he would now have the Grail in his possession. He was close. So close he could almost see it . . . and now he must wait, for there were men here who would heed well his every movement.

Templar Knights. Men of fierce conviction; men who would give little thought to removing obstacles.

He was one man. One knight against four, and these men would be no eager, clumsy swordsmen. If they were here for other than the purpose of relaying the new king's commands, he would have to tread carefully indeed.

Despite the late hour, when he left the abbey he returned to the Tor to search for Aislinn's dagger. It would be light soon; already the sky was a slate gray instead of the inky black of deepest night. The gate was closed, the latch fallen. He opened it carefully, and eased into the meadow.

The spot where Brother Timothy had fallen was still sticky with his blood, a dark pool against the earth. But there was no sign of a dagger, though he searched diligently through the grass. He hoped she had retrieved it.

✝

AISLINN FELL INTO a fitful sleep at last, exhausted from worry and tension. Yet her dreams would not give her rest—vague images haunted her, frightening and imparting a dread that sank like stones through restless slumber.

She jerked awake, gasping, a hand pressed to her throat at the terrifying apparition of Brother Timothy's blood-soaked corpse rising to stare at her with accusing eyes. The image vanished, but left her shaken and wide awake.

She left her bed to go downstairs to her hall, the candle she carried a brave beacon in the shadows. She held it high to shed light on the narrow stairwell that angled sharply to the ground floor.

Silence greeted her. It was hushed outside, the normal noise of day not yet begun, the cart wheels and hooves, shouts of peddlers and carters would arrive soon enough.

It was so familiar she rarely noticed it, save when it was absent as it was now.

The floor was cold beneath her bare feet, and she shook so that the candle wavered erratically. Shadows loomed beyond the faltering glow, shrouding the familiar lines of table and chairs, the ambry that stood in one corner and held pewter plates and cups. A smaller cupboard secured the loaves of bread and a cheese, held the basket of cabbages and apples she had put away. A wooden crock held a fresh supply of oats to last the winter months.

She set the candle on the table, where it cast a feeble light on the wall and painting of the Grail. It hung crooked now, tilted to one side. She moved to straighten it.

"I found the pages, mouse."

Gasping, Aislinn whirled, saw Stephen detach from the darker shadows around him, his dark features barely lit by the single candle. Irritation replaced the shock of fear that had sent her heart to her toes, and she recovered to demand:

"What are you doing here?"

He held up a pale bundle. "The pages of your uncle's journal. I found them."

"In your pack, perchance?"

A dark smile set his mouth in a moody curve. "You had access enough to my pack when we were in the marsh. Did you find them then?"

"No." She pulled her loose shift more closely around her. "But you must have known I didn't."

"How would I know that?"

"What are you doing here?" she asked again, far too aware of the danger of his presence. "I'll be branded as the village harlot before the day is done. Not that I don't already have the distinction of that title."

"So I gathered." His gaze was sympathetic, and she turned away with a tight frown.

"Please, spare me your pity. How is Brother Timothy?"

"Alive." He shrugged when she made an exasperated sound. "That's all I know. He was alive when I left the infirmary. Brother Arnot was working himself into a frenzy with herbs and potions. He seemed to be skilled."

"He is quite skilled. If Timothy can be saved, it will be because of Brother Arnot's knowledge. Oh, God, I wish he had listened to me!"

"Brother Arnot?"

"No, of course not. Brother Timothy." She signaled with a hand for him to be seated at the table and pulled out a stool for herself. "I warned him to be wary, and he promised he would, but he was so excited—" She stopped, aware that she had been about to reveal Timothy's secret.

"Excited? About these, perhaps?" He held up the pages. "I found them in his cell, you know."

"No." She stared at him. "I didn't know."

"I took it upon myself to conduct a brief search before someone else thought of it. I'm glad now I did." He tossed them to the table. "Did you retrieve your dagger?"

"My dagger? Oh. No, it was dark and I was too worried about Brother Timothy. Why?"

"Why? Because it's not there, mouse, and if someone else found it, they may well think you are the person who used it on yon hapless monk." He shoved a hand through his dark hair, blew out a heavy breath. "It stands to reason that if you did not stab him—" He smiled when she voiced a vehement denial. "Then whoever did plunge a dagger into his back was nearby when you found him. It could very well have been you lying there with him, my sweet. At best, they now have your dagger."

She shuddered. "I'm already the village pariah. If I'm accused of doing harm to Brother Timothy—" She did not need to finish the sentence. The implications were clear enough.

"What were *you* doing there?" she asked, suddenly

struck by the realization. "Were you following me?"

"Yes." His smile was dark. "I saw you leave, and it was late. I wanted to know where you were going and why."

"Quite brazen of you, I think."

He shrugged. "Perhaps. Why were you there? It seems an odd place and time to meet to discuss Gaven's health."

"If you must know, Brother Timothy told me he must talk to me privately. He did not divulge any details."

A slight lie.

She felt his gaze on her, a probing stare that seemed to pierce to the marrow of her bones, to search out her secrets and lay them bare. She didn't look away, but could not meet his eyes. Instead she stared at a point beyond his shoulder, the metallic gleam of pewter plate in the ambry holding her attention.

"You're a terrible liar, mouse," he said at last, but not unkindly. "Very well. Don't tell me. It isn't necessary. I can draw my own conclusions."

Her gaze snapped back to his face. "Don't call me *mouse*. I'm not a rodent."

"What a prickly nature you have before daylight. I didn't recall how surly you can be."

"Stephen, please go before someone sees you here. I have only yet given cause for suspicion of my carnal sin, not proof."

"It's two hours before daylight. Only the watch is out at this time of night. Does Glastonbury have a watch?"

"*Please. . . .*" She was trembling, with reaction to him, to what she felt for him, to the realization of all she'd lost and might yet lose. Why had he come back? It had been better when he was gone, when she didn't have to see him and grieve for what would never be.

"Do you really want me to go, Aislinn?"

He said it quietly, an intensity in the words that was

raw and bleak. She wanted to cry out a denial, but did not.

"Yes." She looked down at her hands, clenched into a single fist atop the table, knuckles white with tension. "I want you to go and not come back. I cannot bear it."

"Liar," he said softly, and she buried her face in her palms in silent desperation.

It was true, oh, God, it was true . . . she wanted him to stay, to hold her in his arms and spout silly compliments again, to laugh with her, to kiss her and take her again to that blissful plane where nothing intruded but a need and emotion so deep and powerful it obliterated every obstacle. That's what she wanted.

But the truth was that there were obstacles, elemental differences neither of them could overcome. It would destroy them in the end if they tried.

She heard the dull scrape of chair legs on the floor, felt him come to her, his hand brushing the hair from her cheek and smoothing it over her shoulder. Blindly, she felt him lift her with a hand under her arm, and her hands fell away from her face as he turned her into him.

As his arms went around her, she succumbed to the aching emptiness inside, the loneliness eased even for so short a time. A respite, only a brief lull in the eventual intrusion of the world.

"God . . . Aislinn. . . ." It was a prayer whispered against her ear, his breath warm and ardent.

The quaking need that she had tried to ignore returned, a throbbing, insistent desire that curled from her belly to her spine, seared flesh and resistance and left her clinging to him with fevered surrender.

His hand tangled in her hair, drew her head back so that she stared up into his face, half shadowed in the flickering candlelight. He was the dark knight of her dreams.

"One more night," he muttered, "before I must leave you for a time."

"Yes. One more night."

Scooping her into his arms, he carried her to the narrow stairs that led up to her bedchamber, his boots loud on the wooden steps.

Chapter 24

✝

I T WAS DARK in her chamber, a silky absence of light that heightened their senses and left her quivering in his arms. He was heat and impatience, his hands sure and arousing as he pulled away her shift, touched her breasts, her belly, the pulsing ache between her legs. The ropes of her bed creaked beneath their weight, her mattress a fragrant cushion that rustled slightly with fresh lavender and rose petals as he knelt beside her.

In the darkness she heard him pull off his tunic and boots, heard them drop to the floor with a muffled thud. The dark was liberating; emboldened, she reached out for him, ran her fingertips across his chest, a light exploration of hard muscle that flowed in ridges to his belly. The springy pelt of hair was crisp beneath her touch, thicker below his waist as her hand trailed lower. She found him, a rigid arousal that was hot and soft beneath her palm. Her fingers curled around it, held him lightly at first as his hips thrust forward. Her grip tightened, and with her other hand, she cupped his stones in a gentle massage. He groaned as she manipulated his body, and she exulted in her power to arouse him. It was heady, potent. Powerful.

"Enough," he said at last, his voice thick and hoarse, "enough."

"Cry mercy," she whispered, smiling. "Cry mercy and I may give you respite."

In answer, he shoved into her hand again, a long slow thrust that invited her to retaliate, and she teased him with playful squeezes that earned another groan. His hand caught her wrist, held her, and she felt him shudder.

"Have I displeased you, beau knight?" She twisted to a sitting position, pressed a kiss on his belly, his thighs, the heavy heat of his arousal. He sucked in a sharp breath. Her mouth moved over him in silent appreciation, until at last he pulled away.

"You please me very well." He sounded strained, a tremor betraying him. "Now," he said as he put his hands on her shoulders to push her back into the mattress, "I shall show you the same kind of mercy you have shown me: none."

She laughed softly. "Do your worst, dread knight. I am at your mercy indeed."

She felt his hands touch her face, trace the outline of her lips, skim over her chin and jawline and up to her ear. Light, feathery brushes of his hand wafted over her throat, came to rest upon the swell of her breast. His palm was rough textured, old calluses and new, an abrasive scrape over her quivering skin. Slowly he cupped each breast in a hand, thumbs raking across her nipples in erotic torment, then twisting them between thumbs and fingers until the heat in the pit of her belly moved lower, flared hot and high as he continued caressing her.

When she felt as if she would explode with the tension, he suddenly stopped. She moaned, a sound like a whimper, and reached out for him. Her hands fluttered over his chest, up to his jaw, then down his arms to his hands to bring them back to the sweet torment.

"Please," she whispered, aching for his touch, "please don't stop yet."

"I've no intention of stopping yet, my dove." He pulled away from her hands, but before she could protest, a warm, hot dampness covered one nipple, drew it into his mouth with a strong pull that shot spears of flame through her entire body. His other hand caressed her breast in matching rhythm, until she felt as if she could not bear it another moment.

She arched upward, felt him part her legs with his knee and slide between, felt the silky hardness she had caressed earlier scrape across the aching source of sweet flame. He did not enter her, but slid his body over her in a searing caress. Damp friction increased, the pleasure a powerful sensation that built to a quivering tension that took her ever closer to release. His mouth was hot on her breast, the tug on her nipple stimulating, the heated friction between her legs deliciously exciting.

Her hands curled into his hair, held him as she dug her heels into the mattress and arched upward, seeking that elusive oblivion that burst upon her without warning, a searing, wrenching explosion that left her shattered with ecstasy.

He swallowed her cries of pleasure, muffled them with his mouth on hers, held her tightly to him as she shuddered. Then he pressed her face into his shoulder and slid downward so that his arousal pressed against her. She lay quietly, drained for the moment, still floating.

He entered her slowly, a heavy fullness that stretched and filled her, an exquisite invasion. She rocked her hips up to receive him, and he tucked his hands beneath her to tilt her forward. Her muscles clenched around him, and he made a harsh sound. Contractions of her body drew him deeper and deeper, until the fullness became almost pain. His breath came in shallow pants for air, and he went still at last. She throbbed with the heavy weight of him inside her, blindly aware of every inch of her body and his.

His mouth found hers in the darkness, kissed her with leisurely thoroughness, his tongue mimicking the sex act as he slowly began to move inside her again. The tension began to build, the waiting release hovering just beyond her grasp as he moved, the friction of his thrusts sending bolts of sensation along her spine. Breathless, she held tightly to him, swept along with his increasing movements, the hard driving lunges of his body taking her once again to elation.

When he gave a final, powerful thrust, his chest heaved and he went still—his body gave a hard throb inside her. He did not move for a long moment but finally shifted his weight slightly, an arm still draped over her body.

They lay still locked together, and she pressed a drowsy kiss on his chest. There was no need for words. It would be too difficult to express how she felt.

She dozed, woke only when she felt him strengthening inside her, his body awakening before he did. He began to move, lazy strokes that were pleasure without the searing passion, a comfort and a promise.

Tension was slow to build, and in the darkness he pulled free of her, turned her onto her stomach, his hands beneath her as he pulled her to her knees and entered her in a slow slide of his body. He reached around her, cupped her breasts in his palms, teasing her as he rocked against her. He filled her as if he couldn't get enough of her, as if he would never stop.

Unending hunger, driving need, awakened like a sleeping dragon, all fire and heat and scorching flame—he took her to the heights again, let her float slowly back to earth, then turned her onto her back and eased inside once more. He kissed her fiercely, explored her body with hands and mouth and tongue until there wasn't an inch of her he hadn't committed to memory. She ached with it, yet met each new caress as if it were the first. There was a desperation in them both now, a sense of loss that couldn't be appeased with mere passion.

She rode him, on her knees and astride him as if he were a wild beast, a horse to be tamed, bucking beneath her, his hands on her waist as he pulled her down with savage fervor, impaling her on his body, his hands sliding over her slick flesh to grip her tightly. She groaned and gasped and sobbed his name, the frenzy upon her now, his desperation reaching inside to tear her apart. She couldn't get close enough. Not even the drowning waves of release could ease the pain that was to follow, and they both knew it.

Just before daylight, when the sky was rosy with the rising sun and birds had wakened with sleepy song, Stephen slipped from her bed and left the house. Aislinn could not bear to watch him leave, and could not stem the rising tide of despair he left in his wake.

One night was not enough. A year would not be enough. A lifetime would not be enough.

Yet the night would have to be the end. She could not endure another farewell.

Chapter 25

✝

BROTHER TIMOTHY WAS propped up on soft cushions in the infirmary, one arm in a cloth sling, his chest bandaged with strips of clean white linen. The calico cat perched nearby, watching warily all who came and went, and just beyond, lurked two more cats not quite as brave.

"The cats brought me a dead mouse this morning," he said with a faint smile that betrayed his pain. "A gift to ease me, I think."

Aislinn leaned forward to spoon more broth into his mouth. "They return your kindnesses. I can only stay a short time, and am here by the graces of Brother Arnot. Tell me what you wish me to say to your grandfather."

He looked startled. "I can think of nothing. Tell him I am well and happy."

She sighed. "He will hear of your injury, Brother. He will want more comforting words than that."

"Tell him—tell him I've not forgotten the tales. Tell him I am a worthy man."

The spoon hovered above his chest, and Aislinn stared

at Brother Timothy's pale face. "That is what you wish me to say? Are you certain?"

"Yea, I am certain." His mouth set. "All would know it now if not for this." He indicated his injury with disgust. "It will not stop me. Will you still help me, Mistress?"

She tilted the spoon into his mouth, watched as he swallowed the broth. "When you are able. You must rest and regain your strength now. It's a pity you did not see who did this to you."

A faint frown knit his brow, and he did not reply. She dipped another spoon of broth from the cup, tipped it into his mouth.

"I didn't see, of course," he said slowly and wiped his mouth with a cloth she held out for him, "but I felt that someone was there just before I was struck down. The cats knew. They were restless, and wary. I should have paid more attention."

"Brother Timothy," she said softly, "do you wish to tell me what you know so that I may help you?"

"No." He gave her a slightly petulant glance. "It is my vision. My obligation. Or will be."

"And you are certain *no one* else knows about it?"

He chewed his bottom lip for a moment, concern marking his face. "I don't know," he admitted. "But if they do, they would have done something by now."

"That's true."

She removed the empty bowl, set it on the tray with the clean cloth and a cup of red wine. She thought of the pages Stephen had found in Timothy's cell. When he was well enough to question, she would ask him about them. There was little doubt in her mind that he had indeed taken the pages; the calico cat had jogged her memory of a night at her table, and the mysterious solitary visit from the feline. The cat was never far from Brother Timothy, and it was likely she had not been far from him then. An open window, a chance glimpse of her studying the pages, and it would be easy for Timothy to link his suspicions with Gaven's tales.

But he had not stabbed himself, and that meant there were others aware of the search. It was unlikely to be a random attack.

"Here," she said and held up a cup Brother Arnot had left for him, "a few drops of poppy juice in the wine to ease your pain."

He grimaced but dutifully drank the wine, and when he slipped into an easy slumber, she left the infirmary. She met Brother Arnot in the cloister.

"He rests," she said, and the monk nodded.

"Youth is his ally. An older man might well expire of such a grave wound. It barely missed his vitals."

"I cannot imagine who would dislike him enough to do that to him," she murmured, and the monk shook his head.

"It was someone of like size, for the wound was lateral instead of a downward strike." He smiled when she lifted a brow. "It's obvious from the size and direction of the wound. I have made a study of wounds, you see."

"I imagine you've had many to study, with all the men brought in during the last conflict with the Welsh." She paused. "You are Welsh, are you not, Brother Arnot?"

"Yea, I am, Mistress. Welsh by birth, a Benedictine by choice."

"And we are blessed for that choice."

"It is my privilege to serve. Mistress—" He paused, then continued softly, "I feel the presence of evil within the abbey walls. Be ware."

"Have you spoken to Father Prior?"

"Father Prior is—uninterested in anything he cannot see or feel or hear."

"Ah. I appreciate your warning, Brother."

Reluctant to return home with the memory of Stephen still so vivid in the hall, she chose instead to visit Gaven and take him news of Timothy. She carried a basket to him from her own stores, unwilling to confront Mistress Margaret in the almonry.

The day was crisp, bright with sunlight and a brisk, cool wind that smelled of approaching autumn. The change of the seasons was always welcome to her, even winter with its frigid rain and storms. It was still warm enough to go without her cloak in the warmth of the sun, and she took her time on the walk to the miller's holdings.

Gaven looked stronger than last time, sitting up in his bed with a sharp expression on his face, and she thought of Stephen's suspicion that he could see more than he admitted.

"What did ye bring me?" he demanded, as always. "Did ye bring it?"

"Not this time, Gaven. I will bring it with me the next time I come." She paused, set the basket down on the table by the door and poured him a mug of beer.

He smacked his lips impatiently and held out a hand for it. "Ye dally too long," he complained when she took her time, and with a sigh she moved to his bedside and put the mug into his outstretched hand.

"I've news for you," she said and dragged a stool over by his cot. "Brother Timothy has been injured. He is alive, but recovering from a grievous wound."

"An injury, ye say." Gaven took a sip of beer, the slight shake of his hand betraying his distress. "A clumsy lad, full of visions. He allus were."

"This was not his fault, Gaven. He was attacked by an unknown person or persons who meant him harm."

"Who would mean the lad harm? He's too meek to earn enemies . . . bah! No one could mean him harm. It were a mistake 'tis all. A mistake."

"Perhaps." She looked down at her hands, folded in her lap, and rubbed idly at her knuckles with her thumb. "But I wonder—it happened last night at the Tor. He asked me to meet him there after matins. He said . . . Gaven, he said he knew about the Grail, and needed my help to retrieve it."

Genuine alarm spread over the old man's wrinkled face, and he sloshed beer from the mug over his hand and arm as he made a sharp gesture. "No! Aiie, no, he cannot be so foolish! He is no' the one—"

"He said to tell you . . . he said: *'Tell him I've not forgotten the tales. Tell him I am a worthy man.'* Those were his exact words."

Shaken, Gaven moaned. "Ah, the doltish lad! A nodcock for certain, he be. . . . I never should have filled his head with all those tales. Mistress, there be danger that he will not see, and cannot fight. His heart is worthy, but it takes more than that to triumph. The knight . . . the knight is the one. He can win all. The knight. . . ."

Her mouth set. She stared down at her hands, eyes burning.

"What is it, lass? Tell me."

She looked up. Gaven was staring at her, his eyes thin crescents in his withered face, intent and focused.

"Stephen was right. You *can* see."

He waved an impatient hand, dismissing her accusation. "Tell me what ails thee, lass. He has no' given up, has he?"

"No." She knew she sounded tense, but it was still too raw and fresh. God, she felt so disloyal, but the truth was the truth. She took a deep breath. "You were wrong, Gaven. He has not given up the search, but he is *not* the one to honor the Grail."

"Did he go to Cadbury? And Tintagel?"

"Yes. How did you know?"

He cackled, a thin sound. "I know. I know. His will is strong. He has no' given up."

"No." She sighed. "He has not. He says he will find it, but he hasn't left Glastonbury."

"Ah."

It was a satisfied sound. Aislinn gazed at him for a long moment, frustrated.

"You know more than you tell," she said at last. "Brother Timothy says he knows where to find the Grail, and now Stephen Fitzhugh claims to know where it is also. I am the only one who has no idea."

Gaven's hand came out, fingers strong and wiry as he clamped them around her wrist. "Ye cannot let Timothy search for it, lass. He be in mortal danger."

There was an intensity in his tone that struck her. She shook off his hand, a deliberate note of indifference in her voice.

"That is not my doing. I have no influence over your grandson."

"Ye ha' influence over the knight," he said shrewdly. "He can wait no longer. If he knows where it lies, he must retrieve it now. It will be lost forever if it falls into the wrong hands."

"Tell me where to find it, and I will tell Sir Stephen. If it must be found soon, he cannot waste time searching the wrong places."

Gaven sank back onto the cushions of his cot, closed his eyes against her. The mug of beer remained remarkably steady in his hand.

"It be a quest he must solve himself, lass. I cannot tell him. Nor will I. If he indeed be worthy, he will find his Grail. If he is no' worthy, 'tis best it remains forever gone from him."

A sentiment she fully shared. But Stephen Fitzhugh was not a man to surrender, and when he found the Grail he would barter it away as casually as if it were a prize mare. She said as much now, painfully, but Gaven's eyes remained closed and his breathing steady and even.

She stood up. "If you don't care, I do. Why? Why won't you help me? You know that if he finds the Grail, he will take it away, Gaven!"

When there was no answer, she turned away, filled with frustration and anguish. "If he barters away the Grail," she whispered, "I may never find it in my heart to forgive him for it."

Silence. The mill wheel rumbled and creaked, muffled by the walls. She stared out the door at the rising hump of the Tor in the distance. "Perhaps I'll find the Grail," she said softly. She turned back to look at the old man; he feigned sleep. She drew closer. "I have my own ideas where it might lie. There's more than one king said to lie beneath Glastonbury's sod, and as a child I heard the tales, too."

Gaven's eyes opened slightly. He peered at her from the slits, but remained silent. She smiled. "Faery dust and Celtic kings, cups that are never empty and sacred vessels—all share a common thread. Legend and truth intertwine."

To her disgruntled surprise, he only smiled, and his eyes closed tight again.

A vexing old man, she thought irritably as she walked home, with no scruples at all when it came to the Grail. But what should she expect from an old man who still spoke of wizards and dragons as if they were real? Perhaps there once had been such things, but they were all gone now, gone the way of the griffins and unicorns, the firedrakes that had once inhabited England long before the days of Christ.

Only old bones had been found, and those uncertain. He refused to surrender his old beliefs and convert to the new religion that was a thousand years young . . . vexing, indeed!

When she reached the foot of the Tor, Aislinn paused. Around a curve in the road was the cattle gate where Timothy had been attacked. To the right were the steep ridged slopes of the Tor, and to her left, lay the abbey grounds. At the summit of the Tor, old stones marked a sacred spot where it was rumored the Old Ones once held human sacrifices. More like, it was the occasional bullock or goat, but much had been corrupted in memories of the old ways.

Timothy had come here in the quiet darkness of night to find the Grail. Why?

Deep in thought, she stood silently; the wind carried the sound of children's laughter to her, and she smiled. It was a lovely day, the play of children a fond memory of her own childhood.

Two young girls came running up the hill, laughing as they carried small buckets of water that sloshed over the sides and wet their shoes. One of the girls was breathless with laughter, her cheeks pink. Dark brown curls tumbled around her face, and as they reached Aislinn they came to a halt.

"Did you see our friend, Mistress?" the dark haired girl asked with a giggle.

"Your friend? No, I've not seen anyone on the road. Is she lost?"

Another giggle erupted and both girls covered their mouths with their hands. "She's not lost, she's scared," the other girl offered.

"Scared. What would frighten her on such a lovely day as this?"

"We told about the dragon in the well, and she dropped her bucket. When she went to get it, Rannilt made a funny noise and Suisan thought it was the dragon. She ran away and left her bucket in the well."

"I see." Aislinn studied them gravely, trying to recall if she had ever been quite so mischievous as a child. "And what will happen when Suisan goes home without the water or her bucket?"

Eyes grew wide, and the girls exchanged glances. "We could go back and get it for her," Rannilt said. "Then she may feel better."

"That's the charitable thing to do, and she is your friend so it will make you all feel better."

"Will you go with us? We don't want the dragon to get us."

"Yes, I'll come and help you." Aislinn smiled as the two girls skipped ahead of her, water thoroughly wetting their shoes and hems. It would be a miracle if any water actually reached their homes.

As they reached the steep lane that led to the well, one of the girls set down her bucket and ran ahead. Near the bottom of the incline, water ran down a rock wall, gathered in a small basin, leaving deep reddish stains on the rock.

"See?" Rannilt said, pointing, "it's dragon's blood! We told her and she didn't believe us. Is that what makes the water red, Mistress? Is it dragon's blood as everyone says?"

Aislinn studied the stains gravely. "It's possible, of course. Dragons, firedrakes and griffins once roamed all of England, I'm told. Perhaps one is trapped in the well after all. . . ."

Both girls grew still, eyes wide with excited fear.

Aislinn hid a smile. "Where is Suisan's bucket? I don't see it here."

"Oh, not this well, Mistress. The other well has the dragon in it."

"The other well?"

"At the foot of the Tor. You know the one. This way."

"That well is closed," Aislinn said, vaguely alarmed that the children would go there. "It's dangerous."

"Yea, so we told Suisan!"

She bit her lip to disguise a smile. "The danger comes mostly from children falling in and not being able to get out. Does your mother know you go to that well?"

Silence was ample answer, and Aislinn sighed. "Come. We'll get Suisan's bucket, then you must promise not to go near that well again. It's supposed to be covered with boards."

"Some of them have rotted away, Mistress. The water there is *enchanted*. Oh, it's true. My brother told me. It belongs to the king of the faeries, Sim says, and anyone who drinks from it will never go hungry and never be sick. That is why the king set the dragon to guard it, so he can keep it all for himself."

Aislinn stared at the child's earnest face. The king of the faeries lived beneath the Tor, and it was there the Celtic cup of life was kept—a fable, of course, but if the well was fit for the cup of a faerie king, why not a fit place for the chalice?

Why not, indeed! And complete with a dragon to guard it from intruders. . . .

Deep in a thicket of bushes and trees on a rocky slope, the well was ringed by rocks, and a steep wall of rock rose to one side. The well was half covered with old boards that had rotted in places and been pulled away. Aislinn knelt, peered into the well. Several feet below, water shimmered in a dark glow, reflecting her face, a blur of light brown hair and pale skin. Suisan's bucket was barely visible at one side, tilted awkwardly on some kind of rock shelf.

Stretched out on her stomach, she reached down and hooked the edge of the bucket with her fingers, gingerly drawing it closer until she could grasp the leather handle. She eased it up and rolled over, holding it to her. It was completely dry.

Sitting up, she gave the bucket into the keeping of the girls. "Fill it at the other well, and do not come back to this one unless your mother is with you. It's far too dangerous here, far too dangerous."

"Is it the *dragon*?" Rannilt whispered with a slight quiver in her voice. Her glance at the well was apprehensive.

"Yes," she said with no compunction, and was rewarded with terrified gasps and immediate retreat from the edge of the well. It was difficult not to laugh at the expressions of dismay on their faces, but if it took a dragon to keep them from danger, then a dragon it would be.

When they were gone she pried up one of the boards and leaned into the well. Her heart gave a peculiar thump. At one side, tucked into rock, there seemed to be a chamber of some sort. Thick cobwebs veiled the opening, a sign that it had not been used in some time.

Unlikely miracle . . . but what if it's real? What if this dragon-guarded well truly holds the Grail?

This well had been built by the Old Religion, the Old Ones, the Druids who had once lived in Somerset. Painted men, ancient Celts, the Picts, and the Britons had all invaded and been invaded. The Druids were long gone now, leaving behind mysterious evidence of their inhabitance: huge standing stones on the chalk downs of Wiltshire, which she had seen once when her uncle had taken her to Canterbury with him, and smaller stone rings that served unknown purposes, countless remnants of wells and cairns such as the one atop the Tor—all reminders of a forgotten time.

As was this well. She'd heard Gaven speak of it as the bridge to the underworld. Why had she not remembered it before now?

But perhaps Brother Timothy had remembered it. . . .

She visited him in the infirmary, once more prevailing upon Brother Arnot's kindness, and found the young monk restless and agitated.

"Mistress!" he said when he saw her approach, and he tried to sit up in his narrow cot. Candles flickered in holders at his head, and the smell of herbs was pungent and familiar.

"No, no, Brother Timothy, you must lie still or I fear

Brother Arnot will cast me out. He has a high regard for his patients, you know."

Timothy clung to her hand, stared up at her with anxious eyes. "The Knights Templar are here!"

"Yes, so we have discussed. Calm yourself, Brother. They are in the king's envoy and bring word of his death to Father Prior and Ralph Fitzstephen. Lie still. You are working yourself into a fever."

"Listen to me," he hissed and jerked at her arm to bring her closer, "they are no messengers—they have come here for the Grail!"

"Have you heard them say it then?"

"No. Not to me. But I overheard Father Prior—he has tried to convince them it is not here, but they are most insistent. There were letters from King Henry about King Arthur's grave being here, and the Templars are instructed to continue the search to honor the dead king's wishes."

"King Arthur's grave and the Holy Grail are not one and the same, Brother Timothy."

He calmed slightly. "That is true, Mistress. Yea, that is true."

"And I think *you* know that the Grail does not lie with King Arthur, or with any other king, don't you, Brother?"

Startled, he flashed her a guilty look before closing his eyes and lying back upon his soft cushions.

"And I also think," Aislinn said softly, "that you took the pages of Abbot Robert's journals from my hall. Was it you outside my window that night?"

For a moment, the monk lay there, pale as the white linen beneath him, then he nodded, a brief jerk of his chin.

"Yes, Mistress Aislinn, to my shame I did take those pages." His eyes flew open. "But I did not harm them!"

"Did you learn from them? Did you unravel the mystery of my uncle's riddles?"

Thin fingers plucked at a loose thread in the sheet over him, and he looked miserable. "At first I could not make sense of any of them, but then I remembered tales my grandfather used to tell around the fire of an evening. I remembered how he said the gate to the underworld was right here in Glastonbury, on the slopes of the Tor. 'The keys to the kingdom. . . .' It was the Old Religion who built the well, of course, but I wondered—"

"And I think you were right, Brother Timothy." She put a hand atop his bony arm, thin in the loose tunic he wore over his bandaged torso. "I went there this afternoon."

"Did—did you see anything?"

"I saw that there is a chamber in the well. What reason would there be for a chamber if it's not to hold something precious?"

"Mistress—" He clutched at her arm, cast a beseeching glance at her. "I wanted to be the one to find the Grail. It would ensure my place at the abbey forever. I could never be sent away then, and I . . . I might even be given an office."

"Do you aspire to the office of prior, then?" She laughed at the look of horror in his eyes and said, "Be calm, Brother, for it was only a jest."

As he relaxed slightly she said, "I want the Grail for the Holy Mother Church. It matters not to me if you are named benefactor. All that matters is that it be revered as it should be. When it's found, I will bring it to you, and let you present it to the prior, as you like."

A faint flush rode his high cheekbones. "You shame me, Mistress Aislinn. I have ill-used you."

"All is forgiven and forgotten, if you will regain your strength. Now." She straightened. "We cannot wait for that to happen. I must retrieve it as soon as possible."

"You intend to go into the well, Mistress? A misstep could be dangerous." He frowned. "Don't forget, someone put a knife into my back. Take Master Weaver with you. He can protect you."

"Master Weaver has difficulty escaping garden voles. No, I think that I shall ask Brother Arnot to accompany me. He is most discreet, and very sensible. Would that be acceptable to you?"

"Indeed it would, Mistress. I have a great respect for Brother Arnot. He has been more kind to me than anyone here, except perhaps Brother Daniel, who sees to it that the cats are well fed with kitchen scraps."

A gentle soul, Aislinn thought with a faint smile, for all that he harbored such fierce determination in his thin body.

"Get well, Brother Timothy. I shall seek Brother Arnot and present him with my suggestion."

She did not tell him of Gaven's insistence that Stephen Fitzhugh must find the Grail. The knowledge would only hurt him. Soon, it would no longer matter who had found it, only that it had been found at Glastonbury where Joseph of Arimathea had left it. The abbey would have a superior claim upon the relic that no other church save Rome could make, for if the uncle of Christ thought it belonged here, there was little doubt the pope would consent.

And once the Grail was properly honored, Stephen would reconcile himself to the fact that he could not have it. It would be a bitter thing to accept, but he was, she had observed, a practical man. Cynics usually were.

Pulling her hood over her head, she left the infirmary in search of Brother Arnot.

Chapter 26

✝

DEEP SHADOWS TIPTOED over rock and brush, crept through trees with damp familiarity. Stephen waited beneath the dark shelter of a yew. Garbed in black, he watched for the last of the thin light to fade from the sky. There would be only a short wait before the moon rose. Clouds were scant, the sky still blue and purple streaked.

He needed moonlight to illuminate his deeds, darkness to hide them from watchful eyes.

It was quiet in the thicket, the soft murmur of birds settling for the night a gentle melody. If he succeeded tonight, he would leave Glastonbury in the morning.

But not forever.

He thought of Aislinn as he had last seen her, lying in her bed with the early light a soft glow around her. She had not watched him go, but turned her face to the wall, her shoulders hunched in a sorrow that he felt keenly.

He'd wanted to promise he'd be back, but more fiercely, he wanted to stay in the bed with her and never leave.

Yet it was an impossibility to do either.

Promises were too easily made and too easily broken, and he'd already broken faith with her once. He didn't want to risk another blow to a trust that was already frayed.

If there was only another way, another choice to make—but there wasn't. Essex would never grant him Dunmow if he failed to get the Grail.

The Grail—it had become an obsession. It burned in him with an unholy flame, even more so now. If he failed Essex, he failed Aislinn. How could he ask her to share a life spent living by the sword? He could not. It would destroy her in the end, just as it had destroyed a piece of her to be named harlot in the village.

Blame Mistress Margaret for that, and he would see to it that the hag received her just reward for that evil work.

But now he must succeed, or all would be lost. There was little time. With the Knights Templar at the abbey, he dared not delay.

Another piece of bad fortune, that King Henry should die and these knights be among the envoy come to the abbey. Those warrior monks were single-minded in their pursuit of a goal, and ruthless in purpose. They lived by the sword and for the sword, with God's grace as their shield. They did not fear death, and were more dangerous because of it. If they had come for the Grail, no man would be allowed to stand in their way for long.

He had heard of the exhortation by Bernard, Abbot of Clairvaux, in which he had written to the Knights Templar how blessed it was to die a martyr in the service of God. The killing of an enemy was justified if it was for a good cause.

The Holy Grail would certainly qualify as a just cause.

Now time ran short and this was his last hope. If the Grail was not here, he knew of no other place to look.

He thought of the old man he'd met in Cornwall, on a

coast with fierce winds that carved rocks into grotesque shapes. Surf was an endless roar on that coast, oft obliterating the puny efforts of man to leave a lasting memory. Ruined towers and castles were testaments to the power of the sea and the short tenure of man.

Over a peat fire, the old man had shared his ale and told him of the great King Arthur, echoing the tales Gaven had told for the most part. But he had not relayed his tales in riddles, and was glad to answer questions.

And it was that old man who had told him of the well said to contain the chalice used by Jesus at the Last Supper, and how it had been brought to Glastonbury by Joseph of Arimathea after Christ's death. Joseph had been a tin merchant living in Palestine when Jesus was a child, and he had often brought his nephew with him when he docked his ships along the coast of Cornwall. After the death of Jesus on the cross, Joseph journeyed again to Cornwall, bringing with him the Holy Grail, which now contained drops of the blood of Jesus. This he took to Glastonbury, where Druid priests gave him land to build the first Christian church in the West that would be above the ground, not hidden away in some dark hole for fear of persecution.

Before his own death, Joseph hid the Grail beneath the Tor, and a well was said to spring forth on that spot. When death was imminent, Joseph was said to have cast the Grail into that bottomless well, where it had been for nearly twelve hundred years, safe from those who would use it for ill.

Safe from men like Essex. . . .

Stephen thought of Aislinn and her unshakable faith— the Grail was the holiest of relics to her, precious for its origins rather than its rumored powers.

He stared at the well beyond the leafy bushes. It was unimaginable to him that a cup could summon such dangerous men and devout women. A miracle, indeed.

As shadows claimed the land, blurring the line of sky and earth, a lopsided moon wobbled above the horizon. It shed wavery light, silvery and brittle. He rose to his feet and began to uncoil the length of rope he'd brought. It was sturdy and thick, a stout line for his purposes. He secured it to the broad trunk of a yew tree and tossed the free end into the well.

A deep hush descended upon the thicket, birds were silent and even the wind was still. An eerie waiting seemed to settle among the trees and rocks.

Testing the rope with several strong tugs, he satisfied himself that it would hold and moved to the edge of the well. Loose rock spilled into water far below, loosened by his removal of the boards, and sank with soft plunks.

Slowly, he lowered himself over the side, boots braced against the uneven cobbled walls. Dank and musty, claimed by darkness that the moon could not penetrate, he felt his way to the side, hands scraping over mossy rock.

The chamber was there, as the old man had said it would be, and he slid into it with a grunt of effort. It was tight and narrow, the ceiling low so that he had to bend his head to stand. He secured the loose end of the rope to his wrist to keep it near and fumbled in the pouch at his waist for the flint and candle he had brought for light.

Several sparks struck, then caught at last on the tinder, and he quickly lit the candle. An ellipse of light shimmered, spread a soft glow in the cavern, flickered over walls that glowed with eerie incandescence. As his eyes adjusted, he saw that a shelf had been carved into rock, and the corbeled sides reflected the candlelight in thousands of glittering chips. He blinked, leaned close to peer at the reflective surface, rubbed at it with his free hand. Crystals. Points of light gleamed red and blue and green as he lifted the candle, until he felt as if he were standing in the midst of a rainbow.

Awed, he stood staring at the beauty of the cavern. The flame of his candle flickered, steadied, grew into a bright light as of a thousand torches, until he put up a hand to shade his eyes. He suddenly remembered the powder Gaven had sprinkled on his hand, and how it had shone with just such a brilliance.

The old trickster. . . .

Had he been here, then, the old man? Had he always known of this chamber? There were those who knew of it, like the old Cornishman who was content to let it lie in peace. Or perhaps he believed the Grail was not here, an empty chamber all that he would find.

And it seemed as if he may be right, for there was no sign of a cup or chalice, just the crystal walls and shelf. He stood still, studied the walls that angled upward in an unbroken luster. The illusion of color was just that, for as the candle moved, so did the glints of red, green, and blue.

He turned slowly, holding the candle high, watching for a break in the seamless brilliance.

It was a swift flicker, a subtle alteration in the glow of crystals that caught his attention, and he paused. He moved the candle back again, glimpsed the darker shift of light, and leaned forward to touch the spot. His hand met a small protuberance, and he felt along it carefully. There seemed to be something different here, something other than wall.

He bent, scooped up a handful of dirt from the chamber floor, and cast it over the wall. Dulled by the darker dust, the shelf stood out in relief at once, obvious now that he had found it. And atop the shelf, a crystal casket gleamed, small and undisturbed for a thousand years.

Despite his cynicism, his doubts and disbelief in the workings of man, there was inherent wonder in the mystery of God. His hand shook as he brushed away the dirt and lifted the casket from the shelf. It was small, light, modest with no gold or jewels to adorn the curved lid.

Hardly worthy of the Son of God, but suitable for a tin maker.

Awkwardly, with the rope still tied to his wrist and the candle in one hand, he fumbled with the latch and lifted the lid. At first he thought it was empty, but then he saw the silver vessel that lay on a bed of blue-green moss.

With unfamiliar reverence, he lifted the small chalice in his hand, studied the simple curved lines of bowl and stem. It fit his palm easily, this unadorned cup that bore only a thin line of gold around the rim of the bowl and an ancient decorative gold knot on the curved side. Worthless in value, save for the man who had used it at the most famous meal of all time.

Holding it up, he thought of all the men who had searched for this Grail, who had risked and lost their lives to possess it. It seemed so ordinary, a humble cup that would earn not even an interested glance were it not for the legend that made it extraordinary.

And oddly, it was that very humility that awed him more than a vessel crusted with precious jewels and made of solid gold.

Carefully, he replaced the cup in the small casket and closed the lid.

He thought of Essex—a profane man who corrupted all he touched. He hid behind the guise of religion to work his own misdeeds, used the church as a sanctuary to justify greed.

Aislinn was right. The Grail did not belong to men like Essex. Even if it did not possess the power to restore life and lend immortality, it should not be left in the hands of a man who would misuse it.

Uncertainty settled on him like a shroud. If he did not yield up the Grail to Essex, Dunmow would be lost to him forever. But at what price?

His soul he had always considered unsalvageable, for it had been lost to him years before, buried beneath anger and resentment, the rejection of the church a rebellion against the pain he had been forced to endure at the hands of impious men.

And then he had found Aislinn.

A sweet, bright light in the darkness of his life, a woman of hope and beauty, of steady faith despite trials. She had humbled him, given him glimpses of a world that he had never thought he could attain.

She offered love, when he had known nothing but hate for years. But what could he offer her, other than a life of aimless wandering? He was not the kind of man to be content plowing fields or tending sheep. He had been reared in a knight's household, taught the skills of a knight from an early age, and it was all he knew, all he could give. Of what use was that to a woman?

Candle wax dripped over his hand, hot, reminding him that he tarried too long.

Tucking the casket into the pouch at his waist, he moved to the mouth of the chamber. The rope on his wrist was loose, and he gave it a sharp tug to renew the tension for his climb to the top of the well.

To his shock, the rope slithered free, falling into the well below him, one end still tied to his wrist. He lifted the candle, saw light dance across dark water, then turned to look up. A light shimmered at the top, a pale glow as of a lantern. Shadows briefly blocked it, moved away, then returned.

He knew, even before he heard, what to expect.

"Send up the Grail," Aislinn called down, "and we will throw you another rope."

His mouth set into a taut line. "And if I do not?"

There was a brief silence, and then her voice came down to him, distorted by rock and water: "If you do not, you'd best learn to like living in a well."

He almost laughed. "If it's good enough for the king of the faeries, I suppose I can learn to adjust."

"Stephen, do not be stubborn. You must know that you cannot take the Grail with you."

"Are you so certain there is a Grail to be found? We have chased shadows before, mouse."

Irritation edged her reply. "You have it. I know you do. Send it up to me."

Perversely, despite his indecision on whether to give it to Essex, he resented her demand.

"If you want it, mouse, you will have to come down and get it from me."

There was a whispered conversation, and he wondered who she had brought with her, felt a spurt of alarm that she had placed herself in danger, then she was leaning back over the opening of the well.

"If I come down to get it, will you give it to me freely? Do I have your word of honor as a knight?"

"As a knight? Certainly." A farce . . . he had long ago broken his knight's vows, and breaking another would hardly matter now.

"Then I'm coming down."

Leaning back against the crystal wall, he smiled darkly into the damp shadows as he waited.

Chapter 27

✝

HE HAD WEDGED the candle into a niche in the wall. Light danced and skirted shadows, gleamed on crystal shards and glittered on the black water of the well. Aislinn's palms were damp as she clung to the rope. It was tied around her waist for safety's sake, but she was still afraid.

A plunge into that murky water would be terrifying. She had never learned to swim and would sink like a stone, descending into black eternity in a well that had no bottom.

As she was lowered by little jerks of the rope, she came even with the mouth of the chamber and Stephen. He gave her one of his ironic smiles.

"How pleasant of you to drop in, mouse."

"Give me the chalice, if you please."

"Ah, and if I don't please?"

She stared at him. "You swore on your honor as a knight you would yield it to me!"

"Of all people, you should be aware that I have little

use for honor. It makes a cold supper and a hard bed. But," he added when she gave a sound of frustration, "I'll make a bargain with you, now that you've been so kind as to visit."

"A bargain! Stephen Fitzhugh, I should leave you down here to rot!"

"Angry words, mouse." He reached out, snared her arm in a tight clasp. "You're in a bad position for anger or bargains, I'm afraid. You'll have to trust me. No help for it, it seems."

Dangling over the water, she glanced down, felt the precariousness of her situation, and looked back at him. He met her gaze with a smile that he obviously meant to be encouraging, like a spider in a caterpillar shell, innocent and lethal.

He looked past her to the mouth of the well. "Who holds the other end of your rope? I presume you had sense enough to tie it to a tree, otherwise we might both be left down here to break bread with the faerie king."

"Brother Arnot is quite sensible," she said coldly, "and tied the rope to a stout yew. I shouldn't have trusted you to keep your word, I see."

"Yes," he agreed, "it seems that way. Do make up your mind, mouse, for if we're to discuss the proper disposition of the Grail above ground, we might want to get at it fairly soon. There are others who would be most intrigued to learn what we have found."

"Very well." She swung a foot toward him. "You go up first, while I hold the Grail. While I'm not at all certain I can trust you to bring me up, I'm quite certain you'll be glad to retrieve the Grail."

"You wound me deeply, mouse." His smile was slightly crooked, but he gave a careless shrug. "Won't Brother Arnot be surprised to see the fish he lands."

He pulled her into the chamber, and she found that her legs were weak-kneed when she stood at last on solid ground. His hands lingered on her waist, and she pushed him away, then braced herself against the wall, caught by the beauty of the candlelit crystals.

"It's lovely! It's almost spiritual here, as if I'm in the presence of God. . . ."

"Yes. Quite inspirational. Untie the rope, please. I have an uneasy feeling we've wasted too much time down here. I'd hate for the faerie king to demand the return of his cup, you know."

"Irreverent knave," she muttered, but obliged by untying the rope with clumsy haste. "Ah ah," she said when he stepped toward the lip of the chamber, "first give me the Grail or I will tell Brother Arnot to cut the rope when you're halfway up."

"Vicious lady," he murmured with a taut, strange smile, "I think I've taught you better than I meant."

"Hard lessons to learn, but necessary. The Grail, if you please—or even if you don't please, but I think you're in no position to be too surly about it."

"Enjoy your triumph while you can," he said as he opened the pouch at his waist and removed a small casket, "and don't mind about me. I'm sure I'll be fine."

"I'm sure you will. You always are." She took the casket from him with trembling hands, looked up to find him staring at her with an expression almost like relief. "It's for the best," she said softly, "you know it is. You're a much better man than you credit."

She thought he was going to make one of his caustic comments, but he only smiled and said, "I hope you're right, mouse."

Taking the rope, he began to climb. Hand over hand he pulled himself up with swift, strong movements, a dark shadow against darker shadows. She watched until he reached the top, and she saw him pull himself over the lip and then disappear.

She looked down at the casket in her hands and gave

it a slight shake. It rattled. Her fingers trembled with awe and reverence. The Holy Grail. At last. The greatest prize in all Christendom lay in her hands. It was an answer to a prayer, a sacrifice and homage, and she felt the burn of tears in her eyes.

Taking it for the church was the right thing to do. He would never have given it the honor it deserved, and now pilgrims could come from near and far to worship and receive the blessings of the church.

It had been here all the time, tucked away in this well where men had forgotten to search.

When she heard voices above, she carefully put the casket into the cloth bag slung around her neck. The length of rope unwound toward her from above and she tied it around her waist. Then she looked up expectantly.

There was no pull on the rope, or face peering into the well. It looked dark, save for thin moonlight. Where were the lanterns they had brought? She waited patiently, but not even Brother Arnot appeared to pull her up, and she began to fret.

Doubts formed, but she resisted them. Brother Arnot wouldn't leave her here, and certainly Stephen would not. It was unlikely he would have overpowered the monk. Determined to have the Grail he may be, but he also loved her. She was certain of that. They may disagree on this important issue, but he wouldn't allow that to place her in danger. Nor would he be so cruel as to frighten her just to recover the Grail. It would be far too easy for him to take it away from her by force, and she doubted he would even do that.

But still, as time passed and neither Stephen nor Brother Arnot drew her from the well, fret turned to panic. The candle was burning low, and deep shadows dulled the bright beauty of the crystals. To be left alone in the dark bowels of the earth was a fate she could not contemplate, and she finally called out with only a hint of fear:

"I am ready, Brother Arnot!"

A moment later, light appeared at the mouth of the well and she blew out a sigh of relief when it was superimposed by a man's silhouette. Tension drew the rope taut, and she clung to it with both hands as she was slowly pulled upward, twisting slightly in the air as she was suspended over the water far below.

Hands reached out to help her as she reached the top at last, and she was lifted up and set on her feet. Lanterns cast light and shadow around the thicket, illuminating rocks and men. She paused uncertainly, heart thumping in sudden alarm.

Stephen stood between two men in the garb of Knights Templar, white surcoats bearing a red cross on their chests. Stephen looked grimly mocking.

"It seems that we are not the only ones searching for the Grail," he said softly, and her heart sank.

"Mistress," one of the knights said, not unkindly but firmly, "yield up the prize. We mean you no harm."

"This belongs to Glastonbury," she said with a lift of her chin, "and it will remain here. There will be no conflict over its proper place, for it has been here a thousand years already, and here it shall stay."

"Pardon, Mistress, but that is not your decision to make." The knight's voice had taken a hard edge. He held out a hand. "You will give it to me now."

"I will not. I will deliver it to Father Prior, and he will decide its disposition."

"It is not for Father Prior to decide." The knight took a step forward. "This is no time to be foolish, woman. We will have the Grail, will ye or nill ye allow it. Give it up."

"Give it to them, Aislinn," Stephen said suddenly, and when she shook her head, he snapped, "Do not argue!"

"And why should I not argue?" Near tears, she held the casket to her chest fiercely. Grief clogged her throat and eyes. "You know they will take it away, when it belongs at the abbey."

Brother Arnot spoke up. "No, Mistress Aislinn, they have promised to honor the abbey with the Grail."

One of the knights turned toward him. "We made no such vow, Brother. It goes with us. It belongs to the Templar Order now, where it will be protected. It would be too dangerous to leave it at an abbey where enemies of God can easily take it."

With a soft cry, Brother Arnot stepped forward. "No! It belongs here, as was promised! I did not go to such lengths to keep it safe to lose it now . . . you swore an oath to me that it would be—"

"No, Brother," the knight said harshly, "we swore an oath to honor and reverence the Grail, to keep it safe and where it is meant to be."

"It is meant to be here!" Brother Arnot's face was contorted with rage. "Joseph of Arimathea brought it here to Glastonbury because he believed it belonged here. You cannot take it away. . . ."

Brother Arnot moved swiftly and reached Aislinn before she could move. In the scant light there was a brief glitter of metal as he swung his arm upward, held something cold against her throat. Stephen lunged forward but was held back by one of the Templars.

Brother Arnot tightened his grip on her. "Do not," he warned, "or I will see her slain."

Frozen with fear, Aislinn felt him pull her with him away from the edge of the well. His arm was around her waist, a dagger pressed against her throat.

"Mistress," he said against her ear, "do not struggle. I do not want to hurt you, but I will not allow them to take the Grail from here."

Her hand came up to grip his wrist, and the blade pressed harder against her throat.

"Brother Arnot . . . why are you doing this?" She stumbled slightly as he pulled her along backward, and he jerked her against him. "Please . . . it's not worth your soul to keep the Grail here."

"He has no intention of leaving the Grail at the abbey, Aislinn," Stephen said softly. "Do you, Brother?"

A harsh laugh curled past her ear, and Brother Arnot gave her a vicious tug over a fallen log. "You are more clever than you appear, Sir Stephen."

"Very gratifying," Stephen said dryly, and this time when he took a step away from the Templar, the knight let him go.

"Don't come any closer, I warn you," Brother Arnot said sharply, "or your lady love will die."

"Kill her," Stephen said, "and you will pray for death to release you from your suffering long before you join her."

Aislinn closed her eyes. The menace in Stephen's tone was unmistakable. Brother Arnot had halted, his back against a high rock wall covered in brush. She could smell heather and gorse and knew they were near the road to the Tor.

Stephen paused. The three knights were silent, watchful and tense, their faces betraying nothing. Her heart thudded painfully, and she could feel the tremble of the monk's arm muscles as he held her like a shield against his chest.

"If you slay me, Brother," she murmured, "they will surely slay you."

He made a choking sound like a sob. "Keep silent, Mistress, and you are in no danger. I have no desire to damn my soul for all eternity. But neither do I desire to stay in England any longer than I must. Obey my commands, and I will send you back as soon as I am safely away."

She understood then. "You take the Grail to Wales."

"Yea, that I do. Little enough have the Welsh under Henry's rule, and this holy vessel will earn our freedom and salvation. It was a God-sent miracle, a sign that it's here."

"You never meant for it to remain at the abbey, did you? Why have you not taken it before now?"

His arm tightened slightly around her, cutting off her breath. "For the simple reason I did not know where to find it. If not for Brother Timothy's quick mind—"

Stephen said sharply, "It was you who stabbed Brother Timothy," and Aislinn gave a gasp of shocked surprise.

"I did not try to kill him!" Brother Arnot cried. "I only meant to stop him from telling anyone about the Grail, but he turned and almost saw me so I struck out at him a little harder than I meant. I did not stab him, I swear it!"

He was quivering and tense, and Aislinn feared he would press too hard with the dagger's blade against her throat. The weight of the casket was heavy in the cloth around her neck, and she shifted slightly so that it moved to one side.

"Brother," she whispered, "you are not a sinful man. It is understandable that you wish to help your own people. I am certain that Father Prior will—"

"Father Prior! An obscene jest, mistress, to even think he would lift a hand to help. He cares only for his position and his belly. Peevish man, a blight on the Benedictine house, yet he is cosseted and cajoled, while others who are more worthy must stand idly by and be humble."

"I do not argue that the prior has his faults, but so do we all." She slipped a stealthy hand into the bag holding the Grail, closed her fingers around the casket. She had no intention of being dragged to Wales.

As Brother Arnot worked his way along the rock wall toward the hedges that bordered the road, she managed to tug the casket free of the bag. She glanced up, saw Stephen watching her intently, and he gave a slight nod of his head.

They had reached the end of the hedge fence, and she flung out an arm, letting the casket sail through the air.

"No!" Brother Arnot screamed, releasing her as he lunged after the casket.

But Stephen caught it deftly in one hand, pulling out his sword with the other. "You can come and try to take it," he offered softly when Brother Arnot stumbled to a halt.

Moonlight gleamed on the wicked blade of his sword, a lethal warning, and Aislinn quickly scuttled away before the monk could turn back on her.

Nearly weeping, Brother Arnot fell to his knees, the dagger tumbling from his hand to clatter on rock. She saw with a start of surprise that it was her eating dagger he carried. The jeweled hilt gleamed in pale light.

She gazed at the monk with growing sympathy, though she was appalled that he had been so heinous as to stab Brother Timothy. Never had she thought one of the brothers would do such a thing, though she had always known they were prone to the same human emotions as the secular world.

Giving him a wide berth, she walked toward Stephen, where he stood near the well holding the Grail. His sword was still unsheathed.

"I don't think he's a threat," she murmured. "You can put away your weapon."

"No," Stephen said in an odd tone, "I don't think I'll do that just yet."

She gave him a sharp glance. He stood with legs spread wide apart, balanced as if for attack, the sword held in front of him and ready.

"What are you doing?" she demanded.

"Saving the Grail from unholy brethren, mouse."

Aghast, Aislinn stared at him. "You've run mad. These are Knights Templar, Stephen Fitzhugh! You cannot mean to attack men of God!"

"Why not? They haven't minded attacking me."

She looked at him uncertainly. "They haven't attacked you, though they have held you back."

"Ah, but you are quite mistaken, mouse. I've met that man"— he pointed with the tip of his sword at one of the Templars—"on the road near Cadbury. You were in rather a hurry to leave, as I recall, so missed the pleasure of making his acquaintance. I, however, had the misfortune of close association with the rogue."

The Templar snorted. "Were I to have met you on any road, Sir Stephen, you would not now be here braying like an ass. Put down your weapon and hand over the Grail, and we'll not take you to task for your impudence."

"Of course," Stephen said as if the knight had not spoken, "you were wearing a monk's garb then instead of the red cross you wear now. Neither of the garments suit you."

Aislinn began to understand.

One of the men cursed softly, took a step forward. "You will give us the Grail, or we will take it from you. Then you will lose both the Grail and your life."

"I think," Stephen said, "that you intend to kill us all anyway. I much prefer dying on my own terms. Aislinn, come here. Give him a wide berth, love, for he has no more honor than any cutthroat on the roads these days."

She did as he bade her do and reached his side safely. He put her slightly behind him. "Come along, Brother Arnot, or do you wish to stay here with these wolves? They'll tear you to pieces given half a chance, but the choice is yours."

Brother Arnot, still on his knees, looked up. Tears streaked his face. "I have grievously sinned . . . and am not worthy to live."

"Let God judge that, Brother."

"Yes." Brother Arnot looked down at his hands for a

moment, held out in front of him as if pleading, and nodded. "Yes, God will indeed judge me."

One of the outlaw knights stepped forward, halted when Stephen swung to face him. "Do you hide behind a woman?" he mocked. "A knight of the crown? Come. Leave go of her skirts and fight for honor and the Grail."

"Three against one is hardly a fight—it's a massacre. I have no illusions about my chances against men of no honor such as you." Stephen put an arm behind him, pressed the casket into Aislinn's hands. "Throw down your swords."

"I think," the outlaw said with a curl of his lip, "that we will keep them. And we will keep the Grail, and we will keep the woman as well since you prefer to resist."

Steel hissed as swords were drawn, and Aislinn clutched at Stephen's tunic in terror. He wore no mail, only a leather hauberk that she could feel beneath the wool. He'd be killed by these men!

Quickly, without pausing to think, she flung herself toward the well, fell over a root or rock and smashed to her knees, but held an arm out over the opening. The crystal casket gleamed in the light of the moon and lanterns, suspended over the bottomless waters of the well.

"Throw down your swords or I'll drop it!" she cried between pants for air.

She heard Stephen curse softly behind her.

"I mean it," she said, "I mean it. You may kill us, but what if he kills one of you? Two of you? If the Grail is at the bottom of the well, it will do you no good then."

Silence descended. Her knees hurt where she had smacked them against rock, and her arm trembled with strain and fear as she held the casket over the well. It was small, light, but it felt as heavy as a great stone right now.

"Give it to me," one of the knights said, "and we will free you."

"No. I don't believe you."

"Well, what would you have us do?" he demanded harshly. "I have said you may go free if you give up the Grail."

"Two of you must throw your swords into the well. Once you are disarmed, I will place the Grail here, on the edge of the well, where Sir Stephen will guard it until Brother Arnot and I are at the road. Then he will join us and leave you with the prize."

"A singular idea, mouse," Stephen said, "but what will you do if I decide to take the Grail?"

It was said lightly, but she shot him a frowning glance. "I'm certain that yon knight would take exception to such a betrayal. He will still have *his* sword."

Stephen laughed softly. "There you have it. An impossible choice. What will you do, Sir Rogue? Will you chance it? I may take the Grail, or you may kill me and take the Grail. Or if you tarry too long in making a decision, she will probably drop it anyway, as her arm quivers even now."

It was true. Her arm shook from the effort of holding out the casket, and Aislinn did not bother to hide it.

Cursing again, the outlaw knights conferred briefly, then agreed.

Brother Arnot collected their swords and brought them to the well, where he dropped them. There was a soft hiss before the splash, and Aislinn glanced once at Stephen as she worked her way back from the lip of the well. His face was impassive. She looked at the casket that held the Holy Grail, the most prized relic that would ever grace a church or abbey, and considered letting it drop. Would that not be better than giving it into the hands of men such as these?

But if it were dropped into that well, it would truly be gone forever. Never again would men hope for the chance to set eyes on such a precious treasure.

Slowly, she lowered her arm and set the crystal casket

on the very edge of the well. Should there be treachery, he would have only to nudge it over the edge.

Clumsily, she got to her feet, wiped her hands on the front of her kirtle, and drew in a deep breath. She faced Stephen, held his gaze with her own, prayed that he would not be hurt—or betray her trust. His dark gaze held a pale gleam, his mouth curved slightly in a smile.

"All will be well, mouse."

"If they break faith," she said, "do what you must."

"I always do. Now go, before yon rogue knights think themselves brave enough to try a new trick."

Aislinn turned to the silent monk. "Brother Arnot, please escort me to the road."

The monk gave her a tortured glance and looked back at the casket. "Mistress, they are nearly unarmed—"

"No," she said quietly, "I will not risk Sir Stephen. I have given my word."

It only remained to be seen if Stephen would keep his. . . .

Chapter 28

✝

AN UNNATURAL HUSH descended upon the thicket as light from lantern and moon threw shadows into stark relief. The casket gleamed a temptation, and he saw that these men had no intention of allowing him to leave alive.

"Where are the true Knights Templar," he asked casually after a moment, "or did you kill them?"

"They are alive. Just unclothed," the taller of the knights replied with a laugh. "And naked on a riverbank!"

"I thought as much. The only way any of you three could slay a Templar would be by poisoning. I've rarely seen more clumsy swordsmen."

"You did not acquit yourself so nobly in the wood," the man retorted harshly, "a mounted knight against men on foot! We nearly had you twice, if not for that devil horse you ride."

"Yes, Nero has a distinct dislike for vermin." He smiled at their anger, shifted slightly on the balls of his feet, sword deceptively lowered. "I taught him well."

"The woman and monk should be at the road by now. Step back and give us the Grail."

"I've been thinking about that. Mistress Aislinn often speaks unwisely. But it did seem like the most expedient way of getting her to safety, and as you knaves didn't seem to mind too much, I thought it best not to disagree. But now"—he lifted his sword—"now, I think we should agree on new rules."

"We thought you might." He grinned and held up his sword. "Now it's a bit more even, lad."

"Save for those two dogs at your side."

"The lads here won't interfere. They have no swords."

"I'm willing to wager they have a dagger or two tucked into boots and sleeves, but no matter. Come along then. Let us begin."

They circled warily for a moment, renewing estimates of the other's prowess, gauging tactics. Stephen saw the swing coming, met it with the edge of his blade, and knocked it to the side. The clash of steel was loud in the night, shriek of meeting swords a familiar sound.

It was a mere testing of the other's reaction, and after the first few swings, they got down to the serious business of fighting. It was close, brutal, heavy swords inflicting damage on each other with every swing.

Stephen was focused on his opponent—he let no distraction gain his attention, but fought with savage fury that slowly beat back the other man. Over rock and fallen log, through the brush and into the fringe of trees, they hacked at each other in the fickle light.

Finally, Stephen gained the upper hand, sent the outlaw to his knees, the sword clattering onto the ground.

"I yield!" the man panted, arms flung out to the sides as he lay on his back glaring up at Stephen, "I yield!"

"As well you might." Stephen's breath came in harsh gusts. "Your two companions have fled with the Grail."

The outlaw rolled to his side, stared at the empty thicket and the spot where the casket had been. He swore. "Curse them for dogs! They should have the hide flayed from their backs!"

"I'm sure you will when you catch up to them." Stephen took a wary step back, not quite trusting the two men not to return and attack from behind.

"You'll set me free?"

"The Grail is gone. There's no point in killing you now." He stared at him, and added softly, "But should I ever be so unfortunate as to set eyes on any of you again, I'll not be quite so considerate. And a word of warning—when you return to your overlord, you'll have need of the Grail's miracles."

Staggering and uncertain, the outlaw gave him a swift, puzzled glance as he reached for his sword. Stephen's boot came down on the hilt, holding it to the ground.

"No, I'm not fool enough for that," he said. "Go now, before I change my mind and skewer you."

When the man had disappeared, he hefted the confiscated sword in one hand, weighing it. No point in wasting good steel.

"Stephen!"

He didn't turn around, but continued to inspect the sword, wondering how men who had been good soldiers had come to be such clumsy outlaws.

"Stephen," Aislinn said again, stumbling toward him over the rocks and grass, "you let them take the Grail!"

"I thought that was what you wanted," he said mildly. "Was it not?"

She came to a halt, eyes boring holes into him until he turned to face her. "I *thought* you would best them and keep the Grail. Now it's gone, and wicked men have the most cherished treasure in all of Christendom! You were to push it into the well if all seemed lost—"

"Ah, a noble act, to save the Grail with my dying breath." He shot her a sulky glance. "Is that what you want? A hero knight who sacrifices all for the sake of honor? Forgive me for not cooperating. I've been told I'm perverse. Now it's proven true."

Moonlight lent her face a soft glow, and her lashes cast long shadows on her cheeks. She shook her head.

"Perhaps you didn't want the Grail as badly as you thought you did either," she said after a moment. "Perhaps you realize that men will commit acts of terrible wickedness to have it."

"I've always known that. It has nothing to do with why I wanted the Grail, as you well know." He slid his sword into the sheath on his belt, still holding the other one in his hand. "Aislinn, until tonight, I thought getting the Grail and Dunmow would save me. I thought it would erase all the years of pain and hatred and put everything right again. I thought . . . I thought it was what I wanted more than any other thing in the world. I might have been wrong."

"Might you?"

"Yes. When I saw you with that knife at your throat, I said a prayer."

"You did?" Surprise lit her eyes. "You prayed?"

"Actually, it was more of a bargain with God."

"A bargain! That's not a prayer, Stephen, not the way it's meant to be."

"I think God was a bit more understanding of my reasons than you obviously are." His mouth curved when she flushed. "Not to worry. I'm not that familiar with prayer, and it was probably a bit awkward for both of us."

He reached out and pulled her to him and pressed her face against his chest. The faint fragrance of roses drifted from her hair, and he smiled fiercely against her. She was so warm and precious to him. How could he ever have thought anything was more important than this?

"What about Dunmow?" she asked against his chest. "You have lost it now."

"Dunmow was my past. It was the only place I had

ever been happy. Ever felt loved. Ever wanted to stay. Memories of my mother aren't there. They're with me. I just got it all turned around."

"And now?"

"Ah, and now. Now I have memories of a certain bog marsh that are quite happy." He put his fist beneath her chin and lifted her face to his. "It's all right, Aislinn. I've discovered that it doesn't matter to me anymore."

He kissed her, a gentle kiss of renewal and promise. When he lifted his head, he saw tears on her cheeks.

"What is it, mouse?"

"I love you, Stephen Fitzhugh."

"Yes, well that's certainly a good reason to weep, I suppose," he said wryly. "Must be a confounded nuisance to love a man with no prospects of decent employment. I could make a sight better outlaw than those last, but it's an uncertain future, I fear."

Curving an arm around her shoulder, he turned her toward the well. "Did Brother Arnot return to the abbey?"

She nodded. "He swears he did not stab Brother Timothy. He's quite distraught about it all."

"He didn't stab him. I'm certain one of those pestilent outlaws took advantage of the good brother lying helpless on the ground."

"What do you think will happen to Brother Arnot, Stephen? He intends to make a full confession to Father Prior about his actions."

"Father Prior will be most unhappy about losing the Grail, no doubt. Being the sort of man he is, he may well take it out on Brother Arnot. A hefty penance, indeed."

"Well," she said with a heavy sigh, "now that King Henry is dead and Richard is king, the abbey faces an uncertain future. If it is dissolved, Father Prior will be sent elsewhere. All of them will. Poor Brother Timothy. He will be grieved."

"And you, mouse? What will you do if the abbey is no longer here?"

She looked up at him, a serious expression on her face. "I have my house. I doubt that would be taken away from me, though it is abbey property. All church property would be disposed of, save that which is entailed."

"And if the abbey were to remain? Would you still stay in Glastonbury?"

"Yes, of course. Why would I—oh. Oh, I see. I see."

"Yes. It sounds as if you do." He fell silent, stared past her to the yew trees ringing the well. It had been a foolish idea. An impulse. Why would she wed a man with nothing to offer when she could stay in her snug little hall and live comfortably if not lavishly? He had wanted to know. Now he did.

"Stephen, I didn't—"

He put a finger over her lips to silence her. "It's all right, mouse. Listen to me a moment. I have a confession to make to you." He watched her face, shadowed in the moonlight and lanterns, as he said, "I played a trick on you."

"A trick?"

"Yes, with the Grail. I still had it in my head that the only way to get what I wanted was to take the Grail to Essex in exchange for Dunmow."

"Much good that would do you now. The outlaws took the Grail."

"They took the casket."

"Yes, with the—you took out the Grail!"

"Yes, while you were still sliding down the rope, I put it back in the chamber."

"But I shook it, and it rattled." She paused, drew in a sharp breath. "You meant to deceive me."

"I did deceive you. If you'd done what any other woman would have done and opened the casket, you'd have realized that at once."

"I trusted you."

"Yes." He sighed. "I know."

She was silent for a moment. Then she looked up at him again, her gaze probing, flaying his lies and his very soul. "If I had said I didn't want to stay in Glastonbury, would you have told me about the Grail?"

He frowned. "I don't know. You didn't say that, so it doesn't matter."

"Yes, it does. It matters. Oh Stephen, I love you with all my heart, I do. But I have to know you love me more than anything else."

"I do, mouse," he said softly. "I do."

"You said you don't want Dunmow, and perhaps you don't anymore. But it will always be there in the back of your mind, the uncertainty. The question of how it would have been if you had what you've wanted for twenty years. I want you to do what you must, then come back to me. I want you to come to me when you want nothing more in this world but to spend the rest of your life with me." She put a hand on his chest, and her voice broke. "I want you to *know,* with no doubts at all, that I'll be enough for you."

He stared at her and saw nothing but his own flaws mirrored in her eyes and knew that he risked all if he left her now. But she was right. God, she was right. He had too long hated, too long wanted an elusive prize to let it go so easily. In the end, it would ruin them both if he didn't rid himself of it before he came back to her.

She took a step away from him, hands folded in front of her and her heart in her eyes. "I'm not going to look for the Grail, Stephen. As far as anyone knows, it's gone. Take it if that's what you want to do. It's your choice."

When she turned and walked away, he started to go after her but stopped. He stood there under the moonlight until the lanterns flickered and died, and it seemed as if all the lights in the world had gone out.

Part Three

Chapter 29

✝

A COLD DECEMBER wind blew around the corners of her hall, and Aislinn held out her hands to the brazier to warm them. The chill in her hall was no greater than the cold that seeped through her bones.

It was the feast day of Saint Nicholas, and also her own. She was twenty-five years of age today. A lifetime. When had she grown so old? A veritable crone now, though her body was still straight and strong, still so alive for all that she felt the weight of her years.

There had been no word from Stephen Fitzhugh, no message to give her hope. It was just as well. Hadn't she known all along that there *was* no hope?

What a fool she was to think he could change, to hope that he would choose truth over vengeance. Life over death. *Me over Dunmow.* . . .

Leaning forward, she fed another coal to the fire, watched it burn—as she burned, a cold flame that turned her heart and flesh to ice, froze out the world and left her floundering to hold on to what she'd known before, all the faith that had kept her world upright.

So many betrayals, not just Stephen, but Brother Arnot, who had yielded to the lure of the Grail just as had the outlaws. Just as she had.

How could such a holy relic incite such iniquity? There was good reason it had remained hidden from men for so long, for its very existence threatened mortal souls with eternal damnation. Temptation to achieve immortality was too great a lure, all reason lost in the pursuit of it.

True to her promise, she had not gone back to the well. There was no point in it. The Grail wouldn't be there.

A shiver tracked her spine as the wind soughed in a plaintive cry around the eaves of the house. It was such a human sound, like that of a lost child. Or soul.

Gaven said the spirits of the ancient ones kept watch over the temporal world they had once known, became part of it in shadows, winds, water. Trees held spirits, as did the very earth and rocks.

She almost believed it now.

For all that he wove such intricately imaginative tales of King Arthur and the quest for the Grail, Gaven touched on potent truth at times. It was his gift, she supposed, his offering of truth bound neatly in a web of lies. Stephen was right. One day, it would be impossible to discern fact from fantasy. One day, history may well be viewed as nothing more than the idle dreams of old men.

Above the rattle of wind at the shutters and roof, she heard the quick tapping on her door, and her heart leaped.

As always, Stephen Fitzhugh sprang immediately to her mind, and rising from her chair by the brazier, she smoothed a hand over her rumpled kirtle skirts and moved to unbar the door.

Brother Timothy's familiar form was bundled in hood and habit, and she stepped back to allow him entrance. He was shivering, and she waved him toward the brazier.

"Come. Warm yourself against the chill."

"It smells of snow," he said in a shudder, and moved

to the brazier. He held reddened, chapped hands out to the coals, palms downward. "I came to see how you fare on this special day, Mistress Aislinn."

Pleased that she had been remembered, she smiled as she closed the door against the wind. "I fare quite well, though it is indeed a day to stay inside."

She joined him at the brazier, marking that he smelled faintly of pungent herbs.

"I trust all goes well in the herbarium now, Brother?"

"Yea, though I despaired for a time that I would never learn all that Brother Arnot knew about the herbs. It has been a most instructive few months."

"Brother Arnot had many years to learn what you've been trying to learn in only a few weeks. I hope he is happy now, at the monastery in Wales. Does the new abbot approve?"

Timothy pulled back the cowl from his head. His fair hair gleamed in the light of brazier and candle branch. "He has been most patient with me."

"And Brother Prior—how fares he now that there is a new abbot?"

A smile twitched the corners of Timothy's lips. "He has been most chastened of late. Father Abbot dealt with him on several matters."

"Abbot Henry is said to be a pious man. King Richard could have done much worse."

"Aye, he is indeed pious, and fair-minded, though not patient with those who shirk their duties. Ralph Fitzstephen has been of great help in smoothing the transition."

"Yes, I can see where he would be. Perhaps the future of the abbey is no longer doubtful. The king would hardly appoint a new abbot only to dissolve the charter."

"So it seems. And there is good news to tell you, if you wish to hear it."

She laughed. "Why would I not wish to hear good news? There is little enough of that in the world these days, with rumors of another Crusade being launched."

"You do not approve of taking God's word to heathens? I'm surprised, Mistress."

"I approve of sharing that word," she said practically, "but I am not at all certain that forcing it down pagan throats on the point of a sword does much good."

"It saves their soul at the most important moment, just before they meet God."

"Ah well, we differ on method if not motive. So tell me, Brother, what good news do you bring me on this day?"

"There are two items to share with you. First, it seems that before he died, King Henry had sent an urgent dispatch to Henry de Sully as well as to Ralph Fitzstephen, with new details about the grave of King Arthur. They are to begin digging in a few months when the ground is not so hard. Father Abbot is convinced that this time it will be found."

"That is excellent news, though surprising. I thought it futile after all, but perhaps there is new knowledge that will succeed. And the second news?"

"Yes. The other . . . just a moment." He dipped a hand into his habit, came out with a small box wrapped in linen. He held it out to her. "This is to celebrate your feast day."

Pleasure warmed her, and she smiled. "It has been some time since I've received a gift. I hardly know what to say, Brother!"

"Say nothing until you have seen it." He stared at her intently. Pale eyes were shadowed, and he wore an anxious expression on his face.

"I'm quite certain I will cherish this gift," she assured him as she unwrapped the white linen cloth. Her hand smoothed over the lid of a carved box not much bigger than her palm, carved with intricate knots and studded with tiny pearls. An expensive box, more costly than a Benedictine monk sworn to poverty could manage, and she glanced up at him with a faint frown. "Brother Timothy, this is far more extravagant than I should accept."

"Fear not, Mistress. I have not committed any sins."

When she did not open it, but stood indecisively, he said softly, "Open it, and then you will understand."

Fingers trembled slightly as she fumbled at the latch, flicked it open, and tilted back the small lid. On a bed of dark velvet lay a wooden cross. It was beautifully carved, slender and studded with jeweled chips, gleaming promise and hope on velvet. She touched it reverently, and her fingers grazed a piece of parchment tucked into the lid. It bore writing.

She knew. Even before she opened that scrap of vellum to read the words, she knew. It crackled slightly as she unfolded it, spread it open, Stephen's handwriting leaping out at her.

In strong, decisive script, she read:

A cross for a cross. True faith cannot burn to ash.

The vellum shook in her grasp as she looked up at the monk. "When did you receive this?"

"Before he left. He told me if he wasn't back by the time of your feast day, to give this to you. It's made from the wood of Noah's ark, a true relic, Mistress. Most holy."

Tears stung her eyes. "Most holy, indeed."

Silence fell, the coals hissed, and outside, the wind sighed of memories and loss. Grief rose in her throat, made her want to howl her desolation aloud.

But she did not. Instead she slipped the cross onto a length of ribbon and put it around her neck. It lay upon her breast, a reminder of lost love and renewed faith.

"Mistress? Are you well?"

She looked up at Timothy, read concern in his eyes, and nodded.

"Yes, Brother Timothy, I am well. I have just been

reminded of my own words, a necessary reminder."

And now I know Stephen has gone from me forever....

✝

STEPHEN FITZHUGH RODE into the shadow of Essex Castle for the final time. Black clouds bunched darkly overhead, seemed to tangle on turrets and treetops. The Dragon's Lair. The earl awaited his return.

He was long overdue.

But there were many things long overdue. Justice, for one. Retribution. A day of reckoning that would end with one or both destroyed. He had put it off as long as he could, tarried in anguished irresolution until he was sick with it, sick to the soul and the very marrow of his bones.

He held no illusions about the conclusion of the day's work. Essex had never kept faith in his life. Nor would he now, even were Stephen to be foolish enough to put the Grail into his hands. Treachery was the earl's meat and bread, and the man who believed there was any honor in him was a fool, indeed.

There were ways to avoid total annihilation, and he had taken great pains to ward off almost certain fate. Never had he won a battle with Essex, and it was unlikely he would triumph now, but he would not go tamely to his doom.

Familiar sounds of drawbridge and gates echoed in grim reminders of finality as they closed behind him.

The earl stood behind a massive chair in his solar, and he did not acknowledge Stephen's entrance as he studied an unrolled scroll in his hands. An affectation that didn't fool Stephen for an instant. Eager impatience quivered in the gnarled hands and parchment.

Finally Essex looked up. "You found the Grail," he said tonelessly.

"I'm certain your fraudulent Templars have already given you a full report of my discovery—and their failure."

Essex smiled, a faint, thin stretching of his lips. "I have amply rewarded their incompetence."

"Have you? Ah well. I did warn them."

Rolled edges of the scroll curled with a rustling sound of impatience, and Essex held it in a fist, tapped it against his other hand. "Enough of this verbal swordplay. I would see the Grail now."

"Do you think me fool enough to hand it over without some kind of warranty against your treachery?" He shook his head. "I was taught well, my lord earl, and am not so foolish as you would like me to be."

Essex regarded him coldly, an assessing stare that had always pierced men to the marrow of their bones, for it portended tribulation and ruin.

"Very well," he said at last, "I see that you must have your little diversion. However, the outcome is inevitable."

"We agree on that, at least." Stephen watched as the earl moved to a table, lifted a silver flask, and poured wine into two goblets. He turned, held one out, and shrugged when Stephen refused. Essex curled his lip.

"You've always had the manners of a goat. Tell me what it is you want from me, Sir Stephen, before I lose patience and call my guards to get the information I require from you in a less pleasant way. There are methods guaranteed to work on the most reluctant of men."

"Yes, and I'm certain you know them all." Anger built, stone by stone, fortifying his determination. "What method did you use on my father to make him abandon my mother? The rack? Thumbscrew?"

Essex slanted him a wintry smile. "I used nothing. You don't truly think that even an earl's younger son would wed the daughter of a mere *knight*. A travesty. A farce. Did you expect that he would give up the robes of a bishop to mewl sweet words into a woman's ear? She was available to him. He took what was offered."

As Essex set the refused goblet back onto the table, Stephen moved forward, three long strides that brought him even with the earl. Essex did not retreat, but stared at him with the inbred arrogance of power and long years of rule.

"My mother was of good blood," Stephen said softly, "and she loved honestly, if not wisely. She did not deserve her fate."

"Hugh was always weak," the earl said. "He resisted his true calling, and had to be convinced of it. As the youngest son of an earl, he was promised to the church from an early age. He knew better than to rebel."

"He should never have been forced to it."

"He was *born* to it, just as you were born to your lot. *I* took you above that, you ungrateful churl, and saw to it that you had the education of a baron's son despite the fact that you were born outside wedlock. Do you think your *father* would have done so?" He gave a harsh laugh. "No, he thought only of his own misery and retreated to a cell and prayers. He was useless to me. Your mother did that to him, ruined him for anything other than a weeping eunuch."

"So you destroyed her."

Essex made an impatient motion with one hand. "Pah! I became her father's overlord when my father died. Dunmow was dead, there was no legitimate issue, and so I granted Dunmow lands and title to the church. It purchased you an education and a knight's fee. Did you think I spent my own coin on that?"

"I earned my spurs—"

"And your armor? That expense was borne by the church, in exchange for your grandfather's land and keep. Your mother should have listened to reason and taken her own vows. Instead, she chose to die."

Fury made Stephen's voice taut: "She was refused by church and monastery, and forced into the streets to die alone!"

Essex's stare was bland. "I gave her another choice. She could have accepted my offer of protection."

A shock curled down his spine. He gave a disbelieving shake of his head. "You lusted after her yourself . . . it was not Hugh you wanted to protect, but my mother you wanted to spite for refusing you. . . ."

"Your mother was a beautiful woman, but foolish. She had been ruined. Did she expect marriage? My brother Hugh would never have married her, even if he had been released from his obligations to the church. When Hugh rejected the world and his offices and retreated to a cloister, I offered Eleanor more than she deserved."

Stephen's hand tightened, and he realized he gripped the hilt of his sword. Essex glanced down, then back to his face, and a spurt of emotion flickered in those dark demon eyes for the first time.

"Enough of this, Stephen. Give me the Grail. I know you have it. An empty casket is worthless to me."

"You promised me Dunmow."

"Yes, and you shall have all of it you can inhabit, I assure you." A tight smile touched those thin lips, a travesty of humor. "Hand over the Grail. My patience wanes."

"Dear *uncle,* you must know that I need more assurance than just your word. Pardon my lack of manners, but we churls can be quite distrustful. A family failing, it seems. A trait I inherited from my father's side, no doubt."

Essex stiffened. "Your insolence has gone too far. If you will not willingly yield it to me, I will see what my captain of the guards can do to convince you otherwise."

As the earl turned to summon the guard, Stephen said softly, "Do that, and I shall see that our new king is made aware of the funds you've sent to King Philip. France is his sworn enemy, and Richard is not the lenient man his father was. . . ."

Essex turned slowly back toward him. "I hardly think a dead man can inform King Richard of anything."

"Ah, but should I not return at a specified time, a letter with names, dates, and amounts will be delivered to King Richard. He would be most disturbed to discover that monies he desires to fund his Crusade have been channeled to his enemy—and that the crown has been compromised by one of its most . . . loyal . . . barons. I'm sure he'll be disappointed, but not at a lack for how to deal with traitors. If you have not seen Richard in one of his rages, I have. It's a rare sight, my lord earl. A rare sight, indeed."

"Bastard churl! Whoreson! You would not dare."

"I do dare. I *have* dared."

Pale fury glittered from the earl's eyes, and his lips were drawn back in a feral snarl. "I should have left you in the gutter where you were born!"

"Yes, it would have worked out a deal better for you if you had. But you did not. You were unwise enough to think I could be used and discarded, as was your poor brother. But I have the blood of my father's father in me, as well as the blood of my mother's father, and I can be as devious as well as any legitimate heir. All those years in your service taught me more than you intended. I learned to observe as well as follow orders. I paid attention. And now you will pay attention."

"What," the earl ground out between his teeth, "is it you wish me to do?"

Stephen smiled. At last. Victory was within his grasp. If he didn't lose his nerve. . . .

Chapter 30

✝

THE MILL WHEEL was frozen in place. The River Brue
was a solid sheet of ice that reflected back the dull
grayness of the sky. Aislinn slipped, skidded in a rut left
by wagon wheels, and caught her balance by grasping at
a tree branch.

Icicles dangled from the evergreen needles of the yew,
broke off in her hand as she clutched at a branch, fell to
the ground with a brittle pop. She clung a moment, gasping for air, her breath a hazy cloud in front of her face.

Smoke curled up from the miller's chimney, melded
into the anonymous blur of cloud and sky. Warmth beckoned, and she progressed the last of her journey with wary
steps.

Cordelia came to the door, bundled in layers of wool.
" 'Tis a raw day to be out," she scolded as she ushered
Aislinn inside, "and all for a foul-tempered old man."

Shivering, Aislinn managed a smile. "He expects it
every year. How can I disappoint him?"

Cordelia snorted but waved her toward the back room

where Gaven waited with his usual impatience.

"Did ye bring it?"

The familiar demand in a querulous, imperative tone summoned a smile from her.

"Yea, you know I did. Here."

She placed a pouch in his eagerly outstretched palm, and saw him stare at it suspiciously.

"This not be what the crone allus sends me—what is it?"

"It's nearly the same thing. Your 'crone' has grown too infirm to continue, Gaven. I fear her days are numbered."

"She has, has she?" He nodded with the satisfaction of the aged who have outlived their contemporaries. "I allus knew I'd outlive her. I'm fit as a young man, save for me eyes."

"And you see better than you admit," she said tartly. "I think you could do a good day's work were you not so lazy about it."

A grin split his face, and he cackled. "Aye, that I could if I chose. But why should I, when I have all me needs met and a full jug of ale to warm me?"

"Why indeed." Aislinn drew a stool near the cot. "This comes from the abbey. Brother Timothy sends it to you."

Gaven's jaw sagged. "Timothy? He sends it? Ye are sure? He said he would never—"

"Yes, well Brother Timothy has reconsidered. While he doesn't approve of the Old Religion, he deems certain rituals harmless if precautions are taken. He is praying for your soul at every office."

"Me soul is in no danger," Gaven snapped indignantly.

She noted that his fingers closed around the pouch, and that there was a faint smile on his mouth as he leaned back against his cushions.

"Nonetheless, Brother Timothy has relented in this. It is the solstice. Regard it as his gift to you."

"Aye, he allus were a good lad," Gaven said with a sigh and a nod. "Be he content?"

"He is most content."

Silence fell, and Aislinn flexed her cold fingers as they warmed. The brazier held hot coals that spread heat in the small room, welcome if scant.

"Tell me again of the Grail, lass," Gaven murmured. "I would hear the tale once more."

His eyes had closed, and he clutched the pouch of herbs to his chest. She swallowed the lump in her throat, and said tartly, "You don't deserve to hear it again. You knew where it was all along and made us waste time in searching."

"It would not have meant as much if ye had found it easy, lass. The pursuit separates wheat from chaff."

"Yes." She cleared her throat again. "Yes, that's very true."

"Ah, ye cannot blame him, lass." A wise nod greeted her sharp glance. "Ye knew his intent."

"If you speak of Stephen Fitzhugh, I do not blame him at all. He made his choice." Her fingers curled into the wool of her cloak, knotted it in her fist. "I freely gave him that choice."

"And now ye blame yerself for it, then."

She blew out a heavy sigh. "I mistook my own judgement. I thought he would choose wisely."

"Perhaps he did."

"No, he chose temporal gain rather than spiritual grace. It is a grievous thing to me."

Silence fell again between them. Gaven kneaded the pouch between his fingers, a gentle working of his hands as if for reassurance.

"What of the king?" he asked finally. "What of King Arthur?"

"No grave has been found."

"But the abbot searches for it." He moved restlessly on the cot. "Ye told me he does."

"Yes, he searches for the grave when the ground is not so frozen."

A sigh slipped from the old man. "King Bran lies neath the Tor . . . the faeries tend him there."

Aislinn was silent.

Gaven said after a moment, "But Arthur . . . ah, that good king must lie hidden until the time is right . . . it maun be nigh, for I hear the Old Ones whisper to me of a night."

Alarmed, she leaned forward, put a hand on the old man's arm. "Gaven? What whispers do you hear?"

"They beckon, lass. They call me to the ring of stones of a night . . . remind me of the old ways. Gone now. Gone." He heaved another great sigh. "Only a few remember now."

"Remember the old ways?"

"Aye, when old magic was in all the days. The new magic rules now. The magic of the cross takes the place of all. Me grandson knew it long before me . . . he's a good lad. A good lad. Soon none will be left who can tell about the Old Ones. 'Tis the way of it. Old makes way for new . . . and now 'tis time for kings to rest undisturbed."

His eyes closed, and he smiled blindly.

"The great cycle turns, just as do the seasons. All turns on itself, becomes one. 'Tis how it's meant to be."

When he lapsed into silence again, she waited. There was no sound, not even that of the miller's family to break the hush. It was so quiet she thought he might have stopped breathing, but then he sighed again in a soft snore.

Rising quietly, she took her leave, bundled up against the cold as she returned to her own hall. There was some truth in what Gaven said. Old did make way for new, and the new religion that was a mere thousand years old was still young. There were more ancient religions that still thrived, that would continue to thrive.

How could she condemn Stephen Fitzhugh when she didn't condemn Gaven? Yet how did she reconcile her own faith with a man who had none? . . .

✝

CHRISTMAS PASSED, AND Aislinn felt more alone than ever before in her life. The new abbot, Henry de Sully, had made it clear that he dismissed the gossip of her immorality. Yet the easy association with those she had lived near most of her life had irrevocably altered. Some women drew away as if she was contaminated when she passed them, and she held her head high and pretended she didn't see.

But she did see, and it wounded, continually flaying her spirit with sharp remorse, with humiliation, with grief. It gnawed at her soul, until she felt sick, until her days were tainted with shame.

Not for loving Stephen Fitzhugh—no, never that. There was no shame in honest love. The shame was in compromising her faith. That she had done.

These days, Brother Timothy was her only ally. He came to visit regularly, to bring her baskets of food and insist that she send Master Weaver when she needed more.

"You have shut yourself away, Mistress."

"No," she replied, "I have been shut out. There's a difference. I will not force my presence on those who find it offensive, nor will I force myself through closed doors."

"The doors of the church are never closed to you."

"I attend the offices regularly."

"Yes, like a wraith passing through. I've seen you. A shadow at the rear, standing back as if you have no right to be there." Timothy's smile was compassionate. "You have been my salvation before, Mistress. Let me be yours now."

"My soul is not in peril, Brother."

"Is it not?" His head tilted to one side. "It's my thought that God doesn't want you to be spineless."

"I thought submission was a requirement of monks," she retorted, stung by his assessment.

"Of monks—and submission to *God,* not to vicious gossip that is a sin in itself."

"It is the truth, Brother," she said brutally. "I was with Stephen Fitzhugh and you know that well."

Silence stretched between them, while winter winds were a dismal moan. He looked uncomfortable, still not accustomed to the role he had taken for himself. Then he sighed.

"Have you asked forgiveness?"

"Forgiveness for loving a man? No. Forgiveness for lacking faith, yes." She put her face into her palms. Her trapped breath smelled of the mint she had been chewing earlier, reminded her of Stephen and the bog marsh. Another sin, to cling to such memories.

"Mistress Aislinn, I don't know all the answers. I'm not a learned man," Timothy said softly, "and I have little knowledge of love between a man and a woman, save what I have observed from a distance. Yet I do know this: God put man and woman together on this earth to love and be loved, and the only sin you have committed is in denying that love. If you reject Sir Stephen now, then you have rejected the sacraments put into place for you."

Her laugh was brittle. "You are telling me that unless I marry him, I've sinned?"

"From what I understand of it, yes."

"Marriage as penance. I had not thought it."

Brother Timothy looked abashed, and she relented in

her anguish. "Forgive me, Brother. I don't mean to spurn your comfort. I just find it hard to accept."

"I am not a priest," he said, "but I urge you to seek one out."

"Yes, yes, I'll do that. Your advice is appreciated, Brother."

He seemed cheered.

She didn't have the heart to tell him that her grief was more than just spiritual. She could not ask forgiveness, for if by some miracle Stephen Fitzhugh came again, she'd not turn him away. She was weak. And she had never known it.

But the dreams that inhabited her slumber were vivid reminders of her lack of moral character. So vivid, so real, that she awoke aching and reaching out for him, the blood a hot and heavy pulse between her thighs, the restless desire that churned inside a constant ache.

There was no reconciliation. She had lost all. She had lost the comfort of her faith, and she had lost Stephen Fitzhugh, and there was no help for it.

Chapter 31

✝

SHARP SPADES DROVE into the ground with grinding sounds as lay brothers toiled. Prior Thaddeus hovered with solemn regard, his hands clasped in an attitude of prayer. Stubborn earth was slow to yield, though it had thawed enough to be excavated.

"Dig down another foot, brothers," the prior said when the lay brothers paused, "for Brother Berian was specific in the request for his burial. Father Abbot says he is to be honored just as he wished."

A brisk wind tugged at his cassock, revealing bare white legs above his boots. The prior moved to the shelter of the Lady Chapel, to observe from a less windy position.

"Brother Timothy," he said sternly, "escort Mistress Aislinn to the abbey gates."

Aislinn paused with the basket of herbs she had fetched from the herbarium, vexed that the prior would summarily dismiss her today, when just the day before he had summoned her to assist with the lay duties.

"Yes, Brother Prior," Timothy said calmly, "though it

was Father Abbot's request that she help me."

The prior blew out an exasperated breath. "Very well, I shall certainly not interfere with the abbot's decisions."

"Stay," Timothy murmured when she would have gone on, "for I believe that there is something of importance here."

Puzzled, she glanced at him, but his thin face was intent, eyes locked on the grave being dug for the elderly monk. It surprised her. He had grown more confident in the passing months, reaching the promise of manhood and leaving the uncertainty of youth behind.

And as the weeks had passed, so, too, had she lost the overwhelming grief that darkened those first days and weeks after Stephen left. His loss and the loss of the Grail were no less grievous, but she had come to peace with it. It was a relief, salvation from the shadows that had threatened to claim her.

Brother Timothy knelt to pet one of the cats that were always at his heels, but his gaze was riveted on the grave being dug. There was a tension in him that was arresting, but Aislinn could find no good reason for it.

She set down her basket of herbs, eyes downcast so as not to offend the prior, and bowed her head in an attitude of prayer. Milder weather was a blessing, facilitating the digging of the grave, but the winter winds were still brisk enough to snag the hood of her cloak and whisk it from her head. Her hand went up immediately to retrieve it, and as she looked up, her gaze passed over the two pyramids that stood beside the south door of the Lady Chapel.

The lay brothers were digging Brother Berian's grave between the pyramids, as the old monk had requested. And now she understood Brother Timothy's sudden tension, as well as the prior's rapt interest. Apparently, hope was renewed.

Heads were below the lip of the grave, the men barely

visible in the depths as they worked. The steady scrape of shovels drowned out their labored breaths.

A few moments later, one of the shovels made a clank as it struck something solid, and there was an exclamation.

Brother Prior was instantly at the edge of the grave. His round face was flushed with excitement and anticipation.

"Swiftly, Brother Timothy, summon the abbot!"

Aislinn slipped into the shadow of the chapel, watched as the abbot came, and Ralph Fitzstephen. They spoke eagerly and with great enthusiasm, and soon a pavilion was erected, white curtains enclosing the raw hole in the earth. From where she stood, Aislinn could hear the chink-scrape of digging quite clearly.

Then there was another excited shout, and she moved silently to the edge of the curtains to peer inside. It was crowded with monks, all intent on the work and taking no notice of her hovering on their fringes.

A heavy stone slab lay at the bottom of the hole, and with much effort and grunting and sweating, the lay brothers managed to pull it up. It heaved in a tilt, one end pushed vertically to rest against the side of the hole.

"Look here, Father Abbot!"

Abbot Henry bent over the grave. The flat underside of the slab was now visible, and it could be seen that part of the stone had been carved out to form a niche. Into this cavity a leaden cross of unusual shape had been set. They pried it loose to find strange lettering hewn into the surface, which had been turned to face downward.

"It's in Latin," Father Abbot murmured, and reached out to touch the inscription.

It was quiet, a hush having fallen over the monks, so that the only sound for a moment was the rustle and snap of the pavilion curtains.

Then Father Abbot translated the inscription:

*Here in the isle of Avalon lies buried the renowned
King Arthur, with Guinevere, his second wife*

He looked up, drew in a heavy breath, and said softly,
"It is as King Henry said it would be."

At once, an excited babble broke out and was quickly
hushed by the abbot's uplifted hand.

"We have only discovered the gravestone. Now we
must find the bones, so that they may be properly in-
terred."

With renewed vigor, the lay brothers set to work again,
spades sliding carefully into the earth. As they dug deeper
and deeper, Brother Timothy began to fret.

"Surely it cannot be so deep, Father Abbot! Could it
have already been discovered?"

"Have faith, Brother," the abbot replied, "have faith.
All is not yet lost."

Aislinn felt a hand on her arm and glanced up guiltily,
but was relieved to see Ralph Fitzstephen at her side. He
looked weary, his face grayish in the shadowed light beneath the pavilion curtains.

"I mean no harm," she began, but he shook his head
and put a finger to his lips.

"No harm is done, Mistress. This is a great moment. I
only wish King Henry had lived to see it."

"Do you think . . . it is King Arthur?"

"So says the inscription. If it is not, then the hoax is
beyond my understanding."

It was nearly dark before one of the lay brothers cried
out again, and this time, the coffin had been found. Not
of stone or marble, a simple hollowed-out oak bole lay
over sixteen feet beneath the ground. It was quite long,
and it took gentle persuasion to pry the lid away.

Resting in the top two thirds of the coffin were the
bones of a tall man, evident in the length of his shinbones
and powerful arms. And near the foot of the coffin, at his

feet, lay much smaller bones. A tress of hair, pale as gold and still fresh and bright in color, curved around her skull in a gentle wave.

Overcome with excitement, Brother Timothy leaped into the grave and snatched up the hair, crying out at its beauty and gazing at it in obvious rapture. But as he held it in his palm it dissolved to fine powder, leaving nothing but a pale shadow. He gave a moan of distress and looked up, shamefaced to find Abbot Henry frowning down at him.

"Grant pardon, Father Abbot—"

"Come up, Brother. What is done is done."

Aislinn slipped from the pavilion as the monks worked to bring up the coffin, filled with wonder at what she'd seen. Evening shadows shrouded the abbey grounds, and she retrieved her herb basket and left by the gates, unattended in this moment of great discovery and excitement.

High Street was as usual, cart horses plodding wearily home with faster step now that the end of the day was nigh, and others hurrying home before darkness fell. No torches had yet been lit on the abbey walls, and a soft gloom crept in alleys and beneath walls.

Her hall was dark, and she set down her basket on the floor just inside the door. The only light emanated from coals inside the brazier, and she moved to stir them to a brighter glow, feeding coal until a tidy blaze banished gloom to the far corners.

Holding out her hands, she warmed her palms before removing her cloak, fingers more agile now to untie the strings at her throat. She swept it free, and turned to hang it on a wall hook beside the ambry.

And stopped.

Stephen Fitzhugh stood with his arms crossed over his chest, a negligent posture, watching her with that crooked smile that she had despaired of ever seeing again.

"You've come back," she said softly.

"Yes, my love. Did you doubt it?"

"Every hour." She moved past him with a jerk, hung her cloak on the peg, and turned back to look at him again. Silhouetted against the rising glow of the brazier, he was so familiar, yet so strange. A man she had thought she knew and found she didn't . . . the man she loved beyond reason, beyond hope.

Half in shadow, he seemed as one of her dreams, even when he moved into the flickering light of the brazier and she saw him more clearly. He seemed thinner, taller than she recalled, but there was a dark gleam in his eyes that seemed familiar. A wine-red surcoat was belted around his waist in a double loop, the black cloak he wore carelessly thrown over his shoulder, melding into shadows. Intensity vibrated in him, in his voice.

"You should have known I'd come back for you. As long as there's breath in my body, I'll not let you go." He took a step toward her, stopped when she drew back. "Aislinn. Ah, God. . . ."

"Yes," she whispered, *"God.* You use the name as a curse when I have been taught to use it with reverence."

"That," he said with a slight twist of his mouth into the old mockery, "was actually a prayer."

"Prayer! *You?"*

Was that a flinch? Had she struck a chord of remorse in him? Was he even capable of it? It was doubtful, for the man who could barter such a holy relic as the Grail was beyond redemption.

And yet . . . and yet, she remembered other things, too, the torment in his eyes, the bitter grief in his voice when he'd told her of his father and then his mother's loss. She wanted to believe he was not lost to her, but evidence spoke otherwise.

"Yes, well." He cleared his throat. "Even the devil is known to pray, I suppose, though not for the benefit of others. I'm guilty enough of that, selfish dog that I am."

"I don't know how you have the courage to pray, after what you've done."

His mouth set in a sulky line, and he reached to push a piece of coal into the brazier. "Perhaps I thought God was a mite more merciful than you seem to be. My mistake."

She flushed and bit her bottom lip. "Why have you come back, Stephen?"

"I told you. I came back for you." He glanced up, a swift dark look from beneath black lashes. "Isn't that enough for you? That I came back?"

"No. It's not enough. Why should it be?" Agitation rose in her, confusion and yearning tangled together in a seething knot of indecision and resolution. She could not let him weaken her. It would destroy them both. "Stephen, you still don't see. It's not just that you bartered the Holy Grail for stone and trees—it's that you're willing to do it. That marks the unbridgeable difference between us. We're too essentially opposite in nature."

"Are we? Perhaps you're right." He fed more coal into the brazier, red and gold flames illuminating his face with unholy light as he stared into the fire. "A man who would barter away the Grail is not worthy of your love."

She was silent, watching him. Finally he looked up at her again.

"You have great faith, Aislinn. You can't see God, or talk to Him, or touch Him. Yet you believe in Him. When all around you wicked men spout blasphemy and commit evil acts, your faith in unshakable. It was one of the things I resented most about you at first. You believe in something greater than you, and I could find faith in nothing." He frowned slightly, shook his head. "I've not found much reason to have faith in men. But I believe in you."

His gaze was riveting, potent, and he held her eyes with his for what seemed an eternity. There was raw need in that tormented gaze, and in his hoarse words: "Believe in me, Aislinn. Believe in me when everything tells you not to—I need it. God, I need to know you believe in me. You have so much faith and goodness in you—have faith in me."

Despair rose in her throat, anguish crowding the drumming desire to believe in him, to take the supreme leap of faith in this one man and risk all. But could she? Could she ever hope to find peace in her life if she made the wrong decision?

Can I ever find peace if I don't take this chance....

He was waiting, immobile, tense, eyes a dark fathomless sheen in dim light, and she thought of him that night at the well, when he had offered to relinquish the Grail and she had left him to make his own choice. She had believed in him then. She had believed he would choose integrity over all. He was still the same man....

"Yes," she said on a whisper of sound, "yes, I believe in you, Stephen Fitzhugh. God help me."

He was reaching for her, pulling her to him, crushing his mouth against the top of her head, holding her so tightly she couldn't breathe. A shudder went through him.

"God help us all, my love," he muttered, "God help us all."

His hand tangled in her hair, pulled her head back to stare down into her eyes, and she was surprised at the pale sheen in his eyes. Tears? She put up a hand, touched his cheek gently, and he turned his face to kiss her fingertips.

As she leaned into him, he bent, lifted her into his arms, and moved to the staircase that led to her bedchamber. She rested her head on his shoulder, one arm around his neck as she prayed she had made the right choice.

There was no turning back.

He undressed her in leisurely efficiency, his hands divesting her of garments without haste, despite the tremor of urgency in his voice.

"I've dreamed of you every night," he said softly. "A torture I do not recommend."

"Am I that repulsive, that I haunt your rest?" she asked lightly, and heard his laugh in the darkness that filled the chamber unlit by lamp or candle.

"It was the waking that was torture, for the only ease I knew was the dream of you." His lips moved over the curve of her bare shoulder. "I was tempted to sleep the days away just to keep you near."

"You could"—she gasped as his mouth moved lower, lost the thread of her words, found them again when he shifted to move beside her—"have come back sooner."

"Yes, love." His hand smoothed over her body, tested the cushion of her breast, then spanned her ribs and moved to rest upon her belly. "I could have come back sooner, but for Essex."

Her fingers grasped his wrist, held his hand still. "Is it done?"

"All is well, but now is not the time to discuss it. We have the rest of our lives, and I will not ruin this night of reunion with his name."

When she would have protested, he covered her mouth with his, kissed her so fiercely that she yielded to the urgency in him, and to the rising passion in her body that answered to his caresses. Releasing his wrist, she moved her hand over him, explored his chest, belly, lower, fingers finding him, holding him, measuring his response. A deep growl rumbled in his chest as she applied the movements he had taught her.

Restraint swiftly altered to ruthless purpose. He held her hands in his, pushed them over her head into the soft cushions of the bed. Tension vibrated in him, tightened his muscles as he moved over her, as bare as she, skin hot against her, a throbbing flame.

"Open for me, love," he muttered against her lips, and his knee pressed between her legs as his tongue slipped into her mouth. His weight spread her thighs, and she moaned at the aggressive domination, excited and restless beneath him.

Urgency transferred to her, and she opened eagerly, felt him push against her, impatient hardness seeking entry. All the waiting, the doubts, the fears, were swallowed by a smothering rush of need. In his arms, she could believe that all would be well.

Surrendering all, she met the slow burn of his entry with soft little cries, relished the hard friction of him, the searing heat of his invasion as he filled her. She moved beneath him, matched his rhythm, the fierce pounding of his body into her, the molten fervor of their joining taking her beyond coherent thought, beyond this dark chamber and into a world of light and shuddering sensation.

Only vaguely was she aware of his breath at her ear, a fervent sound, a promise, a release and a joy so intense that she thought she must surely die from it. Pure bliss to feel his arms tighten around her, to feel his body thrust with a last explosive shudder before he lay still atop her, his release a throbbing burn inside her.

And bliss to hold him as he relaxed, his muscles a taut quiver against her, a comfort and a reassurance that it was no dream this time. He was real. And he was here. And there was no thought of the morrow until it came. It would arrive whether she wanted it or not, and now she meant to hold tightly to what happiness she could summon.

The world would intrude soon enough.

Chapter 32

✝

IT WAS STILL dark. No lamp lit the gloom of the chamber where they lay, and Stephen felt the sudden need to see her. Confirmation, reassurance that she was his, that she was here at last and not just a dream from which he'd wake.

She murmured a protest as he rose from the bed, and he smiled as he tucked the covers back around her. It was cold indeed on his bare flesh. Cold enough to unman him if he didn't swiftly retrieve the lamp.

Downstairs he lit a candle from the brazier, stoked the fire, barred the door that had been left unbarred in his earlier haste.

"You really shouldn't be so careless as to leave doors unbarred, Stephen."

The soft drawling voice came from the shadows, prickled his bare flesh with recognition. He turned toward the source and waited.

"Did you think I would allow you to make a fool of me and live?" Essex flicked a contemptuous finger at him as if brushing away an annoying insect. "I warned you."

"Yes. So you did."

"You should have paid heed. And—" He rose from the bench where he sat at Aislinn's table, "you should not have been quite so cocky. Arrogance is a grave sin."

"You should know, my lord earl." He tried to stem a shiver, and his effort did not go unnoticed. Essex smiled.

"You realize, of course, that Dunmow will revert back to me once you are dead."

"I didn't realize I was ill, my lord."

"Sadly, I fear your illness is fatal. Stupidity usually is. Here you are, naked of weapons and clothes, brought low by a woman. Another sin, that of lust."

"And again—you should know that well enough, my lord earl."

"Ah. Well. All in my past. Confessed and forgiven."

"Forgiveness cannot always be purchased."

Essex moved to the brazier, held out his hands over the coals and stared at him thoughtfully. "That," he said after a moment, "depends upon the currency used. Where is the true Grail?"

Stephen was silent. A sick certainty roiled in his belly. He'd noticed the men in the shadows, waiting for the signal from Essex. Never had he felt so vulnerable as he did now.

Essex sighed and shook his head. "Such an admirable resistance will only earn you a great deal of pain. Spare us both the necessity."

When Stephen still didn't reply, Essex snarled, "I did not follow you all this way to be denied now, by the rood! You will tell me where it lies before this night is ended."

The signal he'd been dreading came, and the two men were on him, holding his arms behind him, forcing him to his knees on the cold floor. One man jerked his head back by the hair, held him facing the earl.

"I had thought," Essex said more calmly, "to have to

waylay you in some other place or manner, but this is quite sufficient. Privacy and convenience are most appreciated. Should I not loosen your tongue with my efforts, there is always the woman."

"She knows nothing," Stephen growled. "She thinks you have the Grail."

"Yes, as did I. A pitiful substitute."

"It fooled you," Stephen observed wryly.

Essex glared at him. "I'm afraid I depended rather too strongly on your good sense to prevent you risking such a foolish trick."

"Yes, well, there you have it. I'm prone to lapses in good judgement, it seems."

He suppressed another shiver, felt hands tighten on him, and despaired. He had to delay Essex, hope Aislinn would somehow escape his grasp, or at the least, delay the inevitable until daylight. There was always the hope someone would arrive before the earl could drag the truth from him. And he had no illusions that it wasn't entirely possible. Men under torture were susceptible to spilling all they knew. He'd seen it too often.

"How do you know it isn't the Grail?" he asked, and gave a shrug at Essex's contemptuous snort. "It could be. No miracles are guaranteed, I imagine."

"A Flemish burgher informed me that the cup you gave me is a cheap imitation of those sold in the Holy Land to naive pilgrims."

"What do you expect? Pig knuckles are sold as the bones of saints every day at abbeys all over England. I can't be responsible for every forgery foisted off on unsuspecting fools."

"No, you can't. But you are responsible for this one. Before they died so precipitately, the men I sent to follow you informed me of your discovery in the well. That can be no forgery. *That* is the Grail I want. And that is the Grail you will give me."

Dread locked his jaw as Essex toyed with coal tongs at the side of the brazier. The coals burned red and hot, a solid glow that did nothing to ease his chill, but would sear the skin off a man at close range. Nausea churned as the earl poked in the brazier, lifted a coal, watched his face over the glowing chunk.

"Are you certain you have nothing to tell me, Stephen?"

Yes! his mind screamed, but his tongue would not form the word. He thought of the Holy Grail in this man's profane hands, the sacred cup that would give him immortality being used for wickedness and sacrilege, and could not say the words that would stave off pain. Death was inevitable. It came to all. It should come to the earl as well.

"I gave you the Grail," he said tonelessly, hopelessly. "I gave you the only Grail I have."

"Tch tch . . . such a stubborn fool."

Stephen steeled himself as the earl stepped close, jaw set to hold back a scream that would surely rouse Aislinn and earn her the earl's brutal attention.

The tongs wavered in Essex's grasp, his twisted hands clumsy as he maneuvered the coal. He pressed too tightly, and the teeth of the tongs bit into the coal, shattering it so that it fell in glowing pieces to the stone floor.

Essex cursed harshly while Stephen welcomed the brief reprieve.

"You," Essex snapped at one of the men holding Stephen, "take the tongs! You know what to do."

"Yes, my lord." The man released Stephen's arms and moved to take the tongs from the earl, grinning a little as he turned to the brazier.

Held now by only one man, Stephen drew one leg up under him so that he was in a half crouch, one knee on the floor and the other foot steadying his balance.

" 'Ere now, lad," the soldier said softly as he fished a

coal out of the brazier, "we'll warm you right up, we will, and see if 'at don't make you feel more talkative."

"You really don't have to be concerned about me taking a chill," Stephen muttered. "I'm quite warm enough."

Still grinning, the man advanced. The tongs were steady enough in his grip. There would be no more delay.

Muscles tensed, and when the soldier was almost over him, Stephen threw his weight to one side, twisting so that the man holding him was thrown into his comrade. He screamed loudly as the coal evidently found its mark, and he released Stephen abruptly. Curses filled the air, and the sound of steel being drawn was a warning.

Stephen lunged toward the door, snatched Aislinn's cloak from the peg, wrapped it around one arm as he turned back to meet the advancing threat. A sword would slice through it like butter. The best he could hope for was to tangle the blades for a moment, pray for opportunity.

Retreating, he stumbled back against a solid piece of wood, remembered the ambry filled with pewter plate. It was heavy. He grasped the edge of it with one hand, waited until the two men were on him, then gave a mighty shove that toppled the tall cupboard and sent it crashing over. One man escaped, but it pinned the other to the floor. He screamed with rage and pain as he heaved at it to free himself, and pewter plate spun and clanged on stone, a violent tune.

Another scream rose into the air, high-pitched and filled with pain and terror, and Stephen turned to see that the ambry had knocked over the brazier. Coals spilled over the stone floor, spattered the earl, who beat at them with bare, frantic hands. His rich tunic smoldered, and coals gleamed in wicked red eyes on the fringes of his cloak.

The smell of burning wool curled into the room, and the earl screeched for the soldier to help him, but the man stood uncertainly, attention drawn from Stephen to the

new crisis. Whirling awkwardly, Essex attempted to un-
fasten the cords that bound his cloak around his throat as
tiny flames ignited and threaded upward in greedy lines.
His fingers were clumsy, twisted and useless as he clawed
at the cords.

Stephen started forward. The soldier turned to meet a
perceived threat, his sword uplifted to strike as he snarled,
"Get back!"

"Fool! This is no time for that—" Stephen ducked as
the sword lashed out, the man's attention diverted by the
earl and his companion and the fire that began to crawl
eagerly across the floor as the coals burned.

Using Aislinn's cloak Stephen retreated in a half circle
to the foot of the stairs, and was startled to hear her right
behind him on the steps.

"Your sword—take it quickly now!"

She shoved the hilt of his sword into his hand, and he
grasped it and turned back. Reflected light glittered in
dangerous promise along the lethal blade, and the soldier
jerked to a halt as he realized his quarry was armed.

"Come ahead," Stephen said softly, and beckoned with
his free hand, "or save yourself and your companion before the house burns down atop us."

Hesitation was brief, and the soldier moved quickly to
his companion, shoved the ambry from him, and hauled
him to his feet. They staggered to the door, the weight of
his fallen comrade draped over his shoulder as they fled
the flames that threatened to consume them all. The cry
of *Fire!* echoed into the night as they emerged into the
dark wind. It swept into the hall, a careless draft that set
the fire to a higher pitch, sent it licking up walls and
curtains.

Essex was screaming wildly, and the stench of burning
flesh overpowered that of burning wool. He whirled
drunkenly about the hall, wobbled, ablaze, a human torch.

Stephen rushed forward, attempted to throw Aislinn's

cloak over him, to beat out the flames. Futile effort, for the earl in mindless agony evaded his attempts.

"Stephen," Aislinn urged, and thrust his own tunic into his hands as she pushed him toward the door, "the ceiling will collapse on us if you do not flee!"

It was true. The entire hall was engulfed in flames, and outside he could hear the panicked shouts of men come to fight the fire that threatened to burn down the entire town.

"Get out," he snapped, and gave her a forward shove to the open door.

"No! Not without you! You cannot save him—can't you see? He's already as good as dead. . . ."

Essex had pitched forward, his body in the final throes of death on the floor, while around him walls and curtains blazed.

Coughing, choking on thick smoke, Stephen felt Aislinn trembling beside him, refusing to leave without him. He swept her up, carried her to the door, shoved her out.

"I cannot leave his body here. . . ."

Ignoring her anguished cry, he turned back into the hall, felt heat blister his skin as he stumbled through the smoke to reach Essex. The garments were burned away, so that he had to use the cloak he still held to snare him and drag him to the door, but he made it at last, staggered out into the cold night with the flames a solid wall behind him.

"You fool," Aislinn said on a sob as he collapsed on the side of the road opposite her burning house, "You fool! He was already dead. . . ."

"Yes." Stephen gulped in a draft of cool air, felt it ease the burn of his throat, and let her slip a tunic over his head. "Yes, and now there will be . . . no doubt that it was Essex . . . who died in that fire."

Kneeling beside him, she stared into his face. He returned her stare grimly.

"I want . . . no more impediments to stand between

me . . . and Dunmow. It's mine. At last. He signed . . . the papers . . . before the bishop."

A fit of coughing doubled him over, and when he sat up to wipe soot from his face, she wore a faint smile.

"I don't suppose," she said, "that the next earl will be so foolish as to attempt to take it from you."

"Doubt-ful." He coughed again, spit up soot. "This will be a . . . sterling example . . . of possible consequences."

Aislinn sat down on the ground beneath the abbey walls and turned to look at the inferno that had been her home.

"It seems, Sir Stephen, that I am without a home at present. Do you have any suggestions?"

"Yea, lady fair . . . I do indeed." He hooked an arm over her shoulders and, heedless of shocked stares from those who had come to watch the fire, kissed her full on the mouth. "I am in need," he said with his forehead pressed to hers, "of a goodwife to manage my keep."

"I've been told I'm stubborn to a fault, and that I have a sharp tongue."

"Just the attributes I need."

"And I've also been told," she whispered, as tears made pale streaks in the dark soot smearing her cheeks, "that I'm willful."

"Excellent. We shall deal smartly together, I think."

He was breathing easier now, and heaved himself to his feet, bringing her up with him. He looked down and saw the carved cross she wore on a ribbon around her neck. Lifting it in his palm, he rubbed his thumb over the surface.

"You wear the cross I sent you."

"Yes, my love. How could I not? Is it truly carved from the wood of Noah's ark?"

A moment passed before he answered, then he said slowly, "If you have enough faith and believe in the legend, yes, it is. Faith, I've been told, works miracles. Oak turns to ash, yet is reborn. As are some men reborn, if they are fortunate enough to find love."

Tears sprang into her eyes, and her lips quivered with emotion as she curved her hand over his to hold him and the cross in her tight grip. "I love you, Stephen Fitzhugh."

"Yes, I have faith that you do. Have faith in my love for you, Aislinn. It is forever."

"I know." She laughed softly, "I know."

A shout went up as the roof to her house imploded in a fiery shower of sparks and flames, collapsing upon itself. He turned to look at the destruction.

"I think they could use an extra hand with the fire, my love. Too late to save your house, I fear."

"Yes. So it is." She leaned against him, her hand on his chest. "Go, then. Save the rest of the houses, though it will take a miracle to manage that."

"Say a prayer, love." He meant it lightly, but saw that she took him seriously as she nodded.

"Yes, I have prayed for rain, as it's hopeless to douse the flames with buckets."

He opened his mouth to comment, but a heavy crash of thunder drowned out anything he might have said. As he looked up, a deluge poured from the sky, an instant dousing of rain that was met with cheers from the men fighting the fire. It soaked them to the bone, wet and cold and welcome.

As he threw her cloak over their heads, he said with an emotion akin to awe, "I think I'm finally convinced of the power of prayer."

Chapter 33

✝

CLOUDS HUNG LOW in the sky. It was the first time she had been back since Stephen had left that night in August. Aislinn sat quietly on a rock while he moved to the lip of the well, knelt beside it to gaze into the depths.

"We're the only ones left who know where it lies," she said softly. "Save for Brother Timothy."

He swerved to look at her. Faint blisters still marked his skin, but were nearly healed now. "Brother Arnot?"

"Died last week. Brother Timothy told me." She leaned forward, hunched her shoulders against the cold wind that rattled the green needles of the yew trees. "And he thought, as did I, that the Grail was gone from here."

"Yes. That was my plan, of course." His smile was a bit abashed. "I did hope you would know better. I've never known a woman who didn't let curiosity get the best of her."

"I gave you my word I wouldn't look for it."

"So you did, mouse. I should have believed you."

She met his gaze, an ache in her heart. "And I should have believed in you."

"You do now."

It was said flatly, but there still a faint question in it, a need for reassurance.

"Yes, I believe in you, Stephen Fitzhugh. You are an honorable man."

"Keep it believable, mouse."

She laughed. "Yes, I wouldn't want to accuse you of any good deeds you haven't done."

He picked up a handful of pebbles, dropped one into the well. It made a tiny plink when it struck the water below. A hush descended on the thicket, where the only sound was the soft swish of wind through the yews.

Tomorrow they would leave Glastonbury, and she would begin her new life at his keep—as his wife. A knight's wife with new duties to learn, a brand-new beginning. With the death of the earl, there would be no shadows to cloud their future, other than those that were always unexpected.

She shuddered. She had crouched on the stairs that night, listened to the earl's soft voice, the menace and evil that he spread, and had understood for the first time what Stephen had endured. It amazed her that he was not as vicious and depraved as his uncle.

"Primogeniture," Stephen had replied wryly when she said as much to him, "That right would have gone to his eldest son had he fathered one. Instead, the next earl can lay claim to it, though I doubt he will. He seems a fair man for all that he has the same blood as the rest of us. It's past time for a decent overlord."

And now they were to leave. She'd said her farewell to Gaven that morning, and known she would never see him again. He was so frail, for all that an indomitable spirit burned in him. He'd accepted the news of King Arthur's grave with solemn satisfaction.

"Aye, 'tis as I said it would be."

"Yes," she agreed, smiling at the lie, "just as you said it would be."

"Now I can rest. The mysteries are done." His eyes had closed, until she thought he was asleep and started to leave, and he said, softly, "Has the Grail brought ye happiness?"

"The Grail? No."

"But ye're happy now, aren't ye, lass?"

"Yes."

"Ah. It does not take a magic cup or a Holy Grail to find that which ye need in life. It takes faith."

His eyes opened slightly, and there was a gleam of damp silver dewing his lashes. "That is the true meaning of the Grail," he whispered.

She held that knowledge to her as Stephen knelt beside the well, and she kept her silence. She had found her happiness, and he would have to find his own peace.

Wind ruffled his dark hair, tugged at the edges of his cloak. He moved back from the mouth of the well and tested the length of rope he'd tied to a sturdy yew.

"Strong enough," he said and looked up at her with a faint smile. "This time, try not to sever it."

"I left my eating dagger behind."

Stephen removed his cloak and sword, lay them on the ground near the well. She watched as he lowered himself over the edge, a flash of red that swiftly disappeared in agile inches.

He had not said what he intended to do with the Grail, and she had not asked. She trusted him to make the right decision. At last.

What self-righteous arrogance she'd had, to believe her path the only one! There were many paths to the same destination, yet she had seen only one. How pompous she must have seemed. For the first time, she understood Mistress Margaret's hostility, if not her expression of it. She must have been a thorn in the older woman's side with her prattle of faith and humility, when all the while she'd been guilty of intolerable condescension. She must have reeked of it.

She watched the rope, saw it pull taut again as Stephen climbed back up. The moment of truth was at hand. She would, at last, be privileged to see the Holy Grail.

Rising, knees weak with anticipation, she moved to meet him as he emerged from the well. He eased himself over the edge, sat with his legs dangling over the lip.

"Come," he said softly, and she knelt beside him.

He reached into the cloth bag at his waist and pulled out a plain cup with clean lines. It was silver, gold trim on the lip, a golden knot on the bowl.

"Oh," she said, "I thought . . . I thought it would be—"

"Solid gold? Crusted with jewels?" He shook his head. "No, a simple cup for a simple man. A carpenter. He had no need of earthly wealth. His lay elsewhere."

Pale sunlight gleamed on the surface of the Grail, a soft glow. Stephen held it carefully, and they sat in silence for a time.

Finally he turned to her, said, "This chalice is not meant for men to own. It had one owner, a holy man. It was not left in a church, but here in this well. Part of the earth from which it came."

She met and held his gaze, read sincerity there, and a sense of peace that had been so long lacking.

"You think it should go back to the earth," she said, and he nodded.

"Yes. I do. It will always be a lure to men like Essex, who saw it as a vessel to be used, defiled by purposes that had nothing to do with honor. He wanted it to save his life, to bring him wealth and power. There are many like him. No church can contain it for long. If there are squabbles over the bones of saints, only think what there will be over a prize such as this."

She sighed. "Yes. You're right, of course. And now that the grave of King Arthur has been found on abbey grounds, Glastonbury's future is secure."

A faint smile tucked the corners of his mouth. "Are you saying that now you no longer need it, it's all right to let it go?"

Startled, she stared at him. It dawned on her what he meant, what he'd meant all along.

"Oh Stephen! How blind I've been! I'm as bad as all the others, wanting to use it—"

"No, my love." He slid an arm around her shoulders, tightened his embrace as he pressed a kiss on her cheek. "You wanted it for more noble reasons. Your heart is in the right place."

Silent, she blinked back tears. He was being kind. She recognized how selfish she had been, in the guise of being devout.

"Aislinn." She looked up and met his solemn gaze. "It is time to decide."

"Yes," she said, "yes. Shall we give it back now?"

"Together." He reached for her hand, drew her trembling fingers to the Grail, curled them around the stem. She shook with awe and anguish, both for what the Grail represented and how wrong she had been.

They leaned forward, both of them holding the Grail in their entwined hands. Clouds broke above, and a shaft of light illuminated the air so that the cup took on a sheen as bright as gold, nearly blinding. It radiated with a luminous intensity.

And as they both released it at the same time, a chorus of birds burst into song, sweet music filling the hush that shimmered around them. The chalice disappeared from view, down into the bottomless well at the foot of the Tor.

There was no splash to herald its immersion, nothing but the chorus of the birds. And as it disappeared beneath the earth, the light abruptly left, as if a candle had been doused, plunging the day back into cloudy gloom.

Stephen held her hand in his, fingers entwined, felt her release her breath as if she had been holding it. As had he.

It was gone. He hadn't believed it truly existed until now, hadn't believed it was sacred. Yet how did he explain what he had seen? What he'd felt, holding that sacred cup in his hand? It was as if a weight had been lifted from his shoulders, and the emptiness in him filled at last. There was a sense of peace in him now, where always there had been a restless urgency, a need to move on. Had a simple cup changed that? Did it have the power to change anything? He believed it did, but couldn't say why.

No miracles had occurred, save for the miracle of Aislinn loving him.

And that was enough. That was miracle enough to convince him of divine intervention. Only a power stronger than any he'd seen on earth could have salvaged his life.

He rose to his feet, brought her up with him, held her against him with an arm around her. She lay her head on his shoulder, a simple gesture of trust, faith, and love.

And he knew then what that power was, what it had always been, when he'd been looking in all the wrong places for it—that power was love.

Gratitude swelled in him, held him motionless as they stood beneath the clouds at the foot of the Tor, let the wind sweep around them and the sharp scent of yew mingle with the elusive fragrance of roses that he would always associate with Aislinn.

Gaven was right. His search had ended where he least expected it.

Author's Summation

✝

IN THE LATE 1130's, Geoffrey of Monmouth was a minor ecclesiastic and a creative genius. While decidedly a great writer, he also used proven historical fact as a basis for much of his work. Geoffrey's imagination was generally accepted as fact, and his triumph assured by the support of King Henry II, who encouraged the fascination with Arthurian literature. King Arthur's exploits were made famous, and the "Matter of Britain" took an honored place beside the "Matter of France" and "Matter of Rome" as a proper source of romantic fiction. A convention of fantasy blurred the line between truth and fiction, so that by the last quarter of the twelfth century, Britain was known as the realm of King Arthur.

A Welsh bard told Henry that the site of Arthur's grave lay between two pillars or pyramids at Glastonbury Abbey. The king then discussed this with the current abbot, Robert of Winchester. Abbot Robert reluctantly offered to excavate, as proof of King Arthur's death would be a powerful gift to Henry. It was a halfhearted attempt, and

nothing was discovered, and in time, it was forgotten in
light of more pressing affairs. While reports differ, I chose
to use the version that it was here, when a monk died and
his request to be buried between the pyramids was honored, that King Arthur's grave was discovered, just as I
depicted with much embellishment in *The Knight*. The
account that I used was taken straight from Gerald of
Wales, who wrote of the discovery of the grave in *Liber
de Principis Instructione* circa 1193. Gerald reported that
the shinbone was said to be three inches longer than that
of the tallest man at the abbey, and that he was shown
the leaden cross by Abbot Henry de Sully. The inscription
was faithfully reported, first by Gerald, then by me in this
story. There are, however, five different versions of that
inscription, all very similar.

When the remains of Arthur and Guinevere were rein-
terred in 1278, King Edward I attended the interment, and
at that time the cross was attached to the top of the marble
coffin at the high altar. It remained there until the Dissolution of the Monasteries in the year 1539, after which
it was left in the care of the Anglican church of St. John
Baptist in Glastonbury. The reliable reports of John Le-
land, who wrote in *Assertio Inclytissimi Arturii* that he
held the cross in his hand during a visit to the church
about 1542, mentioned that the cross measured nearly a
foot in length. At this time, the cross's location is not
known; the last it was seen was in the early eighteenth
century, in the possession of a Mr. William Hughes,
Chancellor of Wells, which had long been a rival of the
Glastonbury Abbey. All that remains is a drawing.

As for the Holy Grail and the Chalice Well, I have
taken facts and added my own embellishments for the
purpose of this story. The idea of the Holy Grail has long
been open to conjecture, of course, so the reader is invited
to choose a personal truth. In medieval ages, the church
was a powerful force in politics and in the lives of the

faithful. The bones of saints were revered in a manner that modern readers might find repugnant, but to the people of the time, it was a sacred privilege. Relics were regarded with awe, and one can imagine how the dishonest took advantage of the more credulous; yet men of intellect also viewed relics with reverence, an accepted custom of the times.

While I have described the outer portion of the Chalice Well with a fair amount of accuracy for the time, the actual chamber can only be reached from a spot below the western wall of the shaft. The well is considered to have been built by the Druids, though it was most likely a ground-level spring at that time. Over the years, a buildup of natural silt, as well as the efforts of men, raised the ground level. The water is, indeed, reddish in color and tastes of iron. It is regarded as beneficial to the human body, and I brought home several bottles. While I could not drink the waters of Bath, the water from the Chalice Well was at least palatable. I am happy to report my health is excellent!

As for Glastonbury itself, the town retains an aura of mystery and magic that draws visitors from all over the world. Everyone who visits brings home a tale of some strange event, as did I. I am convinced there are definite forces at work in that ancient town.

Cadbury is very close to Glastonbury, about a twenty-minute drive by car on winding roads that swoop through what was once marsh and woodland. Now it is dotted with ancient stone farmhouses and rolling meadows of sheep and cows. As with the rest of the tale of King Arthur, Cadbury is but one of several sites suggested as Camelot. As it sits near the River Camel—which was named for the ancient fort in the ninth century—it seems the likeliest site. It is impressive and a steep climb that requires good hiking boots and fortitude. In my case, sheer determination got me up that hill, but it was well worth the effort.

Though I used an earl of Essex as a central character, I took pure fictional license with his presence in the story and the events that took place. All derived only from my imagination.

On a final note, some people enjoy scoffing at the notion that King Arthur's grave was discovered, or even that he existed, but evidence of contemporaries and historians cast the light of truth on the reports. There was a sixth-century king of that name, whose fame spread far; whether he is the man of myth and magic is one of those subjects that will always be open to spirited debate. Finding the grave of King Arthur would indeed have drawn pilgrims from all over the world, yet the monks of Glastonbury, after respectfully interring the king and his queen in a marble tomb below the high altar of the beautiful abbey nave, did not capitalize on it at all. It seems that if they had indeed wished to do so, they would have publicized it in a more advantageous manner. Instead, they seemed content to pay homage to King Arthur in their own quiet way. To me, that lends credence to the discovery of Arthur's grave. Alas, during the Dissolution, the bodies disappeared when the abbey that had been known as the most beautiful in England was destroyed.

I hope you've enjoyed my version of the search for King Arthur and the Holy Grail. To read more about Glastonbury and view my personal photos taken of the Chalice Well, the Tor, Glastonbury Abbey, and Cadbury, legendary site of King Arthur's Camelot, please visit my Web site: http://www.ladyofshalott.com